The Tool
and
the Butterflies

Dmitry Lipskerov

Translated from the Russian by
Isaac Stackhouse Wheeler and Reilly Costigan-Humes

Deep Vellum Publishing
Dallas, Texas

Deep Vellum Publishing
3000 Commerce St., Dallas, Texas 75226
deepvellum.org · @deepvellum

Deep Vellum is a 501c3 nonprofit literary arts organization
founded in 2013 with the mission to bring
the world into conversation through literature.

Published with the support of the Institute for Literary Translation, Russia.

Support for this publication has been provided in part by grants from the National
Endowment for the Arts, the Texas Commission on the Arts, the City of Dallas Office of Arts
and Culture's ArtsActivate program, and the Moody Fund for the Arts:

ISBNs: 978-1-64605-039-0 (paperback) | 978-1-64605-040-6 (ebook)

LIBRARY OF CONGRESS CATALOGING IN PUBLICATION DATA
Names: Lipskerov, Dmitriĭ author. | Costigan-Humes, Reilly, translator. |
Wheeler, Isaac Stackhouse, translator.
Title: The tool and the butterflies / Dmitry Lipskerov ; translated from
the Russian by Isaac Stackhouse Wheeler and Reilly Costigan-Humes.
Other titles: O nem i o babochkakh. English
Description: Dallas, Texas : Deep Vellum Publishing, 2021. | Novel.
Identifiers: LCCN 2020041307 (print) | LCCN 2020041308 (ebook) | ISBN
9781646050390 (trade paperback) | ISBN 9781646050406 (ebook)
Classification: LCC PG3483.I448 O213 2021 (print) | LCC PG3483.I448
(ebook) | DDC 891.73/5—dc23
LC record available at https://lccn.loc.gov/2020041307
LC ebook record available at https://lccn.loc.gov/2020041308

Cover Art by Rob Wilson | robwilsonwork.com
Interior Layout and Typesetting by KGT

Printed in the United States of America

THE

TOOL

AND

THE

BUTTERFLIES

1

Mr. Arseny Iratov was sleeping. He never had any trouble falling asleep at night—not because his fifty-odd years had left his nervous system untouched, but because he'd chosen the right therapy. For twenty-five years now, he'd swallow two little pills three minutes before bed and go right to sleep, preferring to lie on his side with his legs tucked up against his stomach.

Sometimes he had nice, bright dreams, and sometimes his dreams had mundane plots, but with an atmosphere of anxiety. He often had no dreams at all, though.

Eventually, Mr. Iratov began to wonder whether taking meds for such a protracted period really was a wise decision, so he went to see a neurologist he knew, who, almost shouting, rebuked him for neglecting to inform his friend of the sorry state he was in—maybe he could have gotten proper professional help, but now he was a full-fledged drug addict . . .

"You have no one to blame but yourself for your nightmares and anxiety!" When he was done with his indignant wailing, the neurologist informed Iratov that there were still treatment options available. He canceled the old prescription and replaced it with a trendy—and expensive—antidepressant.

Mr. Iratov obediently abandoned his "practically narcotic substances" and began taking the costly new pills. After a week, the patient started feeling poorly and said as much to the friend who'd given him the new prescription.

"That's a case of withdrawal—and a nasty one," the neurologist declared. "You'll just have to deal with it." What Iratov had to deal with was aching bones, total insomnia, and an unusual urge to consume copious amounts of food, an urge so strong it made his hands tremble with impatience. Black and blue circles appeared under his eyes, making him look almost like an old man, which alarmed his darling Vera, the thirty-year-old with whom he enjoyed unwedded—but very nice—living arrangements. They got along splendidly. He had set her up on the floor above, explaining that he needed to spend most of his time in peace and solitude and that he was completely incapable of falling asleep in the same bed as a lady. The lovely Vera hardly raised any objections to these peculiarities of her gentleman friend's constitution and contented herself with living in her own apartment in a lovely building in an excellent neighborhood. The couple would lunch in boutique restaurants, visit theaters and museums, and enjoy infrequent but passionate intimacy; ten years into their relationship, they still kissed voraciously, on the lips.

Vera loved Iratov deeply and intensely, like a true Russian woman who was raised properly, with fine sensibilities, prepared to give of herself unconditionally. Mr. Iratov reciprocated his lady friend's strong feelings, worshipping her as an example of the sublime, and he was anything but selfish with her. Quite the contrary, he was never tightfisted where the woman he loved was concerned. The deeds to both apartments were in her name, as was the title to the luxury car, and she had a whole suitcase of treasures and a significant monthly allowance. Most importantly, though, Iratov's bequest to her in his will was as wide as the Volga, even though he had plenty of people among whom he could divide his sizeable fortune.

His withdrawal from the old meds just wouldn't end, though; it had already been dragging on for three months. His once steady blood pressure was hopping up and down like a kangaroo in the bush, and his stool left much to be desired. But worst of all were the episodes of déjà vu—not rare moments of delightful surprise, like normal people have, but torturous hours of hyperrealism that carried Iratov's consciousness away into the past, forcing him to relive times long since gone until he felt as if he were being ripped asunder. His life could hardly be compared with those of the Biblical martyrs, though—it was just a regular life, with the usual ups and downs. Iratov knew very well that hell is shame, not some frying pan full of sizzling oil. Shame elevated to an absolute. Burning in hell is burning with shame. Before you pass the hundreds of people you have wronged in your life—perhaps without even realizing you were doing it— and the shame, multiplied a thousandfold, becomes almost eternal. When Iratov had his episodes of déjà vu, he was burning in shame. Maybe there was someone who wanted it that way . . .

Strong-willed as he was, Mr. Iratov forced himself to resume his daily walks. He typically strolled down the lanes of Moscow's fashionable Arbat district, and, before the onset of his illness, he would derive endless pleasure from the city's architecture. He was a connoisseur, an aesthete, and things of beauty never failed to resonate with him . . . But now he hobbled along, leaning on an elegant ebonite-handled cane, oblivious to the intricate ruffles of the hand-sculpted palaces and all the masterpieces of nineteenth-century classicism. Like some uncouth peasant standing on a silk Persian rug in his muddy bast shoes, not even realizing just how uncouth he was—that's the state Iratov was in.

He suffered panic attacks, dragging himself along and recoiling from everyone he encountered—each passerby appeared as some protrusion from the regular surface of the world, flashing with excessive, celluloid brightness that made them dangerous. Iratov's brain told him that these baleful pictures of ordinary streets with demon cars and pedestrians straight out of a science-fiction movie were just a trick his mind was playing on him, monsters birthed by the sleep of his exhausted reason . . .

He managed to complete his usual route, but by the end he was drenched, nearly swimming in sweat, even though it was the dead of winter.

Things were easier at home. He wasn't afraid there; he could even talk on the phone in his usual confident way, but he had the eyes of a sickly dog, and Vera couldn't stand to see him like that. She hardly left his side in those difficult times, of course. She did all the cooking herself—and there was a lot to do. Iratov requested pilaf with big chunks of meat, pot after pot of pasta, and desserts that Vera would order from Café Pushkin.

All through that wretched time of human suffering, the little pills that Iratov had taken for twenty-five years lay unused in his desk drawer. His subconscious constantly reminded him that all he had to do was take a couple and he would be back to normal within an hour. But his will—the highest value, the greatest distinction for any man—was so firm, so strong that it never wavered for an instant. This is how it has to be, Mr. Iratov told himself. Serenity comes at a price, and I have the will to pay that price!

His will was too strict, though. On long, sleepless nights, his brain searched for justifications for this brutal revenge—and, alas, there was a great deal to find.

The moment came when Iratov realized that he might die very soon. That didn't frighten him; he was just upset at the thought of losing Vera. He wasn't done enjoying her, wasn't done loving her. He'd only drunk a quarter glass of this rare wine, and the chance to savor it, one drop at a time, like the most precious elixir to balance body and soul, would be lost. It didn't bother Iratov that he hadn't fully gorged himself on his material wealth. He understood that human existence is just a brief transition between one state and another, but unselfish love elevates a man in the eyes of God. In the place where he was fashioned, castles had already been built for his immortal soul, standing on an eternal foundation, sublime and indestructible . . . Or perhaps shame would come first. But the shame would end, even if it took millennia.

"I love you!" Vera said, stroking Iratov's shoulder-length hair, black as a crow's wing, with one gray streak that looked like winter. "I love you . . ." And she kissed his handsome face with its demonic features, unhurriedly, at nearly regular intervals. Temple, jaw, cheek—and then her responsive lips slid down to his neck.

In those brief moments, Mr. Iratov thought that he was almost well again; he even started to enjoy himself for a moment—until he realized that he had tears in his eyes. It was just gross—gross!—it was unworthy of his stony structure, the granite that constituted him. There are no tears in stone . . . He gently rebuffed Vera and bade her withdraw.

Iratov tried to make sense of what was happening to him on his own, spending hours poring over every internet source he could find. Thanks to his perfect English, that included professional European medical sites, where he studied G-proteins, beta-blockers, all the chemistry behind his condition, but the deeper he plunged into all that medical terminology, the more he realized that there simply wasn't one single way to treat a disorder like his. He discovered that many truly great people hardly left their homes, tormented by panic attacks for decades until they died alone, and that he, a man crushed under the weight of his own fear, was likely also fated to die like that, cooped up in here, deprived of a normal life.

He spoke to Vera.

"I don't want you to waste your life on my madness!"

"You're not mad!"

"But I'm still an invalid."

"I'm your wife . . ."

"No, you're not. There are no vows binding you to me."

"Oh, don't be such a jerk!"

"You still have your own destiny!" He extended his beautiful hands and stroked Vera's cheeks with his long fingers. "You'll have everything, believe me!"

She wouldn't argue with him, and, whenever he tried to have the big conversation again, she would go to her upstairs apartment, weeping and wondering how she could help the man she loved. She kept on making pilaf . . .

Iratov, who had so recently been a strong, handsome, and statuesque society gentleman, would probably have withered away like a proud flower, and inadvertently dried his darling Vera out, too, but, on one of those melancholy days, he got a call from Israel. It was Iratov's partner from an old, near-dead sapphire resale business. When he heard the brief and tragic story of Iratov's ailment, he answered concisely.

"You do know I trained as a doctor, right?"

"Rheumatology, as I recall," Mr. Iratov answered.

"My specialty has nothing to do with this. Let me tell you something, my dear fellow—when a man finds his pill, that's a miracle, do you hear me? A miracle! Most people never find their pills, never! But the Lord has unveiled yours to you! Hallelujah!"

"But the neurologist said—"

"The world is full of quacks and idiots! Steer clear of those con men and don't confuse willpower with the kind of stupidity that can get you killed! We'll talk business when you're back on your feet. I have this sapphire . . ."

Iratov stopped listening to his Israeli partner. Mighty thunderbolts were suddenly crackling in his head, followed by torrents of rain that drowned his brain like the Great Flood, cleansing his right mind of its husk of hopeless wandering and fruitless searching. Mr. Iratov lunged toward his desk, tugged at the handle of the drawer, eventually got it open, dug out his old pills, squeezed two of them out of the package, and tossed them in his mouth . . .

For the first time in three months, he enjoyed a night of deep, undisturbed sleep and woke in the morning feeling completely refreshed, his head finally clear, his body full of its former strength. Some unbelievable joy had overcome his entire being. He was like a man with some terrible ailment, on the very threshold of death, suddenly recovering and receiving decades of his life back, instead of the mere weeks promised to him. His senses were as they had been in childhood; whatever he looked at, be it a leaf on a tree, a cloud, or an ordinary sunbeam—the most trivial, everyday things—it was a discovery of global significance, except that this man was not obliged to share this happiness with mankind. It's just for you; it's all yours!

Iratov smiled at the sky, whispering words of gratitude, then shouted at the top of his lungs, trumpeting like a whale, announcing to the world that he was the biggest man on earth, the strongest, and now he was bubbling over with fountains of love for mankind and the generous desire to share this new, mighty energy!

"I'm going to live! Live!"

Then he shaved, taking his time, enjoying the smell of the cream and the way the aftershave made his skin prickle. He washed his hair and carefully combed his shining locks, as black as Hammerite paint. He looked in the mirror and was a little troubled by the extra weight he'd put on while he was ill. But he knew that two weeks of tennis and swimming would be enough to rid him of his excess flesh.

He grew hungry, but, for the first time in a long while, his body wasn't trembling in expectation of abundant food. Iratov pulled on a pair of jeans with holes—the ones all the kids were wearing—and a T-shirt with the bold slogan "I love KGB," slipped his bare feet into sneakers, and charged up to Vera's apartment, taking the stairs two at a time . . .

After his usual fried eggs with toast and coffee, he made tender, lasting love to his darling Vera.

"My demon . . . you're back," she whispered delightedly in his ear.

They became one, and it was noon by the time they became two again. Then, happy and pleasantly tired, they started making plans. Theaters, museums, trips to faraway lands, working out together . . . They made enough plans for two lifetimes, but first they agreed to have dinner at a little Georgian restaurant near the Old Arbat.

He went back to his study, feeling like a David who had conquered the Goliath within himself. His imperious thoughts turned toward creating value, and he dialed the number of his brokerage firm in Switzerland. Once he'd heard the indices that had changed in his absence, he issued some instructions to sell energy sector stocks and acquire European bonds. He also exercised some options on currency pairs in the developing world.

Vera appeared between calls.

"What should I do with all that pilaf? There's a whole pot . . ."

"Give it to the doorman! It's healthy food for me from here on out!"

He called his Israeli partner via Skype and inquired about the sapphire.

"Back to your old self?" his partner asked with a chuckle.

"Thank you, Robert!"

"Don't thank me! I need you more than you need me."

"Okay, I owe you one."

"Well, I've got this sapphire that's excellent across the board. If you could only see the color, whoa mama! I know that you've moved away from dealing with stones . . ."

"What kind of weight are we talking?"

"Twenty-eight carats."

"Wow . . ."

Iratov had not been interested in buying and selling precious stones for some time. The fierce competition and serious risks had driven him away from the tears of the earth many years ago. That was what he called diamonds, sapphires, and emeralds: the tears of the earth. Still, he asked Robert about the price of the sapphire—and then asked him for a discount. His partner's offer of 15 percent satisfied Iratov, on the condition that the stone and all the accompanying paperwork would be in Moscow by the following day.

"I will wire you the money posthaste."

"So you'll take it?" asked his amazed partner.

"Yes."

Mr. Iratov understood perfectly well that this was not the time to be purchasing precious stones, but it wasn't the prospect of future profit that led him to acquire the sapphire. He was doing his partner a favor—no, more like returning a favor, paying off a debt incurred by relying on someone else's wisdom. Well, and the sapphire was meant for his darling Vera, of course, a reward for her selfless love.

Iratov was on the phone all day, contacting his architecture firm, then his tailor, Lev, promising to drop by and order a new suit. He called the trainer to inquire how Eros, his beloved thoroughbred, was doing. He planned to do many other things on the day of his miraculous restoration, too.

Meanwhile, Vera, dressed all in white and wearing a white

headscarf, was visiting the Church of the Exaltation of the Cross in the Ostozhenka district, where she lit candles, donated money for the church's needs, bought forty days of prayer, and then went to confession, shedding tears of joy . . . She was pure now, as pure as the sky above Jerusalem. Assistant Rector Ivan Ostyatsky, a deacon, nearly started crying too, astonished by the light shining from her pristine soul.

The ritual words were pronounced by Ostyatsky, and he blessed her many times. Then Vera informed the deacon that she wanted a child, but it just wasn't working out.

"Well, the Matrona is at Donskoy Monastery! Go petition her!"

"The man I live with . . . well, we were never married in a church."

"Then I will perform the ceremony."

"He doesn't even know that I go to church."

"Just open up to him. If he loves you, will he not understand?" The deacon pressed his hands to his heart.

Vera had no idea how Iratov would view the fact that she was a churchgoer and was deeply devoted to Jesus Christ, while he regarded the Son of God as one of mankind's greatest humanitarians, but not His son.

"But Vera, why would the Creator need a son?"

She knew the answer perfectly well, but she wanted to avoid theological disputes at home, so she simply shrugged, as if wholeheartedly accepting Iratov's words. Husband knows best, after all.

"Is your spouse a man of faith?"

"No," Vera answered, "but he knows for certain that God exists."

"But that *is* faith!"

"He says that knowledge of God is more important than faith in Him."

"What an interesting fellow!" Deacon Ivan said with a laugh. "I would like to break bread with him! Bring him with you sometime—I'm sure the rector won't disapprove."

Vera evaded Ostyatsky's offer, knowing that there would be no meal shared among the three of them, and changed the subject to the Matrona.

"I will take your advice and visit the saint."

"Good thinking."

After standing in line for four hours, she realized that at that rate she would be late for dinner with Iratov, so she sadly settled on stepping out of the crowd and back into worldly life, but, at that very moment, a thin, ragged-haired, and hook-nosed old man, who looked vaguely Greek, took her by the arm. He was wearing an ankle-length black coat and a gloomy expression. He hissed that he had someone holding a place in line up ahead, right by the entrance. Before she could even open her mouth, she found herself near the flower-bedecked icons of the Matrona. In front of her stood a strikingly beautiful young woman with dark skin and blue eyes.

"Where'd she come from?" Vera wondered.

"Petition her, petition her already!" the old man urged.

So she began petitioning the Matrona for a miracle for a little boy with black eyes—whispered a little to herself, and pressed her lips against the protective glass.

She was swept away to the exit. Carried along by the flow of people, she searched the crowd for the old man with the Greek features, but it was as if he had dissolved in the descending twilight.

"An angel!" Vera thought. "Or a devil."

Thick, soft snow began to fall, and by evening, the whole city was covered with December manna. The new year was coming . . .

•

Mr. Arseny Iratov was sleeping. No alarming dreams tormented his serene consciousness, just nice little pictures of bygone days, flickering fleetingly. Vera's face . . . it was a miracle how lovely she looked yesterday, clad all in white. Blue eyes under bright lashes . . . A skewer with chunks of meat strung on it, a glass of red wine . . . His mother's smile, somewhere far away. There was only one picture that didn't fit in with the rest of the luminous exhibit—it was too crude, too Soviet—Captain Alevtina Vorontsova, in full-dress vestments, baring her teeth in a baleful smile . . . This last apparition was sent by a full bladder, which forced Mr. Iratov to awaken, though not fully. He rose from his bed on autopilot, without opening his eyes, remaining in contact with his dream, went into the bathroom, suffused with the greenish glow of night-lights, stopped in front of the toilet, pulled down his pajama pants just a little, and reached below his stomach, but couldn't find what he sought, the means by which the body usually rids itself of excess fluid. He had to wake up, regain his coordination. He opened his eyes, braced one hand against the wall and used the other to try and find the primary organ of the male body. It was nowhere to be found . . . Iratov's brain struggled to process this tactile input like an old, lagging computer. He had to bend down and bring his vision into play. Then his consciousness emitted a death cry, as if someone had stabbed it with an electric carving knife.

It was gone! Gone!

Searchlights flashed on beneath his cranium, mobilizing his entire nervous system. Iratov, perspiring in horror, stumbling out of his pants, moved over to the huge, six-foot-high mirror. One foot got caught in his pant leg, and he fell, painfully hitting his knee on a floor tile. He rose to his feet, hoping that it was a hallucination brought on by his ailment returning, but when he flipped the switch and stood there, naked and bathed in light, he was finally compelled to accept it: the member was missing from his reflection, as was the scrotum typically adjoining it.

He recalled an epidemic of jealous American wives cutting off their husbands' manhood—what if . . . ? His knee still bleeding, he looked at himself in the mirror but could find no trace of a wound in his groin area. Probing beneath his stomach with one fingertip, Mr. Iratov felt only a flat, smooth surface, and a little bump . . .

Iratov remembered that he had a magnifying mirror on a telescoping metal arm—the kind often found in hotels. He stood on a chair and moved the mirror toward his groin like a magnifying glass. On the even surface of his skin, so smooth it was as if nothing had ever been growing there to begin with, was a small, neat hole. Mr. Iratov studied it for a long time, like that hole was a wormhole in space, or a black hole sucking up his entire being . . . His brain refused to believe the visual stream it was receiving, but Iratov famously viewed belief in anything at all as nonsense. He was convinced that knowledge alone defined existence. Know therefore this day, and consider it in thine heart!

He got down from the chair, sat on the toilet, and relieved himself like a woman. That black hole was not a black hole, but a urethra. Dumbfounded, he asked himself how something like this could have happened. He stuck his hand into his groin again and again, verifying that what was happening was reality and not a hallucination . . . He sat on the toilet for so long that he wound up emptying his bladder once more, then pulled on his pajama pants, plodded back to bed, conked out, and slept until morning.

It was a bitterly cold night; the snow wrapped itself around the streetlights and then froze, so many of them burnt out.

Of course, the moment he woke up, he plunged his fingers

between his thighs in the hope that it had all been some night-mare vision. He detected only emptiness. He rummaged around in his sheets. Nothing. He did not, however, find this situation as horrible as he had a few hours before. His brain was comforting itself, crooning to his consciousness. *That* wasn't the most important thing for a man over fifty, and one could view this whole situation as ironic or even downright funny.

Iratov just couldn't laugh at himself, though. He set off for the bathroom, where he brushed his teeth, shaved, and made himself comb his hair. The gray streak, in particular, vexed him, as if he were still a strong, handsome man, ready to win another hundred women's hearts.

"That's just how it goes," he declared. "But does it?"

Iratov sat down at the computer without having breakfast, hoping to find an answer on the World Wide Web. Even after an hour, no answer was forthcoming, since he could not even formulate the search term. His brain urged his fingers to type, "Have your sexual organs disappeared?" What utter nonsense! "Did your tool leave you?" It was like something out of a fairy tale. Kolobok, the pancake who rolled away on his own, or the living gingerbread man . . . He finally managed a smile. "How to live without your member."

He answered the phone. It was Vera, inquiring as to whether he'd already had breakfast or if he wanted to join her.

"You may come downstairs," Mr. Iratov said.

She prepared an excellent omelet with tomatoes and mush-rooms, made toast with cheese, and brewed some coffee.

Iratov ate, not without enjoyment, all the while thinking about what problems this situation might cause. He didn't like going to the sauna—he found the whole thing repellant. What about tennis? Well, he could get changed in a VIP booth, and swimming would actually be easier . . . Or maybe he could stick something from a sex shop in his swimsuit? And there was another plus: he could ride a bike without worrying about his groin hitting the frame . . .

Meanwhile, Vera was cheerfully relating something, smiling and chirping away, like a princess from a movie. She was describing some adorable little tykes she'd seen playing outside, romping in the white drifts and making a snowman. Then she was wondering how mothers ever got by without diapers, dietary supplements, and formula. Vera did not consciously realize why she was talking about the neighborhood kids, that it was all leading to the subject that was most important to her, the glorious laurel every single woman dreams will crown her life: motherhood. Iratov could only spare his eyes and face for her, simply letting them react to her tone of voice. He raised his eyebrows, chuckled, and squinted in response, seemingly listening intently, but his brain was considering his new circumstances from every angle, as they were quite extraordinary.

"Well," his brain demanded, "what about your darling Vera? That's the big question. She's singing away about some triviality, like a bird, unaware that her beloved raven has become a chick." That question brought him around to the problem he'd been afraid to consider, the biggest problem: he couldn't just love Vera platonically. She was a young woman who needed the delights of intimacy. On the other hand, Iratov was an experienced man, and he knew many ways to please a woman without using his primary organ. But it was one thing to have options besides the main event, and quite another to have all options and no event . . .

"Do you know the origin of the expression 'sand's falling out of him?'" he asked, interrupting her.

"No," Vera answered.

"In the fifteenth and sixteenth centuries, men, both young

and old, wore hose. Well, they were tight, so naturally, a younger man would have a distinct outline showing through the fabric. As their masculine organs withered, the older men would attach little bags of sand to their family jewels. So when one of those bags broke, sand would fall out of an old man's hose. That's why we say 'sand's falling out of him' when a man's getting old."

"I never knew that," Vera admitted. There was very little in their domestic life that made her peevish, but now she was experiencing a certain displeasure at this story that had nothing to do with what she was talking about, with where her monologue was heading . . .

"He probably doesn't want another child," she thought and bit her lip painfully, becoming truly upset, to the point that it almost made her unattractive. Claiming to be indisposed, she asked to be excused.

"Certainly, certainly," Mr. Iratov answered graciously. "If you need any help—"

"No, no, it's just female things."

At two p.m., he went to visit a doctor he knew, a specialist in urology and gynecology who worked at a private andrology clinic. Iratov had barely seen him since their college days, but he happened upon the doctor's ad in a magazine. A gray-haired man with the face of a butcher promised to solve any men's health problem.

The doctor was a strange fellow. He started making his money in the eighties, just like Iratov. While he was a medical student, the future Doctor Sytin boasted that he was related to the very same Sytin who was the publisher of all publishers. He made a name for himself selling platinum ingots of the highest grade, stolen from a state enterprise. It was big business. It was also a firing-squad offense, but he was never brought in by the Soviet police, not even when they checked his papers. He always had a complete set in his pocket: ID, Communist Youth League card, union membership papers. They called Sytin "the Wizard" because he handled millions of ill-gotten rubles, was admitted to some big-time urology association, but never encountered the law enforcement organs of the USSR, not even on a drunk and disorderly charge. That's because he didn't drink. Iratov was one of Sytin's regular customers. He bought precious metals, and lots of them, while the Wizard treated him for gonorrhea, which almost everyone in the country had.

"Sytin's probably no poorer than I am," Iratov thought as he waited. "But he's still slaving away. Maybe he lost everything in the financial crisis? Or is he using his job to protect his fortune? Passing himself off as a regular doctor so nobody tries to raid his assets?"

A few minutes later, they greeted each other with a hug— they were old college buddies, after all.

"Hey there, Wizard!" Iratov said with a genuine smile.

"How's it going, Yakut!" the speculator with the prominent chin and gray hair answered in his bass voice, taking Mr. Iratov by the shoulders and examining him at arm's length. "Man, you sure are a handsome guy, still looking good after all these years! How about some coffee?"

"It must be my genes . . . Some coffee would be great."

"Marina! Two coffees! Cream for you?"

"I take it black."

"One with cream!" the famous publisher's relative shouted.

They sat down on opposite ends of a sofa and continued examining each other, grasping for memories of their youth.

"Where'd you disappear to, back then?"

"Before Gorbachev, you mean?"

"Yeah, around then," Sytin answered, trying to remember. "I almost went down because of that metal for you. You never

picked up the order! Boy, I lost a good chunk of change! Well,
water under the bridge . . ."

"I did a little time."

"No kidding? I had no idea!" The doctor lit a cigarette and
thought for a few minutes. "I was pretty pissed at you back then,
Yakut. I thought I'd never forgive you. But if that's how it went
down . . . I should be thanking you for not turning me in . . . How
long were you in the can?"

"They promised to shoot me . . ." Iratov didn't enjoy
remembering all that. He went pale, momentarily finding himself back then. "It all blew over. They didn't even put me in a
high-security camp!"

"Yeah . . ." Sytin drawled, sending a stream of smoke at the
ceiling. "Those were some crazy times . . ."

"How come they let you off the hook? How come you never
got caught?"

"Actually, I got caught right away," the urologist answered
with a chuckle. "But then they made me an offer—" Iratov
tensed up at this. "No, no, they didn't make me their mole.
This one guy took me on—interesting character—it turned
out he worked for Andropov. Well, he worked for himself more
than anything. Who the hell knows, though? Anyway, he proposed that I keep doing the same thing but give him a 90 percent cut. He covered for me, and I earned him ten mil. But
after that—sometime in the late eighties—he started divvy-
ing up the cash among the most committed Communist Youth
League guys . . . three of them are in the Russian Forbes top
ten now. I probably wasn't the only guy like that he had . . .
No, I couldn't have been. I put everything I had into government bonds, then I got greedy in '98 and lost everything, so I
went back to my profession, and five years later I'd built my
own clinic, all with legit money."

"There's no keeping you down," Iratov said. "You really are a wizard, if you managed to get your business off the ground in times like these. Rising after a fall is no mean feat!"

"Well, how about you, Yakut? Did you manage to hang on to anything?" Sytin asked.

"Oh, you know, a crumb or two... So are you really related to Sytin, or were you just pulling our legs to look like a big shot?"

"Yeah, I'm related to him . . ." said the urologist/gynecologist/andrologist. "Well, distantly . . ."

The old friends found that they had nothing else to talk about. They finished their coffee.

"Yeah . . ." one of them drawled significantly.

"Yeah . . ." the other seconded.

"Well, let's get down to business!" said the urologist, returning to his desk. "You didn't just come here to reminisce, after all. There's something troubling you, I can see it in your eyes. I'm at your service—this is no place to be shy!"

Iratov didn't know where to begin; he merely muttered sheepishly. The clinic owner waited calmly for his patient to work up the nerve, looking him in the eye intently, as if hypnotizing him.

"Well, what is there to say? I'd better just show you," said Mr. Iratov, finally ready. He got off the sofa, undid his belt, and dropped his pants and underwear to his knees.

The doctor silently examined Iratov's groin, smooth as a piece of cardboard. He looked and thought in silence, while his patient pulled his shirt up to his navel so he could get a good look.

There was a knock at the door.

"Idrisov is on line two," Marina proclaimed.

"Not now!" Sytin barked at the locked door. "Getting ready for gender reassignment?" he asked Iratov quietly.

"Huh?"

"But why do it as two separate procedures?" asked Iratov's old friend, thinking out loud. "Did they prescribe hormone replacement therapy? Why haven't they performed the vaginoplasty yet?"

"No, no way, no!" Mr. Iratov shouted, putting an end to the doctor's wild speculation. "Gah! What surgery?! What vaginoplasty?! What's wrong with you? Are you nuts?"

"Well, what *is* going on, then?"

Then Iratov had to recount the unbelievable story of his disappearing sex organs. His speech was halting, wandering, a far cry from his usual manner of expression, and he broke off after every other word, fully aware of how surreal his story and his appearance were.

"Are you sure it wasn't an assault?"

"It happened last night! I would have bled out a long time ago!"

"That's true . . . You've got blood vessels down there, vein clusters, arteries . . . You would have been gone in an hour . . . Well, what's going on?"

"You're the doctor," Iratov said with a shrug. "What's your hypothesis?" Now wielding a magnifying glass, the urologist knelt and examined the problem area for some time, probing with his fingers. "Does it hurt here? No? How about here?" After about twenty minutes of medical investigation, Sytin was only certain of one thing.

"If I didn't know you, I would say that this is a classic female pubic mound with an undeveloped vagina and sexual organs. That can happen when the endocrine profile—"

"It's not a pubic mound!" said Iratov, beginning to hiss with fury. "Sytin, please, can the theory, what I need is practice!"

"Yes, yes," said the doctor, clearly baffled by his own

theorizing about the origins of this saucy situation, contemplating how interesting it was—scientifically speaking, that is. "A medical marvel," he thought. "There is no rational explanation for what happened . . . assuming Yakut isn't lying, of course."

"How about your libido, your sex drive?" he asked aloud.

"I satisfied my wife a few times yesterday morning."

"Ah, I see there's a reason for all those rumors about you! They said you were a real sexathon man—the whole gang was jealous!"

"Why are you bringing that up now?" asked Iratov, irritated. "I've been left with no dick!"

"Indeed." Sytin agreed. "And no balls either," he added, then instantly caught himself. "I'm not mocking you, simply stating a medical fact! Scoot on over to the cot! No need to put your pants back on yet. Face me, tuck your knees up by your chin. Anything getting in the way?"

"Not anymore," Iratov responded, and all through the prostatic secretions test, with all the revolting sensations that accompanied it, he remained firm in his conviction that what he had lost was not of primary importance, or even secondary, for that matter.

When Sytin had finally obtained the juice he sought, he called in his assistant Marina, and gave her a vial for the lab.

"Strictly anonymous," he said in a near-whisper.

Mr. Iratov finally returned his garments to their proper places and sat in the chair.

"What do you want?" Sytin asked directly.

"What do I want? Ideally, for everything to go back to normal."

"I must admit, this is a unique situation for me . . . no, I must say, for all of medical science! There is no sign of surgical intervention whatsoever. Everything looks as if this was the way nature had intended. Maybe you never had anything there in the first place?" the doctor asked with a sly squint. "Maybe your prolific sexual conquests were all an elaborate tale you spun for our benefit? Were you just born a little different?"

"I have children, Sytin," Iratov sighed wearily. "I don't even know how many. One of them only turned up recently—paternity test in hand. He's grown up, probably wants money, but he says he just never knew who his father was, so he was hungry for answers. I have a gorgeous young wife. Why would she want a guy with no . . . Well, you know."

"Where did that son of yours get the genetic material? Maybe he's trying to take you for a ride . . ."

"We leave our genetic material everywhere! We lose hair at the barbershop and teeth at the dentist, we spit out our gum—"

"Then you're a medical marvel!" Sytin concluded. "A phenomenon that has never been documented anywhere! I have never even heard of such a thing in old wives' tales!"

"Way to make me feel better . . ."

Marina brought back the results of an expedited test. Sytin dropped his eyes to the paper and quickly familiarized himself with them.

"Everything looks normal! No white blood cells, very few epithelial cells, no sign of serious infection detected. The prostate itself is in perfect condition."

"Good to hear."

"Let's see what I can do for you . . ."

"What do you mean?"

"Do you know how far medicine has come? Or what kind of technology I have at my disposal? Looks like you don't! Well, it's expensive—"

"*What* is expensive?" Iratov interrupted, frustrated again. "Talk sense!"

"Penile prosthetics—a panacea for all men who have suffered traumatic injuries, whether at war or in everyday life! We take skin grafts from the back of the thigh and grow additional layers in a special container, then when it's time for the surgery, we combine it with plastic to create a new member and scrotum. Then one prosthetic ball is implanted, while the other will serve as a pump for filling the new organ's built-in erection chamber with fluid. That pump compresses the functional ball like the cuff on a blood pressure machine, which enables you to fill the organ itself with fluid—and an erection is achieved! Note, however, that this is an erection that will never end. You are its master! When you get tired of it, simply deflate the penis and the fluid recedes. Cosmetically, it will be as natural as the original!"

Flushed and satisfied, Sytin concluded his monologue and awaited a response. Iratov sat and pondered. So his problem could be eliminated after all—it wouldn't be easy, true, but it was possible. That conclusion forthwith restored his faith in a brighter tomorrow and a brighter day after tomorrow, too.

"How much does it cost?" he asked.

"Oh, it varies. American prostheses are good, Chinese ones are a little worse."

"I didn't even buy Chinese in the Soviet days!"

"A wise choice! So, the American one, plus the operation, lab work, and surgeons' fees . . . It'll come to between fifty and seventy thousand dollars, give or take. If that's too much, I can still vouch for the Chinese model—"

"Wizard, come on! I have enough for the American one."

"You rascal, Yakut!" the urologist said with a smile. "So you do have a little something tucked away. 'Crumbs' he says! By the way, I forgot to tell you the most important thing—you will enjoy the sexual act as much as you did at seventeen! The nerve endings of your prostate are in perfect condition, so you can get your new dick wet as often as you like!"

"That's reassuring!"

"I hate to break it to you, but you won't be able to have any more children. Creating artificial spermatozoa is currently beyond the power of medical science. Not that you need any more kids!"

"That's for sure..."

As they were saying their goodbyes, the old friends hugged again, agreeing that Iratov would take some time to mull things over, discuss it with his wife, and then inform Sytin of his decision. It was only at the door that Sytin realized he was privy to no personal data whatsoever about his patient; all he knew was the nickname "Yakut." He didn't know his first or last name. "Life is strange," thought Sytin as he closed the door behind his patient but did not pursue any further philosophical reflection—he knew full well the dangers of overthinking things. It was pointless! That superficial interpretation sufficed to ensure that he was capable of getting by in a civilized society . . . Yeah, he didn't know the guy's name—did that change his life or something?

At the same time, Iratov was walking down the stairs, thinking parallel thoughts about Sytin. What was his doctor's name? They'd known each other for like thirty years, and he just called him Wizard . . . But what the hell did he need his name for anyway?

Iratov arrived at his architecture firm, located on two floors of a historic mansion in the Ostozhenka district, Moscow's Golden Mile. As befits a lordly man with democratic values, he went through every department, even shaking hands with the new draftsmen, and asked the department heads how their work on the World Cup stadium was progressing. Everything proved to be coming along just fine: most of the calculations for the utilities and structural elements were complete, and the firm was even set to complete the project ahead of schedule. Their first model, shaped like half a pumpkin, had received a prestigious prize in Amsterdam. The orange structure, its enclosed walkways fitted with windows resembling jack-o'-lantern eyes, didn't just dazzle the Dutch; bids for the idea had come in from nearly a dozen countries. Russia won—the arrangements for the contract work hadn't hurt.

Once he was finished talking to the employees, Iratov proceeded to his spacious office; it was designed in the best traditions of minimalism, but still elegant, showing clients that its master appreciated sophisticated simplicity. The office also had a hidden room with its own facilities, as well as a soft Arabian-style sofa with birds of paradise on the upholstery (and, naturally, tassels) where Iratov could recline. It was also fitted with a bar, a coffee machine, and a bunch of other junk: sketches of old projects, a big-screen television, walls lined with the certificates and awards Iratov had earned throughout his successful life in the international architecture world.

Mr. Iratov visited the lavatory and once again relieved himself like a lady. He could have easily begun dwelling on that, but he'd already accepted the major changes his new situation had brought. Sitting or standing . . .

Iratov returned to his actual office, poured himself a glass of whisky, contacted his assistant, Vitya, and verified that the first part of the plan had been sent to the Russian Football Union.

"Certainly, Mr. Iratov!"

"You remembered about the credit, right?" he asked, automatically twirling his elegant fish-patterned ring around his finger.

"Everything was done in accordance with your instructions.

A new seal was prepared and every sheet was stamped with 'Designed by Arseny and Andrei Iratov.'"

"Well done! What else?"

"A strange middle-aged man who declined to give his name is waiting for you in the conference room."

"Strange how?"

"He has a briefcase handcuffed to his wrist . . ."

"Bring him here."

"Certainly, Mr. Iratov!"

A minute later, an entity with the appearance of a mercenary appeared at his door. Iratov remembered that face. He knew who this was. "Oh, now I've done it," he thought. "Now I've done it." Owing to tragic circumstances of an intimate nature, Iratov had completely forgotten that he had agreed to a major transaction with his Israeli friend just yesterday. He had forgotten to wire the money, but it appeared that the sapphire in question was now in this courier's briefcase. He was a man of about forty, with Middle Eastern features—a former Mossad agent who had worked for Iratov's Israeli friend for many years, and now he was standing on this rug here in Russia, not moving.

"I never transferred the money!" Iratov said. The courier nodded his close-cropped head. "I'll do it now . . ."

In just a few minutes, Iratov ordered an electronic transfer and shifted a six-figure sum into his Israeli friend's account. He nodded to the courier, who promptly extracted a cell phone from his pocket and placed an international call. He said a few words in Hebrew, waited for a moment, then terminated the connection. In one movement, he unlocked the handcuffs, advanced a few steps, placed the briefcase on the desk, turned with almost military precision, and exited the office.

The Kashmir stone was immaculate. Iratov examined it with a jeweler's magnifying glass and a powerful lamp, relishing this natural masterpiece: the color of the Atlantic Ocean, flawlessly cut, with ideal proportions and miraculous dark blue coloring. It was stunningly pure, without a single speck of anything alien.

Mr. Iratov had adored precious stones ever since his college days. At first, he treated them as an investment, as a safer and sturdier harbor than currency, but then the financial side became secondary to him, and he learned to love them as true masterpieces, born in the depths of the earth amid geothermal torment. He had an astonishing collection of diamonds, sapphires, and emeralds. It was kept in a Swiss bank, which Iratov visited at least once a month. He would open his personal safe, take out the little velvet bag that held his treasures, head back to the hotel, and spend a few hours dipping his fingers in the "pure water," drawing energy from the stones, letting them make him just a little younger, harder, and more confident. Then he would bring the collection back to the bank and return to Russia.

The sapphire from Israel was just a hair beneath his standards for the collection, so Mr. Iratov was glad he would be presenting it to his darling Vera today. He dialed her number and asked how she was feeling.

"I'm all better now," his wife reassured him.

"Excellent! I'll be wrapping up soon. Then I'll come by. You remember that we're going to the Bolshoi tonight, right?"

"Of course."

They attended an avant-garde production of *Eugene Onegin*, which was booed off the stage twenty minutes in, when it was revealed that marijuana had been woven into the fabric of the plot—quite literally. The man seated in the presidential box waved his hand, promptly putting a stop to this unworthy treading of the boards, and the audience left the hall.

"How about Italian?" Iratov asked.

"Sounds good!"

An instant later, he heard someone saying his wife's name somewhere behind him, but with a British accent. "Verie, my dearie!" He turned and peered into the crowd, spotting a man with a spiky, snow-white buzz cut, but absolutely no sign of eyebrows or lashes on his face. Was it him? Guess the freaks are out tonight.

There was a little Italian restaurant near their building. It was owned by an elderly Neapolitan man who had brought his children and grandchildren over to Moscow so they could help him run the family business.

Iratov and Vera loved that place. It was a cheerful little island of sunny Italy in the midst of inclement Russia. Alessandro Italianov, as Iratov and Vera privately called the owner, made the best pasta in the city, and he always kept bottarga—cured tuna roe—in stock, only serving it to his most faithful regulars. The excellent selection of Tuscan wines, cozy, domestic atmosphere, and staff who always worked together smoothly—they were family, after all—made it a favored haunt for Ostozhenka connoisseurs. At the end of the evening, the owner would bring out his guitar and sing old Neapolitan ballads in his weak yet soulful tenor. By the time the third song came around, even chance walk-ins were singing along, especially if it was a sad rendition of "Napoli."

It was there, in the coziest nook, that Mr. Iratov and his darling Vera spent their evening. God, that night was such a pleasure. The beauty of that woman! Dressed in soft gray tones, with her hair up, revealing her graceful ears with their understated diamond studs, wearing some sublime, elusive scent . . . To Iratov, Vera looked like the most precious treasure in the universe, and she belonged to him. He simply couldn't help feeling a sense of pride. At the same time, Vera was looking at her husband, still finding him the handsomest man on the planet, even after a decade of living together. Iratov's black eyes enraptured her, a deep abyss she fell into long ago, when she fell for him; his long, thick hair, cascading to his shoulders in a black curtain, shone like the night sky, and his full lips stood out darkly under his prominent nose and white-streaked hair. It was a combination that presented a major threat to purity and holiness. Her tempter demon!

Mr. Iratov ordered for both of them, and they conversed quietly between sips of Tuscan cabernet.

"I want to go back to Ischia," Vera said. "We spent a few days there, remember?"

"That was ten years ago! I'd only known you for two weeks . . ."

"You brought me there on that yacht, with that dazzling white sail . . . I forget what it was called."

"Eleanor," Iratov reminded her.

"The whole time we were there I wanted to ask you who Eleanor was . . ."

"I told you, remember?" Iratov said with a smile. "That's how it's done—yachts are always given women's names. It's an old tradition. It was the previous owner who named the boat. That's all there is to it. Maybe it was his grandmother's name."

"And hurricanes are all men . . ."

"Because men are the destroyers of their own creations . . . and there's nothing to do on Ischia in the winter. The whole island is deserted; it's depressing."

He ate his spaghetti with truffles, and she her ravioli with pears. The owner served the dessert himself, adding two tall, thin glasses of very old grappa to go with it. Iratov produced a little velvet-lined box from the pocket of his blazer and placed it before Vera.

"What's this?" she asked in surprise, as if she'd never received a present in her life. That reaction was to Mr. Iratov's liking; it indulged his profligate generosity.

"Go ahead, open it."

"But what could it be?" Vera's eyes smiled, and her sweet features constituted indelible surprise.

"Just open it."

"But what if there's a scorpion in there? It'll sting me, and I'll die!"

"Oh no, don't worry," Iratov played along. "There are no scorpions in there."

"Do you promise?"

"Go on," he said hastily, nodding. She opened it.

Men only give generous presents to women who know how to accept them generously. So when Vera opened the little box and saw the huge sapphire reflecting the candlelight, filling the restaurant with blue, she looked at it, seemingly dumbfounded, her eyes moving from the stone to her husband and back again, filling with joy, her entire appearance showing him that it was not the value of his gift that had lit a fire of happiness within her, but the fact that she, Vera, was valued, and loved, as strongly as one can only love his own kin. Then she spoke, her eyes lowered.

"I love you, too." Iratov took his wife's hand and began to caress it. "It's such a beautiful stone!"

"Beauty for my beauty," he said. She drew his hand to her face, her blue eyes looking into the impenetrable black gloom of his.

Then they went home, and Iratov related the story of what had happened, how he had lost his private parts under the strangest of circumstances. At first, Vera took it for a joke—and not a good one, either. She didn't like below-the-belt humor. Iratov knew that, so he hardly ever used it. What had gotten into him? Too much grappa? But Mr. Iratov's entire demeanor demonstrated that he was dead serious, that it was the bitter truth, but there was still hope of making him his old self again through surgery.

"Enough already!" Vera said with unexpected abruptness. "I don't like this! It's disgusting!"

Iratov sighed heavily, went into the bathroom, and changed into his bathrobe. He came back into the living room, froze like a statue for a moment, then opened the flaps of his robe with one motion and stood there, tall and simultaneously thick, with his mighty legs, voluminous ribcage, and glowing skin.

Vera looked at the area below her husband's stomach for so long; it was as if she had not processed this picture at all. Then she spoke matter-of-factly.

"Iratov, you've got no fuckin' dick!"

"I don't like it when women use that kind of language," Mr. Iratov answered, cringing.

"Well, I don't like it that you don't have one! It's gone!" she said with a nervous laugh.

"Do you think I like it? I told you: everything can be fixed surgically."

"But it won't be your f—" she stopped herself. "It won't be yours! How could this happen?"

"I'd like an answer to that question myself," Iratov replied with a shrug, closing his robe and pulling the belt tight. "But I don't have one! And I don't have an answer either!"

"This is horrible!"

"What if I went to war and got wounded like this?"

"But you didn't go to war!" She was truly shocked and full of uncharacteristic acrimony. "You just lost it, lost it in your own bed!" Iratov was angry now, too, so he answered harshly.

"If you don't like it, and you can't accept me this way, then get out!"

"You're throwing me out at a time like this?" asked Vera, suddenly looking distraught.

"I was counting on you to support me, not lash out at me! I can't take this! So get out! Now!"

He went into his study and made a great show of slamming the door behind him.

As she went upstairs, Vera rubbed her face as if trying to scrub away some delusion or hallucination. Back in her apartment, she downed two glasses of red wine and collapsed into an armchair, descending into a nervous breakdown that left her shaking and trembling for almost an hour.

"It was aliens!" she thought convulsively. "Instant castration, without leaving a scar or changing the endocrine profile—there's no such technology on earth! Or was it some kind of bacteria?" Ages ago, in another life, when Vera was twenty, she had been employed as a paramedic in her native city of Samara. She saw a lot in her two years on the job. She saw the bloody mush in the crotch of a man who got hit in the stomach with a powerful firework. She was once in the ambulance with a transgender person suffering from appendicitis. There was at least something resembling female organs down there . . . "Yes, it must have been aliens," she reassured herself.

Vera began to feel ashamed. If it was aliens, then why had she been so cruel? Without him, she couldn't even live, just exist, and pathetically at that! Of course, Iratov's loss of his penis would not radically change their relationship. Vera also thought about how she would probably never have children with Iratov. So, if she stayed with him forever, she would never have children at all. She drank another glass of wine, which made her intoxicated enough to be indifferent.

It was him who went to her, realizing that if a urologist was astonished by what he had seen, his darling Vera must have suffered a near-fatal shock. Iratov found his wife sleeping in an armchair, carefully picked her up and carried her to the bedroom. He undressed her and covered her with a blanket.

"Wait!" she cried as he was leaving. He stopped. "Come here."

Mr. Iratov shed his robe and lay down beside his wife. A moment later, he felt her probing fingers beneath his stomach. Then those restless fingers relaxed, and her hand began to pet his pubic mound. Iratov calmed down. He felt warm, good, like a fixed cat getting scratched.

"I love you," Vera repeated drunkenly.

"Thank you."

Iratov turned around and started kissing his wife's naked body. He was particularly fond of the one breast that was slightly smaller than the other. His full lips touched her stomach, his tongue almost tickling her navel. Then Vera drew a sultry breath and her thighs trembled . . .

Relaxing after their one-sided intimacy, Iratov thought back to the distant past, when a legless cripple who got around on a board with ball bearings on the bottom instead of wheels was halted by him and his college buddies with the question, "Hey buddy, how are things in the bedroom with you like that?"

"Everything's dope!" the cripple answered. "I'm married, with two kids!"

"No kidding?" asked Shevtsova in surprise. She was an upperclassman and the head of the Communist Youth League at the Moscow Architectural Institute. "And everything still works?"

"Well, let me tell ya, honey," the guy explained. "Not everything has to work. Nature has blessed me with nimble fingers, a long nose, and a long tongue. So long as I have one finger left, I'm not impotent!"

They applauded the legless man and gave him two bottles of Zhiguli. He accepted them, yet said that he didn't drink.

"Then give 'em back!" the students demanded.

"I'll bring 'em back to my wife. She likes Zhiguli."

"There you have it," Iratov thought. "I'm not impotent, and I'm not a cripple!"

Vera went to sleep, and he went back downstairs, drank some cognac, and lay down, hoping that what he had lost would, sooner or later, be returned to him.

2

Suffering would not leave my soul. I would say that I only endured my protracted anguish because I realized I could relate Iratov's story to the world. And boy can I! I was troubled by moral and ethical questions, though. Do I have the right? Can I complete the act? Is it not despicable to reveal someone else's intimate secrets? And who am I in comparison with such a lordly personage as Iratov, an aristocrat of blood and spirit?! A hissing serpent! A mute worm! Ah, it takes my breath away, it makes me flush with heat! But when I think about doing it! The sudden lightness that comes with bearing the heavy load of another soul and finally consigning it to memory. The temptation to bring a secret out into the open! A secret made public is like a maiden who has lost her innocence; there is no allure there, nothing out of the ordinary, nothing left unsaid . . . Yesterday, sometime after six p.m., when the cubicle mice of Moscow were waiting in traffic on their way home, I thought I spotted that personage, Iratov, in a store on Znamenka Street—one of those places that sells prepared food. He was standing by the counter—no, more like towering over the marble, an aristocrat with a long streak of gray hair down to his Adam's apple, detached from his hairdo. That streak was draped demonically over his right eye, and, with the left, Iratov studied the freshly prepared, steaming hot chicken Kiev. Just imagine, Iratov in a place like that! I was mistaken, much to my chagrin. It wasn't him, no, it couldn't have been! It was a Gypsy I know. An actor, I think . . . Maybe. Well, they look alike. I went into the prepared food section and tried to buy that same chicken, with the warm butter oozing out of it. I was seven rubles short, but I got two Poltava cutlets instead—more food by weight, meatier, more filling. Plus, I got a small side of fried potatoes. That's a bargain, no two ways about it. Let Iratov enjoy his chicken Kiev. God knows he can afford it . . . Then notes of conscience sounded in my heart again. First of all, I have always considered envy a sin, and this was envy for mythical chicken . . . that's beneath me. I need to develop finer feelings. Including the feeling of envy, sure! But it should be envy elevated to an absolute. Not envy for material possessions, but for their endlessly transparent influence on everyone and everything. Envying the man who lives next to you isn't just about being tortured by fantasies of taking his beautiful wife away from him—no, you dream of pouncing on her like a bogatyr! Iratov has his little Vera. Well, she isn't a perfect ten by my standards, but there's something about her that's higher than beauty: a certain tranquility under her pale skin, a fine mind thrumming with the vein in her temple, pure, sublime blue eyes—and the way she looks at Iratov! I can see how well this girl's mother raised her: my man is divine, I bow my head in recognition of his Biblically appointed purpose, but I, too, am enlightened. I am just a little lower than him, so I can shine forth my light for him while he walks the dark road to his goal—and he will take me with him.

The Poltava cutlets turned out to be more air than meat. Those jerks! And it was the most expensive joint like that in Moscow, too. And that Gypsy, the actor, I figure he'll take to his bed for a few days from the indigestion, and some young guy from the same tribe, let's call him Baxtalo, will take his place, and at his birthday party, the scumbag's gonna holler, "He's here, Roman's here!" Roman is truly the most generous of his clients. He's been dragging his whole Gypsy band around for twenty years. On an ordinary day in a regular luncheonette, he'll shower his dark-haired posse with hundred-dollar bills. At birthday parties, he'll hand out whole stacks of them, and then on anniversaries, he'll offer precious stones for God's sake. His uncle, Vladlen Gubaidullin, owns some coal mines, and where there is coal, there are diamond pipes. It's rather strange. We're talking about a family of Tatars, but they hold Gypsies in high regard—like Russian industrialists before the Bolshevik Revolution. But hey—Russians, Tatars, what's the difference? Well, maybe that party made it so Baxtalo could finally buy that Toyota Camry he'd always dreamed of. A brand-new car, at twenty-two! And now that redhead Khmali, this one Gypsy baron's brother's cousin—Baro, the guy's name is—maybe she favored him with the chance to hold her soft, dusky hand in his. The hand he ran over the soundboard of his guitar so tenderly, strumming the strings—he'll run that same hand over his beloved's cheek. Just you wait . . . when spring rolls around, Baxtalo and Khmali will get married, and by then, Roman's uncle Vladlen Gubaidullin's birthday will come around too, and the aging Gypsy actor will stuff his face with something that'll make him sick, get knocked out of commission by that prepared food joint or some other eatery. And the youngsters will be buying themselves a country home.

I was sick all night. I threw up my potatoes and Poltava cutlets . . . it was the Battle of Poltava all over again, but I came off even worse than the Swedes did. I took five doses of Imodium, which tightened me up so much it felt like I was carrying bricks in my stomach for a week.

On the eighth day, liberation was at hand, and I got on a B-Line trolleybus and headed for the Bolshoi Theatre. I had a dress circle ticket for the premiere of an avant-garde production of *Eugene Onegin*. It wasn't hard to get—I saw the gilded corner of a fancy envelope sticking out of my neighbor's mailbox. He's a bureaucratic swine, without the breeding to go to the theater. I always find expired tickets by the trash can.

The little old ushers didn't want to let me in, since I wasn't exactly outfitted for visiting a temple of the arts. My clothes were neat, though—sleek, even. That's my style. I gave the old ladies a wolfish scowl, and they relented.

"It's the fashion!" I proclaimed. "And I have a tie with me."

"Let him in, why not?" the senior usher said in a low contralto. Was she a singer or something? "It's not like he's going to sit in the stalls," she declared imperiously.

"Why not?" the others agreed.

I went up to the snack bar and positioned myself in line for a salmon canapé, but the lingering heaviness in my underbelly advised against eating fish. I'd only just rid myself of bodily disarray—no more of that. So I bought some chocolate and a cup of coffee. I settled in at a little table, crowding two young ladies in ball gowns. My side even brushed one girl's brocade—the blonde (the real blonde—the second was actually a brunette)—but then I remembered I had forgotten to rent opera glasses, so I quickly finished my Mishka, gulped down my coffee, and went back to the ushers. They greeted me like an old friend, equipped me with the requisite eyepiece, and presented me with a program. I rushed back to the snack bar to catch another whiff of crinoline mixed with elegant perfumes and maybe give the blonde a cheeky wink. I didn't run into the girls, though, which made me a little upset. I heard the first call and went to assume my lawful place, lined with new velvet and marked with the number 19 on a mother-of-pearl plaque.

The grand chandeliers burned bright as day and the orchestra tuned up; the woodwinds and especially the oboes were really going for it. The big strings seemed quite lazy to me. Contemplating the burgundy curtains, the light instrumental cacophony, and the susurrus of humanity made me feel so good that I grinned from ear to ear, covering my missing right incisor with my program.

Ah, the theater! What a magical deception! But, as Pushkin once wrote, I am delighted to be deceived!

The second call boomed forth, and, eye pressed against my opera glasses, I began examining the audience in the stalls. I spotted my young acquaintances from the snack bar and waved to the blonde. She was all in crinoline, with a fan and a corset, which made turning around difficult. Well, forget her! I scanned the theater, from stalls to dress circle. So many celebrities here! Designers, politicians, pop stars, gays—and that must be that famous writer over there, signaling with the reflected light from his bald spot. A grand event, to be sure . . . At that moment, I turned my opera glasses toward the boxes, where the richest and most important people always sit. I saw the industrial oligarch Arnold Ivanovich Tyunin hiding behind his wife. Even the president of our Motherland holds him in high esteem. He entrusts him with projects of national importance. I even spotted Mike Tyson in the opposite box, reclining in his seat and flashing a predatory smile. "Oh, yes," I thought. "He has master classes planned in Moscow. I never imagined that tattooed baboon would know anything about the opera . . ." The government box was dark—nobody there. Top officials don't go to avant-garde plays, especially premieres . . . I shifted my opera glasses and suddenly encountered Iratov's face—a close shot—and I instantly forgot all about the celebrities. Even *Eugene Onegin* became secondary.

How could it be him?! How dare he appear before this kind of crowd after what happened to him?! Beside Iratov's face, the face of Vera, my dearie, emerged as if from the very fabric of reality—stunningly beautiful, framed by fair locks. So dutiful, and—once again—beautiful! What is she doing next to Iratov?

What happened to him should have driven such an elegant creature away! I was so agitated that I even rose from my seat a little, examining the couple, twisting the focus knob on my opera glasses to make the image sharper. Someone behind me grabbed my shirt and hissed at my back that everyone wanted to look around. And my back was all they could see! I turned around—a portly old man with a cow of a wife, both with their own opera glasses offering sixteen-times magnification. I made such a scary face that the portly little man muttered an "excuse me" while his better half held out her opera glasses to me.

"Would you like to take a look?"

"Yes," I answered formidably, but I tempered justice with mercy and gave her a crooked smile designed to reveal my missing right incisor. I grabbed the opera glasses and directed them at Iratov's box.

"What a miraculous instrument," I thought as I saw my dearie Vera's face close up. Her magnificently shaped ears were drawn slightly downward by diamond earrings, and on her neck—no, a little lower—in the nook between her breasts—I could see a big, heavy diamond, a real one, pure as water, ringed with a smattering of emerald undergrowth. The facets shone brightly enough to cut my eyes. She wafted some air toward her face with a fan of white ostrich feathers. One of them stuck to her lovely little nose, fluttered in her warm breath, and contemplating this vision filled me with exquisite tenderness.

What the hell is she doing with Iratov? What good is he to her, after what happened? She cannot be expected to carry this cross forever! Poor Verushka! Do you remember that model in the sixties, an unbelievably beautiful gem of a woman who drove grown men out of their minds, whose assets haunted the dreams of pubescent youths?! Her name was Vera, too, but everyone called her by a pet name—Veruschka. Everyone was

in love with her. Iratov's Verushka is that model reincarnated!
But Iratov, that earthbound realist, just calls her Vera, or something disgustingly trite like "my darling." There's no roman-
tic spirit in him, no capacity to understand that beside him is a
dream that has yet to come true, the treasure of treasures, the
sun of suns!

Iratov turned away from Verushka and told an offhand joke
to some acquaintance, who burst into affected laughter, its false
tones reaching all the way to my modest dress circle seat. The
tails of a black tuxedo opened with a flash of burgundy lining.
Iratov's raiment was supplemented with jewelry, after the old
fashion: a chain bracelet coiling around his broad wrist, a ring
protruding from his index finger, laden with precious stones and
elegant designs. I once had the opportunity to observe that ring
from close up, very close up indeed, on the B-Line trolleybus.
Iratov was standing up, holding on to a handrail, and I was sitting, almost directly beneath his hand—it was big, but the skin
was soft—and I studied every detail. Iratov's ring has many layers. It is not some petty merchant's signet ring with a large central stone, but the most elegant ornament I have beheld in all
my days. There was a cavity in the surface of the ring, containing a little fish in a vignette of white gold, seemingly swimming,
along with inserts made of common stone, pieces of marble,
and a thin little line of granite. There was also a luminous ruby,
of course, like blood bubbling under glass, positioned to the
side, adding a dazzling asymmetry to the piece. I even tried to
snap a stealthy picture of that miracle of the jeweler's art with
my phone, but Iratov instinctively removed his hand, clasping
an ebonite-handled cane, then clutched the rail with the other.
But why was Iratov traveling by trolleybus that day when he
had his own black limousine at his heels? Was he taking public
transportation so he could check out the girls? Was he trying to

find out if somebody was tailing his limo? No, he wasn't looking around; he just hopped off near Neopalimovsky Lane without really observing his surroundings and went into a luxury tobacco store. I had to stay on to remain unnoticed, even though it meant missing my stop . . .

The third call sounded, and the guests settled into their seats. Iratov put his arm around Vera, and they disappeared into the shadows of their box. The chandeliers traded their sunrays for moonbeams, the last cacophonous notes ascended to the uppermost vaults of the theater, there was some faint coughing in the hall—and then silence, the magic of quiescence! It only gets that quiet right before a hurricane or in a theater . . . From up above, I had a good view of the conductor flicking his baton. The orchestra opened harmoniously. The burgundy and gold curtains swept to the side, revealing the first scene of Tchaikovsky's great opera.

I knew that it would be an avant-garde production. The advertisements had made that clear. There were rumors that it was going to be quite edgy, but the fact that I found myself observing not the Larins' country estate but an abandoned factory with profanity written all over the walls simply shocked me, just knocked me out. It was as if someone had drawn a black eye on the Mona Lisa. There were also some strange, howling, ghoullike people carrying the lady of the manor, who was dressed in jeans and bearing not the celebratory sheaf of wheat but a bundle of some kind of withered herbs. It smelled painfully familiar. St. John's wort, perhaps? But then the Larins' nanny, dressed in ripped leggings, started boiling some kind of mixture in a big cauldron, stirring her stew with a wooden ladle. Pushkin's words came in from the wings in the voices of jazz singers—Olga and Tatiana Larin, apparently.

"Oh how I love to hear the notes of song, let dreams carry me off somewhere far, far away!" Tatiana sang.

"Oh Tanya, Tanya, always dreaming. I am so unlike you— when I hear singing, it makes me cheerful!" Olga answered.

Filth! Absolute filth! Disgust boiled up inside me. Maybe it's avant-garde, maybe I just don't get contemporary art, but this is certifiable insanity! The director is schizophrenic!

It was then that smoke started drifting off the stage. The workers had lit the bundle of herbs. That smoke was so familiar that it felt like every nose in the hall took one harmonious sniff, drawing in the blue eddies rising from the smoldering grass.

"Marijuana!" came a whisper from behind me. "That's definitely marijuana!"

"What a disgrace!" The little fat man behind me had finally forced something out, but his cow of a wife responded by bidding her spouse shut his trap, saying something to the effect that he had the intellect of a bookkeeper, so what could he know about contemporary opera?

"Shut your ugly face!" she added, getting really nasty.

I was so shocked by what was happening on the stage that I could not utter a single intelligible sound. It was as if my neck were suddenly filled with concrete, and now it couldn't turn, and my Adam's apple dropped nearly to my lungs. I thought I was going to suffocate.

One scene gave way to the next. Lensky, stripped to the waist, sang the grand tenor part in his tremendously deep bass voice, and the corps de ballet performed as a chorus of bare-breasted Greek odalisques, singing of fields and rivers.

"I love you," went the bass Lensky, an actor with a most formidable frame, like an old-school bodybuilder. Well, actually, Lensky was no spring chicken. "I love yo-u-u-u-u!"

"He's probably singing about pot," I thought. "That's the thesis of this production! That's the director's surrealist genius!" The stalls broke into gentle movement and whispering, some inquisitive, some irate.

"I love you!" Lensky sang with mounting vocal power.

The audience in the dress circle is always a heterogeneous mass, rarely familiar with classical art. So those movers and shakers of the food processing, automotive, and other industries sat there as if this was precisely what Pushkin and Tchaikovsky had intended. But the cow behind me hissed to her husband that the civilized world had long since acknowledged the health benefits of marijuana.

"Gala Shmonina has late-stage cancer, and her doctor secretly recommended marijuana!"

Only one part of the hall, the opera's great peanut gallery, fully aware that a full-blown bacchanalia was underway on the stage of the Bolshoi Theatre, suddenly burst into coordinated whistling, as if they were at a soccer game, jeering and throwing crumpled-up programs into the stalls.

"Boo!" the chanting spread upward. "Sha-a-a-me!"

"The director's a fag! Lysistratov's a fag!" said a bass voice from above, so loudly that it drowned out the mounting uproar, and even what was happening on the stage. It must have been some young bass singer from the conservatory. "Fa-a-a-g!" the gifted young artist sang.

The stalls took a while to get going, but they soon began to express their agreement with the peanut gallery in their own way—by trying to clap the actors off the stage. The actors apparently didn't give a damn what the audience thought, so they continued enacting their director's innovations with even greater gusto. The pot had probably helped, as had a heads-up from Lysistratov—that was probably a pseudonym. Their director must have told them that this was exactly how things would go. This is what he was counting on. A scandal. These days, if there's no scandal, there's no show. There was a stupendous scandal at the Bolshoi Theatre today, one for the ages.

A light suddenly came on in the government box, and everyone instantly turned in that direction, seeing a hand extended, followed by part of a pale face.

"Curtains, please," said someone's quiet voice, accompanied by a commanding wave of the fingers.

The conductor threw his hands up, stopping the orchestra. The action on the stage came to an end, and the musicians rose from their places, faced the government box, and began clapping. The actors joined the musicians in applauding the wisdom of the authorities. At that point, the hall could no longer contain itself. Such an ovation had not been heard in the theater for nigh on twenty years. The curtains closed, like two express trains racing toward each other. The light in the box went out, but the lights in the rest of the hall flared up so brightly that the masses clamped their eyes shut.

A gentleman who looked to be from the Caucasus ran in from the wings and proclaimed in perfect Russian that the show had been canceled due to technical difficulties. Tickets would be returnable until the 31st of December.

Once they'd had their fill of pot smoke, the audience in the stalls moved toward the exit. Hardly any of them were disappointed; most of them were laughing, gesticulating, and jostling by the doors. The dress circle was also heading for the exit, sweeping me along like river water.

"Young man!" said a voice behind me. "Young man, please return my opera glasses!"

"Ah, yes." Catching myself, I turned around, removed the eyepiece, and held it out to its owner.

"Who was that?" the middle-aged lady asked. "Up on the balcony?" I shrugged, acting like I didn't know because I was a foreigner. That irritated the lady, who had already noticed that I had the facial features of Russia's titular nation. Her husband kept muttering to her the whole time.

"Rita, what's the hurry? I haven't even gotten hold of the driver yet."

The only one who didn't leave his box was Mike Tyson. The champ didn't understand what was going on, why everything had ended in a flash. He still had three bottles of champagne and a bowl of black caviar left. He'd gotten a bit of a contact high and didn't feel like leaving his nice seat, so he called his manager and instructed him to arrange for a couple of cute black girls to be delivered.

Down in the lobby, I saw Iratov and Vera. Iratov bent toward her and whispered something, and she blushed. Then Iratov stealthily licked her little ear . . .

No. No!

My heart was bursting with rage! My cheeks were burning! "Such lewd behavior!" my soul protested. "And in a theater!"

Instead of slapping him in the face for his depravity, Vera burst out laughing. Many people noticed her beautiful smile, framed by moist eyes and the thin tongue touching her perfect teeth. What a funny little habit! She ran her fingers through Iratov's long locks and kissed him on the shoulder.

Pain. Extreme mental anguish made every muscle in my body clench. My spirit shouted silently along with my soul . . .

Iratov turned around unexpectedly, and we bumped gazes. Just two guys who didn't know each other. But our eyes locked for an abnormally long time, which drew a polite grunt from Iratov.

"Hi there!"

And I answered.

"Hi there!"

Iratov turned around, probably thinking that my countenance was vaguely familiar, and gently took Vera's waist and led her toward the coatroom.

Old Man Fedorych, who has served the theater faithfully since the sixties, deftly produced her ermine mantle. Iratov intercepted the furs and draped them over his companion's shoulders, then took a heavy Chaliapin-style coat with a beaver collar from Fedorych. He slipped the coatroom attendant a generous tip.

I have a coat with a warm zip-up liner. It's universal, good in any weather. I wear it in the spring and fall, then winter rolls around and I unroll my liner. It never goes out of style. Made in Yugoslavia.

Swept away by a human current, I found myself on the street, sadly watching Iratov opening the door of the limousine and Vera disappearing into the soft blue light within. Iratov paused for a moment and then looked around, as if trying to spot someone in the crowd. He looked for a long time. His black hair, streaked with gray, fluttered in the wind . . . Then the limo took off.

I had store-bought dumplings—Palych brand. Then I sat down in front of the television and dialed the number. Long, endless ringing was the only answer I got . . .

A long time ago, I was told that once the worst was over, I'd finally get through and someone on the other end of the line would answer . . . I was very worried that the number was no longer in service—it was given to me a long time ago, when there was no such thing as cell phones, country codes, and so on. The possibility that nobody was ever going to answer frightened me. I tried every possible variation over and over again, every combination. The numbers had all been disconnected, all except one, and its endless, icily unresponsive ringing tormented me . . .

In a panic, I wrote Iratov a letter, saying that the son he'd had with Vorontsova had died almost twenty years ago, that he was cursed for disowning his own flesh and blood. Just like twenty years ago, I received my answer at Moscow's main post office, via general delivery, on a single sheet that read "eat a dick!"

The Bolshoi Theatre scandal was already all over the news; they even aired an interview with the director, Edmond Lysistratov, in which the hack, flashing a delinquent's smile, shared his views on what had transpired. The young monster explained how it took quite a long time for audiences to accept Tchaikovsky's own opera. His own concept for transforming old into new was being rejected for the same reasons—Russian art was almost always backward; it was an ossified country that was only prepared to accept bland academic formulae! Lysistratov went on to declare that now was plainly not the time to work in the Motherland, and that he intended to accept an invitation to work at a Western theater—he had a dozen to choose from. As a parting shot, the monstrous Lysistratov thanked the management of the Bolshoi Theatre for affording him the opportunity for artistic experimentation, and, for some reason, saw fit to inform the country that he had a Swedish passport. In parallel with the interview, they reported on the arrest of a young man with an athletic build, a shaved head, and a thin, shoulder-length Chinese-style braid who was charged with using profanity in a public space. It has to be him—the bass who sang the word "fag" from the peanut gallery! A tremendously colorful character, a tremendously talented singer! The conservatory student stood there in handcuffs, facing the camera, and his eyes shone purely.

"Fag!" the student confirmed, on live TV, but they managed to bleep it out. Everybody knew what he was getting at, of course.

I dialed the number that was so important to me one more

time and listened to it ring, like it was some miraculous music sent down from the heavens. Hope, why do you comfort me in vain?!

I wasn't even that mad at Iratov anymore. Vera's shining image was tickling my imagination—that's all. No, I didn't like her in the commonplace sense of the word; I felt no physical attraction to her at all, and I harbored no amorous feelings, of course. I simply worshipped her, one of the Supreme Being's creations, as one might worship true works of art or delight in the laconic genius of mathematical formulae, or even just the sun.

I went to bed early. In despair, I had decided to reveal Iratov's story to the general public in about a month's time . . . Just as soon as I woke up . . .

3

He could feel, but he didn't know who he was. It was very hot, and he was trying to move, to crawl, to find a cooler spot. But the whole universe was hot. He could hardly see anything, just blurred outlines, as if he were a hatchling with a film still covering his eyes. A little pale pink face expressed unendurable agony, and tiny drops of sweat stood out on the forehead.

"Who am I?" asked his awakening consciousness. But it was lethargic and overheated, unable to respond to its own question. It was only capable of moving its tiny little hands and feet. The creature reflexively began crying—the way a newborn lets the mother know that it is hungry or uncomfortable. Hurry up and furnish me with your milk-filled breast.

But it had no mother . . . It didn't have anyone! It was tormented, body and soul. It just couldn't figure out where it was, or, more importantly, what it was . . . and why it was.

The creature was suppressed by the heat. Eventually, it lost consciousness, incapable of latching on to reality, and its minuscule body relaxed . . .

A girl of about thirteen, named Alice, enrolled at School Number 1 in the town of Sudogda (which is located in the Vladimir Region), was walking home after class. She had to make her way to the edge of town on foot, and then walk another six miles to the village of Kostino, where she shared a simple wooden house—two rooms, big stove, entryway—with her grandmother and their cow, Glashka. Alice got lucky that day: she'd caught up to a horse that was barely stumbling along, hitched to a sleigh carrying a drunken redheaded shepherd—it was Shurka. He was sleeping, revealing to the sky a mouth with half the teeth missing. The girl hopped on to the sleigh, took the reins out of his hands, settled into the malodorous hay, and urged the horse forward with a "get a move on!" It seemed like the mare was as drunk as her owner. She was moving sideways, plodding through the freshly fallen snow. But that wasn't it, of course; the poor critter was just getting to the end of a long life in which she had eaten meagerly, worked a great deal, and seen little joy. She tried to trot when the girl yelled, of course, but her arthritic right foreleg couldn't keep up with her intentions; her hoof skidded, and she nearly fell.

"Come on, you old nag!" Alice said angrily.

The horse responded by trying to turn around, but the bridle stopped her; the iron mouthpieces pinched her tongue and pressed against her worn-out teeth. All she could do was exhale puffs of steam into the frost and move ahead at her crippled pace.

Shurka woke up about half a mile into their ride. It took roughly a minute for his moonshine-sodden eyes to bring the world into focus, and then he noticed that he wasn't alone on the sleigh.

"Alice, my dear!" the coachman said happily, heaving an alcohol-laden sigh and embracing the girl. He was trying to feel her breasts through her sheepskin coat.

"Back off!" she commanded formidably and whacked Shurka's leering countenance with the reins. Blood dribbled out of his nose and down to his pockmarked chin.

"You're so nasty, Alice!" the red-haired shepherd scowled, but cracked a toothless smile as if he hadn't felt the blow at all. "Who else is gonna hug you?"

"I have some takers! Half the school's trying to feel me up!"

"Yeah," Shurka agreed dreamily. "Your mother was the same way. Her boobs came in early. We went to the same school, she was in the other class, though. By the time we were in seventh grade her tits was bigger than the ones on the assistant principal! Those boobies of hers—like two fishbowls! And boy, your mama let us feel her up, too! She was like 'whatever, there's plenty to go around!'"

"I'm in seventh grade, too," Alice said with a nod. "But all the girls at school are F-A-Bs, even the tenth-graders."

"We said the same thing back in the day! F-A-B—flat-as-a-board!" He sniffed, but the blood had already stopped, frozen in the chilly air. "Well, how 'bout you and me get hitched, Alice?"

"Hitched?" the girl asked, wrinkling her nose. "I'm thirteen!"

"I'll give ya another year." The red-haired drunkard tried putting his arms around her again.

"I said back off!" Alice hollered, so formidably that the horse lurched to one side and almost overturned the sleigh. "Or I'll slug you for real!"

"You're so nasty!" Shurka said, shaking his head. "Go on, get off my sleigh."

"Yeah, right!"

"Off, I said! Scat! Or else I'll put my foot up your ass!"

"I'm not going anywhere! This ain't your sleigh!"

"How you figure?" the coachman asked, eyes wide. "Whose is it?"

"Do we pay you for Glashka's fodder?"

"You pay in the summer . . . but what does that have to do with—"

"Where are you taking this hay?"

"To your village . . ."

"Five houses. Five hundred rubles each for hay, right?"

"Yeah . . ." Shurka conceded, feeling the urgent need for a drink.

"As long as you're delivering the hay for our cows, the horse and sleigh are ours. Bought and paid for. It's like a taxi in the city. You rent it, then the car and driver are yours for the trip!" The girl lashed at the mare's skinny croup with the reins.

"Get a move on! Or should I put my foot up your ass? Watch it, I'll throw ya into the snowbank headfirst!"

Something had jammed in Shurka's head. He wasn't familiar with the concept of logic, but he knew that little Alice, with her prematurely developed womanly attributes, was putting one over on him. Not knowing what to say, the coachman decided to take umbrage, so he groped underneath the sleigh and pulled out a bottle of moonshine, as well as a rag, which he unwrapped to reveal a sliver of salo, a quarter loaf of black bread, and a nub of onion. The man swigging straight from a bottle of stagnant swamp let out a groan, then released a protracted burp, produced a knife from the depths of his sheepskin coat, and cut the cured fat into pieces. The warmth the fat had picked up from the rotting hay, the scent of the onion, and the aroma of the heel of Borodinsky bread teased Alice's keen little nose, making her nostrils flare. She turned away involuntarily. He clasped his sandwich, took a huge bite, chewed, and cracked a sneaky smile.

"What're you smilin' about?" The girl was really hungry, but she was too proud to ask for some, so she sat there stewing, swallowing useless saliva. It was still a ways to the village, and she had to feed and milk the cow before evening, then she would only be able to sit down to dinner with her granny after all her chores were done.

"Want some moonshine?"

"I'm thirteen, you lousy drunk! You forget already?"

"And you never touch the stuff, right?" he asked sarcastically.

"Just on holidays—and not that crap. I don't want to go blind, that's the last thing I need!"

"This food is for drinkers only! Don't you know ya have to eat a little somethin' after every drink! C'mon, your mama didn't think she was too good for moonshine!"

"Yeah, and she went and got herself killed while she was tanked!"

Twilight was setting in. The violet-tinged sun was diving behind the trees. Alice stood up on the sleigh, holding on to the reins to steady herself, and tried to catch a glimpse of the sunlight on the windows of the little village houses.

"It's getting cold!" the red-haired drunk observed and swallowed a swig from the bottle. He took another huge bite.

"Fine, pour me one!" Alice relented.

"Huh?"

"Ya got a glass?"

"Yeah, somewhere."

He pulled a table glass out from under the sleigh, blew on it to get rid of the scraps of hay, and smiled.

"Just a dab'll do me!" the girl warned him.

"Yeah, yeah, dabby-do." Alice pulled off one mitten with her teeth, blew on her hand to warm it up, and only then accepted the glass. She exhaled and emptied the moonshine into her mouth. She cringed.

"How do you drink this stuff?" she coughed. Shurka held out a piece of Borodinsky bread with a square of salo and onion slices on top.

"Go on, eat up!" Alice swallowed it like a frog swallows a mosquito and smiled at Shurka. "That'll warm ya up!" he said encouragingly and lit a hand-rolled cigarette. "Can ya feel it?"

"Yeah…" The girl was a little drowsy now, and the prospect of a sad evening slipped into her trove of irrelevant happenings.

"Want a puff?" he said, offering her the half-smoked cigarette and ripping off part of the paper filter with his teeth.

"Never smoked before, never will," Alice declared. "What for? So my mouth can reek like yours?"

"Good for you. It's a rotten habit," said Shurka, flicking the unfinished cigarette away—but he did it so clumsily that the still-burning tip hit the horse right in the croup. The unexpected burn made the old mare want to rear up on her hind legs. She gave a despairing jerk but only managed to rise a few inches off the ground before her full weight came crashing down on the road, overturning the sleigh. Its riders flew off in opposite directions.

While Alice was digging herself out of a snowbank, the enraged coachman hurried over toward the supine horse and nailed it with his felt boot, right in its ailing, distended stomach. All the animal did was exhale steam and give him a crooked glance from under her sparse white eyelashes.

"Worthless bitch!" Shurka cursed, giving her another hard kick.

"She isn't a bitch, she's a mare!" Alice objected, pulling herself out of the snow and rubbing her injured side. "A mare, not a bitch."

Suddenly, Alice was thinking back to a class early in the school year. They were studying a Mayakovsky poem where a horse fell over, and all the passersby started neighing with laughter, while tears ran from the horse's eyes . . . For some reason, Alice felt so sorry for that mare in the poem, and she shed some furtive tears herself. This nag collapsing didn't elicit any sympathy, though—all it did was irritate her. Thirteen years had sufficed for Alice to learn that old age was irritating, not worthy of sympathy. Her grandma irritated her every damn day! Mayakovsky's poem must have been about a young horse.

"Come on, help me!" Shurka yelled.

They unhitched the horse together. Then they grabbed the tack and dragged the damn horse by the neck until she struggled to her knees, and then finally stood on all four hooves. They flipped the sleigh back on to its runners together, and then got the horse back into her collar and shafts. Huffing and puffing, they heaved the scattered bundles of hay back into the sleigh.

"Motherfu—!" he hollered, but stopped himself.

"What is it? Wolves comin'?" asked Alice, turning to face him.

"The friggin' bottle got busted! Two liters down the drain!"

"Why don't ya eat the snow? It soaked it all up."

"You're a genius, Alice!" He fell to his knees, detected the homemade alcohol by smell, and gathered handfuls of wet snow into his hat. "Got a whole cup's worth!" he proclaimed.

The traveling companions sat down on the sleigh and ordered the mare forward in chorus, then continued their journey in silence. Shurka melted a portion of snow in the glass and drank it immediately. It was a little diluted, but the sheer volume was enough to get him drunk, so he began lowing some old song, then fell asleep again, his toothless mouth hanging open. Alice glided over the January snow and contemplated her marriage prospects. How would she come by her future husband if there were no decent men to be found, even in Vladimir? Just drunks and losers. Her village was even worse: three old maids who looked after this one bedridden guy named Vykhin. Then there was Old Lady Ksenia and Shurka. He wasn't from their village, though; he was from Stepachevo, where the store was. More folks lived there, but there wasn't a single boy or man. The only boys who didn't go off to trade school after ninth grade were a bunch of pimply nerds, and the lack of competition had made them far too cocky. They're grabby—let your guard down, and they've got their hands up your skirt the next second! Alice was no pushover. Actually, she could push the creeps around. She'd given a few of them black eyes, too. But they're like flies—swat as many as you want, but they'll keep going after the sweet stuff!

Alice spotted rectangles of electric light. The village was close. She tried shaking Shurka awake. No luck. The horse, sensing the proximity of human abodes, picked up the pace, and soon the girl was hopping off the sleigh and hurrying down the well-trodden path through the snow to her house. She wasn't thinking about Shurka anymore, about how a night out in the cold could do him in. That was his problem. He was a grown man. Plus the mare could always take him back to his house in Stepachevo. At least it was warm there, and he had a patch of hay.

"What took you so long?" her grandmother asked with irritation in her voice. She was actually Alice's great-grandmother. It'd already been eight years since her grandmother was ripped to shreds by stray dogs, or maybe wolves. It was around this time of year. She was running a little late, so it was almost nighttime when she walked home from Sudogda . . . and ran afoul of man's best friends.

"Where have you been?" Granny Ksenia asked. Even though she was technically a great-grandmother, she was just a hair over sixty. She had Alice's granny, Pelagia, at fifteen—the one who wound up being fodder for wild animals and who, fifteen years after her own birth, had also brought a daughter into the world, Alice's mother, Irka Kapronova. The latter bore fruit at fourteen—and they had chicks every time!

As usual, Alice only provided vague answers to her granny's questions. She didn't want to get dragged into the same old conversation about her schooling and her future. She changed out of her school clothes, grabbed an empty bucket, and went out to milk Glashka the cow. She returned half an hour later with the result, went over to the mirror without putting the bucket down, and noticed several ripening pimples dotting her forehead.

"Thought there'd be more." Her granny had crept up silently and looked in the bucket. "Two gallons? Not even!"

"What are ya doin' creeping up on me like a ghost!" Alice yelled, angry at both Ksenia and her adolescent breakout. "Feed Glashka better and you'll get more out of her!"

"Don't get wise with me!" her granny retorted. She took the bucket out of Alice's hand and filtered the milk through some gauze and into one-gallon jars, filling two with a little left over. "Each of the neighbors'll get a pound of farmer's cheese and two cups of milk. That'll buy us some bread and spaghetti— that's if they deliver it to the store!"

"You can go on a diet if they don't!" Alice quipped. "That's the style now."

"And you can go down to the cellar," said her granny, not backing down.

"What the heck for?"

"To make you less lippy! And no grub for you tonight!"

"I'll go to Officer Dyskin! You have no right! You signed the guardianship papers! You're obligated to feed me or else you'll answer to the law!" This unheard-of impudence nearly made Granny Ksenia drop her jar of milk, but she held on to their irreplaceable capital and answered bitingly.

"Your mother was just like you when she was your age— all sass and all about the boys. But where there's men, there's flim-flam and alcoholism! Just watch, you'll wind up dead, just like her!"

"How can you say that about your own granddaughter? You're the one who raised her that way, or else your genes aren't no good!"

Granny Ksenia didn't know what "genes" were, but it

didn't sound like a curse, and there was some hidden truth to Alice's words. The old lady tempered justice with mercy.

"Alright, hurry up and eat! You still gotta wash the dishes and do your homework!"

"Whatcha got?" Alice asked, looking at the pot Granny Ksenia was taking out of the large brick stove with a set of heavy tongs. She grabbed a trivet from the windowsill and deftly slipped it under the scorching pot.

"It's taters and eggs. Go on, get some pickles outta the fridge, and some sunflower oil offa the shelf there. If it hasn't gone and run out already . . ."

They had dinner, and Alice went to her room to watch TV—that's if they got lucky and their antenna was actually picking something up. Their seventies-era black-and-white Rubin-205, which had lived to see practically every innovation in television technology, tried its hardest, yet mostly just showed Channel One. It would sometimes freeze up and lose the picture, so they'd have to whack it on the side. It sometimes showed Channel Two as well, but the only way to prove the existence of that mythical signal was to take some pliers and turn the metal dowel that once held a knob that had vanished before Alice was even born. She didn't feel like it . . . The girl didn't even think about doing her homework—she just flopped on to her bed and idly watched some show where people dressed up like Christmas trees shrieked and grimaced. She was waiting for the singing to end—there was a sitcom she liked coming up next. The leading lady was a tomboy just like her, a little older, though. She moved to Moscow to find love, but those big-city types clipped her wings, used her, and tossed her out on the street. Alice knew for sure that the heroine would turn into a princess and get married at the end of the show—not to a prince, but maybe to an honest cop at least . . . They were just showing a bunch of politicians that night, though, yapping at each other like a pack of wild dogs for the whole country to see, spewing all kinds of insults. The sparks were really flying! Alice couldn't stand politics, so she decided to go to sleep. It was cold in her room. She wanted to sleep by the big wood-burning stove, but that was where her granny always slept, so the girl went in and said in her most honeyed voice that she had caught a cold—probably because it was so damp in her room—and would have to miss school.

"Go sleep by the stove!" Ksenia instructed. "I'll brew up some raspberry tea for you! And don't forget to put a warm shawl on, or you'll freeze your little butterfly shut for good. I'd still like to have some great-great-grandchildren." That was all she ever called what was between Alice's legs: her little butterfly.

"But what about you, Granny?"

"I'll sleep up top," she said, referring to the little curtained space just above the stove.

"Oh, thank you, Grammy!"

"Sly Aly . . . sly as a fox."

Alice hopped up on the stove and stretched out, letting her whole body soak up the warmth from the bricks, smiling blissfully. She was already asleep by the time Ksenia brought her the raspberry tea. For the first half of the night, she dreamed a maiden's childish dreams. A tremendous variety of sweets, fruits whose names she didn't even know, human-sized talking dolls, and a fair-haired boy. It was a miracle how handsome he was! In the second half of the night, closer to morning, her caramel dreams gave way to horrors. Alice dreamed of rats with yellow teeth. They squeaked clamorously, about to attack the girl; the vile, hungry beasts, yellow-toothed, worse than wolves . . . An unbearable squeaking awakened her in the early morning. Whew, it was all just a dream! She scrounged up some matches and lit a candle, banishing the dream for good. The girl didn't have a watch, and she couldn't see the wall clock with the dead cuckoo, but she had a perfect sense of time, almost down to the second, and her little brain was ticking away. Fifteen minutes left until reveille. The stove had almost completely cooled off, so she moved toward the wall, where it was a little warmer. With her cheek pressed against the bricks, Alice heard the despairing squeaking again, but this was no dream. She was awake. Shock flung her away from the wall, and the despairing squeaking suddenly took on a plaintive note.

"Gross, a rat!" Alice thought. "So it wasn't a dream! He's right under me." She wasn't any more afraid of rats than of any other creature—all the little gray rodents elicited was mild distaste.

"You little shit." She began searching for the cheeky creature in the creases of her cotton blanket, then down by her feet, where some birch branches for the sauna were hanging. "Where'd you get off to?" Alice caught an earful of ruckus up by her head, so she turned instantly, leapt like a cat, rummaged under the pillows, and ran her deft fingers over the felt mat underneath. She eventually seized the beast with her right hand. As she was dragging it out into the pure light of day, the girl was already picturing herself flinging the nasty critter against the cracked plaster wall. She was winding up, but then the rat gave an especially despairing shriek, as if it understood that it was about to die.

"It's a baby rat!" Alice thought, loosening her fingers slightly. "A newborn, no doubt about it!" the girl concluded when she saw its pink skin and decided against killing the little creature. She opened her palm—and was struck dumb for a solid minute. In her hand, twitching its little arms and legs, lay a naked homunculus with a tiny, wrinkled face, scarcely larger than Alice's index finger. It was male, and it was shedding bead-like tears.

"He's alive!" the girl finally said with a gasp, titillated by this as yet unobserved miracle of nature. "A gnome! I caught a gnome!" It engendered something like an unexpected celebration in her soul. "A little gnome of my very own!" Then she decided that it wasn't just a gnome, but an honest-to-goodness Smurf, just like in that foreign movie! She had never actually seen it, but a lot of the girls from her class had gone to the movie theater in Vladimir and then talked her ear off about how funny those cute little guys were.

"So are you a Smurf?" the girl asked the tiny person in a whisper. Her discovery stopped crying and was now looking at Alice's face with his itty-bitty eyes. "You're so cute!"

The interminable whispering woke Granny Ksenia, and, unexpectedly as always, she stuck her head between the curtains that separated the stove bench from the upper room. In the first rays of sunlight, she caught sight of her great-granddaughter kneeling and holding something in her hands. It was moving.

"What is it?" she screamed.

Alice shuddered with surprise and accidentally squeezed the Smurf's little body. The gnome, crushed by her childish fingers, cried out like a human infant and cowered like an animal whelp. Once she had overcome her initial fright, the girl turned to face her granny.

"What do you keep scaring me for, you old hag?"

"What is it?" Ksenia hopped agilely on to the bench and reached for the creature moving in Alice's hand. A horrible thought entered her mind, and she let out a single hiccup. She grabbed her great-granddaughter by the hair and yanked. "How could you? You little bitch! You ain't more than thirteen! A miscarriage, I can't believe it! Who knocked you up?"

"You've finally lost it!" Alice shouted back, trying to free her hair from Ksenia's iron grip. "What are you talking about? I'm only thirteen! I'm still a virgin! And this is a Smurf!"

"A *what*?" Granny Ksenia hadn't let go, but she wasn't yanking on her hair anymore.

"A gnome," Alice explained, hiding it behind her back.

"I'll show you a gnome!" said Ksenia, still all worked up. "Right under my nose! A miscarriage at thirteen! You little hussy!" She started pulling her hair again. Alice vigorously crossed herself.

"I swear to God—I am a virgin!" her great-granddaughter shouted in pain. "I'll be damned if I'm lying! I found him right here, on the stove! He didn't come out of me! Stillborn babies don't cry! When there's a miscarriage, there's always blood. Where's the blood, huh?"

The last argument cooled the old lady's temper. She released Alice's hair and rummaged around on the stove bench, looking for a wet spot. When she saw that everything was perfectly dry, Ksenia turned her face toward her great-granddaughter.

"Well, show me!" she commanded.

"Just don't kill him," the girl pleaded tearfully.

"Show me already!" Alice opened her palm, and her granny studied the naked homunculus intently. Now he was lying still, just fluttering his doll-like eyelashes.

"He's cute!"

"That's what I'm saying!" the girl said happily. "My little Smurf!"

"Looks like a late abortion . . ." Ksenia conjectured. "But he's alive . . ."

"Please, Granny, my dear, sweet Granny, can I keep him? I'll take care of him!"

Ksenia pondered that at length. She carefully touched the

gnome with one rock-hard fingernail, and it smiled at her with its tiny mouth full of minute teeth so intoxicatingly that the old lady smiled in reply. Alice cracked a smile too.

"But what will we feed him?"

Alice hopped off the stove and ran over to the window; it was already letting in the sun. She sat down at the table across from it.

"Grammy, he's so little! His dinner will fit in a thimble!"

"What if he gets sick? What are we gonna do, show up at the hospital with a Smurf?"

"He won't get sick!" the girl reassured her. "I'll take care of him! I'll give him hugs and kisses!"

"Dunno . . ."

"I'll do all the chores! I'll chop the wood, I'll fetch the water, I'll milk Glashka in the mornings, too, and I'll scratch your back! How 'bout it?"

"If you're lying, I'll throw him in the well myself!" she threatened.

"I'm not lying, Grammy! I'm telling the truth!"

"You'd better be! And make sure he doesn't just go to the bathroom wherever he pleases, like your parrot!"

"He's not a bird! He's a person! And I'll make him some swaddling clothes . . ."

"One strike and he's out!" the old lady declared, thereby granting her approval for this new resident.

"Maybe I could stay home from school today?" the girl asked. "All we have is geography, then three hours of cross-country skiing. And I'm coming down with a cold," she sniffled. "Plus, you can't leave a Smurf all by himself. It's his first day . . ."

"I'm gonna go get some firewood," Ksenia said. "The fire's gone out—look, there's already frost on the inside of the windows!"

"I'll do it!" Alice sprang off her stool, willing to move mountains.

"Sit down already!" Granny Ksenia set out toward the door. "He's probably hungry. Give him some mashed taters with milk." "Why study geography?" she thought. "Nobody ever goes any farther than Vladimir anyway."

Granny slammed the door. Alice placed the gnome on the rag they used to wipe the table, covered him with one corner, and darted over to the stove, where there was a little left over from dinner. She put some food in a plastic bowl left over from the long-dead parrot, Adolf—who was actually a parakeet and had flown into the hot stove and burned up like a paper airplane—put a drop of milk on top and brought the meal over to the table . . .

He didn't like the smell of the rag the big girl had wrapped him up in one bit. The moist fabric irritated his tender skin, but he bore all his trials and tribulations gladly, since he had just been saved from his seemingly inevitable demise. He ate. The girl nudged the scraps of potatoes toward him with a match and then put them in his mouth. The food proved comestible, and he chewed it exactingly, thinking about who he was and why he was here, in a village cabin, a doll for a girl who was big for her age, but without the smarts to match . . . The word "amnesia" appeared in his minuscule brain, and he understood what it meant pretty well.

"Something happened to me," he thought. "Some kind of physical or psychological trauma." But probably psychological, since his arms and legs were in perfect working order, and he had experienced no physical discomfort aside from the odor of the dirty rag . . . He also got to thinking about the quite palpable difference in his dimensions and those of his environs. He felt like Gulliver in the land of the giants. Did this kind of thing really happen? He had a creeping doubt that his whole being was being manipulated by some hallucination, and he was actually just mentally ill.

Granny came back in with the firewood, tossed it in the stove, and informed Alice that she was going to Stepachevo for the bread and pasta, but first she'd take the milk to the neighbors and see if the farmer's cheese had ripened.

"What should I call him, Granny?"

"Something cute . . . Like 'Aborty.' "

"Eww," went Alice, and that noise made the foreign name "Eugene" flicker in her voice. She pronounced it out loud, in the French manner, which she liked. "You'll be Eugene! But I'll call you Zhenka!" she added. "No need to put on airs." That was nice and simple, short for "Evgeniy," the Russian for "Eugene."

"Why 'Eugene'?" he thought. "What kind of name is that? And 'Zhenka' is far too familiar . . ."

Alice plucked the Smurf out of the rag and carried him to her room, where she had a two-story plastic dollhouse with no front wall set up on the floor. That little house had everything: a bed, a dining room table (two dolls were sitting there now, like husband and wife), and even a bathroom with a tiny toilet. The girl placed Eugene on the bed and covered him with a dolly blankie.

"Do you like it, Eugene? It's all yours now! King in the castle!"

He realized that this was to be his fate: living in a plastic dollhouse with plastic toys and peeing in a toilet that wasn't even hooked up to the plumbing. And he needed to relieve himself— very badly. He tossed the stupid blanket aside, got to his tiny feet, and hurried into the caricature of a bathroom.

"You can walk!" Alice exclaimed. He nodded. "And you can understand humans?!" The girl was absolutely floored.

Suddenly, she found herself thinking that he'd grown a little in the past few minutes—at the very least, he was unmistakably longer than her finger—or did it just seem that way to her? The gnome turned his back to the girl, used the toilet, and then proceeded into the dining room, covering his private parts with his hands, dragged the wife doll out of her chair, and flung her from the second floor of the house. Then Eugene moved on to the husband, but first he undressed him, slapped on his clothes to cover his willy and protect his body from the cold, and only then did he hurl the naked mannequin from his dollhouse life.

Alice was watching everything unfold like she was at some Smurf theater, though the Smurf, admittedly, was utterly alone, if one didn't count the subjugated dolls.

"So can you talk?" the girl asked with bated breath.

He was asking himself the same question. Since he could understand human speech, it followed that he could talk, too—provided he wasn't mute. Eugene adjusted the collar of his shirt and coughed into his tiny fist.

"Yes, I can."

His voice didn't sound childlike anymore; it had taken on a certain adolescent timbre, which he could detect, too. "I must be young," Eugene concluded.

All of a sudden, Alice grabbed him—passionately and less tenderly than she'd intended—and began kissing her precious discovery on his tiny cheeks, nose, and forehead.

At first, Eugene was terrified he was about to be crushed, but he soon realized that the girl's fingers were more delicate than they had been in the morning. He caught himself thinking that he liked the way Alice was kissing him. Her wet lips excited him, making him stronger and suppler. Zhenka felt like he was growing, like his muscles were hardening and his spirit rapidly strengthening. The girl also fancied that her new friend was getting bigger right there in her hand. She knew for sure that his little body, his arms, and his legs had gotten longer, and now his head was covered with little black hairs.

"Are you growing?" She opened her hand.

Sitting on her palm with his legs dangling over the side, Eugene heard his doll clothes ripping.

"Looks that way."

"Can you maybe not grow?" The girl sounded upset.

"I don't think I can."

"What if I don't feed you?" Alice really didn't want the gnome to grow. A grown-up gnome was just a dwarf! She didn't like dwarves, she was afraid of them. And little people, too . . .

"If you don't feed me, I'll die."

"No, no, I'll take care of you!" She started kissing Eugene again, like a beloved doll, while he relaxed and relished his mounting strength. "You're so wonderful!"

He reciprocated the girl's affection, kissed the edge of her lips, but she didn't even notice. She kept kissing him and kissing him, until she suddenly realized that the gnome was growing again. He was bursting out of her palm; he was twice as tall as when she found him on the stove, and his doll clothes had come apart at the seams and fallen to the floor.

The girl put Eugene on the table, realizing that, while he had once been a boy the size of her little finger, he had now grown bigger than a pickle jar, and he was standing before her, hands on his sides, unabashedly displaying his nakedness. Alice was embarrassed that her eyes had settled on the place where boys are different from girls. For the first time, she felt subtle impulses transforming her from a curious girl into an amorous woman. She blushed and reluctantly looked up at Eugene's face, noting how attractive he was . . . Then a defensive wall flashed into existence in her brain—the memory of the time when, out of curiosity, she had visited O, the only sex shop in Sudogda. The experience had left her with a vile feeling, like she was some special kind of dirty . . . Alice suddenly realized that she was being tempted by the same impurity now as she looked at Eugene's naked body. She crossed herself.

"If you keep growing, I'll throw you away!" she declared.

"Everything is in God's hands!" the growing gnome said resignedly.

The doors squeaked in the entryway, and the girl realized that her granny had come back from Stepachevo.

"I'll hide you and tell Ksenia that you ran away."

"Do as you think best," Eugene agreed. She hid him under the blanket on her bed and was about to run out to meet her grandmother, but then she lifted the corner of the blanket.

"Please, don't grow! And don't make any noise!" she warned him.

He lay there, weary from their fly-by-night kisses, breathing in the smell Alice had forgotten in the bed sheets, feeling intoxicated and almost pleased. Eugene stopped thinking about who he was, how he'd wound up in this village cabin of all places. He simultaneously felt like a newborn and an adult, since he could think rationally but didn't know his own growing body. Utterly unexplored, it was developing according to its own laws—rapidly, as if his life would consist of one winter day. Hidden from the white light by a warm blanket, he probed his anatomy and checked how it felt, in both senses of the word, as if he had spent an eternity paralyzed and insensate, and now everything had unexpectedly come back to life, and his body was experiencing the joy of the Resurrection.

"Where's your Smarf?" Granny inquired as the girl was putting the groceries away.

"Smurf . . . my Smurf disappeared!" Alice broke into

natural tears, like true misfortune had befallen her. "I looked everywhere, but I . . . but he . . ." She even threw in some masterful sobbing. "He ran away!'

"Maybe he fell through a crack?" Ksenia suggested. "Down into the cellar?"

"I looked everywhere, I checked everything!" Alice wailed.

"Quit whining! Fiddlesticks to him! It's a disgrace, living with some stranger's abortion! Now he won't be going to the bathroom God knows where."

"It's sooo sad!" the girl howled.

"Want some cheese to go with that whine?"

"We don't even have a cat!"

"Cause we don't have mice! I'm going to Vladimir tomorrow."

"What for?"

"They didn't adjust my pension for inflation! I'm gonna take care of it!"

"Go for it!"

"I'll spend the night with Lyudmila and come back on Saturday. No skipping school!"

"Fine," Alice agreed dully.

"Not 'fine—' school! Now stick the pot on the stove, we're makin' pasta! Go down to the cellar and put some cabbage in a bowl!" The old lady and the girl had lunch.

As Alice washed the dishes, the sky turned from white to gray, and it was grim inside the lightless house, where Ksenia forbade her from turning on the overhead light until it was really dark. She always said, "There's no such thing as an electric bill being too small!" The old lady thought the best thing you could do in life was learn to be thrifty. The only entertainment the family had was the TV and a radio set that could only pick up one station.

Ksenia would often listen to political programs, with her ear right against the speaker. Her opinion almost always differed from that of the professional politicians, but she never shared it with Alice, saving the results of her deliberations for the store in Stepachevo, where the women from the five surrounding villages would gather at a specific time to buy fresh bread.

"I'm going to my room," Alice announced once she had finished with the dishes and dried her hands.

"Homework!"

"Fine!" The girl shut the door behind her and neatly put the hook in the eye. "Are you here?" she whispered.

She lifted the corner of the blanket and nearly shrieked with surprise. Her toasty discovery, which had so recently been the size of a pickle jar, had grown rapidly in the brief time she was gone. He now very much had the shoulders of an adolescent, and Alice was hesitant to pull the blanket any lower. How could this be? She stood there, mouth agape. Maybe the Smurf had been replaced with something else? How could a gnome have gotten as tall as her?

"Eugene, is that you?" She shook his shoulder. "C'mon, wake up!"

The sleeping young man did not react to her decisive command; he just groaned quietly in his youthful bass and parted his big, juicy lips. His long, shiny black hair was spread across the pillow. Alice found herself involuntarily admiring the handsome Eugene, and the nearly imperceptible smell of sweets drifting from his half-open mouth stirred the girl's soul with its novelty. Without intending to, she started stroking his head but then jerked her hand back as if she was afraid of getting burnt. But then she started touching him again, touching his face with her fingertips, and not withdrawing them, lightly caressing the soft skin of this fabulously beautiful youth.

He wasn't asleep, just pretending. He liked the feel of this girl's little fingers. They trembled faintly from her childish inexperience, and his eyelashes quivered.

"You're awake!" the girl said, pulling her hand back.

"Yes."

"And you have been for a while?"

"I have."

Alice blushed and launched into a whispered rebuke directed at this impudent entity that had transformed from a gnome to a guy almost as tall as her in half a day. How dare he grow when he promised he wouldn't? And why would she want a guy in her bed? Now Granny would kill her!

"You're a liar!" she hissed. He sat on the bed, hands behind his head, and smiled.

"I never lied to you! You asked me not to grow, but that proved beyond my power. I grew. I don't know who I am or where I came from, but I am grateful for your warmth and benevolence, since I'm quite comfortable here. That was very kind of you, not letting a defenseless creature die. And I'll be going tomorrow, don't you worry!"

"Going? Where?"

"I have to get to the city."

"Vladimir?"

"Moscow."

"What for?"

"I don't know what for. I just know that I have to."

"No, stay." the girl said. "You'll walk me to school!"

He reached out to Alice, who was overcoming the excessive speed at which her little heart was contracting, and she placed her hands in his mitts. He drew his savior very close and pressed her to his chest, gently stroking the girl's hair, and she whispered in alarm, "No, don't, my hair ain't clean . . ." He smiled in the twilight of the fading day, and she thought that here was her prince, though he had come to her by a strange route, as a miniature gnome, then turned into this miraculous youth. How divine he smelled . . .

"Homework!"

"I'm doing it!" Alice answered and pressed her tense lips to Eugene's.

Oh, what sweet torture! The girl could not resist. Her lips relaxed and submitted to his. This kiss was nothing like the nicotine smooches of the nerds from her school. Sensuous and sublime, it was a magical key that opened the maiden's heart to her first, most elevated love. She lost any sense of time, although she still automatically answered Ksenia's occasional questions, then greedily returned to his lips, as if she wanted to drown in this bottomless kiss. For a time, Alice detached her reason from her body, which her butterfly connected with his naked flesh in unison with her fluttering heart . . .

Nine months later, Alice would give birth to a boy who would become the first male in their chick-laden lineage. Of course, this future was beyond her ken—all she knew was the entrancing pleasure that had seized her whole being. She was swimming in warm, primal happiness, letting out involuntary groans, and he covered her mouth, now with wet kisses, now with his strong hand. Then her breath was seized by a spasm, her whole body became suddenly hot, and Alice pronounced a short "Ah!" like the toll of a bell, rose to where angels sing, and then soon, so soon, returned, remitting her rapid breathing and detached reason to their tenuous balance. She noticed that Eugene was breathing heavily, too, his hot cheek resting on her breast. Alice embraced her prince powerfully.

"Stay!" she said plaintively.

"I can't," he whispered in reply.

"How can you leave me . . . after everything . . ."

"You will remain renewed, and you will remember me all your life."

"But I love you!" The girl held the young man even tighter, as if she thought she could keep him in her life that way.

"Everyone's first love is short. That is how it is meant to be. Either you will remember it as none too happy, or it will become your guiding star. You will measure everything that happens in your life by this first feeling!"

"Are you Jesus?"

"Who?"

"Jesus Christ, I mean."

"Who's that?"

"'Who's that?' God, that's who!"

"No," Eugene answered firmly. "I am not God."

"So who are you?'

"I . . . I don't know . . . All I know is that I have to go to Moscow!"

After that, she cried for a long time, not like a little girl, but like a grown woman, furtively wiping away the tears, and he stared into the vast sky, or maybe not into it; maybe he was directing his gaze into his own stupor. They sat there in silence until morning. Alice heard the door squeak. Granny Ksenia had set out on her journey to Vladimir.

"Soon?" the girl asked.

"Yes," Eugene answered dryly, and Alice realized that he wasn't there with her anymore. Her prince was already out on the road, leaving her alone forever.

"You need clothes . . ."

"Yes."

"Ksenia's got some in her closet. Some gentleman caller left them here . . . twenty long years ago."

"Uh-huh."

"But you'll never get there without any money!" This change in Eugene's mood hurt Alice's feelings, but, oddly enough, she wasn't mad or upset. She somehow understood that her prince had his mission and she had hers. She came back with the clothes. "Here, try them on!" As the young man was getting dressed, the girl got a little bank shaped like a formidable owl out from under the bed and smashed it open with a hammer. Eugene jumped and turned around.

"What's that?"

"Money. You won't even get as far as Vladimir without it."

"Oh yes . . ."

The young man, dressed in a black shirt, black pants, and an ankle-length black coat, bent over the shattered bank and began gathering the coins. He nicked himself on one of the shards and stuck his finger in his mouth to stop the bleeding. She loved him so much in that moment! Alice thought that her heart would never be capable of such an acute, powerful feeling ever again. She decided to throw herself into the ice-fishing hole.

He stuck the money in the deep pocket of his coat, then put on a pair of black wingtips. He looked at himself in the mirror and permitted Alice to comb his black hair until it fell in waves on to his collar.

"Ksenia's gentleman caller worked at the funeral home in Sudogda . . . is it okay?"

"It's perfect." Eugene turned to face the girl and kissed her on the lips. There was no passion in that kiss, much less love. That is how a man kisses a person he is indifferent to, a person he will never see again. "Farewell." When he was on his way out, Alice told him that Shurka, the red-haired drunk, would be heading to Sudogda.

"He'll drop you off. Just tell him you're related to Alice . . ."

He crunched swiftly through the snow, away from Alice's house. His rapid stride spoke to his determination, and his long black hair fluttered in the wind.

"A demon!" Alice whispered behind him. "A demon . . ."

4

I've slept . . .

I've scratched . . .

I'll resume . . .

The boy's mother, an English teacher, came up with his first name. There was no need to come up with a patronymic, since that was derived from his engineer father's name, Andrei. Hence, his name, in total, amounted to Arseny Andreivich Iratov, born 1960. Immediately after he was born, Mr. Iratov made a face like he could already tell that he was to be a millionaire.

There is no reason whatsoever to linger on Iratov's childhood. It was just like everyone else's, until he was around fifteen. That's when he suddenly found himself with a handsome face. His whole appearance held rare allure for women both older and younger. Iratov made good use of that gift, and by seventeen, he had already gorged himself on the fairer sex to the point that he was utterly spoiled.

When the young man was in college, he often had five relationships going at once, and there were times when he was skillfully shuffling a hand of up to seven girls, not to mention winning the affections of the provost. He enjoyed spending his nights with Ms. Ivanova. The provost was of that age when the flower is still full of beauty and vitality, but you can feel the little fissure at the very peak of its blossoming, inevitably followed by barely perceptible wilting. There is such sweet enjoyment at the onset of that rapid plunge, when you catch the petals' piquant scent . . .

Iratov's other partners all seemed like the same chick: pliant body, greedy and insatiable as teenagers pouncing on a bowl of ice cream. He welcomed their attentions cordially, but the lack of variety wearied him, thoroughly exhausting him when they were only a third of the way through the night. Iratov would have pleasant dreams of his partner leaving before he woke up.

It wasn't like that with Ms. Ivanova. She was in no hurry, and she encouraged her student to be the same way.

"There's time," she promised, looking into his eyes, her warm fingers tangled in his tar-black hair. "For everything." And she twirled dark strands around her fingers.

She cooked for him. Simple, tasty meals. She got his clothes in order, mending and ironing and gently instructing him that a man ought to pay attention to his wardrobe and select his things exactingly—if he has the means, of course.

"Just don't look like anyone else! Dressing simply, yet tastefully is fine, but, for God's sake, don't make yourself look like a puppet!"

There was a certain slowness about both her motions and her thoughts. Iratov examined her in the first rays of morning light, and it seemed as though she was floating, "as stately as a peahen," as Pushkin once penned.

Her movements were so slow, just fluttering along . . .

He recited English poetry to her in the original: Milton, Keats, and, of course, Shakespeare's sonnets.

Never once did he want to run away from Ms. Ivanova— Svetlana, she was Svetlana to him then—in the middle of the night and go back to his youthful life. When it happened on the weekend, he would always sleep in and open his eyes to meet the dark, moist gaze of his lover.

"What?" he'd ask.

"Nothing," she'd answer.

"Did something happen?"

"No, I just wanted to look at you."

"What for?"

"You're handsome . . ."

"And you're beautiful . . ." her young lover whispered in reply.

"I know . . ." Then she would stroke his hair again, and his breath would quicken—and he'd fill up again . . .

He gave her an expensive French nightgown for Valentine's Day—a size too large, so when Svetlana bent over him, he could steal a glance down her silken neckline and see her breasts.

Then Svetlana—Ms. Ivanova—married a distinguished scientist, the jungle explorer Gryazev, a well-known dandy, and left the Soviet Union soon thereafter.

Mr. Iratov was very upset—even he was surprised at this unfamiliar sense of loss, which had seemingly been completely absent from his life. He even tried to make himself puke to purge that torturous sensation.

Six months later, he found a package slip from the Congo in his mailbox. He fiddled with it, knowing full well it could only be from Svetlana, studied it nervously, and found that her message consisted of only three words: "I have wilted."

Arseny wanted to rush to the airport; he was sure that Svetlana wasn't happy with Gryazev. But what could he do as a kid of eighteen? Just hitch a ride to Sheremetyevo, face the suspicious eyes of the cops he knew all too well, and withdraw into terra incognita?

Iratov turned in the slip at the post office and received a little crate with wax seals, but then, for the longest time, he couldn't bring himself to pry it open—or go back home, either. He just sat on the back of a bench, smoking anxiously and watching the stoplight change. By the two thousandth flicker of yellow, he was chilled to the bone, so he ran all the way to the top floor of his five-story, prefab Soviet apartment block and locked himself in his room without even saying a word to his parents. The little crate was on the floor and the young man was on his pull-out bed, smoking cigarette after cigarette. He eventually mustered up the nerve . . .

Under the thin, non-Soviet paper was Svetlana's smell . . . or, more precisely, a French nightgown that smelled like Svetlana, a gift she was now returning to him. There was nothing else in the parcel, not even the shortest of messages.

Long into the night, Iratov pressed his nose into the nightgown, kept breathing in Svetlana's smell, down to the very roots of his lungs, until it hurt. Then he got mad, flung the nightgown into the far corner of the room, hissed, "Bitch . . . bitch . . ." and fell asleep.

For a few months after that, second-year architecture student Iratov put Svetlana's nightgown on all his pliant chicks and had rough sex with them, as if he were taking revenge on her. Volleyball girls, Communist Youth League girls, Ready for Labor and Defense of the USSR girls—they were all delighted by the young man's zeal, and they didn't give a damn what was in Iratov's head; so long as he kept up the pressure and kept the orgasms coming, those patriotic young ladies were happy.

"C'mon, Iratov!" wailed Katya, an attacker from the volleyball team. "Spike it!"

"Whoa mama . . ." sighed Shevtsova, the secretary of the student Communist Youth League. "Now I know who'll be getting their Party card next!"

"Can you go again?" Mykina, the fifth-year swimming champion would ask—she'd usually wake him up at around five in the morning. "You're as big as a dolphin!"

"You've been with a dolphin?"

Then the smell was exhausted, and Iratov tossed the nightgown on top of his wardrobe and forgot about Svetlana. He continued his studies and used the female population so much he practically used them up.

Just a few months later, Arseny was leafing through *Tourist* magazine in the barbershop when his eyes stopped on a photograph of a middle-aged man with a face like Aznavour. Dressed in shorts, sleeves rolled up, looking lean and muscular, he was posing in front of an Egyptian pyramid. There she was, standing next to him, leaning on a closed parasol. Svetlana! The caption read: "Distinguished archeologist and traveler Dr. Gryazev and spouse." The next photograph showed a reception at the Moscow Geographical Society, where the same Gryazev was smiling broadly at the camera and holding a glass of champagne. "Dr. Gryazev returning to the USSR after a series of unique discoveries."

It was the latest issue. Iratov suddenly realized that she was in Moscow.

He rushed out to go to her place. He couldn't wait for the bus; he ran faster than the speed of thought, so the tension of his muscles was too much for the top button of his shirt, which shot off, and then he was already at her building, running up the stairs to her seventh-floor apartment, at her door, almost knocking his forehead against it. He pounded on it with his fist so hard that it almost ripped off its hinges.

"Open up!" he yelled. She opened the door. His Svetlana.

"What are you doing, honey?" Her voice hadn't changed, or at least it seemed that way. Her soothing, melodious tone suddenly made his contorted mouth mute. "What are you doing, honey?" she repeated, stroking his bare chest. "What happened to your poor buttons?"

All he could do was grope for air with his mouth and hoarsely utter her name. Then he threw himself on her and dragged her to the bed.

Then he loved her and she loved him, and later they were sitting in the kitchen—naked. Svetlana told him that Gryazev was at his own apartment, that they'd had an unforgettable trip, and maybe now it was time to start a family.

"Good lord, the things I've seen!" she said, talking a mile a minute. "The pyramids, an Aztec city, the Great Wall of China, Sophia Loren, the Eiffel Tower! And boy, Gryazev knows so much about wine and fashion!"

The melodious quality had disappeared from her voice. He was hardly even listening to her. His nostrils flared, as if he were a hunting dog, trying to detect just one molecule of Svetlana's smell, but something had stamped it out—either her French perfume or something else. Svetlana gesticulated vigorously and exclaimed ecstatically, while he stared at her bare, slightly saggy breasts . . .

He realized that he didn't love her anymore. Yes, she had wilted . . . He left in surprise, citing his workload and promising to drop by later that week, went home, took the silk nightgown off the wardrobe, and threw it out the window like a useless rag. It hung on a tree branch until the sweeping winds of winter arrived, an old banner of love and rabid sex just dangling there, and then disappeared in December. Apparently someone had found a use for it.

Incidentally, about a year and a half later, Gryazev went to the States and never returned. He petitioned the American government for political asylum. Svetlana was left alone with a year-old baby in her arms, practically no means of sustenance, and the disdain of every neighbor in her apartment block.

It wasn't because she was the wife of a traitor, but because she had been abandoned. How good could she be if she got dumped like a dog by the railroad tracks?

Thus concludes the story of Iratov and Svetlana. It seemed

as though she hardly left a trace on his young, promising life, but many years down the road . . . Well, who knows what'll happen?

Iratov was about to graduate from the Moscow Architectural Institute, and he was planning to become an architect and build something that would stand tall for all of Moscow—well, all the world, obviously—like that young Japanese guy, Kenzo¯ Tange. He fancied himself the capital's next Boris Iofan . . . But, during his fourth year, he got involved in speculating—foreign currency checks, which you could use to load up on valuable goods from the special stores that offered Western clothes and electronics. The young Iratov was fantastically successful in that difficult and dangerous business. He would appear by the foreign currency stores in the mornings, dressed like a real fop, and use his rubles to buy dollars, deutsche marks, and francs. He was saving up, determined to leave the USSR by hook or by crook and become a world-renowned architect. To hell with Iofan. He had no real political motives; it was just that his tremendous desire to create something beautiful and live inside it was so passionate that it overcame his fear of prison. He knew very well that he was risking his freedom, that this was practically a firing-squad offense, but he wasn't afraid. Go big or go home!

Even the KGB spooks had taken a shine to him. The handsome, ever smiling fellow knew the names of their wives and kids—and, more importantly, their needs. Perfume, children's clothes, Swedish treats for the holidays . . . Basically, he was a good guy to have around.

The department that oversaw the Tishinka district was headed by KGB Captain Alevtina Vorontsova, who personally arrested Iratov near a foreign currency store. She was thinking about sending him up the river, but by the first interrogation, his demonic beauty had already conquered her. The young man evinced no fear and seemed eager to take her to bed. That's how it looked to her, at least.

"Why should a good-looking guy like that rot in prison?" she reasoned. "He can work for the good of the Motherland!" And work he did—he went to work on the captain's portly body like a tractor. Alevtina, still single, nearly fell in love with the young speculator, but she suppressed her tender inclinations with the help of her KGB conditioning.

"You'll bring in a thousand dollars a month!" Vorontsova declared. Those were her conditions.

"But that's . . ." Iratov had a curse on his lips, but he restrained himself and started to say that she was talking about enough dough for a working man to get by for a year and a half in the "white" economy.

"Oh yeah? But you aren't a working man! You're wearing two-hundred-ruble jeans and a pullover—and you've got gloves on in the middle of summer! Why? Is that supposed to be stylish or something?"

"They're motorcycle gloves!"

"So you have a motorcycle?" Alevtina sipped from her glass of Martell cognac, bit into a slice of lemon, and sent a stream of smoke from her Camel at the state-owned, Czechoslovakian-made lamp hanging from the ceiling of the safe house. "And cowboy boots," she continued. "I've got a guy in an eight-hundred-ruble outfit talking to me about being a working man! Speaking of which, you've got some work to do in the bedroom . . ."

"It's either the grand a month or the bedroom!" Iratov had never been that angry in his life.

"Nice one!" Alevtina neighed like a horse. Her plump body trembled, and she coughed hoarsely from all that noxious nicotine. "Oh, you're fuckin' killin' me! You young people, I tell ya!" Then she was instantly serious, her large features stony. "Two thousand and two safe house nights a week!"

He sat there, pale and angry, looking into Alevtina's eyes, harshly and fixedly. Captain Vorontsova easily withstood his gaze, thinking that she could make a good officer out of this kid. "He's got tenacity, perfect English, plus his looks—he could really do some wheeling and dealing!"

Captain Alevtina Vorontsova decided on the spot to recruit her black-eyed lover . . . what was the harm in mixing business and pleasure? He would finish his studies soon, then two years of training and he'd be a junior lieutenant. If they whisked him away for "illegal" work abroad, then she'd get a promotion out of it. It would take a while, but she was in no hurry . . .

"Deal!"

"Huh?" The recruiter was still lost in contemplating Iratov's prospects.

"Two grand a month and two pumps a week! Just don't forget that I'm still in school! I'm on the dean's list!"

"Good for you!"

"Free access to Sheremetyevo Airport, none of your guys trying to pinch me! I know that isn't your turf, but you'll set it up . . . and access to the duty-free store!"

"You've got some nerve!" Alevtina said, throwing up her big hands in surprise, like a penguin trying to fly. "Think you're a real badass now?" She was actually prepared to accept that transaction; she was just acting tough for show. She didn't answer yet, just smoked another cigarette down to the filter, hit the button on her Japanese-made tape player, and let Vladimir Vysotsky accompany her—"I will spread out the fields for loooooovers!" She nodded her large head. "De-e-al." She pursed her meaty lips like the pope's nose and made a smooching sound. "Ready to get to work? Locked and loaded?

Get in that bed and serve the Motherland!" She went over to the two-person sofa bed, moving like a hippo. "Let them sing, sleeping or waaaaaaaaking!"

"You got your pump for today! Second one on Friday! Money tomorrow!" Iratov put on his corduroy jacket and headed for the hills.

"Where you going, bitch?" Vorontsova snapped out of her reverie, raced toward the door, nearly face-planted, stayed on her feet, and burst out into the stairwell, but her minion in the motorcycle gloves was already turning the corner . . .

Neither of them broke the agreement. Without fail, the student brought in the currency and hit the target punctually. He was allowed into the duty-free store, and soon Iratov was dressing the entire Moscow Architectural Institute. In one year, the young man made so much money that, by Soviet standards, he would be set for life. Through some mystical means, he managed to find time for his studies and his final project . . . He was simultaneously developing contacts in the shadow economy, where he dealt in metals and stones. Even then, Iratov knew not to keep his wealth in paper money.

Alevtina aged rapidly during that time and ballooned until she looked like a police officer straight out of Saltykov-Shchedrin. Her fat-choked heart turned into a money-grubbing muscle, and her enormous body grew greedier and greedier for the pleasures of the flesh. The officer's mind was as clear as ever, though, and her thoughts were sharp.

One time, when they were sitting in the safe house and Alevtina had already gotten her monthly gifts, she suddenly started talking in a folksy way, like she was Iratov's grandmother.

"Well, well, my dearie," she began. "I brought you a little something, betcha can't guess what it is!"

"I don't know," the speculator answered discontentedly.

"Your present will probably put me on the hook for a mil. I don't like presents!"

"Oh no, my sweetums!" Captain Vorontsova scooched over. "I'm cutting your taxes." Iratov looked at her suspiciously. "What I'm offering you is . . . well, it's nothing special . . . it's a new life!" She neighed with laughter.

"With you?"

"We'll see how things go from there. What you've been doing so far is just small potatoes—or small tzimmes, as Zanis would say."

"Who's that?"

"A Latvian guy who works for my unit. He's a hard worker, like you, not scared of firing-squad offenses . . . but he isn't such a love machine . . ." She broke into laughter again, sounding just like a bittern.

"Get back to the big tzimmes."

She gave Iratov a harsh look, like a true officer, and began delivering her business proposal.

"You're a sharp guy! You can handle complex systems—"

Iratov was certain that he was about to face a firing squad. He interrupted her to save his life.

"Let's do it the usual way. I'll give you a bigger cut! How much do you need?"

"Come on, don't be scared! You're no coward! And I'm not talking about a dead-end job here!"

"Then what are you talking about?"

"Well . . ." Then Alevtina came out with it, imparting what she was expecting of him, a young, promising, college-educated man with full proficiency in a foreign language. "You will become a lieutenant and have control of your own life!" The captain produced a small red object from her uniform pocket. "Do you know what this is?"

"Your KGB badge!"

"And do you know that this badge opens every door in the USSR, even in the f'ing Baltics?"

"I'd gathered . . ." Iratov answered, realizing what she was getting at. He hadn't expected this at all. He was ready for anything except her trying to recruit him. "But I want to be an architect! I studied . . . dammit, you're out of your fucking mind!"

"But you're a currency speculator!" Alevtina said angrily. "Plus, being an architect is a fabulous cover."

"That's beneath me, working for a bunch of spooks! I read samizdat copies of Solzhenitsyn and Efraim Sevela! I am an anti-Soviet speculator undermining the economic progress of the communist system . . . not a KGB officer!"

"Not for a bunch of spooks—for the Motherland!" Captain Vorontsova hissed. "See the difference? Read what you like! Read the Kama Sutra for all I care! Then practice on me!"

Iratov downed some cognac and had a stiff think, while Captain Vorontsova watched him affectionately. He really was handsome. Vrubel's demon! She had the great artist's ceramic in her collective apartment and another demon head at her dacha.

"I have to think about it."

"You do that," Alevtina answered, sadly, because she had no husband or children after devoting her whole life to the Motherland . . . oh, how her heart ached! "Is three days enough?"

"Yeah."

"That's what I like to hear. Now how about my 'pump' for today?" She hiked her uniform skirt up to her chin, got on all fours, and rested her elbows on the sofa . . .

All through the next day, Iratov's brain was burning, like a grenade had gone off in his head. No matter how hard he strained, he could not gather the thoughts he needed. By evening, the flame had waned; dawn broke in Iratov's skull, and he realized that he needed help. He went through everyone he knew, from store managers to businessmen, but he couldn't think of anyone who could snatch him from the clutches of the KGB. Refusing the offer to become a spook would be a brief prelude to prison.

By the following evening, a desperate decision came all on its own, and by midnight, it had firmly convinced Iratov that it was both right and inevitable. That same night, he visited the luggage rooms of Moscow's four major train stations, where he picked up six suitcases.

The architecture student loaded everything he had amassed into the trunk of his Zhiguli, parked it in Lubyanka Square at seven in the morning, approached a massive door, and rang the bell. An instant later, a soldier rounded the corner, his insignia identifying him as a warrant officer in the Internal Troops, accompanied by two subordinates. The door still hadn't opened, though.

"You can't park your vehicle here!"

"I'm here to turn myself in," Iratov declared. His face was still pale, but his eyes burned with masculine decisiveness.

"Parking here is still prohibited! We are impounding the vehicle and arresting you."

"Well, that's why I came!"

The door opened, and a young major leaned halfway out and dismissed the guards with a careless flick of his pale wrist.

"Please come in, Comrade Iratov."

That was a cute trick to play—it usually worked, especially on the youngsters—but the speculator knew it well. They just ran the plates on his Zhiguli. Simple as that.

"Thank you."

They took him up to the fourth floor in the elevator and pointed to the corridor leading to the right. The major followed, guiding him with crisp commands.

"Bear right. Straight. Bear right."

Iratov had never seen internal architecture like this. This was more than corridors veering to the left or right; it was like some kind of labyrinth. Anyone finding themselves in this building for the first time would be uneasy, to say the least.

"Stop!" the major said, either asking or ordering. "Here we are, Mr. Iratov."

A minute later, Iratov was sitting across from a small man: lieutenant colonel's uniform, the face of a little beast, and the eyes of a fish. Despite his repellant appearance, the lieutenant colonel gave him a welcoming smile from the other side of a huge table with a black intercom panel on the right side. That's how people smile just before they knife somebody in a dark alley . . . There was also a metal cage containing a chair with a collapsed seat.

"How much do you have?" the beast inquired in a quiet voice.

"Excuse me?" Iratov was confused at first.

"What's the total, in those suitcases?"

"Suitcases?" Here was a trick Mr. Iratov didn't know. He couldn't imagine how they had managed to move his car so quickly, not to mention search it. It had been seven minutes, tops. They hadn't even arrested him yet! "I . . . I don't know the exact amount . . ."

"Your best estimate, please."

"Eight hundred thousand, maybe more . . ."

"In rubles?"

"Foreign currency." The lieutenant colonel noticeably tensed up. He pressed a button on the intercom and issued his instructions.

"Stenographer and all material evidence pertaining to the Iratov case, immediately." Apparently, they had been keeping tabs on him for some time, but, clearly, Vorontsova had been true to her word, and she'd been covering for him as best she could.

Full name, where and when, come on, you're a Communist Youth League boy, hundreds of questions in the first thirty minutes. They brought in the suitcases and counted the money until the next morning. The lieutenant colonel kept looking at Iratov the whole time, like he was scanning his brain.

"I came to turn myself in, honest! I—"

"Hold on there!" the man-fish-beast interrupted. He continued staring in silence, sipping black tea from a glass in a silver holder with an engraving of Felix Dzerzhinsky.

"Eight hundred twenty-three thousand, sir," they reported.

"Rokotov was shot for a million . . ."

"But I came forward voluntarily!" Iratov exclaimed nervously. "And Rokotov was back when Khrushchev was in power! These days you get eight years, but I came forward voluntarily—"

"Relax, Mr. Iratov. We'll set everything straight. The fact that you came forward voluntarily is good, but one way or another, you'll have to do some time. Precisely how much is entirely up to you. By the way, where did you get the nickname Yakut? You don't look like a northerner to me. Now please step into the cage!"

"I have access to information that I am prepared to trade for my freedom," the confessed speculator declared, deciding to take a new tack.

The escort guard pushed Iratov into the cage and cuffed one of his hands to a metal loop.

"Very interesting, please continue!"

"Do I have a guarantee?"

"Is your watch new?" the colonel asked.

"Huh?"

"Is it a Rolex?"

"It's a Schaffhausen . . . almost new." He automatically looked at this left hand and noticed that the handcuffs had cracked the glass, and the gold band was all scratched.

"There you go, it has a lifetime guarantee! But only in Switzerland . . ."

Iratov didn't want to go to prison, though he'd imagined it many times. His whole life down the tubes . . . Time to take a risk. He stood up straight.

"You won't give me more than eight years. I'll keep my information to myself!" he announced.

What came next was a long and torturous palaver, complete with threats that his parents would not be spared, that the Politburo intended to revive good old Mr. Khrushchev's practice of taking dickwads like him and smearing brilliant green dye on their foreheads . . . They kept him in a cold cell, turned on a klaxon so he couldn't sleep, and informed him a week later that they had arrested his mother and father, and his mom was on the verge of a heart attack. They even brought his old sexual partners from the institute in for questioning. The chicks came in with no makeup and their hair done like old Bolsheviks, with their Communist Youth League pins on over their push-up bras. They maintained, each more adamantly than the last, that they had no idea he was secretly involved in currency speculation. Katya, the volleyball player, stated that she didn't even know who Iratov was; sure, she'd seen him on campus a few times, but she spent all her time practicing. Shevtsova, the Communist Youth League secretary, furrowed her Party brows and muttered between her teeth that she herself had suspected Arseny of criminal activity for some time. She had received some signals, and they were preparing a response . . . Another dozen or so chicks made similar statements, but he just smiled slightly, studying his bedmates, knowing full well that, underneath those dowdy Soviet dresses and blouses, their pliant tits and tushies were ready to be stripped of the high-class Italian lingerie gifted to them by a criminal named Iratov. You could have asked the investigator to undress this whole Communist Youth League bordello, and all those young ladies would have been sent up the river along with him for incitement to commit a crime. Well, that would make his time in prison much more pleasurable. Iratov didn't wish the girls ill, though, so he kept quiet. What can you do with these women? They're all whores! You can't expect a whore to be faithful!

"So how many of them, Yakut?" the lieutenant colonel inquired.

"How many . . . what?"

"How many have you poked?"

"A lot of them, sir," the prisoner confessed. "A lot." They slowly and methodically pumped him for information but weren't offering anything in return, hoping that, sooner or later, the tried-and-true methods would loosen the student's tongue. But a week passed, then another, then a whole month, and the speculator still wouldn't talk.

Then they unexpectedly offered him his freedom—if his information proved truly significant. The lieutenant colonel gave him his word of honor.

Iratov waited that proposition out, too, despite how thin and red-eyed his windowless torments had left him. They didn't shave his head, leaving him with long hair, which was soon infested with lice. The bloodsuckers tortured the student far more than the nighttime alarms. It was as if they were scurrying over his exposed brain and sinking their little teeth into his heavy thoughts.

"Come on already, Iratov," sighed lieutenant colonel Ivanov. "What do you know?"

So Arseny told them about Vorontsova. When, where, what currency, how the aging captain had induced him to enter a sexual relationship with her. He related every detail, omitting nothing, dreaming of freedom. His tale of Alevtina's exploits was recorded, chapter by chapter, with exacting care. They let him read it and make corrections, which he initialed, and when there was nothing more to tell, the lieutenant colonel inquired whether or not that was everything. Iratov nodded with a sigh.

"Yes, every last bit of it."

The wind of freedom, its marvelous scent, banged against the barred windows.

"Well, that's good." The colonel looked pleased for some reason. He pressed a button on the intercom. "Send Captain Vorontsova in, please," he instructed.

Alevtina entered the office in her full dress uniform: white shirt, tie, state medals on her chest.

"Comrade Lieutenant Colonel of the Committee for State Security of the Union of—"

"No need for that, Alevtina, it's just us. Is the shop in order?" Mr. Ivanov asked, then answered himself. "It is, I know it is. Have a seat."

She looked at Iratov like he was some pathetic animal in a cage—why'd the shameless critter have to bite his mama?— then turned her monument-still face to the lieutenant colonel.

"He didn't work out!" Vorontsova admitted with chagrin. "Yakut here refused to work with us. An incorrigible subversive and a hardened criminal, at such a young age! The Central Committee's decision to reinstate firing squads was well-timed! How's the family, Mr. Ivanov?"

"Thank you for your kind interest, Alevtina!" the lieutenant colonel said pleasantly. "Well now, your testimony has been included in the case file, Comrade Captain. The audio recordings you have presented make it abundantly clear that this young man, Arseny Andreivich Iratov, born 1960, does not love the Motherland, and thus refused to help us expose enemies of the Soviet Union—quite the contrary, he disseminated anti-Soviet literature and repeatedly attempted to bribe a KGB agent, i.e., you. American currency was received from you against signed receipt three months ago. He has robbed the law-abiding Soviet peoples of one million dollars. He did knowingly undermine the economic might of the USSR! Sign here, please." He made a checkmark on the paper, and Vorontsova scribbled her signature there. "Well, everything is perfectly clear here. The investigation is concluded!" Then he turned to Iratov's cage. The young man sat there, as still as an embalmed corpse. "Maybe they will shoot you after all, if they get tough and charge you with undermining the economic might of the USSR!" He turned back to the witness. "You really ought to come work with us, Alevtina!"

"Thank you for saying so, Comrade Ivanov! But I can't. I'm used to being on the ground. I've learned to dig out those weasels like a truffle pig! And it makes me so happy!"

"Then you are dismissed, Comrade Captain. Thank you for your service!" said the lieutenant colonel, starting the standard call-and-response.

"I serve the Soviet Union!"

"Give Galina my best."

"Absolutely, Comrade Ivanov!" Alevtina Vorontsova left the office. Then the lieutenant colonel started writing something and kept at it into the night, eventually switching on his desk lamp to check it over. In the wee hours of the morning, he looked up at the cage.

"I forgot about you, Mr. Iratov! I'm so terribly sorry." He

turned to the intercom again. "Remove the prisoner . . . And here's some information for you, Comrade Iratov. A trial will be held soon. The evidence will be presented to the prosecutor today, then, a couple weeks later, it's goodbye Comrade Iratov!"

The trial was held seventeen days later. Iratov was relieved to see his parents in the audience—so those fuckers had been putting one over on him the whole time. Those little Communist Youth League girls were out in force, their eyes burning with indignation. During the proceedings, he made eye contact with each of them in turn, and every last one bestowed a longing, amorous look on him, as if to say "if it were up to us . . ." A lot of people had come in the hope of hearing the ghastly verdict: "For this grave violation of socialist law, this court imposes the severest possible punishment—death by firing squad!"

It was soon revealed, however, that the president of the Moscow Architectural Institute had come forward as a character witness and provided an excellent letter in Iratov's defense, emphasizing that he was an extremely talented student. His final project had been awarded a gold medal in Tokyo. Both the Japanese judges and the representatives of several other countries had evinced an inclination to commission this Russian architect's brainchild . . . And the president had been in the Party for forty years. Who could ignore that?

The burly, chubby-cheeked judge grew curious and asked what exactly this project was. The president's representative turned over a sheet of Whatman paper with a sketch on it, and everyone gaped at something their eyes had never beheld before. Standing up proudly among ordinary buildings, swathed in green plants, soared a gigantic self-tapping screw. Yes, really, like the kind a carpenter would use to attach the baseboards in an apartment. Giggling could be heard in the gallery; then the audience burst into laughter.

The Honorable Judge Chubby Cheeks suppressed a smile with difficulty and called the court to order. A juror whispered something in his ear.

"And how much are the bourgeoisie offering for this . . . design?" he inquired.

"Two million dollars," the president's representative answered, and the crowd fell silent at once. Them regular Soviet folks had never even fantasized about that kind of money. "The entire building is designed around the shape of a perfectly ordinary screw." Someone in the crowd let out a nervous hiccup. "The architect used the principles of engineering to demonstrate how elevators would move along the threads of the screw, while the top floor, which would house something important, you know, like the main bureau of the Ministry of the Space Industry, would be located near the head of the screw. You could launch a Vostok spacecraft from the roof if you wanted," the representative joked. He also reported that the architect had made it very clear that he specifically wanted this innovative structure to be built in Moscow, the capital of our glorious Motherland. Thus, it would not be entirely fair to accuse this young man of hating our glorious Motherland.

A recess was called. The judge consulted various layers of the government hierarchy. The party structure urged mercy, as well as closing the trial to the public to prevent journalists from continuing their coverage of this high-profile case.

"We won't let them shoot a talented man like that," said a Central Committee member with a smile. "Who's going to do the building if we put our geniuses against the wall? Plus, these are more humane times. Nobody wants to bring back firing squads for speculating . . . well, except the old guard . . . they're always pushing on us . . ."

"They shot Gumilev," the judge reminded him. "He was a genius, too!"

"Did anybody offer two million dollars for Gumilev's poems? Answer me that! You have to make some mistakes when you're young or you'll be a complete idiot when you're old . . . Come on, the building's a screw!"

"Fifteen years?" the judge asked.

"Five." The Central Committee member admonished the judge once again for his excessive harshness and warned his chubby-cheeked honor that consuming too much sugar could cause diabetes. Just think about that, getting your foot cut off . . . . That was an outcome he dreaded himself.

"Plus, we'll knock some time off for good behavior . . . Then we'll see . . . Leonid's a nice guy!" Five days later, Iratov was sentenced to four years and seven months in a work camp—not even a high-security one. They gave him two hours to say good-bye to his parents, then it was off to the woods near Vladimir.

Iratov had a pretty easy time adjusting to the camp. He was neutral toward everyone, and some people even found him useful. He steered clear of the guys with connections and cautiously established contacts with the ones who did business. Plus, the warden was building himself a little dacha, and there wasn't even a decent engineer to be found. Iratov came in handy—he drew up the plans and even managed the construction work.

"Good goin', Yakut!" said the thin-as-a-churchkhela warden, slapping the architect on the back. "You sure whipped up a top-notch hacienda! And it only took ya six months! I woulda been putzing around for fifteen years! You've got talent! I'm gonna tack another nickel on your sentence! Don't look at me like that, I'm kidding! You can sign on as a volunteer worker.

Do you have any idea how many people I know around here? We'll build castles for all of them and rake in some serious cash! And women! Plus, no oversight! What the hell do you want to go back to Moscow for?"

Iratov laughed the whole thing off and presented himself as some Muscovite lordling who would never contemplate such a thing. He had made up his mind what he wanted in life, and it certainly wasn't working for a bunch of screws! But for the time being, he willingly obliged, even putting out a wall newspaper where the screws were transformed into national heroes.

His mother often came to see him, never missing a single opportunity. Those visits were absolute torture for him. There was a time or two when Shevtsova came out and fucked him for his full two-day leave, which was enough to colorize his black-and-white camp life. The screws would take turns peeping, but the young couple didn't give a damn. Boy, there was nothing Iratov and his guest didn't try! She was every bit the virtuoso Iratov was, spinning and swinging like crazy, getting into these wild positions—the amazing elastic girl! They burst out laughing when they heard a bass voice saying, "Fuck, I'm gonna come!" The uninhibited Ms. Shevtsova aimed her bare ass at the likely location of the peephole—no reason they shouldn't get their virtual jollies over there!

A month later, his mother arrived again. She told him that his dad was often ill, that the principal was being unfair, and that almost all the plaster had fallen off the ceiling in their apartment.

"I'm all alone now."

Then she didn't say anything for a while, and Iratov munched on cheese sandwiches and cold dumplings from a glass jar . . . Then the aging English teacher, born Countess Rymnikova, took the night train back to Moscow. She had to make it back in time for her second-period class.

The very next day, he was summoned for another rendez-vous, and a family one at that—i.c., with his supposed wife. He had been granted another forty-eight hours off. Even the screws were surprised—getting leave twice in a row was unheard of!

Iratov was intrigued, and as he walked to the family section, he pondered who could have been so brazen. Claiming to be his wife! Was it Katya, the volleyball player? Or maybe it was Comrade Shevtsova again? She couldn't stand going without sex unless she was in class, or maybe a Communist Youth League meeting. And she had spectators here, too! The memory of Shevtsova's naked body was enough to make Iratov almost happy.

There's no logic to life. You're driving down a straight road, convinced that it will go on forever, then a pit opens up, and you're . . . frigged!

Alevtina was waiting for him in the room set aside for conjugal visits. Captain Vorontsova, in the flesh.

She was of tremendous dimensions and had grown even more corpulent since Iratov got sent up the river. She settled in between the pillows on the bed, crushing its springs into the floor. Dressed in simple civilian clothing, with no makeup, the officer almost looked like an old lady.

"It's y—" Iratov was stunned.

"Yes, it's me."

He was standing in the doorway, gobsmacked, staring at his former handler. Yeah, this fat sow wasn't Shevtsova . . . there's the pit!

"I'm . . . Alevtina. Don't you recognize me?" She coughed thickly, breathing spasmodically like an old man taking a drag on a hand-rolled cigarette full of the coarsest makhorka tobacco.

"Sure . . ."

She lit one of her Camels and bade him step into the room.

Rooting around in some bags, she deftly spread the delicacies she had brought on the table. A little bottle of precious vodka was soon on display, with another flat one, which had to be French cognac, beside it.

"There's some ham, too—it's Hungarian. Look how pink it is! And some lovely sprats, and some meat with mushrooms—I braised it myself! I made the potatoes, too. You aren't actually that far from Moscow. I wrapped it all up in newspapers and blankets. I drove a hundred and twenty-five miles! Have a seat, baby! Have some pickles and cucumbers! Come on, you must be starved!"

"What the hell did you come here for?"

"Who, me?" Alevtina was breathing heavily, as if she'd unloaded a truck full of watermelons instead of laying out a spread. "To visit you!"

"What the hell for?" Iratov felt a tide of anger rising in him; he wanted to kick her right in the gut.

"To see you, why else?"

"Gather up your crap and beat it, you old bitch! You made me potatoes! Potatoes!"

"Why are you so cross with me?" Alevtina splashed some vodka in a glass. "Or have I done something wrong?"

"What?!" He went crimson with hate. "You wanted to fucking shoot me! Shoot! Me! I don't think so! I'll get parole in a few years. My country needs me, how about that? I hope you croak before I get out! I'll dance on your grave!" God, he was so handsome in his rage, with sparklers under his black brow and that incorrigible hair! Alevtina couldn't help but admire him.

"Shoot you? Are you off your rocker, honey bunny? You were the one who turned me in so they'd let you off! You wanted me to go to jail instead. Or have you forgotten? You're the rotten one, honey! You're as handsome as a god, but you're no god!

I was just doing my job. You were trying to save your skin! See the difference? And don't act tough with me! I know this is like a resort for you! How about cutting down trees in Magadan? How about the mines? Fucking limp-dick prick . . ."

"You used me!" He grabbed his own shoulders and strained his muscles until they hurt to keep himself from choking the old viper then and there. Vorontsova crunched into a pickle. "I hate you!"

"I used *you*?" She spat the end of the pickle on the floor. "Didn't you make millions? You ungrateful swine!"

"What millions? It's all gone!" He took a threatening step toward her.

"Just don't be an idiot, I'm begging you," she said, smiling to reveal teeth stained brown with tobacco film. "And your millions haven't gone anywhere." Alevtina looked into his black eyes with a smirk. "What, do you think I don't know? Me?! You turned in eight hundred thousand! Rokotov was small fry compared to you! I'm Alevtina Vorontsova, working with the security organs for twenty years without a single reprimand, and you think I'm stupid? I have a report on every transaction you made! I know where you buried the dollars and where you stashed the gold and stones! You think you'll just waltz out of here in a couple years, pick up your caches, and go straight to the West? Stick that screw up your ass!" There was a neigh of laugher in her vodka-cleaned throat. "If I had revealed the extent of your crimes back then, you'd be in a mass grave with the serial killers and pedophiles! You'd already be done rotting! I took pity on you, you idiot!"

Iratov sat down at the table, filled a glass to the brim with Stolichnaya, and poured it straight into his belly.

"Boy, you can drink! Where's the money?"

"Where it was."

"You're lying!"

"What for?" The captain sliced off a generous piece of pink ham, put it on a white bun, and held it out. "Go on, eat something!" He took the sandwich, bit into it like a frightened dog, leaned back in his chair, and began to chew.

"It's Hungarian . . . I remember . . ."

"I told you it was delicious! Just as good as what they have in the West!" Alevtina caught two sprats with her fork. They dove into her enormous mouth, and only then did she go back to the vodka.

"How come you didn't take the money?" He, too, crunched into a pickle, then swallowed the brine. "You could have gone to the West yourself . . ."

"How should I put this . . . ?" Alevtina wiped her greasy lips with a rag. "I came here because of a . . . weighty . . . matter. The West can wait!"

"Get to the point already!" He twisted off the top of the cognac bottle. "Want some?"

"Nah, don't want to mix grains . . . and I don't really drink anymore."

"How come?" Iratov took a giant swig.

"Well, I'm pregnant, Arseny," Alevtina informed him matter-of-factly. "It's coming in a few weeks. Wouldn't want to hurt the baby . . ."

"Pregnant? You?" He stared at the captain and laughed out loud. His long laughter tore him up and bubbled in his throat. Then he sputtered to a stop. "Whose is it?" he asked, suddenly hoarse.

"You see . . . I'm sure you understand . . ." Alevtina hadn't stopped eating her presents.

"Whose is it?"

"Yours, honey! It's your son! That's the weighty matter!"

"You're full of it!" Then Iratov suddenly went limp and started crying like a child who'd lost his mommy in the supermarket.

"Tears of joy, I hope! Why would I lie? He'll be born soon— and you'll see he's yours. I can tell it's going to be a boy . . . I keep getting this bitter taste in my mouth. They say that happens when the baby's hair is growing . . . And man, you've got a full head of hair! Ooo, he's kicking! He gets a kick out of it when I talk about him . . . That's why I didn't have them really throw the book at you, you goof! A boy needs a father! A man! And a man of means."

Iratov had almost been annihilated by the enemy's superior forces. He sat there, surrounded, like General Paulus, sensing that his life was coming to an end, like a man on the verge of committing suicide: face pale, eyes wandering, extinguished. He looked like a maniac in an asylum.

"Go on, talk to him!" Alevtina invited Iratov to touch her stomach—it was high time he felt his father's touch, after all. Iratov threw up, right there on the table. "Who consumes that much alcohol on an empty stomach? Yuck, it got everywhere!" She rose from the compressed bedsprings with difficulty, wet the rag in the sink, and cleared the table. "Basically, you register as the father and a week from now you walk! Or else you can wait for your case to be reviewed. And then . . ."

What could he do? To be in a bind like that, when he'd had his whole life planned out . . . He sat at that table until nightfall, not eating, not drinking, just thinking, while Alevtina snored in the conjugal visit bed. Her stomach, full of his seed, rose aloft and then descended, gurgling thunderously, like a volcano about to erupt.

5

I woke up in February. Nothing in the fridge but rotten eggs. It was warm in the apartment, though. I brushed my teeth, washed my face, put some gauze on my jeans and ironed them until they had perfect creases, got dressed, and went outside. My neighbor, Ivanov, was sitting on the back of the bench, so hungover he was shaking. He really wanted something to make him feel better, even just a bottle of beer—he had a splitting headache, and he grinned when he saw me.

"Fuck, man! Wow, it's you!"

"Sure is," I concurred. "I don't have any money."

"We all thought you'd kicked . . . Not even thirty rubles?"

"Thought I'd kicked what?" I inquired, still not intending to offer my neighbor any monetary aid whatsoever.

"Kicked the bucket!"

"What? Why?"

"You haven't come out of your apartment for a month and a half!"

"What are you, my parole officer?"

"No . . ."

"My brother?" Ivanov grew weary of answering my questions—especially since he had the shakes so bad his jaw had locked up.

"I kept going over to your door, you know, the keyhole, to smell . . .":

"What?"

"Well, to see if you were rotting in there. I had a mouse die behind my wardrobe once. It stank for two weeks!"

"I'm not a mouse!"

"Yeah, I can see that you're alive . . . Well, happy New Year!"

"The new year starts in September, idiot!"

Our conversation was soon exhausted, so I set off for Danilovsky Market. I walked down the rows, pinching sauerkraut from the stalls, sampling pickles and marinated garlic, which wound up being my breakfast . . .

It's freezing outside, the streets aren't plowed, and cars drown in pure snow. Breath comes easy, white drifts reflect the sunshine, eager to cast its rays into your eyes. I enjoyed a pleasant sneeze. And another! And a third!

I walked through downtown Moscow, sometimes breaking into a run and skidding on the frozen asphalt. My route took me to Petrovsky Boulevard, home to a little barbershop where an old Greek man with a patchy, gray beard—Antipatros was his name—cut my hair, leaving me with just an eighth of an inch. That was the way he'd always done it, with the clippers. For the last thirty years . . . His assistant was a thin, exceptionally beautiful mixed-race girl with striking blue eyes. She brought him everything he needed, then he put some cream on my face and shaved my cheeks with a wicked razor. He put a hot towel on my clean skin, held it there until steam rose from my forehead, then sprinkled me with chypre. Where Antipatros got that skin-tingling chypre remained a mystery. Maybe he stocked up, back when you could buy it? He trimmed the hair protruding from my nose with manicure scissors.

He never talked to me, or any of his other customers for that matter—not one word in thirty years. The Greek wasn't mute, though. He had a reputation as an exceptionally proud man, and he did not care to bandy words with the masses. But what if he had to buy a ticket to Prague? Well, he didn't go anywhere. He actually lived in his shop, and there was nothing in

Prague he needed . . . But I know where Antipatros used to live, way back . . .

In the early evening, I visited Ms. Senescentova, an Honored Actor of the Soviet Union. I could often be found at her home, drinking linden-blossom tea and listening to her stories about what life used to be like in the theater world.

I might very well have been the only one who visited the old actress. I chased away the scam artists who tried to take advantage of her in the troubled nineties—and punished them severely. Everyone had forgotten about her service to the people, convinced that Senescentova must have long since departed this world, like a wondrous angel, but she just stopped appearing in any productions, much less in other public spaces, in '64, and stopped answering calls from journalists and film studios. She preferred that the audience remember her as young and beautiful.

She was childless, purportedly an old maid for all her former beauty, always wearing powder and a touch of scarlet lipstick. She called me her nephew, and I liked that. When I answered her questions, I would unfailingly use the simple address "auntie." That was very much to her liking as well. For example, when she would ask me if I had been at some interesting gathering, be it the theater, the cinema, or the zoo, I would answer, "No, auntie, can't say I have," or, "Yes, indeed, auntie." Yes, our conversations were full of mutual affection.

"And how have you been doing, my dearest nephew?"

"Well, how to put it, auntie . . . Same as always."

"I went to the cemetery yesterday. Everything is in order . . ." Senescentova pulled a burial contract out from under the tablecloth and indicated the blue official stamps. "I've already paid for six months of upkeep on the grave." She handed it to me. "Here!"

"Oh auntie, don't you think this is a little premature! Have mercy!"

"You promised!"

"I know, I'm not saying no. But you're rushing things, auntie! Come now, life is not a hundred-meter dash!"

"My dearest nephew, I will give you my icon of the Mother of God this instant and sign a deed of gift!"

"Not the icon, anything but that! Count me out! Come on, auntie, what's got you so worked up? You've still got years ahead of you!"

"We'll have no more of that, young man! I know that it will be soon. I will be one hundred and three years old in March!" She rose from the table, strode over to the buffet, opened a little drawer, and fished out an elegant cigarette holder. "Take this, if the icon is not to your taste! It's a classic art deco piece, made of ivory with platinum inserts. Sell it and buy yourself something new—it is a little worn out, though, look."

"Elegant indeed," I agreed, accepting the cigarette holder and examining the seal. "Raymond Templier . . ." I securely secreted it in my shirt pocket. "Alright, let me have your documents."

"They are to bury me in the dress from *Timid Night*," Senescentova said, beaming and beginning to enumerate the instructions that I had known by heart for twenty years. "You know the one, when I exited with Tsyganov in the final scene. Remember? A simple coffin, nothing extravagant, but my face simply must be covered with white, translucent chiffon. Come to my requiem at Donskoy Monastery completely alone. This is positively *not* to be a society function. And no tears are to be shed, my dearest nephew!"

"Certainly not, auntie!"

"All the paperwork for the apartment has been taken care

of . . ." She paused, suddenly remembering something. "By the way, I saw that acquaintance of yours at the cemetery. He's quite an imposing fellow, and the lady with him—goodness, she was miraculously beautiful—highborn!"

"What acquaintance?" I asked, pricking my ears up.

"Iratov, of course! And do you know the most startling thing? He recognized me. He kissed my hand and spoke so very earnestly and tenderly. A very pleasant gentleman!"

"How do you know him?" Something jolted in my stomach. I could feel some kind of knot in my guts.

"Through you, you silly goose! It was you who told me about him! And do you know, he did not look as unsightly as your descriptions led me to believe."

"But how did you know what he looks like?"

"Now I remember!" The old woman looked concerned as her mind raced into the past. "He's the architect of my building! Back in '88, when the Union of Cinematographers gave me an apartment here, he spent six months going around to all the residents and asking if everything in the building was alright. Evidently, he was feeling a little anxious—after all, it was his first project, as I understand it . . . He had linden-blossom tea with me, just like you! There I was thinking you meant the other gentleman of that name . . . There are a great many Iratovs!"

"The man with black hair?"

"That's the one, my dearest nephew! Long, black hair, with one gray streak—and it looks most handsome!"

"But what was he doing there, auntie?"

"I couldn't tell you," Senescentova shrugged. "Presumably he wanted to visit some grave or other. Tell me, nephew, what else would one do at a cemetery?"

"Wasn't there anything else you noticed?"

"Well, I was rather preoccupied! I was outside when he addressed himself to me, and then I went inside to warm up. It was bitterly cold yesterday!"

"I see . . . I see . . ." I muttered to myself.

"Oh, no!" The ancient Senescentova slapped her hands together. "I remember now!"

"What, auntie?" I nearly jumped out of my chair. "What is it?"

"Here's what, my dearest nephew. He was there to meet a young man. Your friend Iratov stepped about ten yards away from his young lady and exchanged greetings with a young man. Then they had a conversation—and a rather brief one. That's why I forgot for a moment there!"

"What did the young man look like?" I was in a real frenzy. My guts tied themselves tighter and tighter.

"Not terribly tall, not terribly short . . ." Senescentova said, trying to recall. "Very thin, like a sugarcane plant—and his face was much like Iratov's—as if he were his own son! Is that who he is? Pale, like he was ill, and all in black, like an undertaker!"

"What did they talk about?"

"Oh, take pity on your auntie! My hearing is not what it once was . . . and I am not generally disposed to eavesdrop."

"Damn!"

"Why are you in such distress?" the former actress asked in surprise. "That's not like you! They had a conspiratorial look about them, though . . ."

"That snake . . ." I hissed.

"Just what is going on?!"

"Do you recall what I told you about Iratov's younger years, auntie?"

"I perfectly recall the unfortunate story of that talented

youth. But such were the times! The law was firm with those who trespassed against it! But . . . his trespasses are permitted now, if memory serves . . ."

"That is not the point, auntie! My story hardly scratched the surface, and I softened some details so as not to trouble your frayed nerves! My tale was told for your amusement!"

"What do you mean? What did you not impart?"

"Not now, auntie." Senescentova was curious, like all old ladies without social connections, the ones who have outlived their girlfriends and the devotees their talents won them. She was as thirsty for information as an astronaut is for oxygen . . . but she didn't like watching TV.

"But what happened?" She scurried over to the old buffet and then put a box of sweets on the table. "Chocolate-covered marshmallows! Korkunov brand!" she declared. "And there's some gummies here! In just a moment, the kettle will start to sing, and we'll sit down with our linden-blossom tea, and I hope you'll calm down, my dearest nephew, and save me from my boredom. And he who saves shall be saved!"

"Well then, auntie!" I said, making up my mind. "If you wish to know the whole truth, I'm at your service!" I collected myself, bit into a chocolate-covered marshmallow, and began.

. . . Iratov was not as I described him earlier. More precisely, he was a different entity entirely! If my tale has heretofore been a lighthearted one, that is due to the author lacking the literary prowess necessary to depict the cruel, coarse, contradictory character of the man in question. But I will try.

I related that Iratov's genitrix spent her whole life teaching English. As the daughter of an émigré who had lived in the English city of York until he died, she grew up listening to endless stories from her father, Count Rymnikov, about how leaving revolutionary Russia in 1924 had been the most horrendous mistake of his life. He deserted his country, for God's sake! Since that day, his life had been no life at all, just a square of film depicting foggy Albion. Her father had remarkably dark hair until the day he died—he either had Georgian roots or had mixed in some taboo blood somewhere along the line . . .

His daughter Anna was scarcely twenty when his lordship passed on prematurely, having never come to terms with his nostalgia, and was buried in York's municipal cemetery. A month and a half later, the young maiden, who did not remember her mother because of the latter's early death, went to the embassy with a petition to be granted Soviet citizenship as an ethnic Russian. Her petition was soon granted, and she moved to Russia, where she was awarded a room in a communal apartment on Tverskoy Boulevard and the title of English instructor at a nearby school in Moscow, the capital of her new Motherland. Anna almost immediately realized that leaving Great Britain had been a mistake, but, not wishing to lead an exiled life of constant grief for her lost country, like her father, she soon adapted and learned to masquerade as a simple Soviet citizen.

Time marched on, and the young English teacher became acquainted with a young man studying construction at the nearby technical school—Andrei Iratov—whom she married a year later. She never regretted that decision, since her spouse proved to be a kind, considerate man. He was striving to better himself through education, so he minded his wife's words and made good use of his season pass to the conservatory.

A few years later, the couple had a son named Arseny.

"Who'd he get that black hair from?" asked the surprised young father, who had a full head of reddish hair.

"His grandpa!" said the delighted mother, as she nursed him. "My father!"

Before he had even reached his third birthday, the boy could speak fluent English and Russian. He matured into a wondrously handsome and intelligent young man, did pretty well in school, and would have been a delight to his parents in all things if it had not been for his utter lack of interest in his future. Not a single one of the disciplines he studied at school touched his spirit. Everything was featureless, boring, mundane.

"Perhaps you would like to join the diplomatic service?" his mother inquired. "Your English is better than mine! You've read so many books in the original! What's the Shakespeare play with Orsino, the Duke of Illyria?"

"*Twelfth Night, or What You Will* . . . But I'm the grandson of an émigré duke; do you really think they'll let me study international relations?"

"Good point . . . How about being a translator? An interpreter! God knows you have the memory for it! Yes, *Twelfth Night*, of course . . ."

"Next you'll be telling me to become some rotten schoolteacher!" said the peeved sophomore Iratov.

"Why not?" His mother wasn't letting up. "I'm satisfied with my lot!"

"Well, I'm not! Why the hell did you leave England and come to this idiotic country run by a bunch of senile paraplegics? You left Britain! The United Kingdom! Maybe it wasn't democratic enough for you?"

"If I hadn't left, I wouldn't have met your father!"

"Big deal! I could have had a different one!" Arseny just kept getting angrier and angrier at his mother.

"But you wouldn't be here," she said, shocked.

"Yes I would! Just with an English father!"

"You should be ashamed of yourself!" his mother

reproached him, tears welling up in her eyes. "Your father gave up his whole life for you! He works all day and then sketches all night! And this is how you thank him?!"

"Did I ask him to do any of that? And what's all that hard work got him? We live in a tiny apartment and eat what we can get from the corner store! We can't even afford to go to the movies! We're the family from Gogol's 'Overcoat'!"

"Have you no shame?"

"Leave me to my overcoat, mother!"

Arseny's father, Andrei Iratov, was a quiet man who was wounded by every harsh word, every glance full of ill will—that's how delicate his sensibilities were. To hide from the gray mundanity of the real world, he would seal its sounds out with earplugs and sketch architectural designs all night, for buildings so improbable and fantastical that they looked silly and absurd, like something straight out of *Alice in Wonderland*. Looked silly to whom, though? His wife and son, of course!

Anna supported her husband's passion, like any wife should support her husband in everything, but, deep down, she saw her husband's hobby as bizarre yet touching. Mushroom-shaped apartment blocks? Really? She imagined a giant boletus mushroom next to the Kremlin, people walking in and out of the stalk and living on the cap, and broke into a shy smile. She loved her husband and didn't shoot down his latest pipe dream; instead, she just kissed him as tenderly as she had once kissed their infant son's rosy cheeks.

The young Iratov loved his father, like any son. He was a gentle, good-hearted man, always hunched over his drafting board, sketching his fantastic visions on Whatman paper, physically weak, with an unexpressive, smudged-looking face that elicited no respect from the teenaged boy, just occasional pity. Iratov often thought about that paradox. How could he simultaneously love someone and have no respect for him—even sometimes feel scorn for him?

The young man could find no answer to that question at home, so he wound up on the street more and more often, where he got his kicks, smoked, and drank a little "port"—Caucasus or Solntsedar or what they called port in the Soviet days. He also amused himself with card games. There were always plenty of kids hanging out on the benches by their building, and boy did he sweep up the cash. Games of bura and seka brought him a tidy monthly income, most of which he put away for the future. He later studied an article about card tricks in *Iskatel* magazine, which brought him an even bigger income. Everything would have been fine, but then Interlopin, their twenty-two-year-old neighbor who had just been released from jail, paid the young-sters a visit. They'd sent him up the river for stealing a sparkling water machine. He set it up right in his apartment! The cops were cracking up when they arrested him, and they made that moron drag the two-hundred-pound article of evidence in ques-tion down five flights of stairs. He caught Iratov cheating and then deigned to inform the callow youth what the big fish did to people who tried pulling that stuff in prison.

They all beat him up. Even the fat-assed, foul-mouthed Kielbasova, the only girl in their group, gave him a smack on the ear. The boys showed particular fondness for checking the strength of his ribs with the toecaps of their boots. They punched him in the stomach over and over again. They sam-pled many varieties of violence. It only stopped when Iratov's face was round, swollen, and puffy from the repeated blows. His unseeing eyes had turned into Asian-looking slits.

"Ooo, look at that mug!" Kielbasova laughed. "He's got slanty eyes like a Yakut!" That nickname stuck.

"That'll do, fellas," Interlopin commanded. "If you kill

him, that's an Article 102 offense! Get this dope on his feet!" They held the swindler up straight, since he could no longer stand, and his head, round as a soccer ball, dangled on his thin, rooster-like neck. "You're gonna give back all the scratch you took off these boys," Interlopin ordered. "By tomorrow! Got it?"

"Don't have the money." Iratov lisped with his bloody mouth.

"What's that?"

"Don't have it."

"Where is it, Yakut?" Interlopin was bewildered by his temerity.

"Gave it to my mom . . ."

"Then take it back!"

"Fuck you!" Iratov spat blood on the sadist's shoes. "Fucking chump glass of flat water."

They beat him up again, and they hassled him the next day, and for a whole month after that. Every day after school, he would be cornered in the park and given a powerful blow to the nose, so the cartilage that had already been damaged by his first beating bent into different shapes like it was rubber.

"Pricks!" Iratov unfailingly answered. They nailed him in the stomach, the old one-two punch: head, torso. Same answer anyway. "Pricks!"

Then they left Iratov alone. The neighborhood gang just got tired of the same routine every day.

What about his parents? Certainly, his mother was devastated that her son was suffering such an indescribable nightmare. She tried to go to the police, but she received such a barrage of anger from her son in response that all she could do was cry and apply lead lotion to his face.

For Iratov, that was the first lesson of his life. The takeaway was simple: you have to be smarter and slicker than them, never crack, and never fess up . . .

Now an upperclassman, he changed his tactics and only played cards with adults. In the summer, he'd go to Vodny Stadion, where Moscow's suckers came to swim, tan, and slurp down the cases and cases of Zhiguli beer they'd stocked up on for the occasion. In the fall, he would play at the little tables in Gorky Park with everyday people who'd come to relax. He'd learned from his days of playing in his own neighborhood that he had to not win too much at one table and leave before they got suspicious.

By the end of his junior year, Iratov had saved up a tidy sum, enough for three two-room cooperative apartments.

Early that fall in Gorky Park, two men joined him at his table in a Czech beer bar called the Pilsner. They were adults, both with gray faces and arms blue with prison tattoos. One of them—the slightly bigger one—took a sip from his mug and revealed that he was missing his two front teeth. The other had all his teeth, but his nose was tinted lilac.

"You shark?" the first asked with a toothless grin.

"Huh?" went Iratov.

"Looks like we got a real smart guy on our hands, Lilac. You shark? You play cards?"

"Well, yeah . . ."

"'Well,' he says. If you were a well, you'd be full of water. Well, go play already."

"Nope," said Iratov. "I only play when I feel like it."

"Wow, looks like he's the boss around here, Lilac!"

Lilac was in no joking mood. He'd had a killer earache all week. He used a compress, then some drops, but nothing helped. He even tried pouring some vodka in there, but that only made it hurt more.

"Listen up, Yakut." Lilac was speaking for himself at last. "We know everything about you! We've had your number since last month!"

"So am I next in line?"

"What a comedian . . ." There was a flash of steel—a Finnish puukko that had imperceptibly sliced through Arseny's brand-new jacket and pierced his skin. A runnel of blood flowed on to his jeans. He felt its long, hot trail.

"We like to joke around too," the toothless one admitted. "But not during business hours! Listen up, buddy boy, we're not some bottom-feeders. We run this park. You're gonna pay us half of your takings every week. You're gonna bring it to Lilac in the pool hall."

"How come so much?" asked Iratov in surprise, one hand clutching his bleeding side.

"That's the tax for interlopers!"

"I'll go somewhere else then!" the schoolboy threatened.

"Who've we got at Vodny Stadion?"

"Gregory the Ferryman and Kesha Mengele," Lilac said.

"You're really gonna get it over there, kid!" the tooth-less one predicted. "Do you know who Doctor Mengele was?" Iratov took a sip from his mug, shrugged, and admitted that he'd never heard of him. "He was this Nazi doctor during the war. He did experiments on prisoners. Well, that German doctor is small fry compared to Kesha! Didn't they teach you that at school?"

"Listen, son, do you know what I can take for an earache?" Lilac asked. "It's a full-on October Revolution here. I'm getting shot in the head."

"I don't know. I'm not a doctor."

"I need a quack and I got a shark . . ." he said, neighing with laughter but being careful not to shake his ear. Then they didn't say anything for a while.

"Thought about it?" Lilac finished his beer, hiccupped, bit into a salted slice of black bread, and gave Iratov a look that was almost affectionate.

"I really don't know anything about ears, honest!"

"You think about my half?"

"How come it's so damn much?" Iratov turned red with spite. "I do all the work. I put up the cash, I take the risks! There's cops all over, and the suckers have given me a couple of beatings! Isn't that enough?"

"Do you know how many good people are doing hard time right now? You think they get fed like they did in mama's house?"

"Don't thieves take care of their own?"

"You see . . ." Lilac began in a satisfied voice, but then the criminal caught another bullet in the ear, and his face contorted into a grimace of pain.

"So, here's how it's gonna be," the toothless one said. "We'll keep the cops off your back and take care of it if one of the suckers starts shit. Plus, you eat for free at all the BBQ joints in town. That's nothing to sneeze at! If you wanna go to Vodny Stadion, we'll make sure Kesha Mengele is wise to our agreement."

"Fine," Iratov said with a nod. "It's a deal. After all, it's like they said in the war. We have nowhere to retreat to—Moscow is behind us."

"Then our negotiations are concluded!" Lilac smiled through the pain, and the parties to the new agreement shook on it.

Then the two men, their skin blue with tattoos, disappeared from the Czech bar. It was like something out of a cartoon—the Road Runner vanishing in a cloud of dust.

As he stood in the shower, washing away the dried blood,

Iratov thought about his immediate future. He didn't feel like taking orders from those criminals, and he most definitely had no desire to meet Mengele. He would have to come up with something else. In the meantime, half it was . . . damn them! Iratov swore to his own reflection in the mirror that he would live in the West one day—and live comfortably, far from these snarling convicts!

Iratov graduated from high school with all A's and B's, but as June came to an end, thoughts about what profession he would like to pursue failed to appear. They went through every available institution.

"Maybe the Meat and Dairy Industry Institute?" his worried mother asked. That was where absolute degenerates went in those days, because there were always more slots than applicants. "It's still a degree, and they say you don't really have to do anything there, just show up once a week . . ."

"How about I just go to trade school to be a lathe operator? Or a circus clown! I'll be the next Nikulin or Shuydin!"

"Nikulin would be good . . . He was terrific in *When the Trees Were Tall*!"

After all those fruitless conversations, his mother would go cry in her room, and Iratov would hit the streets and broaden the horizons of his young life with piquant pleasures.

It had already been a year since he first identified Café Lira on the corner of Tverskaya Street. There weren't all that many people there or anything, but they were all well-off. They didn't let working stiffs in. That rule was enforced by a curly-haired bouncer nicknamed Artemon. Speculators, black-market dealers and their children, plus other interesting characters hung out at the Lira, dropping crazy money—for the time, anyway. Iratov was set when it came to cash, always packing a bunch of fifty-ruble bills in the inner pocket of his jacket. He was always ready to treat himself, and he loved buying pretty girls champagne cobblers, the specialty of the house. On one of those evenings, two gal-pal, MAI-frosh types latched on to him. Nice boobs, nice butts, looking as cute as strawberry ice cream. The cheerful future architects made eyes at the handsome dark-haired guy, then dragged him back to their dorm once they were good and drunk, where they taught the generous youth the ménage à trois—and a few fancy tricks to go with it. With his looks, Iratov obviously had some experience—he had lost his virginity in eighth grade—but those chicks really blew his mind. They suggested—and demonstrated—things he couldn't even imagine. The Communist Youth League girl was sweet, and the volleyball girl was pleasantly sour. Iratov himself proved to be more than a "certified hunk." He had some serious stamina, too. He learned his new bedroom tricks eagerly and easily, and kept going until it was nearly morning, then griped over a sausage omelet that there was no vocation for him—he was a worthless creature who would be dragged off to the army in the fall if he didn't go to college.

"Then come here!" the girls suggested. "We'll get the sketches and designs ready for your application. You'll definitely get in! What a good idea!" they exclaimed.

"Shevtsova, you're the head of our Communist Youth League chapter, you can pull some strings!"

"I will!" the patriotic young lady promised. "And you talk to the athletic department, Katya. Tell them he plays volleyball or he's a boxer or something. You don't happen to play a sport, do you?"

"I can play strip poker," Iratov answered. "But what would I do here, build pre-fab apartment blocks? That sounds so boring!"

"What about us?" Shevtsova asked reproachfully. "Nothing pre-fab about us!"

"That's right," said the volleyball girl. "We're custom projects! You can spend all your free time on us. Does that sound boring to you?" She drew her bathrobe away from one perky breast.

"That's the only good argument for higher education I've ever heard!" Iratov said with a laugh and reached for the boldly bare maiden.

. . . Iratov was sitting in the bleachers at Vodny Stadion, cleaning out a fresh set of suckers, when it suddenly hit him what he had to do. His hopeless thoughts made him jerk suddenly, and so inopportunely that the winning card, the ace of spades he'd stashed away, suddenly slipped out of the sleeve of his summer shirt, soared skyward like a bird, singing out to the band of beefy men that they were suckers getting cleaned out by some high school kid. Heavy with all the beer they'd drunk, the aggrieved gang was eager to rip him to shreds. Some of them were already yanking boards out of the bleachers, others were twisting Iratov's arms so hard the joints crackled, on the verge of breaking. Fortunately, his prison-tatted backup arrived in the nick of time: Gregory the Ferryman and Kesha Mengele. Both of them were wearing the red armbands of volunteer patrolmen, and even a young beat cop who had come there for a Ready for Labor and Defense of the USSR swimming competition got involved. The criminals snatched the hapless card shark from the hands of those honest working men and promised that he would be punished to the fullest extent of the law, up to and including death by firing squad.

"Ain't that right, flatfoot?" asked Gregory the Ferryman, tugging on the cop's tunic. The young patrolman, feeling a newly arrived ten-spot from Kesha against his thigh, answered cheerfully.

"We'll shoot him, no doubt about it! Or drown him!"

The suckers obviously didn't believe the two bruisers with rings and rising suns tatted on their arms, but nobody wanted to pick a fight with them. The presence of the patrolman had confused them, too. Long story short, they got Iratov off the hook. They let the flatfoot run off to his swimming competition and had a brief, harsh exchange with the card shark.

"What the hell?" Gregory the Ferryman inquired.

"It was the heat," Iratov replied. "Sweaty fingers! So it just hopped out of my—"

"Bring a damn handkerchief!" Kesha advised. "Around here, if you're all thumbs, you're getting all ten of them rammed up your ass, you get me?"

Iratov was on a stepladder half the night, rummaging around in the crawl space his family used as a storage area. He went through hundreds of his father's designs, amazed at how he'd managed to produce so much junk. The paper alone must have cost a pretty penny! It would have been one thing if he meant to show them to someone, but he was doing it for himself . . .

Iratov selected three sets of sketches and blueprints. He'd decided to go with a completely deranged vegetable theme: the Tomato Building, a cucumber skyscraper, and a stadium shaped like a carved pumpkin drew Homeric laughter out of him!

"Well, alright," he thought. "These designs will be the portfolio portion of my application. I'm a misunderstood genius! And it'll get Mother off my case for a while . . ." Iratov studied the details of the drawings with great care, submitted them to the admissions committee, and then promptly forgot about them. He shifted his attention to more relevant and worthwhile matters.

A while back, he had noticed this very fashionable grifter sitting with a whole bunch of speculators in Café Lira—and observed him paying their tab with an American ten-dollar bill.

He slipped it to the bartender under a napkin. Ho-ly shit! Iratov instantly decided that he would never try to make money playing cards again, and all those Lilacs and Mengeles with their three- and five-ruble chump change could eat a dick. He had found his vocation now! If a ten was enough for a whole gang to eat and drink, then if he had a wad of hundreds, he could stuff the whole of Moscow until it burst and douse it until it sloshed! This wasn't Gorky Park and Vodny Stadion anymore! It was a clean business: no suckers snarling at him with their ugly soused mugs, no getting in bed with ex-cons. It would be risky, sure, but that'd make it more rewarding for him . . . and his ego. Iratov was already imagining having skills that were transferable anywhere, counting for something on the world's financial markets, knowing the real movers and shakers. His mood soared and the whole universe swelled with high spirits.

"My vocation," he whispered over and over as he lay in bed that night, unable to fall asleep, grinning like Mephistopheles.

The future currency speculator spent a few days patiently waiting for the grifter to show up at Café Lira so he could make his acquaintance and discuss business, but he seemed to have vanished without a trace. As anyone can tell you, youth and patience seldom go together. Iratov was determined to make his entrance into the world of currency speculation, so he sat next to the bartender and spoke without preamble.

"I need five thousand dollars."

Lyosha, the bartender, who drove the only Volvo in the capital, gave the young man a condescending look and answered him in an equally condescending tone. "Have you gone bonkers?"

"I mean it!"

"What makes you think I deal currency?"

"I've seen you!"

"Wow, Mr. Eagle Eye over here. You're a card shark, aren't you? Yakut, right? You hustle in the parks! Sharks don't deal currency! That's a different ball game."

"How do you know about me?" Now it was Iratov's turn to be surprised.

"That's my job," the bartender explained. "Knowing who's doing what and where. Want a drink?"

"I'll pay an extra ruble for every dollar. Pour me some Chartreuse."

"Do you know about the four main castes in India?"

"What the hell would I want to know that for?"

"First there are the Brahmans, the priests—they're the highest caste." The bartender splashed the liqueur into a glass. "A little bit lower, you have the Kshatriyas—they're the warriors. Then after them are the Vaishyas, the artisans, and the Sudras, the laborers and servants. Then there's the untouchables, too. Anyone who touches them becomes an untouchable themselves! They're the lowest caste, and—"

"Why are you telling me all this?"

"Jumping to a higher caste is impossible. You can only fall. You can't become a Brahman if you're a Kshatriya. Not with family, not with money, no way, no how. If you're born a Vaishya, you'll die a Vaishya! If you want an example they'll have covered at your school, I'll quote you some Gorky. 'Those who are born to crawl shall never fly.'"

"So what you mean," Iratov deduced, "is that if I'm a card shark, I need blue blood to deal currency? Is that it?"

"There you have it!" said Lyosha with a smile. "Want another? On me."

"How about you have one on me?"

"Count your blessings, kid! At least they don't put you against the wall for card tricks."

"Three."

"Three what?"

"Three more rubles for every dollar. Are you really gonna get that on the black market?"

"God, you're such a pain in the ass! Don't you have enough money as it is?"

"That's not the point." Iratov wouldn't give up.

"So what is?" Lyosha took an orange wedge from a dish and shoved it into his mouth, peel and all.

"Brahmans can stay Brahmans, but the caterpillar crawled and crawled until it could fly! You'll be the middleman. You can keep a third for yourself. You'll make fifteen thousand rubles on this transaction. You can buy Zykina's dacha with that kind of money! Seven and a half acres! Three houses, a sauna, and your own lake! I'll introduce you to the broker!" With enviable calm, the bartender replied that he would think about it.

"Wait here for a moment. How about some julienne? Or caviar on toast?"

Iratov waited nervously. He was almost shaking with impatience. Lyosha had gone off somewhere, probably to some back room where he was talking on the phone, consulting somebody. He didn't come back for a long time, then he returned with a plate of bloody beef languette. He put it on the bar, cut up the meat, and began to eat slowly. He chewed tediously, like a cow chewing its cud.

Another half hour went by. Then another. The fan on the bar chirred. Iratov looked at the bartender, watched him masticating like a camel, and waited.

The bartender finally finished eating and picked up the last pea. He examined it in the light as if it were some precious treasure, then nodded for Iratov to approach and delivered a brief admonition.

"One mistake and it's a bullet. For both of us. Got it?"

"Got it. How come that took so long? Tough meat?"

"Brahmans chew every piece up to sixty times. Tomorrow morning at eight. Right here."

"How come you're so sure you're a Brahman? You could be an untouchable . . ."

"And count the dough right!" Lyosha ignored Iratov's jab. "I'll take care of it."

They made the exchange the following morning. It all happened quickly and easily. An old Moskvitch pulled up. A little guy in a rumpled hat with tiny eyes behind his Coke-bottle glasses who looked like an accountant from the housing department came into Café Lira, where Iratov was already waiting for him, eating a curd snack. Lyosha was bustling around nearby, nervously wiping the tables. The cocktail wizard wasn't as calm and collected as he had been yesterday. He was scared. Scared that this kid could just hand him over to the spooks, that there could be some fateful foul-up, some monkey wrench—but fifteen large! Lyosha was well aware that he was risking his life. He was sweating, but it felt like his balls were full of ice.

The little guy came in, ignoring Lyosha's invitation to have some breakfast. He pulled a chubby envelope with an Avia stamp on it from his coat pocket and carelessly flung it on the table.

"Here?" He nodded at a duffel bag hanging on the back of a chair.

"There," Lyosha confirmed.

"Yours?" He turned toward Iratov.

"Mine."

The little man slid Iratov a business card, took the bag, instructed them to call if anything happened, and withdrew without a backward glance.

"What's that?" Iratov asked, looking at the envelope.

"What you wanted." Lyosha's anxiety was still going from momentum alone, but hot blood was running into his buttocks, warming up his icy balls. "Where's my fifteen large?"

Iratov looked into the envelope and found a wad of hundred-dollar bills. So this was what five thousand dollars looked like! And in the same instant when his brain realized that a sum that could fit in a little mailing envelope was enough to buy a vacation house in Sochi with his own palm and his own peach tree—in that moment, it was as if his consciousness had expanded boundlessly, exploding like a supernova, and it announced to his soul, "Now *I* can do anything! Youth isn't wasted on *me*!" His soul did not react to that declaration. His soul and his consciousness were not on speaking terms.

"Where's my money?" Lyosha's interruption prevented Iratov's euphoria from taking his entire being into captivity. "Where'd you go off to just now?"

"Everywhere!" the newly minted currency speculator said, coming out of his reverie. He tugged the bottom of his shirt out of his pants, pulled out a homemade plastic money belt, and tossed it to Lyosha. "Here, Zykina's dacha is yours!"

"What the hell, motherfucker?!" The bartender caught the money belt. "You'll give us away!" He quickly stuffed the money behind the radiator.

"Keep your cool."

"Couldn't you have brought it in hundreds? Is this all tens or some shit?" Lyosha asked angrily.

"There's tens, fives, and threes. Come on, you know that black market dealers pay 10 percent. That's all of it—fifteen thousand minus one and a half. Want me to exchange them?"

"Oh, go fuck yourself!" the bartender cursed. "I want hundreds next time!" Iratov rose from the table and headed for the exit. He turned around in the doorway and addressed Lyosha with a smile.

"There won't be a next time!" He waved the business card the little man had left behind. "Goodbye, Mr. Brahman! Or are you an untouchable? It wasn't the dollars I needed, it was the contact! The dealer will call you tomorrow."

Lyosha understood that he was never going to grow to the uppermost levels. He knew that he was a fuckin' chump, and that upset him once again, but the thought of the fifteen thousand rubles in the money belt was still enough to warm his balls up to their normal temperature. Sure, maybe he was a chump, but he was a chump with a great big dacha! And do chumps make fifteen thousand rubles in one day just for being the middleman? Nah, he was no chump! Those working stiffs getting on the metro over there—they were the chumps!

That same day, Iratov took a taxi to the foreign currency store and walked in like he owned the place, nodding at the greasy suit looming by the door in a way that said, "Yes, I am in fact a KGB agent," went up to a pretty clerk named Masha, and inquired, in perfect English, where he might find their outerwear department. Masha had been working there for over two years already; she smiled in reply, stars sparking to life in her eyes. She'd been dreaming that some foreign service officer would notice her; after all, she would make an excellent wife and mother in Europe, or, better still, America. She saw this handsome black-haired man as a potential choice, hoping that he was the son of some important diplomat, and—leaning over whenever possible to show off her inarguable loveliness—led him through their displays of French winter suits, Finnish sweaters, and Irish fur coats with innocent fervor.

Iratov was reeling. It was a miracle he didn't faint. Good thing he had his back against a rack of hangers. Of course, he had fantasized about what foreign currency stores looked like for a long time, and sometimes flipped through imported magazines. But the fact that every object, every piece of this store, even the sales princess and the spook, was an incomprehensibly powerful culture shock for him, a mighty flood of endorphins, was something he could never have foreseen. Countless cans of the kind of fish that was always in short supply in regular stores, every kind of ham, the juice of exotic fruits that he had only read about in adventure stories, a meat and fish section, six- and twelve-piece packs of gum, and innumerable cartons of Marlboros—it all spun in his consciousness, an unreal, unfathomable world he had finally gotten to. And now it was getting to him!

When he saw the price tag on a fur coat, written out in dollars, he calculated that instead of a vacation home in Sochi, he could only afford to buy five mutton coats. Sure, they were fashionable, but good God! His arithmetic stunned him, drove him into a deeper stupor when he realized that this one store alone held millions of Soviet rubles' worth of goods . . . Iratov looked in the mirror and saw the face of a moron. Crimson, with an idiotic smile and the eyes of an orangutan who had just seen the zookeeper's bucket of bananas for the first time. He realized that he was an inescapably Soviet person who only had the means to buy himself two suitcases full of getups from this *other* world he'd stumbled into by accident, and maybe stuff himself with some foreign canned food too, if there was any money left . . .

"Have you found anything to your liking?"

"Indeed I have, Masha. I would like to buy some orange juice, a bottle of champagne, and a carton of cigarettes."

"Excellent!" The clerk, fluttering her eyelashes all the while, put everything into a plastic bag. "Thirty-five dollars and forty cents, please. But how did you know my name was Masha?" That was a tried-and-true trick, but it had never worked on Iratov.

"The name tag on your chest. How much does the bag cost?"

"Bags are free here. I always forget about that name tag . . . Let me double-bag these for you, just in case. Here is your champagne. Are you celebrating something?" Iratov was automatically calculating that bags like that, with a foreign cigarette logo on them, could be resold for five rubles a pop, ten total.

"Oh yes, I am . . ."

"How lovely!"

"The champagne's for you, Masha! I wouldn't mind celebrating you . . ." Iratov went over to her place at eleven-thirty. A huge celebratory moon hung above Moscow and Masha's skin shone in the dark. Very pale, as if sprinkled with flour, soft and responsive . . . She moaned and whispered, "Alex," trying to time her slim hips to his motions, kissed him hotly and eagerly, and finally cried out so loudly that Iratov had to cover her passion-parched mouth with his hand to keep her from waking the neighbors.

"Hush, Masha, hush . . ."

When he was pulling on his jeans in the dawn light, he said, "good morning" to the happy, sleepy Masha in English first, then in Russian.

"Your pronunciation is great!" the girl said, gently kissing his cheek.

"Masha, I'm from here, from the USSR! No need for English! My name's Vasily!"

There was a pause . . .

The magnificent Masha fired a string of curses in his direction, far filthier than he had heard from any man. To the accompaniment of enraged shrieking, Iratov quickly pulled on his

T-shirt and raced out of there without even tying his shoelaces. As he ran down the stairs, he neighed with laughter, listening to last night's fairy princess shriek increasingly florid obscenities at him. Her cries of hatred were just as despairing as her cries of ecstasy, and they pierced the concrete of the apartment block's walls while the satisfied young Iratov loped down the stairs, four at a time, feeling that life was beautiful, that his happiness had only just begun and would never end! The last thing he heard as he burst into a warm Moscow morning filled with the smell of blooming lilacs and the splash of street-washing machines, was "I'll turn you in, asshole!"

Iratov had no way of knowing that his visit to the foreign currency store was immediately reported to the KGB unit responsible for overseeing the Tishinka district. It was the lieutenant who did it, the one who had it written all over his face that he was a spook. He had an extremely peculiar name: Photios Prytki.

"Soviet?" the commander asked.

"Absolutely, and he's only just starting out. I can always tell when someone's not a foreigner."

"That's why we have you working currency, Lieutenant! You'll be handling the duty-free store before you know it! Maybe he's got relatives that go abroad? Diplomatic service? Did he spend a lot?"

"No, chump change," reported Photios Prytki, whose monthly salary was three times less than the cost of Iratov's purchase in dollars. "Maybe he's got relatives . . . But they would've had to convert their currency to checks, and he paid with a hundred-dollar bill."

"That's true . . . Okay, you all keep an eye out. If he shows up again, you sing out."

"Yes sir!"

"How about the salesgirls, are they whoring themselves out?"

"If they are, it's not with me . . ."

"Vigilance, Prytki!"

. . . An envelope addressed to Arseny Iratov arrived in the mail from the Moscow Architectural Institute informing the applicant that his sketches had been accepted and he would be permitted to take the entrance exams but would first have to come to the president's office for an interview. His mother opened the dispatch and met her son with surprised delight.

"I always believed in you!" Tears of joy ran down her plump cheeks. "I never lost faith! Why did you hide it? Andrei, can you hear me?" She turned to her husband. "Our son is well on his way to becoming an architect!"

This news surprised Iratov, and he looked at the bent back of his father, who seemed not even to be listening to his wife's triumphant announcement. For an instant, Arseny felt a rush of tenderness for this man who shared his blood. His eyes clouding with mounting tears, the son looked at the back of his father's head: the dimming red hair, its wild plumes sticking out in every direction, the little bald spot on top . . . The flashes of tenderness passed, the tears dried up . . .

The interview was conducted by a panel of the institute's instructors, headed by the president himself. Iratov later learned that he was a legendary figure in the world of architecture, who, on Khrushchev's orders, led the creation of the now ubiquitous five-story buildings that provided the people with their own apartments—minuscule as they were.

President Staroglebsky's head towered over those of the other admissions committee members. He was a tall, gray-haired gentleman resembling a monument erected in honor of some heroic polar explorer, his walrus mustache hanging down to his chin. Its ends had been colored yellow. Staroglebsky was an inveterate pipe smoker, and the dark amber of nicotine had eaten its way into his mustache and the tip of his thumb.

"State your name for the record," commanded the secretary of the admissions committee, who, concurrently, was Staroglebsky's wife. She was much younger than her husband, but her hair was just as gray. She smoked, too, but preferred unfiltered cigarettes that sent clouds of radioactive smoke into the atmosphere. She loved her husband, took great pride in him, and tried to be as faithful a comrade to him as she was to the Communist Party . . .

Iratov was later to become the president's pet, and he took on the modest duty of presenting him with elegant pipes for his collection. He didn't forget Staroglebsky's wife either. He always managed to get her unfiltered American Lucky Strikes. But that was all to come later . . . Now he was listening to laudatory words from the president's own lips about how such unusual ideas had come into such a young head.

"You've got a spark in you, Iratov! A pumpkin, I tell you!"

"Try and turn that spark into a fire and not a pumpkin, though!" said his wife, sending a puff of smoke at the ceiling.

"As you are no doubt already aware, your projects are for the distant future," the president explained. "What Soviet people need now is simple, comfortable modern housing." He spoke grandly, as if he were at a Party meeting. "We must design new proletarian cultural centers. Not just some buildings where they can have dances and sewing circles, but real centers! Hundred-thousand-square-foot buildings equipped with theaters and exhibition halls, where talented Soviet artists will have access to the facilities they

need and the guidance of their more seasoned peers . . ."
Staroglebsky broke into a coughing fit and stopped to drink some
water out of a table glass. "Tell me, young man, do you know
who invented this item right here?" He extended a long, bony
hand, holding the glass as if it were a torch.

Iratov had no idea that glasses had to be invented.

"This simple table glass that can be found in any Soviet
kitchen?" the president continued. "It was the great Vera
Mukhina! All of us will die, our children and grandchildren will
pass into oblivion, but Mukhina's glass will endure forever, for
it is a work of art!"

"Yes," concurred Iratov, who had never heard of Mukhina.
There wasn't a single architect he had heard of. Once again,
the son felt tenderness for his progenitor. That feeling was both
painfully vexing and torturously pleasant.

"Start studying for your exams!" the president concluded.
"You have a spark in you!"

Iratov's two gal pals were waiting for him outside the door:
Shevtsova, the Communist Youth League chieftainess, and
Katya, the volleyball champion, both with the same mute ques-
tion on their lovely pink-cheeked faces.

"I made it," Iratov answered.

"Hoo-oo-oo-ray!" the college girls shouted in glee. "Party
time!"

It turned out there were some bedroom tricks they had yet
to teach the recent high school graduate. They celebrated his
successful interview by guzzling Soviet champagne and wolfing
down custard éclairs. The chicks got so carried away that their
lips suddenly met in a passionate kiss. The stunned Iratov, lying
naked on bedsheets spread over the floor, laughingly asked if
they'd gotten something mixed up. He was ready for action over
here, wasn't that more appealing? But there was no tearing the

girls apart; they were breathing hard and had apparently forgotten all about Arseny.

He had never even suspected that such things existed, and in his frenzy, he thought that this was a little too much, but in mere seconds, his brain had abandoned thinking; it was running on instinct alone. The sight of two girls making love had left Iratov with no sensory organs except his eyes and nose. The latter was detecting something unfamiliar, something animal, disquieting, something that made the young man's body shiver feverishly. He clutched his shoulders with his hands. Charged to the limit with lust, Arseny kept drawing closer and closer to the two lovers, moving like a dominant chimpanzee, and when Shevtsova began to groan quietly, signaling that the peak of her pleasure was near at hand, that the air was full of molecules of love, he exploded like a compressed spring and leapt on the girls like a wildcat . . . Three human bodies reached the culmination of one event together, then lingered long, entwined in a tangle of shared consciousness, skin clinging to skin . . . A few minutes later, when consciousness had returned to his sprawled body and overcome his instincts, Iratov once again thought that everything was just beginning, that man was created to be happy and his newfound happiness was here to stay.

6

Sorry, I'll start up again soon. Just needed some water. Dry throat, you know. I leaned toward the faucet and greedily sucked at the lukewarm stream until I'd had my fill. The ancient Senescentova was sleeping, slumped back in an armchair.

"Now I can eat the chocolate-covered marshmallows, too," I thought and then returned to the table. I tried one. Hard as a rock. Weird, I thought they would be fresh. I glanced out the window and noted that the white snowbanks were sinking, and streams of springtime water were running out of their blackened foundations. I cracked the window and heard the clamor of birdsong. "It's spring alright," I thought. "How did I let the time get away from me like that?" An unexpected hunch drove me to approach my auntie, move very close to her, bend down, but I knew. I had already smelled it, if you will. She was dead. I can always smell death . . . Senescentova, Honored Actor of the USSR, my "adoptive aunt," had passed away . . . "She really was clairvoyant," I thought with a chuckle. "She sensed it coming a while ago."

I had to go home for a bit, but first, I lifted the lifeless body—it felt light and dry—from the armchair and laid it on a rug. To make sure that the body would really be lying down and not just sitting there on the floor like a dressed-up doll, I straightened her petrified joints, tied her chin in place with gauze, took another look around, and got out of there.

Moscow is magnificent in the spring! The smell of the new, the aroma of rebirth, tickled my nostrils. Even the cars stuck in traffic no longer looked so hopelessly bleak. All the buildings had splashed spring rain on their faces and stood there looking renewed.

I went to see Antipatros on Petrovsky Boulevard. The Greek shaved me in his customary fashion, trimmed my hair with the clippers, and removed my excess nose hair. On my way out, I inquired how he was doing, but he was as silent as usual and paid no attention to my inquiries.

"How do you ask them for a ticket to Prague at the train station?" I asked as a parting shot. "Or do you never have to go there? No, everybody has to go to Prague! How does he buy tickets?" I asked the mixed-race girl who worked there, but she just blinked her blue eyes and hid herself away in the basement, leaving behind a faint whiff of sweet musk. They're all mute here.

Near the entrance to my building, I saw my neighbor Ivanov, who, as always, was so hungover he was trembling.

"I don't have any money," I fired off instantly.

"I thought that you'd kicked the . . . you know, from . . ." He mimed chugging straight from a bottle.

"You thought I kicked *what?*"

"Well, that you were dead! You haven't left your room for three weeks! I already sniffed through the keyhole and arranged for Georgadze the locksmith to pry the door open!"

"You're supposed to call the police in those situations, not pry open other people's doors!" I growled. "I don't have anything valuable in my apartment! What gives you the right to intrude on perfect strangers? What are you, my brother?"

"Gimme fifty rubles," my neighbor pleaded. "If I don't kill this hangover, I'm gonna do something criminal! I'll stick up Zinka's store!"

"Why not the bank? I don't have any money, I'm unemployed!"

Ivanov rapidly muttered something, but I was already on my way up the stairs, agitated by a single thought. What if my luck turns? This can't go on forever!

I sat down, put the old stationary telephone in my lap, and stared at it for a long time . . .

I couldn't muster the resolve to call on my mobile phone, but that old black rotary machine somehow filled me with optimism. I dialed every combination of numbers I knew. Nobody picked up on the other end. I just heard it ringing, the same note over and over again. C-sharp, two quarter notes . . . I even whined in tune . . . I waited at the phone for a few hours, and then I detected the smell of something burning coming in through the open window.

I looked outside and saw the little tent that housed Zinka's corner store burning down beyond the row of old poplars and instantly understood that my neighbor Ivanov really had stuck it up. "Yes," I thought. "A man with a perpetual hangover means what he says." I heard the sirens of a fire truck, but I was already bored with all of that. I had pressing business that could not be delayed. I shook the contents of the trash can into a bag, stepped outside, and . . . Sitting in his usual spot was my neighbor Ivanov, looking contented. There was an open case of beer on the bench next to him. Three cans were crumpled up in the dirt. I threw my bag into the dumpster . . .

"Is Zinka alive?" I inquired.

"Why wouldn't she be?" he asked with a smile. "She kept hollering, though. I shoulda torched her, too!"

"But she's going to turn you in!"

"She can suck it! And what are you so worried about? Are you my brother or something? You gonna bring me care packages in jail?"

"That's true," I thought. "Why the hell am I always conversing with this idiot? I have numerous urgent matters to attend to . . ." I went back to Senescentova's apartment. The old woman was lying on the rug. Well, it's not like she was going to go anywhere. I rummaged in her writing desk, opened a drawer with a little key, and fished out a bundle of papers, including a document signing over the deed to her apartment— to me, of course. I opened a folder and found the actress's ID, as well as a card from a major bank. A piece of paper with the PIN written on it had been thoughtfully attached to the back. I put everything I had found in my breast pocket and called the local cop. All in accordance with the law! While I waited for him to arrive, I gnawed on the marshmallows again, but even my tough teeth proved unequal to the task . . .

The policeman arrived shortly thereafter. He stepped into the apartment and gave the corpse the faintest inclination of his head.

"So you decided the rug was the place for her?"

"Precisely!" I reported. "The meat wagon orderlies are always annoyed when they find a dead person in a seated position."

"And how do you know that?" the policeman inquired. He looked tired, but he showed no sign of shirking his duties and inspected the apartment exactingly.

"Nowadays, practically everyone has some experience with matters funerary!"

"That's for sure . . . Where's her ID?"

"I have it right here!" I handed it to him.

"Wow!" I could hear that the policeman was intrigued. "A hundred and three!"

"Oh yes, many people live for over a century these days! But then others barely make it to retirement, or don't even make it at all! You pay taxes your whole life, then you croak a year before you start collecting your hard-earned pension and the government grabs all the money!"

"I won't be getting my pension for a while . . . but yeah,

that's what happened to my uncle. He died at fifty-nine, just a year to go . . ."

"What illness did he die from, if you don't mind my asking?"

"It wasn't an illness. He just blew himself out . . . One time, this huge machine tool at his factory came off its base and slid along a bunch of pipe they'd left lying around. Just negligence. It weighed three tons, and my uncle held it up for ten whole minutes until help arrived."

"But what for?"

"To save the gear."

"Whose gear?"

"That's what I asked him before he died. They were like, 'Uncle Victor, what the hell for? It's not like it was a state enterprise—it was some crook oligarch's factory! What, you didn't want to see the poor capitalist's property get damaged?' He said 'I don't know what the hell for, it just kinda happened that way . . .' and then he died. How were you related to the old lady?"

"She thought of me as a nephew . . ."

"Let's have your papers, I'll write down your information." We discussed various social issues for a while, as well as a scandalous television program. This cop was a decent conversationalist!

The doorbell rang, announcing the arrival of the meat wagon. Its crew surveyed the landscape morosely.

"Give me that paperwork," the policeman commanded. "I'll sign off. Fill them out yourself." He turned to me. "You will receive the death certificate tomorrow, provided there is no sign of foul play."

"Foul play? You must be joking!"

The policeman shook my hand firmly and excused himself, saying that he had duties to attend to. The morose young men put Senescentova on a stretcher and carried her down the stairs feetfirst.

"I'll ride along with you," I declared sternly as they pushed the stretcher into their old Gazelle van. The morgue employees shrugged. They didn't care. They didn't even ask me for any money. It was a shaky ride.

"The old lady died a long time ago," stated the employee who was broader in the shoulders. "She got mummied!"

"Mummified," I corrected him.

"Huh?"

"Nothing to worry about," I reassured him.

"Like Lenin," announced the second one, who was narrower in the shoulders. "Lenin's a mummy, too."

"He was embalmed," I said, striving for precision. "This is different. My auntie lived a righteous life, so her body is not rotting now that she's passed."

"I'm definitely gonna rot," said the broader one.

"Me too," the narrower one said with a nod.

The orderlies turned to me expectantly.

"I don't know," I said, vacillating. "Nah, I do know. I'll start rotting in an hour, just like you guys." I didn't want to upset them.

That's how our little group came together, around a common understanding of the things that really matter. The broader one pulled a bottle of vodka from his uniform pocket and the narrower one produced some plastic cups. They promptly poured.

"To us!"

"To us!"

Yeah, I repeated the toast. But they didn't have any pickles or anything to follow the shots . . . The orderlies bent over the old woman and took deep breaths to get rid of the smell of the vodka. I abstained . . .

We arrived at the morgue of Hospital 36. The orderlies knocked on the metal door and a woman of about forty with a large head and a tiny surgical cap opened it.

"Paperwork!" she commanded, sparing them only the briefest of glances. The orderlies presented the papers to the coroner.

"Are you in a mood, Nina?" asked the broad one.

"You're the one in a mood, Gregory!" she answered. "I can smell the vodka on your breath from here, and I've got a ton of work! Get moving, stick her on slab eight." The orderlies carried the stretcher into the morgue, and I scampered after them.

"Pardon me, Nina, but I'd like to address you properly. Would you mind telling me your patronymic?" I asked the coroner.

"Solomonovna," she answered harshly.

"Your father was granted a most worthy name!"

"You aren't allowed to come any closer!" She took a can of Coca-Cola out of her pocket, neatly opened it, downed the bubbly beverage, and covered a burp with her hand . . .

"Well, you see, the thing is," I began, trying to explain myself. "It was the departed's last wish that I, and I alone, prepare her body for its final resting place. She only trusted me—"

"And you are?"

"Me? Well, I suppose you could say I'm a makeup artist . . . This is Ms. Senescentova, the actress, you may remember her from—"

"No, I don't. I don't care who's gonna do her up. Just kindly come back the day after tomorrow at seven in the morning. I'll be done examining the body by then."

"Could we forgo the autopsy?" I asked. "She's a hundred and three years old! Natural causes, you know . . ."

"I will conduct a visual inspection. I won't cut into her if I don't have to."

"Thank you!" I said happily.

"Senescentova . . . no, never heard of her. See you later."

I bowed out. The next order of business was going to the nearest ATM and taking out a decent amount of money. I flagged down a car and asked the guy to take me to Herzen Street.

"Five hundred if you show me the way."

"Too steep! Come on, knock off a hundred for navigating."

"Hop in, Mr. Navigator!"

The car stank, and there was something sideways about the way it moved, but the driver—he was from Uzbekistan or maybe Tajikistan—was cheerfully singing along to his people's music . . . We got there alive, glory to the Almighty. I held out a five-hundred-ruble bill.

"Don't have change!" came the typical reply.

"No? Oh well. Then I'll just take your music in lieu of change." I reached for the car's tape slot.

"Ey!" yelled the startled driver. "Don't touch music!" My hand had a death grip on the dashboard. "I'll give ya it, hold on! So anxious!"

Hundred-ruble bill in hand, I went into the theater supply store, where I bought two yards of translucent white chiffon and a case of stage makeup. I also purchased a kolinsky sable-hair brush, some mascara, and a pair of ballet slippers . . .

On my way back, I broke the one-hundred-ruble bill by buying a pack of unfiltered Primas, took Senescentova's Raymond Templier cigarette holder out of my pocket, stuck one in, borrowed a lighter at a kiosk, and lit up . . . Until that day, I had never tried tobacco, so I wholly surrendered myself to these new sensations. Despite blowing the smoke through my nose and rolling it on my tongue, I could find nothing joyful about smoking . . . and nothing sad, for that matter . . . I tossed the butt into a trash can yet decided that I would still occasionally emit columns of smoke like the fearsome volcanos of Kamchatka, just to show off.

The next stop on my journey was a clothing store where you could buy Italian brands off the rack. After a few trips to the fitting room, I chose a dark suit, two dress shirts—one black and one white—and three colorful, fashionable bowties. I also picked out some shoes and a couple pairs of socks. On my way out, I came face-to-face with Iratov. It made me shudder. His eyes stopped on me longer than one generally looks at a stranger. Struck dumb, I stared at Vera's incomparably beautiful legs. I walked out of the boutique sideways, wondering how Iratov could get by without his tool. What use was he to Vera now?

I returned home, pleased to think that I could be sure I wouldn't see my neighbor Ivanov. The government would be paying the rent where that lowlife was going.

You may well imagine my surprise when I saw my pleased neighbor in his usual spot on the bench in front of our apartment building. Furthermore, he was not alone; he had his arm around the waist of a curvy woman with dark circles under her eyes, her hair dyed a raspberry color that had not reached her gray roots.

"Meet my lady Zinka!" my smug neighbor Ivanov gnashed and began shamelessly pawing her. "I'll bet you thought I was already halfway up the river!"

"I was sure of it!"

"Quit it," Zinka said in her bass voice as my neighbor tried to slide his hand up her blouse. "Not in front of a stranger!"

"What stranger?" Ivanov asked, surprised. "Neighbors are never strangers! A neighbor can be even more important than a wife. He keeps me from raising hell!"

"What, pray tell, were the virtues that inspired a lady of quality to forgive you?" I inquired.

"I invited my darling Zinka to become my faithful companion for all the time my liver has left. She was generous enough to agree. Isn't that right, Zinka?"

The retirement-aged Zinka, lowering her dim eyes to the ground, nodded and answered in that bass voice worthy of Chaliapin.

"Yes . . ."

"Zinka will be living in my apartment, in consideration for which I will have the status of a lawful stakeholder in her store! Fifty-fifty! The apartment, the booze, and the grub!"

"But didn't the store burn down?" I asked, surprised.

"Sure it did," my neighbor agreed. "But not Zinka's, it was Tamarka's! Our store just got a little singed."

"So was it you who burned down Tamarka's store?"

"You're my brother, so I'll give it to you straight. It was us. We had a family meeting and decided to remove our competition."

"And Tamarka wasn't inside, I hope?" Zinka and Ivanov exchanged glances at this.

"We didn't check . . ."

"If your competitor burned up," I said, kindly enlightening them, "and you get caught, you might be going away for a long time—twenty years. Well, that's your problem! I have no time for you!" Then I switched to a threatening tone. "I will have no spitting, no improper disposal of cigarette butts, and no consumption of alcoholic beverages in front of the building! Young children can see through these windows! Otherwise I will turn you in myself. Is that clear?"

"Perfectly clear . . ." my neighbor answered cheerlessly, as Zinka seemed lost in thought about Tamarka's fate. They were sisters, after all . . .

I went up to my apartment and dialed the same phone number . . . I shouldn't call so often—if I'm too much of a nuisance, I risk never getting an answer.

I used my cell phone to order some sushi from a restaurant two blocks away. I had a quick, pleasant lunch . . . Then I went online to pay for the coffin, hearse, and carnation wreath for the day after tomorrow. It seemed like everything was in place, so I set my alarm for six in the morning the day after tomorrow and fell asleep with a clear conscience.

At 6:45, I was already ringing the bell at the morgue, two bags in hand. The coroner opened the door at once, since she had only just arrived at work herself. She had not even managed to change out of her street clothes and into her uniform, so she had a sweet, domestic look about her.

"You're a little early!" She pointed to a chair. "Have a seat!" Fifteen minutes later, she came back and called to me.

"I'm ready!" I sprang to my feet and followed her into a large hall that seemed to be brightly lit.

"Will you bury her today?"

"Oh yes, certainly," I answered, examining the doors of the refrigerated compartments. "Goodness, you have a lot of those!"

"This is the largest morgue in the city."

"Then where are your assistants?"

"Late, as usual, the bums! By the way, I finally remembered that Senescentova of yours. Or my mom did, I should say. She's eighty-six . . . She said Senescentova was a legendary beauty, and her films enjoyed great success."

"May I begin?" I inquired. I had limited time to work with, after all.

"Get to it! Compartment four. I didn't cut into your actress. The table has wheels on it. Push it over to the refrigerator and then roll the stretcher over there, too. Can you handle that, or do you want to wait for the orderlies?"

"That's nothing. I can handle it . . ."

There was nothing difficult about transporting the old lady's naked body. Five minutes later, it was lying on a stainless steel table, and my efforts commenced. I took all the necessaries out of my bags. The first order of business was to unwrap a little parcel that had been in my care for almost three decades. It contained the nightgown that Iratov had once given to Svetlana, his first love, on Valentine's Day, the one he put on all his college girlfriends, the precious object he had thrown out the window in a fit of pique . . . Then came the time when I collected it and preserved it in good condition.

I arrayed the ancient Senescentova in that silken garment of love. Imbued with hundreds of shades of passion, that nightgown radiated mighty energy that would adorn the actress's dismal virginity . . . Soon my auntie's dry soles were shod with ballet slippers, and I moved on to her face. I did indeed once work as a makeup artist. It was not a film director or television studio that provided me with employment, though, but a photographer by the name of Beskrylov who specialized in erotic material. I was his assistant back in the 1970s; I took the pale faces of his girls, dimmed by poor nutrition, and got them fixed up. Beskrylov was soon arrested for producing pornography and sent to prison. I went free and never worked as a makeup artist again, but I maintained my skills.

After fifteen minutes of work with the brushes and specialized wands, the dry, sunken-eyed face of the old woman was transformed. With vibrant, pink-tinted skin, the scarlet lips she loved so much, and false lashes, the ancient Senescentova looked almost alive, as if she had simply dozed off before her evening tea and chocolate-covered marshmallows. I covered her skinny little body with the translucent white chiffon. Peeking through the cloth, the actress's face looked almost childlike.

"Boy, you know what you're doing!" said a voice behind me.

"Thank you," I answered, turning to the morgue director. "I did my best."

"I hope somebody does that for me when the time comes!"

"Well, now is not the time to think about that. But beauty will matter little to you when they call you up to heaven! It only matters to the living . . ."

"What're the slippers for?"

"Her Juliet costume. That was her first role. They say she was so lovely you couldn't tear your eyes away."

"They've delivered the coffin," the coroner reported. "My orderlies can help you put her body in now. Here's the death certificate, by the way." She held out an envelope.

"Thank you." I bestowed a warm smile of farewell on her, and we parted as well-wishers. A professional always respects a fellow professional!

The hearse moved down car-choked streets. The sun seemed the very soul of profligacy, so much light did it pour over the city. The light filled up the entire space of the world; myriads of sunrays were dispatched into the darkest niches of nature and city alike. People sneezed and squinted in the glare, and the flowers that had been perishing during the long winter in their windowsill pots returned to life and bloomed colorfully in reply. Only one policeman was vexed by the light. It shone right in his eyes, like a searchlight, hindering his attempts to regulate traffic. Spring! On a day like that, even a burial is a joy!

"Should I take her in for the requiem?" the driver asked as the hearse pulled through the gates of Donskoy Monastery.

"No, go straight to the allée."

"Good," said the pleased funeral worker.

"What's so good about it?" I inquired.

"Oh no, that's not what I meant! Not singing a requiem is bad, of course! I—"

"You'll get out of here an hour early," I said, finishing his thought. "That's right."

"What do we need a requiem for?" I thought. "I'll sing it myself." A couple of burly, taciturn guys neatly lowered the coffin into the ready-made grave, spent a few minutes covering it with dirt, and then laid a wreath at the top bearing the text "to a beloved aunt from her nephew." Then the crew accepted their five-thousand-ruble payola and dissolved among the gravestones.

The next grave over had a bench for relatives to sit on when they visited. I sat down and gave my auntie a heartfelt rendition of Elvis Presley's "Love Me Tender."

. . . "So, where were we, auntie?" And with that, I resumed my story.

Ten days later, Iratov walked through the prison gate and began his parole. The warden he'd worked for had arrived to accompany him, and he kept exhorting him not to quit the Vladimir Region, to build private homes in their thousands for "my guys," make use of his mighty talent, and reap the boundless benefits of his creative genius, unhindered by the scrutiny and reprimands of Moscow.

"I built you a house, didn't I?" Iratov asked.

"And what a house it is!"

"Then leave me the fuck alone!"

"You ungrateful motherfucker, I'll—" The warden's faced swelled with wrathful blood.

"You'll what? Trying to scare me again?"

"I'll take you out, you traitor! In the course of an escape attempt!"

"Do you know who arranged my parole? Or are you really that dumb? I'll survive prison, but you'll be done for! Be happy with what you got outta me and keep riding the gravy train, but do it without me. Got it?"

The warden figured out that this currency speculator's parole had been arranged by the KGB and realized that meant he couldn't do anything. He was dying of hatred . . .

To be more precise, it wasn't the agency or even Captain Vorontsova that Iratov owed his parole to, but her friend Galina. She told her minister husband that an injustice had occurred, and bam, he was free! And she did it all for Iratov's stones, the best of the ones he'd managed to hide from the government.

Alevtina was not there to meet him, so the ex-con took a little bus to the commuter train station. He bought a ticket, endured the embrace of his fellow citizens on the packed train for three and a half hours, then finally arrived in the capital.

He made it back by dinner and pressed his mother against his chest with particular tenderness, kissing her face, wet with tears of joy. As for his father, he just gave him a firm hug. Iratov's hunched, prematurely aged progenitor huddled against his strong chest and cried too. Not just because his son had been let out of the prison camp and because he had survived, but also because he had contributed to his child's happiness with his own plenty. Even if it was through his son, Andrei Iratov had finally achieved his true calling. He had made something of himself. He had become a man. A gold medal in Tokyo!

We must give Iratov his due. After his Moscow Architectural Institute exams were over, he never used his father's work again. Some hidden harmony drew him in after that. He designed the self-tapping screw building himself. It seemed like God really had passed talent from father to son, but the younger Iratov's gift was on a far larger scale.

Later that evening, he called Alevtina Vorontsova. The young man's unmoored heart nearly froze from the foretaste of that hoarse voice, the fifty-five-year-old mother of his future child, but it wasn't her who picked up.

"Who's asking for her?" answered an unknown man's voice.

"Her husband . . ."

"What husband? She isn't married!"

"Not technically her husband . . ."

"Ah, Mr. Iratov?"

"Comrade Iratov! I've got my Soviet passport in my pocket! Who are you?"

"Come on over! Come on over immediately, Comrade Iratov!"

It turned out Alevtina Vorontsova's apartment was full of people, all smoking, including a photographer who was taking pictures of every single item. A pool of still-wet blood reflected the harsh light of the chandelier.

"Committee for State Security Captain Photios Prytki," said a man with familiar features. "I spoke to you on the phone."

"What happened? Do I know you?"

"The thing is," Prytki began. "Two hours ago, Alevtina Vorontsova was fatally wounded—"

"Fuck!" went the disbelieving Iratov. "Fatally wounded? Murdered! Is that what you mean? Huh?"

"Wounded, to be precise. While she was dying, she managed to crawl to the telephone and report the name of the killer."

"I just arrived from a prison camp out by Vladimir! I've been at my parents' apartment for the past few hours. They can vouch for—"

"You are not under suspicion, comrade."

"Fuck!"

"Alevtina Vorontsova was fatally wounded by one Zanis Peterson. Your colleague, by the way."

"Colleague?! From the institute? Is he an architect? Or a speculator?"

"Peterson is a speculator, just like you. He hit an elderly woman in the head three times with a hammer."

"Yes, I think I remember Alevtina mentioning his name once . . . but what now?"

"Now the doctors are struggling to save the child's life." Photios Prytki stepped aside for a moment, whispered something in his colleague's ear, and then returned to the dumbfounded Iratov. "Do you remember your first visit to the foreign currency store a few years ago?" Arseny gave the agent a questioning look. "Come on, think back!"

"Now it's coming back to me! You're the spook from that store! On Vasilyevsky Street?"

"Precisely."

"And now you're . . ."

"And now I am an investigator responsible for matters of the utmost importance to the state, Mr. Iratov."

"Congratulations."

"My career began with you. Who would have thought? I expected to be watching foreign currency stores forever. I'm just a simple country boy from out by Vyazma, but when I caught sight of you, my bosses soon became aware that you weren't just some hustler. You were a fish that was rapidly gaining weight, almost a whale. That's when they promoted me and transferred me to the duty-free store at Sheremetyevo. I watched the monitors, staked the place out, found all your stashes of goods and fall money . . . Do you remember Aleksei?"

"I know a lot of Alekseis," Iratov said with a shake of his shaggy head—too much information too quickly.

"He goes by Lyosha. Remember now? The bartender at Café Lira?"

"That rings a bell . . ."

"The idiot went ahead and bought Zykina's dacha! Imagine that, a bartender buying a dacha that belonged to Brezhnev's favorite singer! They dragged him out of the lake when they took him in, and he crapped himself. Pardon me for sharing that detail. Lyosha cracked as soon as they got him to the detention center. Something went wrong upstairs. It was the fear. He just kept repeating that his balls were made of ice . . . He got a life sentence, but not in jail. Now they're trying to warm up his balls in a psychiatric hospital . . ."

"What are you telling me all this for? Are you trying to scare me? That's an odd choice, considering where I just came from. I don't give a red-hot shit about his icy balls. I've got totally normal balls. How about you?"

"What are you talking about?" Prytki's voice was reassuring. "That was just for your information!" He took a puff to get his cigarette going, enjoyed a greedy drag, and continued. "Do you remember Masha? You know, the salesgirl at our foreign currency store. The real looker. You pretended to be a foreigner, went back to her place that same night, and gave it to her in all three holes?"

"Masha . . ." Iratov said, letting the sound of the name carry him back into the past. A year . . . two . . . three . . . It surfaced in his mind and made him smile.

"Remember? Yeah, I can see you do. Well, the day after you screwed Masha, she got picked up by the scruff of the neck and thrown out of the system—thanks to you. The poor girl didn't know that you were a fellow Soviet national, so she got canned.

Then she got thrown out of the Communist Youth League and... Well, nobody would hire her with that black mark on her record, but Masha was pregnant. She had the child in abject poverty, and it was taken by social services. A drama worthy of the Moscow Art Theatre—"

"Sorry, but what's your name again?" Iratov asked, interrupting the agent. "Phokios—"

"Photios Prytki, at your service."

"What are you doing, acting out a Dostoyevsky novel? Fuck, we've got ourselves a Porfiry Petrovich here! Have you ever taken an honest look in the mirror? With that country-boy mug of yours—sorry, but it's true—all you can do is watch monitors! If you need a Raskolnikov, go catch Peterson! He's the one who bashed Alevtina's head in, not me! Now give me the address of the hospital!"

"I will momentarily," Prytki promised. "But confiscation specialists have already been dispatched to the locations of your stashes. Alevtina is dead. Who will protect you now? That means a new case. I'm already hard at work, believe me! There'll be a new sentence, too."

"And a big promotion for you?" Iratov asked with a sneer.

"That too . . ."

"You're screwed, Photios!"

"Au contraire, Mr. Iratov, you are the one who can expect to get screwed!"

"All those stashes have been moved to new places! Alevtina was hard at work, too, before she died. It was like my birthday when I got her letter! I can tell you that now that she's kicked the bucket. Vorontsova made sure our child would be taken care of. So you can go back to working that store and forget about your new stars, Phokios! Or maybe they'll just tell you to fuckin' get lost! You ruined Masha's life for nothing, you son of a bitch."

Prytki could roll with the punches, but his ears turned as red as molten metal.

"Do you know why Peterson bashed Vorontsova's head in?"

"Knowing that is your job! I've gotta run!"

"Your lady friend was working with Peterson the same way she worked with you. She kept him on the hook, coerced him into giving her regular—what do you call it? Pumps? She stashed away everything her tenderhearted Latvian friend had accumulated and kept blackmailing him . . . The odds that the child is yours aren't too high! She worked with a whole bunch of Iratovs and Petersons, not just you!"

Iratov burst into sincere laughter. He even permitted himself a squeal of pleasure.

"You're such a stupid prick, Photios! I wish there was a foreign currency pay toilet so they could station you there! Even now, you just don't get it, you cannot fathom how glad I am that Peterson did that old bitch in! If it weren't for him, I would've done it myself. If only he'd smashed her with that hammer a hundred times over! Screwing old spooks isn't my calling. And I don't want anything to do with her bastard brat. I'm free, Prytki, free as a bird! Now give me the address, ya little prick!"

Iratov went to the hospital, but they wouldn't let him see Vorontsova. As he walked down the long hallways looking for the exit, he happened upon a ward full of sleeping newborns. He meant to walk right by, but he stopped for a moment, looked through the huge glass window, and suddenly saw the tiny, doll-like leg of a child with a tag attached just above the pink heel. Written clearly, in blue pen, was the name "Iratov . . ."

7

The train car taking Eugene to Moscow was cold, crowded, and smelled insufferably sour. The red-haired Shurka had taken the young man to Sudogda. He was visibly sick with a terrible hangover, but still as suspicious as a dachshund chained up in front of its master's house and expected to guard it like a German shepherd.

"How exactly are you related to Alice?" the coachman asked. The interrogation had commenced.

"Is that a horse?" Eugene inquired, ignoring the question.

"Sure is! A mare. You a city boy? Never seen a horse before?"

"She's old," the young man concluded.

"She's still got a little more in her," the coachman reassured his fellow traveler. "Since when does Alice have relatives in the city?"

"She has relatives in America, too."

"Come on, you're pulling my leg!"

"Way back in the late nineteenth century, one of Alice's ancestors moved to Texas, where he would later invent the television, the automobile, and the locomotive. He patented everything and became a billionaire. Every generation of his descendants multiplied his capital, but his great-great-great-granddaughter Jackie Kennedy was childless, so Alice might have some serious money coming her way. After Jackie dies, of course."

"This city boy's fucking with me," Shurka thought, suddenly tense, his nasty hangover forgotten. "What if he ain't, though? If he ain't, then I've gotta go make Ksenia sweet on me, so's she'll let me rent out a younger horse from her after this Jackie lady dies . . . I won't pay those village capitalists, of course. They got more money than a dog's got fleas. Maybe I could borrow some money from Ksenia, like fifty thousand rubles, and not give it back?" Shurka wondered what would be better for him—if the city boy was telling the truth about the relatives in America or if he was lying. Sure, he'd have a new horse and lots of money, but on the other hand, Ksenia and Alice would be up in the kingdom of heaven, throwing money around at the store in Stepachevo. Did they deserve that kind of wealth? What made those dames better than Shurka? "No way! I'd rather have this city boy be lying," he decided. "To hell with it, the new horse, the millions, everything's fine the way it is! We don't need any upheavals around here! We won't stand for a capitalist revolution! We'll drop the bomb on America! I'm a man who means what he says!"

"So who exactly are ya?"

"I told you, I'm her relative." Eugene hopped off the sleigh and started walking beside it, rubbing the old mare's croup. She happily swished her tail, welcoming the good treatment of horses.

"I mean what do you do for a living?"

"I'm a student."

"And what are you studying to be, Mr. Student?"

"A scholar."

"Scholars are dirt-poor these days."

"There's no changing your vocation . . ."

Shurka didn't want to jaw with Alice's guest anymore. He got off the sleigh, too, and turned away from the wind. He loosened his pants and began to rid himself of excess fluid, but then he screamed at the top of his lungs.

"Oooooow! I'm never buying a stranger's moonshine

again! That crap was fake, fudge pudge! I've got the frickin' DTs, I'm dyyyyyyyyin'! Frig me sideways!" Then he suddenly fell silent and ran to catch up to the sleigh, holding up his pants with both hands. "Hey, Mr. Student!"

"What do you want?" Eugene asked, turning toward the coachman. "What are you yelling for?"

"You're a scholar—"

"Still just a student."

"Wait up, Mr. Student!" Shurka stopped, unclenched his shaking hands, and let his pants fall right on to his felt boots, baring everything below his stomach. "Well?"

"What?"

"Go on, look!"

"I am." Eugene looked at the coachman's white pelvic area.

"Did my dick really disappear, or is it the DTs?"

"It's gone," the young man said and began to climb the hill toward the bus stop. Shurka ran to catch up to the horse, which had managed to turn around and start heading home.

"I can't stop drinking," he said in a voice that hardly sounded human. "I'm an addict!" he shouted into the woods.

"Dick . . . dick . . . dick . . ." answered the echo.

Eugene started feeling poorly on the train. There wasn't enough oxygen. It reeked intolerably of unwashed human bodies. One man was eating hardboiled eggs, another was chewing mint gum to cover up the alcohol on his breath. Little tykes were hollering, and one of the young mommies was unabashedly feeding her spawn from her giant red breast.

Eugene was afraid he'd lose consciousness, especially in a place like this. He was holding it together, but there was still a hellish hour and a half to go until Moscow. The train jerked, people bumped into him from every direction, and his nose started bleeding.

"Hey, snot-nose, get the hell outta here! Go between the cars!" commanded some thug with a mug like a pit bull. "You'll bleed all over everyone! Make way, citizens!"

The compliant crowd squeezed Eugene into the vestibule, where he wiped the blood away with the sleeve of his coat. That was of no interest to the smokers standing out there. His innards twisted from the cigarette smoke, like someone was turning them on a spit, and his vision blurred, but a small, short man grabbed his arm to support him and drew him into the vestibule of the next car.

"Go ahead and barf, kid," he suggested as he rifled through Eugene's pockets. "Go on, let it up."

Eugene vomited a green substance and almost instantly felt better. He took a deep breath of brisk air and the clattering of the wheels cleared his head. Meanwhile, all the little guy found were coins amounting to about two hundred rubles, if that. No ID, no wad, not even a set of keys . . . He cursed his bad luck. Somebody had already cleaned this sucker out! He nailed him in the back of the head with his set of lead knuckles and went back inside to look for his next victim.

Eugene was unconscious when he arrived in Moscow, Russia's capital city. Somebody called the police on their way off the train, and his insensate body was dragged off to the nearby precinct, where Kipa, the senior duty officer, with all of fifty-eight years to his name, chewed out the two sergeants for bringing in another drunk.

"Nah, don't think he's drunk," the junior sergeant said with a shrug. "Doesn't smell like booze."

"Doped?"

"Damned if I know!" the senior sergeant replied. "His mug's all bloody. Maybe somebody popped him one in the nose?"

"Then why in holy hell didn't ya call an ambulance? What'm I supposed to do with him here?"

"Alright, Kipa, call an ambulance then. He woulda frozen to death out on the platform . . ."

Potap Kipa had been working at the Kursk Station precinct for thirty-eight years. They'd made him a cop after he finished his military service. That was a peaceful time: no organized crime, just pickpockets, muggers, and card sharks operating on the trains. The pay was decent, too, so Kipa hunkered down in the warm station and spent almost four decades there. Once he'd risen to the rank of staff sergeant, he married the lady that ran the pharmacy right there at the station, and they had two children. Not too long ago, Staff Sergeant Kipa became a grandfather for the fourth time. He had a calm disposition and avoided the lawless practices favored by the next generation of cops, yet he never interfered or moralized, so they viewed him as a father figure and would slip him some of their takings. Kipa didn't turn his nose up at that money; he invested it in his grandkids and his fishing trips.

"Sure, sure," said the staff sergeant. "I'll call the ambulance. Stick him in the holding tank for now. Give him a bunk, too—toss those brown guys on the floor. What are they, Tajiks? Who cares? Make sure you elevate his head, too."

"You got it!" one of the sergeants replied.

The ambulance arrived two hours later, and it was determined that the young man had suffered head trauma. Eugene was immediately loaded on to a stretcher, carried into the mobile ICU, and taken to the 1st City Hospital with the sirens wailing. In the admissions area, they moved him to a gurney, brought him up to the second floor, and put him in the queue for the MRI machine. Two hours after that, Eugene's brain was scanned. Nothing critical was found, just a minor concussion, and even that was doubtful.

"So how come he's unconscious?" asked the physician's assistant.

"Stick some ammonia under his nose!"

Physician's Assistant Lilia Zolotova had only been working in the ICU for a little over two months and had already seen things far worse than any horror movie. The previous week, they'd brought in a lady who worked in a big factory that made dumplings. She had fallen into the rapidly rotating blades of a giant meat grinder. What they delivered to the hospital was a bloody hunk of meat with open eyes. All of her bones had been ground up, and her head was crushed, like she'd been run over by a steamroller. Her ribcage had been cut open, yet her exposed heart was pristine, beating like she was perfectly healthy. The doctors performed their duties in silence, injecting something into the ground beef, stitching up veins and arteries, draining away the blood. They kept working to the end. Zero brain activity—there wasn't really a brain, just gray mush—but they kept working for two hours, and the heart just kept ticking away rhythmically—sixty beats a minute. There was no way to measure blood pressure—no arms or legs. They kept stitching and stitching, all in silence—seven hours straight. Finally, the inexplicable phenomenon came to an end. The beautiful heart fluttered like a tulip in the wind, changed color from red to lilac—and stopped. They tried to restart it with electric shocks, but their efforts proved futile.

It was only after the surgeon had announced the time of death that the operating room heard a chorus of choice profanity more magnificent than any that had ever graced it before. The surgeons had done seven hours of pointless work, knowing full well that there was nothing they could do. The heart just kept beating! But why?!

The surgeon informed her husband that she was dead. He

broke down crying, but not because of his own grief; he was thinking about their four daughters, aged five to fourteen.

"What will they do with no mother?!"

"That was why the heart was beating," the surgeon thought. "For her children." Then he went to a birthday party for the cute, chubby resident from Unit 3.

Physician's Assistant Zolotova walked up to the patient and stuck some cotton soaked with ammonia inhalant under his nose. The young man's nostrils twitched, his face twisted, and his eyes opened. He pushed Lilia's hand away.

"Can you hear me?" she asked, looking right into his pupils.

"Yes," Eugene answered weakly, casting his eyes about, trying to figure out where he was.

"You're in the hospital," Lilia said reassuringly. "You were struck on the head with a heavy object. Can you understand me?" He nodded. "But you'll be fine! Fortunately, you have not suffered any serious trauma."

A moment later, Lilia was examining the patient, his remarkably handsome face, his humongous eyes that drew her in like black holes in space that consume everything and all things, without exception. This mysterious cosmos drew Lilia in, too. She instantly felt a flood of amorous chemicals, and, if they had been there alone, she would have kissed the youth right on the lips — or bitten him. Wholly consumed by tenderness, she announced that she would escort the patient to the ward herself and transfer him to the care of the head of the relevant department. The physician's assistant rolled the gurney into the freight elevator and pressed the button.

"Thank you for being so kind, dear," Eugene said gratefully.

Lilia smelled the uncanny aroma of his breath—it was somehow like incense, but mixed with some other elements that drove her mad. She, too, was reeling, but she held it together.

"'Dear,' huh?" The young woman wanted to purse her lips into an aggrieved grimace and furrow her brow, but she just couldn't. Instead, she smiled indulgently. "Well, 'dear' is nice, but you can call me Lilia, too. What's your name?"

"Eugene." He took care of himself just fine, moving from the gurney to the bed, taking off his black garments, and putting on the hospital gown, but Lilia sat on the edge of the mattress and cheered the young man up, promising that his strength would soon return and she would visit him in the meantime.

"If you don't mind, of course?"

"Could I perhaps have something to eat? Or some tea?"

"Of course! I'll be right back!"

She walked out of the ward at a businesslike clip and had a tête-à-tête with Petya Savushkin, the resident on duty. They had been in the same premed class, and he'd even tried courting her, but nothing came of it, and then a future psychiatrist got Petya wrapped around her finger, and they later married. He'd resembled a psychiatric patient ever since.

"Listen, Petya," Lilia said firmly, "he needs to be fed!"

"Dinner is at seven," Savushkin answered nasally.

"I'll be back soon with some food. Keep an eye on him, please!"

"Why? Is he special or something? And since when do you give the orders around here?"

"He's special."

"More special than me?" Petya's eyes filled with disappointment, and then he sneezed.

"He is to me. And you're married to that psychiatrist. And you should wear a mask, you've got a full caseload today!"

"Those bastards gave it to me!"

"Do you get me, Petya? Come on, take care of him, sweetie!"

"Is he a relative?" Savushkin had softened at the word "sweetie."

"Yeah . . . I gotta go, alright?"

"Run along now, Zolotova!"

The assistant scurried off to the staircase, and Petya Savushkin, suddenly remembering his wife and comparing her to his classmate, heaved a sad sigh and shuffled off to check on Lilia's relative. He stood at the ward doors for a moment, surveyed the patients harshly, and gave a formidable cough so that they would know he was the boss around here. Only then did he stride sedately into the room and approach the newly admitted patient's bed.

"How are you doing, good sir?"

Savushkin himself found that "good sir" slightly off. After all, they weren't living back in Chekhov's day! On the other hand, the face of Lilia's protégé, pale, with an enfeebled gleam about the eyes, looked like something unearthed from that era.

"My head hurts a little," Eugene admitted.

"You have sustained no particular trauma," Petya reassured him. "This pill will help you. Meanwhile, we can fill out the admissions form. Last name, please."

The young man started thinking hard, his brow furrowing with tension, and his nose began bleeding again. The doctor took a piece of clean gauze out of his pocket. Once it was all soaked with blood, he instructed the patient to tilt his head back.

"Please repeat your question," Eugene requested.

"Don't strain yourself. We can forgo the questions for now and just take your blood pressure." Savushkin turned on the machine and cinched the cuff over the patient's forearm.

"My name is Eugene."

"No talking yet, please. Breathe normally. Come on, just relax." He quickly filled the rubber bulb with air, extended the stethoscope, and listened to his patient's pulse. "Well, every-thing seems normal. 120 over 80. Your heart rate is somewhat elevated, though. The bleeding was caused by dystonia. Do you eat fruit?"

"No . . ."

"Meat? Cheese?"

"No."

"Well, what do you eat?"

Eugene thought for a moment.

"Potatoes . . . and milk . . ."

"Are you a student or something?"

"Yes."

"I was a student once too," Savushkin said with a cheer-ful laugh. "I was poor too—but poverty is no vice, as they say! Lilia's gonna feed you soon. Boy, she can cook!" Petya said dreamily. "Her cutlets, her rollups, her casseroles! Why did she decide to study medicine anyway? She should've stayed home. She'd make a fine wife . . ."

The conversation's turn to this culinary theme made the patient go visibly pale, and he nearly swooned clean away once again. At that very moment, though, Lilia came back with a bag, dismissed the now superfluous and supernumerary Savushkin to the staff room, and laid out the foil-wrapped food on the table.

"Eat up!" she commanded.

Eugene ate with such rapidity that one would have thought his life depended on it. He bit off half a cutlet, nodding approv-ingly at Lilia, chewed it briefly, and swallowed. Then he moved on to a piece of the egg and gribenes casserole Savushkin had praised so highly, plus little salads, assembled with the most exquisite taste; it all got packed away at lightning speed.

"Do you like it?" Lilia asked.

"This casserole smells like you."

"Like . . . what do you mean?" she asked, blushing.

"Molecules of your body wind up in the food you prepare, and then in me," Eugene explained, now nearly sated. "I can feel every one of them. I think that may well be the origin of the saying 'the way to a man's heart is through his stomach.' When a man swallows the food his wife prepares, he also swallows her— in minute doses—and then he can't quit her. She has become his drug. On the other hand, men rarely love their wives. They just have to swallow them whole!"

"Hold on, what are you majoring in?" Lilia asked, somewhat surprised to hear him fantasizing about acts of cannibalism. "And how old are you?"

"I'm studying engineering, and I'm as old as you want me to be."

She didn't know what he meant by that, but she spontaneously decided to sign up for the night shift. She watched Eugene's face gradually growing flush, his cheeks taking on the color of a crimson sunset, his lips swelling, now exuding not incense but something utterly unknown. Lilia steadied herself and analyzed the barely perceptible processes going on in her nose like a medical professional. She arrived at a logical conclusion.

"It's pheromones."

"What?"

"Are you full?" she asked, feeling that the bra under her medical gown was unexpectedly too small for her. The undergarment's cups were sticking out a little, revealing their blue lace to the young man.

"Thank you."

"You can thank me later, when you get your strength back," Lilia said with a sly smile, openly adjusted her bra, and walked out of the ward, tormented by the energetic fluttering of butterflies in her stomach.

All medical professionals are rather callous people. It's a defense mechanism they pick up from their instructors. It's impossible to empathize with every sick and dying person. No heart or brain could withstand it; your soul will just burn out completely. You can only empathize with your family and close friends; that's all your body is designed to handle. Furthermore, empathy is an emotion of the heart, and when you think with your heart, you should expect disaster. Human reason, untainted by emotion, almost always arrives at the right decision, for reason is the only thing that separates us from all other living things. But once your profession has made you callous, you start to see everything around you that way.

Lilia was a product of her medical instruction; she had ended her love affair with romance once and for all, learned to dispense with the palavering, and become accustomed to expressing her desires harshly and clearly. As she rode the elevator down to the general surgical area, she concluded that she definitively wanted to enjoy physical love with that young man, despite his philosophical eccentricities. She recalled the aroma of his pheromones, juggled them on her tongue . . . and her vision blurred again.

She went to get him a little after eleven, woke him up by stroking his cheek with the back of her hand, then put her finger to his lips. She leaned close to his ear, so close her button nose brushed it, and whispered torridly.

"Let's go!" Without asking where or why, Eugene rose from his bed and followed her, his steps rapid.

She had been making exacting preparations for this meeting ever since she'd demanded to be assigned to the night shift. She'd put sheets on the cot in the staff room, set out sweet champagne and fruit on the bedside table—she'd had an orderly run to the store for them—then spent half an hour in the shower, shaving her legs with a scalpel, checked her armpits, neatened up the butterfly below her waist a little, then applied a French cream with the barely perceptible scent of Japanese cherry blossoms. Only then did she put on her medical gown, dispensing with undergarments this time. She was all hot and bothered, since she assumed her chosen lover was inexperienced and guileless. She wanted to teach him everything she knew, and Lilia fancied that she knew an awful lot.

When she despairingly shed her gown, baring her charms to him, he didn't just leap on her, like young men are wont to do, but he didn't fall into a stupor either. Eugene calmly drew closer to Lilia and unhurriedly examined her nude form, beginning with her slight knees and ending with her delicate neck.

For a second, Lilia felt like she was undergoing a medical examination, but in that same second, Eugene took her head in his hand and kissed her on the lips so skillfully, then so sweetly, so penetratingly moved his caramel tongue that the young woman's body instantly turned hot, like a fiery river of molten lava was oozing out of her. It was only afterward, when she had collected her thoughts, that she realized this strange young man had made her feel like an inexperienced yet lustful virgin. He played her body like a virtuoso playing a piano, the tips of his fingers hitting all the right keys and striking the most challenging chords that made Lilia's throat sing mezzo-soprano. Then he moved down to the bass part of his instrument and penetrated its essence. An instant later, the musician made assertive additions to his improvised score, and Lilia sang again, her voice as low as a woman's can be. The whole hospital heard her contralto, and everyone—at least everyone who could feel—felt the culmination, the apotheosis of the performance, in that moment. There was even a miracle in the intensive care unit; two men emerged from comas, and the monitors indicated that they weren't planning on going back anytime soon.

Later, lying next to him on a mangled sofa, she felt that she was spent to the absolute limit, beyond which there was only death. The young woman felt that he had been inside every one of her cells, taking her body captive like a cancerous tumor, an abundant shower of dizzying morphine. At the same time, Lilia, her skin wet with passion, realized that she had bitten into her partner heedlessly and boundlessly, like she had to fill up for later, drink him endlessly, like a diabetic drinks water at death's door.

After a while, when dawn had announced its arrival, when strength gradually began to return to her body, she suddenly realized that from that minute on, she would be the unhappiest woman on earth, that nothing like this would ever happen to her again, that she was never again to taste such epic pleasure! Her hips felt his now cool skin, and she was absolutely sure—he was a demon!

"I was with a demon tonight!" she thought.

He adopted an unexpectedly dry tone with her, asked her what time it was, listened to her answer, got dressed, and headed for the door.

"Where are you going?"

"I have to get back to the ward."

"There's a few minutes left . . ."

"For you, not me. I'll be discharged at nine."

As he was leaving, she wanted to shout that they wouldn't just discharge him, that the police had to question him first . . . But she didn't. She just whispered.

"And you don't have any ID, you little demon!"

Naked, shamelessly dangling a leg that now smelled like

sex over the side of the sofa—that was how Savushkin found her when he showed up for his shift. Thinking that this dish had been prepared for him, he leapt on her naked body like an animal, sneezing twice, and then face-planted as he tried to take his pants and underwear off at the same time.

"You're such a prick, Savushkin!" Lilia said, reaching toward the bedside table and downing the last of the champagne straight from the bottle.

The naked Petya, who was in the manly state and utterly beside himself, insulted yet aroused, didn't hesitate. He firmly threw his classmate on her back. He took her—like a victorious knight, he thought—and she suddenly stopped trying to resist. She relaxed.

"Just don't come in me."

"Uh-huh."

She felt nothing: not Savushkin's pinches, not his snotty kisses, not even him inside her. Lilia's indifference to what was happening made Petya finish quickly, like he was running a hundred-meter dash.

Ten seconds, and the gong announced his victory. Visibly upset, Petya dressed quickly.

"You're frigid, Lilia! You're a wrapper with no candy!"

"You're right, Savushkin. I'm frigid!" The trauma specialist made her get dressed, showered her with lewd insults, and ordered her out. He tidied up the staff room himself and found many traces of passion not left by him . . . this was not the work of his hands. He suddenly realized whom the physician's assistant had spent her energy on and experienced a fit of rage. He called his wife, told her how stressed he was, and asked her for a psychotherapeutic session on the spot. Fuming, he told her how many bad people he had around him, how nasty and two-faced they were, how it was making him lose faith in himself, question whether there was anything special about him, and undermining his masculinity . . . His wise wife offered her support, but she suspected that something fishy was going on, so she tried to ascertain the actual sequence of events. Savushkin muttered something about how Lilia was crazy, how she'd tried to seduce him when he came into the staff room and found her naked. But, he, faithful husband that he was, stoically rebuffed her advances. Petya's wife was a highly intelligent professional, and she instantly figured out what had really happened. Her significant other was no stoic. He'd been pining after Lilia since his college days, but when he finally got to sleep with her, something had gone awry during their intimate encounter and made him hysterical. She had a rough idea of what it was, too: she knew Savushkin and his physical capabilities, his tendency to shoot fast and miss the target. It had probably happened again that morning. She didn't dig any deeper, though, just pretended she was entirely on her husband's side, then told him that he was the best and that work was the best sedative. Savushkin was immeasurably grateful to his wife, since he really had calmed down almost immediately. The trauma specialist made a vow of love and devotion to her and began preparing for his morning rounds. There was only one thing dampening his mood, and that was the fact that his inspection would compel him to come into contact with the patient they admitted yesterday, the one with whom Lilia had apparently spent quite the wild night . . .

"Trash!" our dear little Petya grumbled huffily.

Meanwhile, Eugene, now arrayed in the black garments bestowed on him by Alice, was at the free phone booth in the hospital's entry hall. He inquired if Mr. Iratov could come to the phone, and, when asked what his business was, he replied that it was personal and was told that they could not connect him without knowing what it was regarding, so the best they could do was put him through to Vitya, Iratov's assistant. Seasoned aide that he was, Vitya instantly realized that this was no mere petitioner and could even be someone important to his boss.

"Personal business?" he asked.

"Precisely . . ."

"Mr. Iratov is not in the office at the moment."

"Well, why didn't you say that to begin with?"

"Not to worry, I will connect you to Mr. Iratov's mobile phone . . ."

8

The morning after he and Vera fought and then made up proved depressing. The gray sky was falling along with the snow, causing fits of some peculiar despair. The inadequacy he felt upon making a trip to the bathroom only deepened his foul mood. Iratov caught himself thinking that he wanted to grab his tool like a real man and send a taut stream into the toilet—or at least near it.

For some reason, he didn't want to see Vera at all. Some new attitude toward her had settled in his chest. He understood that a person who can't do it almost always experiences feelings of enmity toward those who can . . . and do. Iratov tried to chase those thoughts away, telling himself that he could overcome all of it, and that what he'd lost wasn't the most important part of his relationship with the woman he loved.

He drank some coffee with a splash of cognac.

"It's a bit early," he thought. "Not even nine yet."

With a menacing squeak, all the computer monitors in his study turned on at once. Leaving his unfinished coffee behind, Mr. Iratov ran over to the desk, glanced at the graphs displayed on the screens, sat down, visited several business websites, and realized that he'd lost something on the order of fifty million dollars that morning. The stock markets of China, Japan, and all of Asia had collapsed, falling by almost 7 percent.

One must give Mr. Iratov his due, though. He always kept his head in those situations. He held that both triumphs and reversals on the market were inevitable, and they generally balanced each other out. There would always be busts, various Black Mondays and Fridays, but there was no precedent for markets failing to return to their historical maximums, even if it took them a while. Patience was the most important quality for an investor. Slumps come and go, but the green rally will still lead humanity ever upward. Iratov wrote a few emails to his brokers and instructed them to minimize his losses by betting against the currencies of developing countries, telling them which pairs would be most advantageous.

Mr. Iratov turned away from his financial affairs and looked at the news. Not finding anything of interest, he could think of nothing better to do than type his own name into the search bar and press enter. There was no news about him personally either. Not even knowing why, he pressed the "images" button and saw numerous versions of his face. He looked at his young self winning various architecture prizes, then posing in his Bentley with some hip girl band, whom he'd unhurriedly plowed one after another, followed by endless parties and gatherings of every kind. He saw a rich, steady, confident man with a magical face that had enchanted a great many members of the opposite sex, from small-town airheads to Hollywood stars. Next came photographs where he was already with Vera. Formal events, the fashionable catwalks his wife loved, theater premieres, and even an official photograph of Mr. Arseny Andreivich Iratov receiving the Fourth-Class Medal of the Order of Merit for the Fatherland from the President of the Russian Federation.

Iratov finished with the public photographs and moved on to his personal collection. He looked through the shots from his life, sometimes happy and sometimes less so. He even had a photo from his trial, when he was young—full face and in profile. He found himself remembering the prison camp near Vladimir, but he chased away those negative thoughts by clicking on the album labeled "USA." Then he was young again, a rich speculator from Moscow who had just emigrated to America through

Israel—tremendously rich, in fact, by the standards of the time . . . There he was, meeting the drivers of his own fleet of taxis. A hundred émigrés who owed their medallions to him, assembled and harkening to his speech. Iratov had been the one who figured out how to chase the Indian drivers and the other old-time aces who had historically dominated the New York taxi business out of Brighton Beach. Outsiders and yellow cabs were only allowed to bring passengers into Brighton. There was no taking them the other direction; they'd always run empty. The residents of that half of Brooklyn could, and did, hire their own drivers—and much more cheaply, too. It couldn't have been done without the help of the numerous boxers who had come to seek their fame and fortune in the American ring, only to fall one after another, like unripe apples in a strong wind. It was them, the sorcerers of pugilism, hungry as wolves, who ousted the interlopers from Brighton Beach . . . Then some gangster types tried to gain influence over him. They had arrived in the Land of the Free to hide from the Motherland's justice and were once again appropriating other ethnic groups' spheres of influence. They even knifed a couple of young athletes, who retaliated by gunning down some gangsters . . . But as a young man, Iratov had sworn that he'd never get mixed up with the pigs, and he had kept his word, despite all the problems dealing with gangsters had caused him. He resolved them quietly, with the help of a few diplomats who were actually GRU agents. Dealing with cops was beneath him, but spooks were cool . . . Photographs of his mother and father. They had both died while he was abroad. His father had a massive heart attack, then his mother followed him into the next world—quietly, the English way. She withered away without her husband and son . . . But for some reason, Iratov thought of his father more often—his head hunched over his drafting table, a funny little man with nearly red hair . . .

Then he returned to Russia, a renewed country concealing within itself unlimited opportunities for those seeking to rise to Olympian heights of success. Mr. Iratov thrived. Thanks to his enormous financial resources, he opened his own architecture firm and assembled an energetic young staff. Within three months, he had designed an apartment building for major theater and film figures, which was erected right in the heart of Moscow. He ran around like an errand boy, visiting all those Honored Artists and Actors of the Soviet Union, making sure everything was set up properly, the interior design was comfortable, and the bathroom containing both toilet and shower—nearly unheard of in the Soviet Union—wasn't too much of a shock . . . In memory of his father, who had given him his unrealized talent, Iratov had decided to bring his ideas to life, though he modernized them and added his own visionary spin. Naturally, it was impossible to put up buildings like that in Moscow; it was just boxes full of tiny apartments there—no creativity, not a drop of innovation. On the other hand, his ideas were in great demand elsewhere, both East and West. He built in Dubai, Japan, and Panama. He signed every design with his father's name as well as his own.

Iratov would sometimes visit Staroglebsky, the former president of the institute who had allowed the ex-con to graduate and receive his diploma as an architect, and his wife. He'd bring the elderly, poverty-stricken old couple the finest groceries and, just as in his college days, present him with pipe tobacco and her with Lucky Strikes.

All his girlfriends from the institute—Shevtsova the Communist Youth League organizer, Katya the volleyball star, and all the rest—had long since gotten hitched and popped out kids. They were women now, not girls, and good for them! Iratov remembered when Shevtsova visited him after he'd returned from abroad. He had only just bought the office and started to put things in order. Chubby-cheeked, broad-bottomed, with DD breasts, she had asked nothing of him, not money, not special treatment for her husband. She just took a bottle of Moskovskaya out of her shopping bag, along with a half pound of choice sausage. She poured some vodka into the glasses she'd brought, proposed a toast to their reunion, and poured hers into herself. Iratov didn't know how she got him going, how he wound up squeezed between her mighty legs, but Shevtsova neighed and rode him like a cavalryman. Iratov was as happy as his old girlfriend, especially when he saw her huge, firm breasts bouncing up and down—like basketballs . . . Then they sat there, naked, on newspapers spread across the floor, their bodies smeared with fresh whitewash, and finished the vodka.

"Do you know who invented those table glasses you brought?"

"Do glasses really have to be invented?" Shevtsova asked with a surprised laugh.

"The famous architect Mukhina came up with the idea of a glass with facets. She improved the design of nails, too!"

"No kiddin'?"

"Yeah."

"Don't worry, Iratov. I won't come here again. I'm not unfaithful to my husband. I just wanted to remember the old days!"

"Where's Katya?"

"Katya?" The former Communist Youth League girl was already dressed and adjusting her skirt. "She was working the Hotel National for a while, then she bought the farm in Turkey . . ."

"Strange times . . ."

"I'm off," Shevtsova declared. "Gotta pick the kids up from school. Take care!" Iratov never saw her again.

Once he had finished setting up the office and gotten to work on the practical aspects of architecture—in close collaboration with the mayor of Moscow—the line of visitors at his door was as long as at Lenin's mausoleum. These were people who had come to see him personally. Some of them were proposing joint projects, going into oil or what have you, but he always refused.

"Me, go into oil, really?" he'd say. Others suggested doing some joint design work. It was a boundless field, but he knew what he was about. What the hell did he need partners for? But mostly they were petitioners: old acquaintances, his friends, his parents' friends. He threw the swindlers and interlopers out on their ears but helped the ones he actually recognized as best he could.

One day, when Iratov was busy negotiating with some shifty businessmen from Singapore, his assistant, Vitya, informed him that an older woman had showed up with a kid of about fifteen.

"Move it to tomorrow!" Mr. Iratov instructed.

"She is prepared to wait. She said she won't have the nerve to come again."

"Why can't it be tomorrow?"

"She is not certain that she wants to see you, but this seems important."

"Did she introduce herself at least?"

"Yes," Vitya replied. "She says her name is Svetlana." He turned that name around in his mind for a while, but it didn't ring a bell. He still asked his assistant to have the petitioners give him another fifteen minutes.

"Bring them in during the break."

"Very good, Mr. Iratov." When the aging, simply dressed woman and the kid stepped into his office, he was fully convinced that he had no clue who she was, but the boy . . . He said hello, asked them to sit down, and inquired to what he owed this honor.

"I told you he wouldn't recognize me," the woman said, turning toward her son. Iratov really didn't recognize her. But that voice! There was something in its melody that sent his soul into the past, into his late teens. He thought hard . . . "Let's go," she said quietly to the kid.

They rose from their cozy armchairs, the woman apologized for disturbing him, Iratov nodded in both parting and pardon . . . He sat there for a few minutes, his gaze detached, still lost in remembrance of his youth. When he had almost broken loose, flown out of his heavy meditative state, when his thoughts had nearly jumped over the boundary dividing past and present, Iratov burst from his stupor, suddenly remembering. It couldn't be! He sprang out of his chair and, leaving his jacket behind, his collar unbuttoned, charged after that strange pair, running down the street, looking in every direction, searching for her with pain and passion in his eyes. When he saw them standing by the trolleybus stop, poplar fuzz falling on their shoulders, he shouted as he had once shouted in his youth, in blinkered impotence and despair.

"Svetla-a-n-a!" The name carried down the avenues and alleyways of Moscow. "Svetla-a-n-a!"

She turned around. He was already running toward her, and his hair fluttered in the wind. He stopped in front of her, still breathing rapidly.

"Svetlana! Is it really you?"

She nodded. He convinced her to come back to the office and led her into his private room, where he made coffee and broke up a big chocolate bar.

"So . . . how are you?" he asked, taking her hands in his. Her palms were soft and moist.

"Well . . . how can I tell you about my whole life?"

"You're right . . . Maybe the boy can take a tour of the office in the meantime? We have a big sheet of Whatman paper you can draw on," Iratov said, turning toward Svetlana's son—and once again, he felt like he had seen that face before. "We have a thousand felt-tips!"

"Okay," the boy agreed, and a minute later Vitya had taken him away to explore the architecture firm.

"Well, how are you?"

"You already asked that," she said with a smile.

"Yeah . . ."

He sat there in silence, suddenly realizing that he had nothing to say to her. Their shared past had been so fleeting, like a single night and day, but it contained his first love and his first true suffering.

"How's that husband of yours?"

She shrugged, and Iratov felt an unbearably strong desire to hold the past against her: the package sent from an exotic land, stealing his naiveté. But he just couldn't. It's impossible to be mad at the aging woman who saved you from spending your life with an aging woman. You just have to thank her!

He put his head in her lap, and she stroked his hair just as she once had, twisting his black ringlets around her fingers. Iratov realized he could only do this with her—bury his face in her lap and let himself be a little weak. His mother was dead, and it had never even occurred to him to put his trust in the women who came in and out of his life. He asked her son's name.

"Arseny . . ."

"Like me. Did you name him after me?"

"No, after the poet, Tarkovsky."

"Oh yeah . . . that's good . . . Arseny Gryazev."

"Arseny Iratov," Svetlana corrected him, and her knees were suddenly tense.

He had never given serious thought to children before, nor was he inclined to now. Hearing such startling, fateful information that could change his life forever didn't even make Iratov flinch. For an instant, he thought that Svetlana was pinning Gryazev's kid on him, but he immediately understood that it wasn't like that. He also realized what he had recognized in the boy's face—himself, his own face at thirteen.

"What should I do?" he asked, lifting his head from her lap.

"I don't know," Svetlana replied. "I just thought that you should know about your son."

"Why are you only telling me now?"

"You wouldn't have believed me before. I was never your wife . . . and why ruin your life? You were a splendid young man . . ."

Iratov looked out the window, and, for a moment, he felt like he could see it—the nightgown he had once given her, fluttering on a crooked poplar branch, saturated with the smell of all those bitches who had slept in it after Svetlana, whom he'd banged in it with primal, animal intensity, as if he could eradicate *her* smell from his nostrils . . .

"I don't want to be in his life," Iratov stated harshly. "The decision to keep the child was yours. You were living with Gryazev back then! While I was almost dying." She rose from her armchair. Her expression had not changed.

"I had to tell you at least. All the best." She left the room.

Embarrassed by his surge of nostalgia, he wasn't planning on running after her again. That embarrassment had turned into vexation mixed with resentment, and he had to drink a large serving of cognac to expand his blood vessels and neutralize his adrenaline. Vitya reappeared.

"Your son?" he asked, smiling widely and showing his luxurious white teeth.

"Go screw yourself!" Iratov growled furiously. His face was contorted with rage his assistant could not comprehend, and his eyes were protruding from their sockets. "Go screw yourself!"

He stopped remembering. It wasn't any fun . . .

Let it be noted that he later tracked Svetlana down and helped her out with some anonymous bank transfers. He wasn't driven by a sense of duty; it just seemed like the sensible thing to do.

Iratov turned off the computer and went into the kitchen, where he made himself three fried eggs with tomatoes in silence. He ate, trying not to dwell on those bad memories, and then drank about two shots' worth of cognac.

Mr. Iratov decided not to go into the office that day. Instead, he had to go up to Vera's apartment and try to sort out how the current state of affairs would affect their relationship. He wanted to play a doubles game at four and then visit the massage therapist . . . actually, he could forgo the massage for now . . .

He was already closing the door behind him when he heard his phone; he'd forgotten it on his desk. He had to go back and answer it. It was his assistant, Vitya, calling, the one he'd chewed out not half an hour ago.

"What do you want?" he asked somewhat gruffly.

"May I connect you with downtown, Mr. Iratov?"

"Is it urgent?"

"The young man did not introduce himself, but he is being terribly insistent—as if his life were at stake!"

"Come on, Vitya, somebody's life is always at stake . . ."

"Shall I tell him 'no'?"

"No, connect me, if it's life and death . . ."

"Okay . . ." Iratov heard background music for a few seconds, and then there was a click, followed by an unfamiliar voice. The man it belonged to was apparently quite young indeed.

"Mr. Iratov?"

"Yes . . ." The man didn't sound nearly as desperate as Vitya had led him to believe. "Who am I speaking to?"

"Yourself . . ." the voice informed him.

"I regret to say that I do not have the time to spare for idiotic jokes!" Iratov answered harshly, already planning to give Vitya another tongue-lashing—one more screwup like this and he'd find himself out of work. Mr. Iratov wanted to sever the connection, but then he heard a warning on the other end.

"Don't hang up! I'm calling about something very important to you!"

"Is that right?"

"I know what happened to you."

"I don't follow . . ."

"Have you lost anything important recently?"

"Start making sense or I will end this call."

"Have you lost a certain part of your body recently?"

"Who was it?" Iratov wondered. "Did that prick Sytin sell me out?" Nobody but him and Vera knew . . . No doubt about it, they were trying to blackmail him, a mighty man as hard as stone.

"I don't give in to blackmail!" Mr. Iratov warned him. "Moreover, I respond to such acts harshly, and, rest assured, you will soon find out how harsh I can be."

"I know very well how harsh you can be. More precisely, I know everything about you, down to the most trivial detail . . . Well, for example, you lost almost fifty million dollars today and made a big bet against the yuan. I know that you personally gave the order for Interlopin to be tortured in prison . . ."

"Who's that?"

"That petty criminal who once caught you sharking when you were in high school. Then they punched you in the face every day for a month, and so you got the nickname 'Yakut' because your face was so swollen. The year before last, when they cornered Interlopin in the Vyatka prison camp and stuck a shank in his liver, they accompanied the deed with the words 'Remember Yakut?' You're Yakut, if I'm not mistaken. No, I'm not mistaken! By the way, while Interlopin was dying, he still couldn't remember who Yakut was . . ."

Iratov didn't say anything. Powerful legs spread, head down, he looked like a bull enraged by brazen picadors. He wasn't afraid, but, unlike a bull, he had no target in front of him, which made his belly burn from the inside with crackling fury.

"What do you want?" he muttered into the phone.

"Want? Well, nothing at all, really. Perhaps something to eat? I'm hungry."

"You want some money for a couple of hot dogs?"

"Let me visit you. I'll only need an hour. Meanwhile, you can have Vera whip something up. I'm far from finicky."

"Now you listen here—I don't know your name—" Iratov said with a scowl.

"Eugene. My name is Eugene."

"Well, Eugene, Vera has nothing to do with our . . ." He wanted to say 'business' but he edited his own inclination. "Problems. She can stay right where she is—but you can come see me."

"At your apartment?"

"Precisely."

"As a matter of fact, Vera has a great deal to do with our problems," he said, emphasizing the last two words. "A great deal! I know you're fuming right now, but please believe me, I am not a toreador, and I have no desire to thrust a sword into your heart!"

"Fuck! Just get over here, you weasel!"

When the buzzer went off and Mr. Iratov went over to the door, he'd already regained his composure, his powerful fingers gripping an engraved Makarov pistol. The desire to kill the stranger was so strong that Iratov was afraid he would snap and shoot him right through the forehead instead of in the leg.

"Who is it?"

"It's me, Eugene. However, I must ask you to put the weapon away. It has the potential to harm both of us."

Iratov raised the hand with the pistol, intending to strike the blackmailer with the butt when he came in while the other hand opened the lock for him. When Mr. Iratov saw the man's face, he instinctively lurched back. Standing in the door was . . . him—just thirty years younger. The black-clad youth was smiling, pale, and feeble-looking. Mr. Iratov lowered the pistol.

"Are you Svetlana's son?"

"Whose son? Ah, of course . . . No. I'm . . . how to put it . . . well, don't blow your top. Let's not stand here in the doorway, I really am quite hungry . . ."

"Follow me!" Mr. Iratov commanded, still holding the pistol, the barrel pointed at the ceiling.

"Alright . . ." They went into the kitchen. Mr. Iratov opened the grand refrigerator. "Be my guest!"

Eugene broke off a third of a baguette, grabbed some sliced pork roast with his hands, and began eating greedily. He took a bite out of a tomato and a red splash painted the wall. A fly— God knows why it had awakened in winter—instantly went for the bloody stain. He drank a bottle of Mozhaisk milk and politely released the air he'd swallowed into his clenched fist.

"You were saying?" Iratov inquired when the young man was finally wiping his mouth with a napkin.

"Yes, of course." Eugene coughed briefly, clearing his throat. "I am not Svetlana's son . . . I am . . . Well, how should

I put it . . . The flesh and blood of Andrei Iratov and Anna Rymnikova. Your parents . . ." Iratov felt an overwhelming desire to shoot him. His knuckles went white.

"Are you trying to say that we're brothers?"

"What? What are you talking about? Of course not!"

"So who are you?" Iratov was losing his composure again.

"I've already told you. Do you really not get it?"

"I'll blow your head off!"

"I am you! What don't you get?"

Mr. Iratov went up to the young man and pressed the muzzle of the pistol to his forehead. "Start talking. You have twenty seconds!"

"A short while ago, you lost a body part, a rather important one, under strange circumstances . . ."

"Who gave you that information? Sytin?"

"Oh no, Sytin has his own problems to deal with. May I ask you to move that pistol away from my brain?" Iratov trained it on Eugene's heart, worrying that Vera may've been the one responsible for the leak.

"Keep going!" he commanded.

"Your blood pressure is through the roof!"

"Yours is about to be nothing!"

"Why are you so dense?" Now Eugene was getting angry. "I'm trying to explain to you that I am the body part you lost! That's me!"

Iratov gave the young man a short, sharp blow to the head with the butt of his pistol, and he slid down the wall and on to the floor, staining the silk wallpaper with blood.

"Bastard!" Iratov barked, but Eugene couldn't hear him in his newly unconscious state.

Mr. Iratov settled into an armchair and studied the pale, placid face of this new arrival. His resentful rage had passed, and he was struggling to understand what all of this meant. These events seemed strange, to put it mildly, rather peculiar and theatrical. Iratov tried to systematize this information, starting with the recent past. The loss of his copulative organ, Sytin, the sapphire, the market downturn, his darling Vera . . . it all interwove into a knot of meaninglessness, but he had the strangest feeling he could see something inside.

"What nonsense!" Iratov said aloud.

He kept staring into the new arrival's pale face, seeing himself as a young speculator. He unexpectedly realized who the injured man was, got up, took a bottle of water out of the refrigerator and dumped half of it over his head. Eugene groaned but opened his eyes almost immediately.

"You really did hit me!"

"You really managed to piss me off."

"You just aren't listening to what I'm saying!" The young man touched his head and then looked at his bloody fingers. "Why did you have to go overboard like that? I didn't ask you for anything. I didn't do anything to you, and you're whacking me in the head with a gun . . ."

"Are you Vorontsova's son?"

"Oh come on! You have a logical brain. I'm barely eighteen, and Alevtina was killed in '84. So if I were her son, I would be thirty, at the absolute least. Do I look thirty?"

"No . . ." Iratov admitted, throwing his guest a kitchen towel. "Clean yourself up."

The young man gathered his wits and suggested deferring this conversation, inasmuch as it was going so poorly.

"Perhaps we should meet in the afternoon, once we've all settled down a bit?"

Mr. Iratov did some figuring. What might the risks be if this young man revealed such compromising information about him? "Well, how do things stack up?" he thought. "Suppose he says I'm missing my sexual organs. Who would believe him? What if he talks about Interlopin? There's nothing to tie me to some small-fry con getting murdered on the inside—I'm a distinguished citizen. He knows I lost some money. Who gives a damn?" No, he didn't see anything dangerous about it.

"Where?"

"Where will we meet, you mean?"

"Precisely."

"How about the Donskoy Cemetery?"

"Why a cemetery?"

"You've never been to your parents' grave before. I hope that being in their presence will make you calm enough to be no danger to me. Would five o'clock be convenient for you?"

"Sure."

Mr. Iratov did finally muster the resolve to go up to Vera's place. She greeted her husband with a bright-and-early smile, though it was fast approaching noon.

"How are you?" she asked, kissing him on the cheek.

Iratov thought back to the events of his day, from hearing that the market had crashed to paying himself a visit—nuts, right? Granted, he was about forty years younger, but still . . .

"Everything's fine, my darling."

"Well, that's marvelous. Have you had breakfast?"

"Yes, I got up very early. I'll have some coffee, though." Vera smiled her sublime smile and headed into the kitchen. Iratov studied her from behind and thought about how perfect she was: back straight as a ballerina's, flawlessly cast butt, and legs that made your head spin with their sheer interminability. His eyes filled with tears. Mr. Iratov turned away and hopelessly put one hand between his legs.

"Lord," he whispered. "I really do believe in you. And I

believe that your acts are always just . . . ! I give thanks to you, my Lord. May your hallowed name shine through the ages!" He thought of the suffering of Job, comparing it to his own and regained his confidence that instant. Job was the one who really had it rough . . . The Lord giveth when he sees fit and taketh away when he sees fit. Granted, the angels were the ones who stirred things up this time, but still . . .

Vera returned with a tray. She served the coffee and inquired if he would like a newspaper. He thanked her, but since he had already heard the news of the day, he ventured the opinion that it would be far more enjoyable to drink his coffee and look at her.

"Have you thought of something to do with the sapphire?"

"No . . . should I have?"

"No, not if you weren't so inclined. Would you like to come to the cemetery with me?"

"Has someone died?"

"Oh no. I'd like to visit my parents' grave . . ."

Iratov didn't know why he had invited Vera. It was like one of those troublemaker angels had pulled him along by the ear. But she was so happy for him she was nearly glowing; he was finally ready to do something he'd never done before, and not doing it for so long must have been weighing on his soul like some great sin. Perhaps now that sin would be forgiven, and his soul would be at peace . . .

"Good for you!" she said approvingly. She was also very pleased that he was taking her with him, treating her as the person closest to him, as his wife. In that instant, her desire to become a mother returned very strongly, to have this man's child and live happily ever after with him. He had seemingly overheard her longing.

"You do understand that my member is gone, right?" he

asked in such a casual, everyday tone that he might have been telling her he'd just had a shave.

"Yes . . ." Vera replied, her large eyes downcast.

"What do you think about a prosthetic?"

"That's for you to decide."

"Of course . . ." He finished his coffee, rose from his armchair, and promised his wife that he would come back for her at 4:30. For now, he was off to play doubles, as he did every Tuesday. "I have to sort myself out! I'm either half dead from quitting my meds, or I'm . . . well . . ." he said resignedly and then left.

Stacking the coffee service on the tray again, Vera thought despairingly that things would never be the same . . . The word "never" was as frightening as a terminal diagnosis. She was scared! Really scared . . .

9

I figured I would move in to Senescentova's place. After all, it was a private apartment, not a single room in a communal one like I had, and the deed was in my name. Sometimes it's good to change your place of residence, especially when you're drastically improving your living situation. I changed the sheets, got cozy on the old featherbed, and stuffed myself with chocolate-covered marshmallows—she had a strategic reserve of them. How come she bought so many? Then a savings book, marked "payable to bearer" fell out from under the mattress. The account held eighteen million rubles and change. On the first page, written in plain pencil, were the words "to my nephew." Oh auntie, you sweetheart! This wretched wanderer thanks you for not spending your wealth on yourself and leaving it for your faithful conversation partner to live on! You know how often I've found myself in need, and now all of my tribulations have been repaid in one fell swoop!

Fortunately, Senescentova also had an old rotary landline telephone.

I went to Sberbank, filled out the paperwork to withdraw a million rubles and handed it to the young teller, her eyes cloudy with sleep.

"An amount like that has to be requested in advance," the girl whined.

"An amount like what?" I asked angrily.

"Like the one you've indicated—"

"What?! Why on God's green earth should I have to request my own money?"

"Those are the rules!"

"Your manager!" I demanded.

"Grishechkin!" she called over her shoulder, then yawned cavernously. Was she raised in a barn? In answer to her summons, a pimply windbag of indeterminate age emerged from his glass box of an office, arranged his face into a smile, and came over.

"He's demanding a million rubles and my manager!" the girl explained.

"At your service," he said with a smile.

"Are you Grishechkin?"

"The same. Senior manager of this branch," the windbag answered, not without a certain degree of pride.

"I have no need for you, Grishechkin. I have a need for one million rubles. You are a means to that end. Just approve my withdrawal!"

"We have a rule about—"

"I hereby close my account and demand its balance, in full and in cash!" I announced, feeling perfectly relaxed; I had ample free time, and they had no other customers. "And you, Grishechkin, will be held personally responsible for the loss of a large account! You think the stars will favor you after that? Incidentally, what's your ethnicity?"

"I'm Russian . . ."

"Well, there you go. Your stars can align any way they please! There are no stars for . . . well, I won't burden you with that information. Just think about it, Grishechkin. There are a lot of people in this rat's nest who wouldn't mind taking your place in that fish tank!"

I was invited into the thirty-foot glass chamber that the senior manager wanted so desperately to keep. A machine provided me with coffee of dubious quality, the transparent walls closed their blinds, and Grishechkin began our interview.

"You were saying something about a star . . ."

"I'm always talking about the stars, my friend! Astrology is a subtle science, yet very reliable."

"So you're an astrologer?"

"I know a thing or two." Grishechkin's face flared with curiosity at this. He had always been eager to believe in anything and anyone: faith healers, sorcerers, the president, and, of course, astrology. He had a very important question about the future . . .

"I am hereby authorizing you to withdraw a million rubles!" the senior manager said decisively. "The girls go too far sometimes. That's understandable—they don't have a million rubles to withdraw! But could you give me your professional opinion on something?"

"Are you a Gemini?"

"How did you—"

"All I had to do was look at you. I work proactively. You were born at 8:45 on the ninth—"

"Oh my God!" Grishechkin threw his hands in the air.

"No," I said, crossing myself. "I am not Him. I am an astrologer. You, Grishechkin, have nothing to worry about. Elena Glassova might not love you, but she will marry you. She sees promise in you. That Khabarovsk country lady of yours needs to bring her daughter up somehow, and she'll need money to do it!" The senior manager listened, mouth agape.

"What dau—" he eventually gasped.

"I see that you don't know about her daughter?"

"No, of course not! That's the stars for you . . ."

"Well, if they favor you, she may be sent to an orphanage. But anyway, do not weary me with your nickel-and-dime problems, just give me my million rubles for this information!"

"But . . . but . . ." The manager's expression instantly turned gloomy.

"Women are all bitches!" I said bracingly. "They have been since time immemorial. Ever since Eve. She was the Ur-bitch! So how about that million?"

"Just a moment." The manager put his sprawling signature to the document.

"Good goin'! As my way of saying thank you, I'll tell you that Elena Glassova's daughter suffers from mental retardation, so your beloved's pedigree is subject to question. Do you really want a mentally retarded child?"

"It's all so . . ." Grishechkin mumbled incomprehensibly in response.

"Well, the good news is that you will live a long life and die on your birthday."

Leaving Grishechkin's office behind, I went over to the little window and handed the half-asleep teller my signed document. The electronic counter portioned out two hundred five-thousand-ruble bills. The money was separated into two bricks and passed over to me, granting me the right of free pilotage.

"Don't lose it, mister!" the girl cautioned.

"You should have the birthmark on your right breast removed. That's why your boyfriend doesn't want you. Not that he can do much for you anyway . . ." I headed for the door, but Grishechkin wailed after me before I could leave.

"Hey! How long am I going to live for?"

"Live as long as ya want!" I replied. Nobody could take those thirty-two years from him. Then he'd drown in the bathtub—that would be Little Ms. Barbiturate's way to acquire his worldly possessions.

I went to a nearby café that specialized in crepes. I put away a couple hundred, accompanied by sour cream and honey. I could have had more, but the waitress was looking at me like I was some kind of monster.

"I won this year's European Crepe Speed-Eating Championship," I informed the eatery attendant. "I have a medal and everything. Want to see it?"

"I'd rather see some money."

I paid my bill, finished my seventh cup of tea, and peered through the glass window, watching the people plodding through the falling snow. Almost all of them looked despondent, like the majority of the population inhabiting the East European Plain. Conceived without joy, they live in sorrow. How are they to know that the snow falling around them is a blessing? Everything that comes from above is a joy, nothing that comes from below is any good. Let's say a man goes ass over teakettle, bangs his head on the ice, and dies. If he's fortunate enough to hit the back of his head, he'll die facing the sky—but if he should perish with his mug in the dirt, that is a cosmic disaster.

Lost in thought, I remembered Grishechkin, and the magical coil of that memory led me to another story directly tied to Iratov.

When Alevtina Vorontsova was killed, when she was already dead and under the scalpel, relinquishing her progeny to the world, when Iratov strode past the neonatal ward and saw the pink heel of an infant sharing his surname, I was right there, in the role of happy father. I don't mean I had a child, I mean I was losing myself in that dramatic role. As Mr. Iratov walked past me, I looked into his eyes and easily discerned his cruel heart. Vengeance had been taken. He seemed to have triumphed. I am not at all opposed to vengeance, myself. Order could not exist without it, whatever you mighta heard about eyes and cheeks—the old law is truer than the new . . . Well, Iratov had been avenged without having to get his hands dirty. He celebrated his liberation, his deliverance, in all of Moscow's finest restaurants, while I held his child in my arms—and this was no Peterson, he was an Iratov, the newborn fruit of Arseny's loins. One mishap did await the doctors, who would state the next morning that the infant's brain was 80 percent sabotaged by oxygen deprivation and what have you. A terrible sentence would be passed on the baby; the best he could hope for was to develop to the level of a three-year-old and be sent to a special institution. They did track down Captain Vorontsova's relatives, but they flatly refused to take on a "future retard." There you have it, conceived without joy!

Iratov's baby boy was very handsome, which helped him to survive his first three years in the reformatory nursery. Very few lived to such a venerable age. The entirely unkind caretakers, who were prone to stealing the food meant for the wretched children, looked into the boy's deep black eyes and experienced something akin to religious reverence. When he reached three and his black hair grew to his shoulders, the caretakers started to view him as an angel. A little raven angel. They doted on him, to the extent that was possible in such a state institution, fed him amply, and even brought him morsels from home.

The young Iratov was named Joseph in honor of the Nobel Prize-winning poet who was expelled from the USSR for social parasitism. Yevdokia, a young caretaker, came up with that name. She was very young, no more than sixteen, and had come to the capital from Yakutia. She was half Buryat, and "Joseph" struck her as a classic Russian name. Yevdokia's own biological father, the second secretary of the regional Communist Party committee, did not acknowledge her, since she was born unofficially, hastily conceived in a reindeer-hide tent. The young woman, who'd already been betrothed to the foremost local herdsman, was taken by force at a Party conference. The Party man ripped off her furs and thoroughly enjoyed the local color. That was how Yevdokia came into the world with narrow eyes, pale skin,

and a lovely figure. She grew up among the reindeer and studied the only book in her tent. It was a manuscript that, according to legend, had been left behind by her biological father when
he raped her mother. It turned out that the Party man read samizdat on the side and had a taste for the sublime. That taste was
the origin of Dasha, as Yevdokia's mother called her. The reindeer herder who married her just couldn't accept another man's
spawn; he drank for a few years and then died along with his
herd, which was decimated by some sullen illness. Once Dasha
was old enough, she left her hopeless situation for Moscow,
where she found a caretaker job at an orphanage for mentally
challenged children at sixty rubles a month—barely enough to
live on. She tirelessly emptied the potties, washed urine-stained
sheets, fed the infants with a spoon—basically, she was always
on her feet. What little free time she had was devoted to baby
Joseph. She even tried to teach him to talk. It was all in vain,
though; despite his angelic appearance, the child was absolutely
vacant and emotionless . . . The rest of the staff consisted of
aging women lacking any semblance of education who called
their charges "vegetables." Only Ms. Bella Yurieva, the director of the facility, had been accredited by an institution of higher
learning. Her nasty, grubbing subordinates just called her "the
college bitch."

Lingering over the daily goings-on of a Soviet residential
facility is hardly enjoyable and far from necessary. The only
thing that can be lingered on here—briefly—is little Joseph's
relationship with his caretaker Dasha. When the time came
for the boy to leave the facility as the last survivor from his
group, he snuggled up to Dasha's knees like they belonged to
his own mother, and the compassionate girl burst into sobs
from the coming loss of her favorite. For the first time, the boy
had showed a sign of emotional expression, which stirred her

youthful soul. She dried her eyes, appeared before the director, and asked if she could keep Joseph—i.e., adopt him. This question prompted the director to think that it wasn't just her charges that were idiots—that applied to her staff as well. What else could she expect from an Eskimo, though?

"But you're just a kid, too! How old are you anyway?" she asked with faint disdain.

"I turned eighteen last month."

"So what do you want this degenerate for? He was born without a foreskin, for God's sake—wretched thing!"

"Now I love him with all my heart!" explained the guileless Dasha. "He's beautiful and harmless, like a little flower!"

"And do you realize that this little flower is going to start smacking you around when it grows up? Right now he's like a wolf pup, meek and sweet, but when he turns fifteen and the hormones hit that brainless head of his, he'll break your neck and not even remember he did it!"

"You shouldn't be like that, Ms. Yurieva!" said Dasha, going pale. "Not everything in life is so bad. There are miracles, too—"

"What will you live on, you dope?"

"The Lord will guide me—"

"Like hell he will! You'll get tired of him and give him back to the orphanage. You aren't the first and you won't be the last! And if you fall in love, it's a short way to smothering him to get him out of the way. We had this one tenderhearted nurse that took a Down syndrome girl home. Then a gentleman caller came into the picture, and when the question of him or the wretch came up, it was answered promptly. A pillow over her face and it went down on paper as an accident. Then the murderess and her gentleman had a baby, and it was a girl with Down syndrome. Talk about an irony of fate!"

"People are all different, Ms. Yurieva. I'm not like that at all."

Hardened as it was by her profession, Ms. Yurieva's heart could feel that Dasha really was a good girl, self-sacrificing, like the Russian women in movies from the fifties. Much to her own surprise, she went over to Dasha, patted her on the head, and drew her to her ample breast.

"Alright, alright! Listen to your heart! You can stay in the dormitory for now, and you'll work here like before. You can bring Joseph, and we'll give him a little extra to eat. He'll get free clothes, too. How does that sound?"

"Thank you, you're so sweet!" Dasha grabbed her director's hand and started kissing it. Ms. Yurieva snatched her hand back and turned away, hiding her own meager tears by studying the portrait of the minister of health.

That was how Joseph Iratov's fate was decided—for a time, at least.

It would be equally pointless to get bogged down in the details of Dasha's trials and tribulations, how hard the life of a girl trying to raise such an unfortunate child was, what was going on in Joseph's dark soul. Yeah, it was tough going, but that's just how it goes . . .

I, on the other hand, undertook a series of attempts to compel Arseny, Joseph's true father, to help raise his offspring, unwanted as he might have been. I sent the young architect and businessman an anonymous letter, in which I tried to persuade him to be involved in the life of his deficient firstborn, even if it was only financially.

"Go screw yourself!" was the swift and decidedly disgusting response to my general-delivery letter.

I am a hot-tempered gentleman, most keen and vengeful. In reply to his "Go screw yourself," I sent Iratov a subsequent missive, in which I insinuated knowledge of several critical details of his criminal deeds and promised to reveal his unlawful activity to the relevant law enforcement agencies. I almost immediately received an invitation to meet by the Gogol statue on a dark November night.

I prepared for the rendezvous exactingly, not wishing to reveal my true appearance to Iratov. As previously mentioned, I have experience as a makeup artist. I attached a goatee and whiskers, aged up my face—the bags under my eyes were especially well-executed, if I do say so myself—and put on a wig with a little bald spot. I arrived shortly before the designated time and surveyed the area. My watch showed two minutes past eleven when a human shadow appeared near the bronze figure of the great Russian writer, and then the entity itself emerged from behind the pedestal. I peered into the darkness, trying to discern Iratov, straining my eyes to the breaking point. Was it him or not? When the tension was at its peak, someone who had come up from behind whispered right in my ear.

"Are you here to meet Arseny Iratov?"

"Yes," I replied, without even turning around.

"Mr. Iratov has a message for you."

"Well?"

"Here!" Instead of a written message, I received a powerful blow to the back of the head with some kind of metallic object and collapsed into the wet snow like a tree that had outlived its Christmas. Out of the corner of my eye, I managed to spot a dark figure peeling itself away from the monument and darting in my direction.

They weren't beating me up. They were killing me. First the blows rained down on the back of my head, then homemade lead knuckles were smashing my teeth, breaking my jaw and eyebrow ridges. One of the villains gouged my eye out, whispering,

"Die, bitch!" Then they both started kicking me with their sharp, heavy boots. Back then, it was fashionable to stick pieces of lead in your footwear to make your lower extremities the ideal tools for smashing ribs and internal organs.

"To hell with this," I thought. "I should just die already." I stopped breathing. They kept beating me for a while, until they were convinced that my body was dead and, therefore, my personhood had perished. Then they let up.

"Gone?" one of them asked.

"Oh yeah," the second man replied. The criminals took a polaroid of my corpse and left to file their report. Just to be safe, I lay there a while longer, unmoving, all ears. You never know, those malefactors might have had a guy hang back to finish me off, if necessary. The coast was clear, though, so I started getting up—slowly, so as not to misplace my bashed-out teeth—and peered around with my one eye. Rising to my knees, I suddenly saw a three-ruble bill, goaded along by the wind, catching the dim glow of the streetlights, twisting faintly as it flew past me, as if it had a specific target in mind. Snatching the money, I was unutterably pleased that I would now be able to hail a taxi and return home in comfort, without the risk of being detained by a police patrol.

I caught a cab with surprising speed and bade the driver make for Dorogomilovskaya Street, where I resided at the time. The older driver did not even glance at me in his rearview mirror; he simply nodded and stepped on the gas. My journey lasted a mere six minutes. We pulled up to my apartment building, and I extended the three-ruble bill to the driver, muttering with my maimed mouth for him to keep the change. I had opened the door and was halfway out of the car when the driver yelled.

"Stop!" I did, without turning around.

"I'm not going anywhere."

"What's this you gave me?" The driver switched on the light and turned around, waving my three-ruble bill.

"It's three rubles," I explained, revealing my destroyed face to the driver in the process, but he seemed to think it was no business of his that I was almost a corpse: bashed-out teeth, missing eye, blood everywhere. He continued shaking the bill, and what he had to say was most curious.

"This is from before the reform! It was taken out of circulation in '61! You want another punch in that bloody mug of yours? Give me some real money!"

Well, how do you like that? An optical illusion! A kink of fate! A pre-reform bill—that's just the damnedest thing. How did it show up in our time, just blowing down the street at night?

"How about an exchange?" I offered. "You brought me home, so I will reveal a piece of information that will be worth three rubles to you."

"What? What information?" The taxi driver was getting more and more agitated. "I have a quota to make!"

"Your little daughter, Svetlana, who lives with you and your spouse, has an abscess on her lower third tooth. I assure you, no mouthwash will do her any good. Furthermore, you must take the girl to the hospital immediately so it can be lanced, otherwise the rot will make its way to her brain before morning!"

The older man stared at me, mouth open. Pictures were flashing in his mind of little Svetlana's suffering, her cheek swollen with periostitis. He realized that the situation could end tragically.

"Jesus Christ, Son of God—" that's all he managed to utter.

"No, I'm not! I'm not the Son or the Father!"

"Can I go?" the driver asked.

"Godspeed!" I said graciously, now that the exchange had been completed. The tires of the checker-patterned Volga screeched, and it sped into the opaque night. I climbed the stairs to my communal apartment, turned on the light in the entryway, and instantly crashed into Old Lady Morozova, who was sneaking toward the bathroom in her slip.

"Viy!" she pronounced. "It's a ghost!" She slammed the bathroom door behind her.

"Don't forget to turn off the light!" I reminded her and went into the room with the bathtub, where, fortunately for me, I did not encounter any of my neighbors. I shed my clothes and examined my face with my one eye. I wasn't much of a Viy, but I could certainly have passed for a plane crash survivor. All of my front teeth—typically situated in my mouth—were now in my fist. I washed them in the sink and stuck them back in my gums one by one. I washed off all the blood, felt my broken bones, and trudged off toward my room in my underwear. I ran into Old Lady Morozova again in the hallway.

"The cyclops!" she squeaked.

"Don't you want to wash your hands?" I inquired, then quickly headed to my room without waiting for an answer. As I shut my door, I realized that I had left my street clothes in the bathroom. I didn't give a damn. I settled into bed posthaste and slept until December.

I woke up to a brisk day with the new year just around the corner, feeling wonderful. The eye they'd gouged out had healed, and now I had the sight of an eagle. My bones had knitted themselves back together perfectly, and every last tooth had taken root. I called again, but there was no answer. Not enough time had gone by.

"Well, well, my dear Mr. Iratov," I released a decisive sigh. "It's time I set to work on you in earnest, since you did try to kill me and all . . . and I offered no resistance, though it was in my power to do so . . ."

I walked out of my room, and, much to my chagrin, all of my neighbors were at home due to the fact that I had awakened on a Saturday. Someone was frying potatoes with salo, arousing my appetite, and someone else had occupied the bathroom and was apparently playing war in there. Old Lady Morozova was nearby, sitting on a piece of shared furniture in the hallway and observing the bubbling activity of our communal apartment. I passed her on the way to the shower, little towel on my shoulder, when she spoke.

"Boy, you're made of stern stuff! You just won't croak!"

"I bid you be well too! Burials are getting so expensive lately, you wouldn't believe it! Cremation is a lot more affordable!" Then I finally got to shave. The confident face of a hale and hearty man looked back at me from the mirror. I stepped into the kitchen.

"Would you salo enthusiasts care to tell me who absconded with my clothes?"

The fat-bottomed middle-aged ladies didn't say anything; they just clicked their knives even louder as they cut up their respective ingredients. The smell of salo and potatoes grew even stronger. Only Medvedev, our eligible bachelor, answered, coffeepot in hand.

"What was even left of those clothes? They were all torn and bloody. Did ya kill someone?"

"Well, where are they?"

"Washed 'em and ripped 'em up for rags . . ."

I went back to my room and put on my athletic clothes. In view of my lack of other footwear, I stuffed my feet into my ski boots, left the apartment, and got down to business. I knew where Iratov had hidden his ill-gotten gains. I walked to Donskoy Monastery and then went into the cemetery. Even before he went to prison, Iratov had bought up several burial plots. Two for his parents, as I understand it, and two in reserve, hopefully for himself—guess he likes to stretch out. He had placed granite plaques at the heads of the graves, but there were no inscriptions, since nobody had died yet. The plaque at plot 432 moved easily, positioned as it was on a wheeled track. This was home to one of Iratov the speculator's secret stashes.

Once I'd moved the plaque out of the way, I extracted a little bundle wrapped in plastic. I rooted around inside, finding a brick of foreign currency and a transparent stone the size of a dove's egg. Then I put the now empty bundle back and defecated into the hiding place. Only after the deed was done did I replace the plaque.

I spent a few minutes outside the Shabolovskaya metro station, begging for a two-kopek coin. Some college girl gave it to me and asked me where my skis were.

"My skis are always on the track, Miss!"

"I like skate skiing myself," the little coed offered, holding out another two-kopek coin. "Here, take this too!"

"May you marry well!" I said gratefully and ducked into the phone booth. I dialed the number and waited for an answer.

"Hello, Mr. Iratov!"

"Hello . . . who is this?"

"I am the gentleman whom you saw fit to murder a month ago—and in cruel fashion, I might add—rather than help your own son."

"You lived? Boy, you're tough!"

"Drop the sentimentality, Mr. Iratov. I warned you that I was privy to certain information. Now I have been forced to take more decisive action. I just visited Donskoy Cemetery, where I took ten thousand dollars and a twenty-karat diamond for the boy."

"Bastard!"

"Oh, and I almost forgot! I took a shit in the hole, too!" I hung up.

Retaining several hundred for myself, I—naturally—passed the money on to the narrow-eyed Dasha—not directly, but through an anonymous transfer, including a note reading, "So your little son will be happy!"

I exchanged the money at Tishinka and then bought myself some clothes. You can't really walk around in a ski suit all day, can you? A tail was put on me, but I ditched it neatly by ducking into the metro and blending in with the crowd . . .

I toiled away in despair, creating several brilliant plans that were meant to chip away at Mr. Iratov's covert power, to trip up this man who was accelerating to terrible, all-destroying speed like some mighty ship. Sublime thoughts took shape in my head, each more vivid than the next, and I smiled in anticipation of the thunderous downfall of Arseny Iratov.

Two weeks later, I dialed the number of the abovementioned gentleman. I suddenly encountered a feminine timbre, informing me that her precious Arseny wasn't there.

"When will he be back?"

"Never," the woman replied, with sorrow in her voice.

"Is he dead?!" I exclaimed, unable to contain myself.

"What? How could you say a thing like that? Surely you walk without the Lord!" As it happens, I was in fact walking with Him.

"Well, what happened, then?"

"My precious Arseny has emigrated . . ."

"So it follows that you're his mommy."

"Yes, I am his mother," the woman answered proudly. "And who might you be?"

"Where did he emigrate to?"

"Israel."

"Israel? The Holy Land?"

"For now, yes . . ."

"But he isn't Jewish!"

"He found something on his father's side."

"So what is it that you are cooking?" I asked. "I smell fish."

"That's just it . . . jellied fish . . ."

"You love jellied fish, huh?"

"My husband is partial to it . . . and my precious Arseny loves it . . ."

"Your precious Arseny loves his belly. If he loved fish, he'd throw them back in the lake, or the river, or whatever!"

"I see what you're doing!" Iratov's mommy suddenly sounded strict. "I may be an English teacher, but I have a decent feel for the Russian language, too. You're using 'love' in the Christian sense of the word, loving a person—but it has other meanings, too. You can say you love potatoes with herring, champagne, or even yourself! Why not? But what lake should you throw yourself in?" This lady was far from dumb; she was just lost in a whirlpool of misapprehensions.

"I am not speaking from any sort of Christian position! It is sheer impertinence to say so!"

"Are you a Mussulman?"

"Perish the thought!"

"Then what?"

"That's the question!" I declared grandly. "Bull's-eye! Where should a man throw himself back! Your question already contains an error of cosmic import. Man has no right to let himself go anywhere. He is not a horse. Man must force himself to follow a defined path. The clearer and more conscious that path, the more defined his future!"

"I get it. You're in a cult."

"Of course!" I agreed, disappointed. "That conclusion

follows directly from what I've just said, doesn't it? I won't keep you. Your fish will dry out if you leave it in the oven too long!"

"Hang on, who are you? Are you one of my son's comrades? And how did you know I was cooking fi—"

"A tick that can't make rent in Moscow is a fit comrade for your son!" I hung up.

Hearing Iratov's mother say that he had emigrated almost took the ground out from under my feet. Due to certain circumstances (my periodic calls), I could not leave Russia, and I would have to postpone hounding Iratov until better days.

For some reason, I trudged off to the barbershop, where Antipatros gave me a shave and a haircut, silent as always, unmoved by the fact that I'd had my tonsorial needs attended to just two days ago. Back so soon? He, too, had to pick up the phone sometimes and listen to the unresponsive cosmos, so he didn't give a damn how often his clients visited.

I went home pissed off, like a bull who had been prevented from goring a stumbling toreador. Plus, my neighbors stuck their noses into the hallway to give me challenging looks. Old Lady Morozova was peering at me with particular suspicion, as if she would personally be entrusted with shooting me after my sentence was passed.

"Well, what are you gawking at?" I inquired. The apartment community was tongue-tied, shifting from foot to foot, until Medvedev the Bachelor steeled himself for his speech.

"You have lived in our apartment for two years already," he finally began.

"And?"

"We don't even know your last name! Not to mention your first name."

"And?"

Medvedev the Bachelor tried to continue, but Old Lady

Morozova beat him to it. "We don't trust you, hon! We suspect you might be an enemy of the people."

"Is that a fact? Are you going to hang me now or may I visit the water closet first?"

"We want to write a letter to the authorities about you," Medvedev the Bachelor continued. "You are a suspicious person! You show up covered in blood! First you've got nothing but a ski suit, then you're dressed to the nines!" he exclaimed with an oratorical sweep of his hands.

"And he doesn't come out of his den for months on end!" Old Lady Morozova added. "What does he live on?!"

"Yeah, yeah," whispered the rest of the neighbors, hiding little kids that smelled of dirty diapers behind their mighty backsides.

"Well, what's the problem, comrades? You can write to anyone you want!"

"But we don't know your full legal name!" Medvedev the Bachelor persisted. "We don't know who to report!"

"Pardon me," I began indignantly. "I have to pay for the electricity, gas, water, and radio just like everybody else. How do you imagine they collect my money with no legal name?" I loomed over Old Lady Morozova with my entire frame. "Don't you see a little issue here, Grandma Yaga? Or are you accusing me of not paying my bills?"

"No, all of your bills have been paid on time," Medvedev the Bachelor conceded.

"Well, they have my name on them, smart guy!"

"Now you pardon me!" said the bachelor, increasingly convinced of the rightness of his case. "I have the form right here! You wrote 'E' under first name, 'E' under patronymic, and 'E' under last name! So your full name is, what, EEE?"

"Precisely," I said with a nod. "Let me take this opportunity to introduce myself to those of you who don't know me. My name is EEE."

"There's no such name!" the old lady wheezed. "EEE! Hully gully!" she screeched.

"That's right!" every other little Mrs. Communal Apartment and her husband chimed in.

"Shall I show you my ID?"

"Please," Medvedev agreed. I fished my ID out of my inner pocket and held it out in front of me. Old Lady Morozova was about to grab for it, but the bachelor beat her to it and began to read.

"First name... 'E,'" he stated. "Patronymic and last name... 'E' and 'E.'"

"It's a fake!" the old lady wailed.

"Oh shut up, you fucking hag!" Medvedev snapped, then regained his composure and continued studying my ID. "Ethnicity . . . Altic . . . I don't know, maybe they meant to write 'Baltic' and they left off a letter?"

"Certainly not, comrades! The people of the Baltic lands belong to numerous different ethnicities, and I will have you know that I am Altic!" I said indignantly.

"What the heck is that?" asked the old lady, showing no sign of shutting up. "Are you Jewish?"

"I'm honored you would think so," I said with a nod. "But no . . ."

"So where ya really come from then?" one of the big-bottomed mommies chimed in modestly. I paused theatrically, cast my eyes toward the ceiling, then lowered them to the dirty floor, and answered the common folk just as modestly.

"I am the son of Comandante Che."

Suddenly, the silence of the grave reigned in that communal corridor. I could hear Old Lady Morozova's stomach rumbling.

"So your father was . . . Che Guevara? Is that what you're

saying?" asked Medvedev the Bachelor once he had collected himself again.

"The same."

"But then what are you doing here?" asked one of the bolder mommies.

"This is where the authorities placed me," I said, extending my hands. "This is a minor affair . . ."

"How come they didn't give you your own apartment?" she asked, trembling with malice.

"Shut up, Irina!" Medvedev the Bachelor commanded. He must've actually been living with her in a common-law marriage, so the kid was his bastard. "They're hiding the guy, don't you get it? They know what they're doing!" He examined my ID further. "His official place of residence matches. Watch out, Morozova. When you give up the ghost, Comrade E will get your room!"

"I don't give two puffs on a guerilla's pipe what happens after I give up the ghost! Especially what happens to my room! Well, there you have it. Got a comandante living with us!" The old lady was no fool, I had to give her that. I immediately suggested organizing a feast that very evening to celebrate the restoration of harmony in the communal apartment.

"It'll be my treat, of course!" I added. "And let's move a few more tables in here, otherwise all the food won't fit!" The community's mood changed at this. A free lunch can make the dead rise from their graves and the executioner and his victim switch places.

"Hurrah!" The woman who cohabitated with Medvedev cheered like a young Pioneer.

"Hurrah!" seconded the rest of the neighbors. Only Old Lady Morozova was nervously shifting her dentures around in her mouth.

"Oh, and could I have my ID back?" I asked.

"Of course, of course!" Medvedev handed it to me and added that if we would be enjoying some vodka at our banquet, he just so happened to have a jar of salted milkcap mushrooms that would pair well.

"It'll all be my treat!"

"What time?"

"I think seven o'clock would be perfect! Sound good, comrades?"

"Sounds good!" my neighbors agreed. I locked myself in my room and, without getting undressed, spent a long time listening to the phone ringing. Nobody picked up. I had no desire to celebrate with my communal apartment neighbors, all those ex-Party members and representatives of the lumpen proletariat. Especially after such a resounding failure with Iratov.

10

Iratov and his darling Vera pulled up to Donskoy Monastery right on time. They bought some flowers there at the gate and walked arm in arm between two rows of trees and up to the Church of the Icon of the Mother of God. Only Vera went in, crossing herself at the entrance and once again in response to voices singing last rites for a departed soul by the name of Zimmerman — probably a convert. Then Vera went to the kiosk, bought forty days of prayer for Iratov, wrote some notes for so-and-so's health and in so-and-so's memory. She collected her candles and left two large bills for the lady who worked at the kiosk.

"Whatever is left over is for the church!" she instructed.

She approached the icon and lit her first candle. She asked the Mother of God to intercede for her, to work a miracle and give her a chance to experience the joy of motherhood . . . The young woman placed some of the flowers in a vase beneath the image, crossed herself, bowed, and then withdrew. She spent some time vacillating about whether or not she should approach the crucifix, but, for some reason, contemplating what the result might be provoked fear in her, so she ran away from Christ and toward Iratov.

"How come all the candles?" he asked.

"You can never have too many. We'll put them on your parents' graves." They spent quite a while trying to find them.

"Everything's different!' Iratov said, trying to justify himself, although it had been a long time since anything had changed at the cemetery of Donskoy Monastery. It was a historic place, and there were very few burials, with the exception of laying bodies to rest in or near existing graves when the spots were bought up. Even the crematorium was gone—the black smoke from its chimney was too scary . . .

The thing is, Iratov had never been to the cemetery where his parents were buried. He had issued all the relevant instructions by telephone from New York, and his people had organized everything and filmed the process. Iratov and Vera had to go to the cemetery director's office and stand in line. Then they found themselves in the tiny room where the director earned his burial fees. The way he greeted the new arrivals was far from friendly; he even tried to excoriate them for neglecting to pay the monthly fee for maintaining the burial plots, but Iratov thwarted that attempt with one look, making it clear to the director that he was dealing with a personage of colossal significance who could step on him like it was nothing, squash him without even noticing.

"I humbly ask your forgiveness," the master of the dead said, tempering justice with mercy. "I didn't recognize you!" He extended his tremendously broad hand. "Gleb Aristarkhov!"

Iratov didn't shake hands; he merely shared what he had observed.

"You have dug your fair share of graves . . ."

"I worked my way up through the ranks," the director agreed.

"Which boss did you work for? Back in the nineties, I mean."

"I don't follow. How about a spot of tea? It's awfully cold out there!"

"The Izmailovo gang maybe?"

"Oh well, you know what it was like back then . . ."

"The Izmailovo gang still has some pull around here . . ."

"I'm an old hand and this is an old business. Who are you with? Feels like I've seen you around . . ."

"I'm a 'have gun, will travel' type. Would you mind showing us the graves, my good man?"

"Not at all!"

Single file, like ducks, they walked down a narrow path in the snow trod by previous visitors, moving farther and farther from the main entrance. They passed the grave of Maya Kristalinskaya, a singer Iratov could remember well from black-and-white TV. The engraved faces of war heroes, distinguished Soviet workers, generals, actors, and artists followed their progress with their sad eyes.

"Almost there," the director said encouragingly. Vera's feet were freezing in her thin, elegant boots, but she didn't show it, just curled her toes to try and get some blood flowing.

"You don't shovel the snow!" Iratov said irritably. It had gotten into his pant leg and started clumping around his ankle.

"Well, nobody pays, so no shoveling gets done."

"Fair enough . . ."

"Here we are. Your graves are on the other side of this wall," the director informed them. "The walk back will be easier now that you've made a path through the snow. There they are, over there!"

Iratov and his darling Vera stood near the fence dividing the graves and looked at the discolored engravings on the stones. The graves themselves had sunk into the fresh snow, and a red-breasted cemetery robin was pecking at the frozen berries on a rowan tree.

"Shall I be on my way?" the director asked.

"Okay."

"I will be in my office if you need anything." He took the same path back. Iratov held Vera, and they stood in silence.

Out of the corner of his eye, Mr. Iratov saw the stoop-shouldered figure of Eugene trudging up the path in his black garments. His black hair fluttered in the winter wind, and Iratov found himself involuntarily admiring his copy.

"I'm going to try and find some kind of shovel," Vera said. "Or a broom, at the very least." She gave her husband the flowers, saying that they should be put on a clean grave. Eugene approached Iratov as soon as she had walked away.

"I'm not late, am I?" the young man asked. "I don't have a watch, you see . . ."

"Right on time," Mr. Iratov answered.

"They were wonderful people," Eugene said, bowing his head.

Iratov had difficulty containing his irritation. If it were up to him, he would have blown Eugene's black-haired head off and stuck his corpse next to Ivan Burygin, a business owner whose bust was gazing at them from the other side of the path with the confidence of a bulldog.

"How's it going?"

"You're angry again!"

"How would you like me to feel?"

"Feel some humility! You'll have to sooner or later!"

"Aren't you afraid I'll rub you out?"

"Rubbing me out is like shooting yourself—"

"Quit your yapping! This is all gibberish."

"Do you remember you had this little birthmark on your tool? The one they burned off with liquid nitrogen when you were little?" Iratov glared. "The one that looked like the letter V? Over time, the spot became almost invisible . . ." Eugene suddenly tossed his coat into the snow and pulled his sweater up to his neck, revealing his back—a pale pink V covered its entire expanse. "Look! Do you see it?"

Iratov looked at Eugene and thought that this was a surreal situation worthy of Dali. Some young man assiduously trying to prove to some personage that he is his sexual organ! Well, the loss of that aforementioned article was already no less absurd than the works of Kafka.

"Put your clothes back on!" Iratov commanded. Eugene pulled on his sweater and slid back into his coat. He was trembling faintly from the cold, but he looked at Iratov questioningly.

"Did you see it?"

"Yes."

"You handled me well, I have to give you that! You're a virtuoso, it was like Paganini wielding his violin, the way you—"

"Oh, shut up already!" Vera had appeared from behind the wall, leading two grave keepers—they had the faces of alcoholics, but at least they were armed with shovels. "So, basically, you're my long-lost son Eugene. I've only just met you myself," Mr. Iratov commanded.

"Got it," the young man agreed. "There's no need to befuddle a fainthearted woman."

At the next plot over, Iratov suddenly saw the face of an old lady. She was somehow familiar. He figured she was probably some Moscow Art Theatre actress. It was only that night that he would remember the legendary Senescentova, who took up residence in the young architect's first building, where she welcomed him with linden-blossom tea and chocolate-covered marshmallows . . . When he turned away from the old lady, he saw Vera with such indescribable surprise on her face that his own contorted in response, but Eugene's expressive, sinful features made Iratov freeze like a statue once again. They did look the same, that was true . . .

"My son Eugene," Mr. Iratov said, introducing his copy. "My wife, Vera . . ."

"Ah . . . the resemblance is staggering . . ." She extended her hand in its elegant kidskin glove. Eugene shook it gently, but that "gently" caused instant changes all through Vera's body, as if every particle of her had changed its charge from minus to plus. Her legs were suddenly warm, and it was like someone was unceremoniously investigating all the most intimate parts of her body, and she was delighting in these manipulations, like the whore of Babylon.

"Well now!" Iratov's voice wrenched his wife free from the bondage of her illusions. "Time to get the snow off these graves. Get to work, guys."

"The gal promised we'd be gettin' five hundred each," the older grave keeper stated.

"Well, there you have it," Iratov said with a smile. "Just do it quick!"

"Can't do it quick," the younger one objected. "Wouldn't want to scratch the marble. Gotta do it slow and steady."

"Well, get going!" The workers proceeded to their objective and began dexterously clearing the snow.

"I've never heard of you before," Vera admitted uneasily.

"Well, I only just found out about him myself," Mr. Iratov said, patting Eugene on the back. "I thought he was an impostor, but how could I not believe him with that face?"

"The resemblance is striking," Vera conceded. "Who is your mother?"

"My mother? She's . . . dead."

"Why did you never make yourself known before?"

"The powers that be prevented me from doing so."

"Well, thank God you've joined us now." Eugene smiled, enjoying Vera's courteous welcome.

"Should we clean the pictures?" the senior worker inquired.

"With due caution," Iratov said imperiously. Something about the worker's face seemed familiar, but then he shifted his focus to his darling Vera's eyes, to that bright, sunray look that was usually reserved for him. Now all the luxury of her gaze was directed at Eugene. Mr. Iratov wanted to get angry, nip these childish glances in the bud with a harsh growl, but no anger was forthcoming in his breast, no matter how hard he searched.

"Will you be visiting us for a while?" Vera inquired, her curiosity piqued.

"Well, I was robbed by a rather slick thug on the train. He took my money and ID and for some reason saw fit to bash me upside the head, too. It all worked out, though, since I spent a warm, well-fed night at the hospital . . ."

"That's just awful!" Vera said, fluttering her frost-tinged eyelashes. "We're going to help Eugene, aren't we?"

"Well . . ." Iratov said, clearly vacillating.

"You know how hard it is for young people these days. We have to help him get his ID back at least!"

"Thank you," Eugene said.

"We'll help him," Iratov agreed.

"That's it, chief." Iratov turned toward the voice and found himself face-to-face with the older grave keeper. "All done. Gimme that thousand!"

"Lyosha?!" Iratov asked, recognizing him at last.

"Yes, I'm Aleksei Ivanov."

"Lyosha, the bartender! Do you remember the Lira? The way we partied, the stuff we pulled!" The past flared up in his eyes but then burned out.

"No, I don't remember . . ."

"What? Come on, you were my currency middleman!"

"You're confusing me with someone else . . ."

"Are you Lyosha? Lyosha who bought Zykina's dacha?"

"Come on, there's lots of Lyoshas in the world! Right there, my son's named Lyosha, and we're upstanding guys.

Let's have that thousand!" Iratov took a hundred-dollar bill out of his fancy wallet.

"We don't take foreign currency!" Lyosha exclaimed, and his son nodded in agreement.

Now Iratov was angry. He tried to do people a good turn, and they spat in his face!

"Then you can both go screw yourselves!" The worker turned around and started walking, his son in tow. "That's right, I'm glad you got dragged out of Zykina's dacha! You're a sucker and you should live like a sucker! Some Brahman you are!"

"Who was that?" Vera asked, startled to see her husband losing his self-control.

"Oh, just someone from my past . . ." By then, Iratov's glands had slowed down their testosterone production by 60 percent. He didn't know it yet, but his hysterical outburst was actually the result of that process.

The flowers were laid on the Iratovs' graves, now free of snow. Eugene took his time arranging the bouquet, like he was a president laying a wreath at a photo op.

"Let's go to Alessandro Italianov's place," Vera suggested. "I'm hungry, it's getting late!"

This time, they ate abundantly. Eugene deftly twirled his spaghetti on his fork and smiled familiarly, as if he had long since adapted to his new circumstances. They had their fill of dessert and wine, then sang "Napoli" with the owner. Vera's face shone with an extraordinary light; she twittered like a little bird and looked as if she were no older than twenty. Iratov bounced between two feelings: hatred and indifference. There was still some testosterone in his body, albeit an insignificant quantity, and his brain was trying mightily to shore up that hormone and engender the desire to knock the wind out of this handsome carpetbagger Eugene, who had now fully ingratiated himself and was even making her laugh.

"He can eat a dick," Iratov thought. "But any way you slice it, he's me . . ." Mr. Iratov was feeling rather tipsy. He asked the waiters to pour some limoncello in his dessert glass. His thoughts were skipping all over the place, as one would expect of a man in his cups: he was thinking about his darling Vera, his lost sexual organ, and its reappearance in the form of his pseudo-son Eugene . . . He saw that Vera was talking to him, but her magical voice was somehow coming from far away. He nodded out of sync with what she was saying, trying to keep up the façade of a man who was master of all he surveyed, but his red eyes and his alcohol-twisted face made him nothing but an older guy in a state of deep inebriation . . . Vera paid the bill herself, and the waiters helped Eugene get Iratov in the car. She tried to remember when her eyes had last beheld her husband in such a shattered state, but couldn't.

They got out of the elevator and stopped near Mr. Iratov's door.

"Arseny will take you in," Vera said with a smile.

"No!" Iratov flatly refused. "I have to work in the morning, and I don't have a guest bedroom!"

"I'll spend the night in the train station," Eugene answered promptly.

"Iratov's son, sleeping in the train station like a homeless man?!" Vera was indignant. "Stay in my apartment! I've never known him to be such a lout!"

Iratov wasn't feeling too hot. He barely managed to drag himself into his apartment. He sank on to the couch in the hall and thought vacantly that just a few days ago his darling Vera would have nursed him through the night with aspirin and cold compresses, but now . . .

"Bitch!" Mr. Iratov cursed. "To hell with both of you!"

He fell asleep right there in the hall.

Vera and Eugene sat in the kitchen and drank red wine, trying to draw out their wonderful evening. The flushed Vera, seemingly driven by momentum, continued talking about her husband, about how unique and generous he was.

"Indeed, a worthy man, no doubt about that!"

The young man munched on pistachios, and his eyes gazed into the most secret niches of Vera's soul. To him, she was an open book, and he could read between the lines most easily. He could see how strong her feelings for Iratov were, how gracious and affectionate she was toward her husband, but, at the same time, the faint chill of dashed hopes was fluttering in her stomach. She was like a tightrope walker crossing an abyss but feeling, down in the depths of her innards, that she was about to fall to her death. Eugene knew that he would be the cause of that fall. He would enjoy these home comforts for another fifteen minutes or so, and then he would take what was rightfully his.

"Just wait here a moment, I'll get your bed set up in the guest room."

"Please don't rush on my account."

Then Vera offered him a towel and invited him to shower. He washed unhurriedly, enjoying the smell of the expensive shampoo, then walked out barefoot with the towel wrapped around his hips. Looking at his bare torso, Vera tried to modestly lower her eyes to the floor, but her pupils just wouldn't move. Quite the contrary, they gawked greedily at his young, muscular flesh. Vera had already fallen from her tightrope and into the abyss, but she had yet to realize that she would soon be plunging irretrievably.

She couldn't fathom how she'd wound up in her bedroom, completely naked, trembling with desire, Iratov's son pressing his hot lips to her neck, and it was as if those kisses were the confluence of all the amorous secrets of all the world's Byrons, Casanovas, and Rasputins.

Driven by momentum once again, Vera continued describing how tender her husband was in bed, even as her body, draped in the young man, was melting like butter. She felt his tiny nipples against her breasts—it was like they had been carved from marble. Her armpits were suddenly moist and joined the butterflies fluttering out of her stomach in exuding the smell of the summer haymaking, awakening a startling quantity of pheromones. Eugene replaced the amorous old-world swallowtails inside Vera with himself, which stilled her breathing for a full minute. She exhaled, and for the first time in her life, her body trembled as if from an electrical current. Her legs trembled ever so slightly, and Eugene looked into her wide-open eyes with mild indifference. He knew what he was doing. He possessed Vera masterfully, drawing every trace of other men out of her, filling her with himself. She squeaked in delight like a mouse that had found a whole wheel of cheese, gasped for air again, feeling that she would die from an excess of everything, and then, for an instant, she imagined that her husband was standing in the doorway, lustfully watching their illicit coitus.

"Come join us!" She beckoned. "Come on!"

"There's nobody there," Eugene whispered and painfully bit her breast—the smaller one that Iratov loved so much.

Vera shrieked and turned her attention away from the mirages birthed from this tumult of feelings and sexual revolution. She submitted herself to Eugene entirely, bent to his every whim, bared her supple buttocks, then, like an awkward teenager, thanked him with her beautifully defined lips, puckered so as not to mar the young man's genius with her perfect white teeth.

She was no longer thinking of her husband, even when they took a break and sat in the kitchen, devouring everything that was in the fridge. She was sure that this was Mr. Iratov himself before her; he had simply bathed in the hot milk that had rejuvenated the little humpbacked horse . . .

Iratov left for the andrology clinic early in the morning without waking Vera. His head was still pounding from the night before when he met Sytin.

"I'll do it!" he barked from the doorway.

"Just wait a second . . ."

"Why wait?" It was only then that Iratov noticed the unnatural, deathly pallor of his friend's face. "Has something happened?"

Doctor Sytin stood up from his desk and removed his white coat. Then he undid his belt with one lightning-fast motion and dropped his pants and underwear.

"See?" Iratov looked—the doctor practically had a pubic mound.

"You too?" Mr. Iratov exclaimed. "It happened to you too?!"

"Let me tell you something else . . ." Sytin pattered over to Iratov, pants still down. "I've had twelve patients like this in the last two days!"

"Put your pants on," Iratov requested. "And ask your secretary for some coffee!"

"She brought her husband in today," Sytin whispered conspiratorially, pulling up his pants. "Two coffees!" he shouted.

"And?"

"Him too. Nothing! No balls, no dick!" They sat on the couch and maintained an austere silence as they waited for their coffee. Iratov was nearly stunned by these events. The secretary brought the coffee, and the men watched her leave—but the way they looked at her was more questioning than sexual.

"Is it an epidemic?" Mr. Iratov asked.

"Maybe . . ." Sytin rubbed the crotch of his pants. "We could make a killing on an epidemic. You put up the money, I'll assemble a team of surgeons and teach them to perform the phalloplasty procedure. What a great idea!" Some vague clumps of thought swirled in Iratov's brain, but he just couldn't collect them.

"Can't think straight . . ." he admitted.

"That's your testosterone dropping! I measured myself and my patients. Our levels are crashing!" Sytin suddenly beamed. "We have to buy up testosterone on a strategic scale! Band-Aids, gels, all the accompanying medicine that reduces estrogen in the body and stimulates male hormones! Let's say fifty-fifty?"

"I watched a stranger fuck my wife last night," Iratov said suddenly.

"What?" Sytin groaned.

"Well . . . imagine this: this young pup shows up, and he's an absolute copy of me. Who do you think he said he was?"

"A long-lost son?"

"He said he was my member. And he presented incontrovertible evidence. He's part of me, so he fulfilled my marital duties. He took my darling Vera up one side of the room and down the other . . . I mean, *I* fulfilled my marital duties, but I was watching from the sidelines at the same time . . . And I have to admit, I experienced feelings that were completely new to me—it was like insane jealousy, but at the same time, my brain was so turned on!"

"Well, that's quite common," the andrologist explained. "Especially when people are tired of classic sex . . . but still, this guy was your member?!"

"Precisely."

"Maybe it was just your nerves acting up? An illusion? A hallucination?"

"There's nothing wrong with me."

"I don't doubt it . . ." Sytin went over to the pharmacy cabinet, took out a box, and handed it to Iratov.

"What's this?"

"Testosterone gel. Rub it on your chest every morning."

"What for? My member has detached from me like a module from a space station, and now it's operating autonomously . . ."

"Look, Yakut, who's the doctor here?"

"You are."

"Above all, testosterone is essential for the brain! You need it to think straight! To reason! Testosterone is what makes us men. What makes us dominant! Just think about it! Why are women incapable of thinking rationally? Because they're testosterone-poor, that's why!"

"Alright," Iratov agreed. He took off his shirt, squeezed some gel into his palm, and rubbed it on his powerful chest.

"If you're gonna be on top of a woman, you've gotta wash it off, otherwise hair'll sprout on her breasts like weeds, he-he-he!"

"Why would I be on top of a woman?"

"Good point . . . Well, how about starting that business? It's a sure thing . . ."

"Do you remember why I came here?"

"Regarding a phalloplasty."

"Then schedule the operation!"

Iratov went to his office on foot. The city was in the power of a thaw; everything exuded water, and Mr. Iratov's light shoes sank into the slush. His car followed beside him.

"I wonder if my driver has a penis . . . or did he lose it,

too?" He wanted to inquire about that intimate detail without delay, but just then a man pulled even with him. Mr. Iratov recognized him immediately; he had seen him in the crowd at the Bolshoi Theatre. He also thought he'd heard this man say his wife's name with a British accent—"Verushka!"

"Hello, Mr. Iratov!" said the freak.

"Do we know each other?"

"I know *of* you."

The car window opened, and the driver called out to his boss and asked if everything was alright. Mr. Iratov waved him away.

"Do you need something from me?"

"Strictly speaking, no. Not anymore."

"So you needed something before? What was it?"

"Do you remember, some twenty-five years ago, you gave the order to kill a person who had somehow found out your secrets?"

"I never—"

"Oh, spare me! I do not represent any law enforcement organ. I won't write anything about you. Your guys almost killed me!"

"But they didn't . . . Yeah, I remember. So I suppose you're the one who took a dump in my stash?"

"I won't deny it."

"Why do you hate me so much, if you don't mind my asking?"

"Oh no, I'm not capable of hatred. I simply have a sense of when what's happening is right."

"Oh lord, so are you from the Church?"

"God forbid!"

"Then who are you?"

"You wouldn't understand if I told you. Incidentally, I know all about your problems."

"Oh yeah? And what problems would those be?"

"You have no sexual organ, and now your sexual organ is pleasuring your wife and his name is Eugene. There's nothing in the universe that can surprise me now . . ."

"Next you'll be telling me that you're my balls!"

"Goodness gracious! I am not worthy of such an honor!"

"Well, that's something at least."

"I could have taken revenge for everything you have done in this life—I would have done so with pleasure twenty-five years ago, but you left your country for Israel and then the USA. By the way, do you really have Jewish roots?"

"Oh yes. My father's grandmother was Jewish . . ."

"Uh-huh . . . but apparently you didn't feel like converting?"

"No. The American lifestyle is more to my liking."

"Being Jewish is not a lifestyle!"

"Whatever you say . . . I'm not religious, but I do know there's a God."

"How can you know that but not be religious?"

"It just worked out that way . . ." Iratov stopped, and his companion slowed down, too. "How about you? Do you have a penis?"

"No, and I never have."

"Well, what are you pestering me for then, huh?"

"That's uncalled for. I approached you politely, and you're—"

"How come you think you're better than me?"

"It makes no sense to compare us. I am of a different substance entirely!"

"Oh sure, of course. You have no penis for higher reasons!" Iratov sneered. "And I have lost mine for my sins—"

"I have been without one since the moment of my creation! It was not part of the plan!"

"Do you have anything else for me?" Iratov could already see his office building and was losing interest in talking to this freak.

"Actually, it's you who has something for me."

"Well, what is it?"

"We'll save that for next time!"

"Thank God." Mr. Iratov smiled at this strange entity. "I'm here and I have to work!" He skipped toward the entrance, sticking to the dry islands.

"Just so you know, my name is Mr. E!" the freak called after him.

11

I would now like to continue my story about the fate of Iratov's unacknowledged son who was later adopted by the young Dasha, for it is directly germane to the future that is now ahead. That little Buryat girl proved to have a strong spirit; she never snapped at little Joseph, no matter how hard it got. She never even complained to anyone about how rough she had it. She may've cried into her pillow in despair some nights, but those moments of weakness were extremely rare. The girl's fortitude won her respect at the orphanage; the director gave her a seven-ruble raise, her colleagues helped her out for free, and life went on, as it does. Joseph kept growing and repaid his adoptive mother's love with his handsome face and the clarity of his gaze—which had no thought behind it. The boy's brain hadn't been completely destroyed. He had the mind of a three-year-old, but the sexual domain was fully intact. Joseph never made in his pants. He had been trained to use the toilet and received a cookie or a piece of candy as a reward every time he did. When the boy forgot himself and peed against the wall, Dasha would chide him and threaten to not read him a bedtime story. Then Joseph would grab a rag and clean up after himself.

Dasha mostly read him Brodsky poems from the worn sam izdat manuscript she had inherited from her mother. Joseph didn't understand the meaning of the text, but, in that respect, he was identical to his mother, from whom all the intricate currents of the Nobel laureate's poetry were just as hidden; it was only the musical qualities that awakened beatific joy in her soul. She thought that Joseph Brodsky was her father who had forgotten his book. He didn't even know that Dasha existed, since he had been expelled from the country for social parasitism. The girl's duties often brought her to the orphanage library, where they kept children's poetry, and she logically concluded that all those Marshaks, Kushaks, and Chukovskies were expelled for social parasitism along with her father and had been excommunicated from the Motherland for good.

The girl herself thought that poems didn't count as work; they were just little splashes of feeling. She did real work, hard and important, with a future nobody wanted, which made it altruistic, and therefore she was certain that she would never be dismissed from the orphanage for mentally challenged children and teenagers. Director Yurieva got less bitchy with age and gradually lost her sight, so times were thin at the orphanage. There was a lot of theft, and the mortality rate among the children significantly exceeded the officially allowable limit. Yurieva was put out to pasture with a pension and an Award for Valiant Labor. Everyone cried at her retirement party and promised to visit her every day . . . In the five years left to their former boss, nobody visited her once. The Lord took her away early one morning; she suffocated a minute after her heart stopped.

Director Yurieva was replaced by a successor of the male sex, Vladlen Stepanovich Catov—a demotion for him, since he was previously the deputy minister of transportation. He'd gotten into some trouble, so they shipped him off to head the orphanage. He was a strong man who did not surrender to despair at having fallen so far. Quite the contrary—he was of the opinion that everything happens for a reason. So Director Catov reduced the budget for feeding the developmentally disabled children by a factor of three, convinced that the government had put him there to cut fodder expenses and surplus population, and the mortality rate at the orphanage climbed even higher. Theft practically came to an end, since the food situation had begun to resemble the siege of Leningrad. The children were so weak that they hardly moved and mostly stayed in bed. Interestingly enough, Catov did not embezzle the food funds; instead, he spent them on beautifying the grounds, repairing the building, and other maintenance needs. Basically, Catov was an idiot with big ideas who really ought to have been placed in the institution for developmentally disabled adults that was right there on the other side of the woods. But who was going to do that? The bosses at the District Commission for Public Education were satisfied with the former deputy minister's work. For some reason, they appeared not to notice the mortality rate among the children under his care; evidently, there really had been some instructions about cutting the population passed down from on high.

That's as may be, but Dasha's situation at the orphanage became much worse, too, since Catov's eye fell on her maidenly loveliness, and he unambiguously suggested that they meet each other's physiological needs during naptime. Dasha had not given the slightest thought to relations between men and women, remembering Yurieva's admonitions that any sexual contact she had might reflect poorly on little Joseph. She categorically refused Catov's advances, and he retaliated by forbidding Joseph to eat at the orphanage's expense. The situation became desperate. Dasha couldn't afford to feed two people, so she didn't get enough to eat and withered away right before her colleagues' eyes. That was when I had to intervene.

I met her when she was walking to the dormitory, holding Joseph firmly by the hand. The kid was hollering, since he had used the toilet but not received his reward. He was squirming, tucking his knees under him and making Dasha drag him. I approached from around the corner and laid my hand on the boy's head. He instantly calmed down and began walking peacefully beside his mother.

"How did you do that?" asked Dasha, surprised.

"Oh, that was nothing," I said with a smile.

"But who are you?"

"I am kind."

"I can tell . . ."

"Your name is Dasha, right?"

"How do you know that?" Dasha was surprised again, narrowing her already narrow eyes at me.

"Oh, that doesn't matter. I know a lot of things. Well now, Dasha, there is nearly a full brick of American dollars waiting in your dormitory room. You are most likely unaware of their existence, but you probably remember that you got a package containing a bundle of funny little green slips a few years ago."

"Yeah . . ." she said. "Yeah, I remember something like that. I used to slide those slips under the flowerpots, make a little 'X.' It was pretty."

"So where are the slips now?"

"They're somewhere . . . the flowers dried out, so I don't have any use for them."

"Our kindhearted government has seen fit to furnish you with three thousand rubles for adopting an ill child. The dollars, however—those funny little green slips—will be reallocated elsewhere, given the fact that you do not require them."

"Are you joking?

"Why would I?" I took an envelope full of rubles from my breast pocket and handed it to her. "Here, please make good use of this. Let's go back to the dormitory. You'll have to fill out a form indicating that you have received the full amount."

When she saw the envelope full of money, the girl seemed to have been struck dumb; her round, flat face looked like a fresh crepe, joyful and delicious. We arrived at the dormitory and completed the agreed-upon procedures. Dasha's pencil scratched over the form, then she returned the remaining dollars, which she'd tucked under a stone. I had to spend some time explaining what such an enormous sum could buy. I enumerated it for her: she could rent an apartment downtown, eat well for three years, buy new clothes for her and the boy, and take taxis sometimes.

Her mouth was agape when I left her, and I was astonished by how many little teeth she had. She took my advice, rented a one-room apartment—not downtown, of course, it was a little one way out by Belyaevo—bought new clothes—but just for Joseph—and resigned from the orphanage, much to Director Catov's dismay.

"I'd like to drown you like a ca—" He stopped, his superstitious nature preventing him from invoking a curse linked to his own name. "I hope you die like a dog!"

Dasha spent more than half the money on hiring the best doctors for Joseph. They spent a year examining the boy, prescribing the latest medications, and assembling expert panels, but all of that failed to yield any positive results, just financial losses. Joseph peed against the wall in the office of the country's foremost neurologist, and his treatment was terminated forthwith. The sentence they passed was final and was not subject to appeal: mental retardation.

"Well, so what," Dasha thought. Life goes on, and it goes on a lot easier if you don't spend money on false hope. She got a job as a janitor in her own apartment building so she'd always be near the boy . . . Things changed with time. Joseph kept his angelic features as he entered adolescence, but, just as Director Yurieva had warned, he was soon tormented by hormones, which instantly gained the upper hand. His brain wasn't up to understanding what was happening to his body; he would often run around the apartment naked, his young manhood standing tall, yanking it back and forth, trying to break this little thing that was the source of his torment, until it suddenly squirted fluid, which brought momentary relief. From then on, Joseph spent almost every moment interfering with himself. He even kept at this most interesting new activity while he was eating. Dasha would wind up threateningly with a towel, but what could the poor woman do? She just had to put up with it. One time, she came out of the bathroom with her robe slightly open. Joseph's eyes began to sparkle, he broke into a sweat, and what little gray matter he had put two and two together. There it was. That was what he had needed all along; the sweet fruit was right in front of him. The boy overcame his mother easily. She was in such a state that she defended herself rather limply. Thoughts about a perverse connection between mother and son slid through her mind . . . He was already inside her when she reached the conclusion that a mother must use any means to help her sick, suffering child. They weren't related by blood, after all. Physically, she didn't experience anything, not even from the bites and scratches, which she'd gotten used to over the years. What was going on between her legs was of no interest to her . . . After that, Joseph would lay Dasha down on the bed five times a day and continue interfering with himself in the intervals. She actually used the fact that her son was such an insatiable animal to her advantage, resisting and thereby forcing him to sweep the apartment or wash the dishes and only then giving herself to him as a reward for his labor.

It went on that way for a few months. To Dasha's delight, Joseph grew calmer and his moments of aggression waned. Then he called Dasha by her name, which she found surprising. Of course, he had managed some simple words, like "mom," "eat," and "potty . . ." It wasn't like her name was hard to pronounce or anything, it was just that it was happening for the first time. Then it went on that way, not "mom" but "Dasha."

About a year later, she missed her period. Dasha didn't pay any particular attention to that, but when her stomach started to swell, she panicked, since she had seen all kinds of illnesses in her long years of caring for the child, including a huge stomach tumor—it was a man who had it, but still. She left Joseph with the janitor who worked the other shift and dashed to the neighborhood clinic, where she signed up to see the oncologist. Dasha awaited her fateful hour in terror. She wasn't afraid for herself, but for Joseph, who would live a year, max, if she died and passed into the world where deer lived after they'd been eaten . . . A week later, she saw an externally indifferent oncologist, who laid her down on the examination table and spent a few minutes touching her swollen stomach.

"Well, this isn't my specialty," he warned her. "But all the evidence leads me to believe that you are pregnant—very pregnant, as a matter of fact."

"How could I be pregnant?!" the terrified patient asked.

"I'm sure a gynecologist could explain that to you!"

After the woman left, her face looking like a crepe that had gone stale, the oncologist complained to the nurse at great length about the population's near-universal sexual illiteracy, stunned that women didn't know what IUDs and birth control were, or even product no. 2.

"What's product no. 2?" asked the nurse.

"She doesn't even know about her own situation!" said the oncologist, throwing up his hands. "How will she take care of that unfortunate child? And product no. 2 is a rubber!"

As she left the clinic, Dasha fully understood that there was a little person living inside her. She distinctly remembered living inside her mother's belly, how sweetly she had slept there, how warm it had been in the shoreless maternal ocean . . . She didn't need any gynecologist to understand the unchanging essence of things. Nature explained everything itself, bypassing her brain and transforming into emotion.

When she got home, Dasha informed Joseph that she was carrying a child in her belly, her son's little brother or sister. Then she suddenly realized that the father of her child would be her own son. Her heart clenched with horror, but another thought instantly came to her rescue—Joseph was adopted. There was no reason at all he couldn't be born perfectly normal!

It was only the janitor who worked the other shift who sensed that something was up and began looking at Dasha's belly suspiciously. One day, her curiosity got the better of her, and she asked straight out.

"Do he force himself on you?"

"What?"

"That retarded son of yours."

"What?" She didn't understand. All she could do was ask again.

"Did your son knock you up?!" For some reason, the other janitor was mad.

"What? No!" Dasha had finally gotten it. "Why would you say that?"

"Who was it then?"

"Brodsky, the poet! I am carrying his offspring!"

"Poet? What poet?"

"Just a regular poet. He's a Nobel laureate."

"Oh!" went the other janitor, putting two and two together. "A con? A guy in jail?"

"Yeah," Dasha said, just going with it.

"You were pen pals first?"

"Uh-huh . . ."

"A tale as old as time, really . . . He got out, had his way with you, and took off, like a crowded bus that won't stop to pick you up!"

"Yeah, it was just like that."

They commiserated about women's rough lot awhile and then went about their business. Dasha toiled away cleaning the stairwells, her stomach growing all the while, the child's birth coming closer, one stretch mark at a time, and Joseph continued to use his mother's body to keep his destroyed brain more or less balanced.

She had to have the baby at home—there was nobody to watch the sick kid. She was not afraid of this process; after all, where she was from, women would sometimes even give birth out in the tundra, like reindeer. The only person Dasha could seek help from was the other janitor; she didn't know anybody else.

"How about I call an ambulance?" her gal comrade asked.

". . . I'll do it myself . . ."

"Whatever you say . . ." They got all the towels in the building ready and boiled a bunch of rags. The last of the woman's water ran down her legs as her labor continued, but she paid not the slightest attention to that, ignored her accelerating contractions, and kept on ironing some gauze to disinfect it. She took a pair of regular desk scissors out of the locked cabinet and boiled them as well.

"They're dull," the janitor winced.

"They'll do."

"I sure don't envy you, honey! Maybe I should call that ambulance after all?"

"It's starting!" Dasha warned her, pulling off her pregnancy belt and lying down on the bed. Like all women do, she screamed from her labor pains, pushed as hard as she could, while Joseph, locked in the kitchen, yowled like a dog, as if someone had died. Five hours into the process, Dasha's relief from her burden resulted in a miraculous baby boy.

"Congratulations!" the janitor said with a smile and cut the cord with the scissors. "Well, time for my shift."

That was how Dasha gave birth to a son—a biological son this time—whom she named Joseph in honor of his father and her father, with a patronymic to match as well, so the full name on his birth certificate was "Joseph Josephovich Brodsky."

"That's a Jewish name!" the civil servant declared. "You registered his ethnicity as Russian!"

"Well, let's rewrite it then. I didn't know." The lady at the registration office produced a new form, filled it out, then wrote the word "JEWISH" in thick letters in the box labeled "ethnicity," not without a certain degree of satisfaction.

"Here is your birth certificate!" Then she smiled nastily. "How does that look?"

"Looks great!"

Dasha redoubled her efforts, toiling away in those stairwells where her righteous neighbors gave her scornful looks—two bastard children and she's acting like she's as sweet as a dandelion. The janitor who delivered the baby just threw fuel on the fire of their ostracism.

"It was a con who put that whoreson in her. The kid came out with a head full of black hair . . . And I didn't get dime one for helping her! Those slanty-eyed types are all the same!"

Joseph Josephovich grew up strong. The little tyke sucked greedily, but, if anything, Dasha produced an excess of milk, like a little dairy farm. While his father, Joseph, was in the process of fulfilling his sexual needs, he, too, would drink his fill.

Life went on, as it does. The children grew, and the younger

Joseph was just as handsome as his father, but his brain worked like it ought to—actually, he even outstripped his peers.

Dasha's biological son had long since moved on from his mother's milk. He turned seven and started school. They agreed to enroll him instantly, the moment the assistant principal saw the incredibly handsome boy with his big, sad eyes and hair as black as piano polish that cascaded on to his shoulders. She could see him vividly, in white gloves with the school's banner in his hands at the opening day ceremony.

"He doesn't look like you at all," the assistant principal commented.

"He's the spitting image of his father."

"That can happen when the father has dominant genes."

Dasha tried to make sure Joseph Senior never had her in front of Joseph Junior. Well, he was the boy's real father, so you could say they were a normal family . . . She'd even kept making the milk that her adopted son and husband loved so much.

Then Joseph Senior got sick. It all started with an ordinary cold, just coughing and a runny nose. The twenty-three-year-old didn't understand what was happening to him or why there was so much bad stuff going on inside him. He no longer sucked on his mother's breasts with his now-dry mouth, lost all physical attraction to her, and did little but hold his head in his weakening hands, trying to squeeze the unbearable pain out of his skull. He tried to roar, but the strength in his body was waning rapidly, so he sounded more like a cat than a lion. Dasha tried everything she knew, even melted deer fat, both rubbed on the skin and taken internally. It was futile, so she decided to call an ambulance, which took both of them to the nearest hospital, while little Joseph stayed at an after-school program where he beat everyone at chess, even the upperclassmen.

"He has neurological problems!" Dasha repeated over and over again at the hospital. "He can't answer your questions by himself," she told the nurse.

It turned out that there was no need to explain anything. The elderly doctor with a beard just like Kalinin who came out to meet the mother told her that he had some kind of nasty meningitis.

"Why did you wait so long to seek medical help?" the doctor griped. "Go say goodbye." She still couldn't make any sense of all this.

"Is this going to take a while? I'll just wait here on the couch . . ."

"He's dying. Oh yeah, it'll be a while. A long while."

She stood in the hallway, feeling her legs growing into the floor, as heavy as if they had been poured from concrete. When the meaning of what she had heard reached her, she staggered toward the ward where her son and husband was dying. She went in, her legs almost too stiff to walk, looked at the doctors hovering over Joseph, and, barely able to open her lips, asked everyone to leave, to just let her have two minutes of his life . . . Then, when they were alone together, she lay down on the hospital bed, took out her right breast, brought it to her son's lifeless mouth, and pressed on it, forcing out a drop. Joseph stuck out the tip of his gray tongue to catch the milk, pulled it back, and then was gone in an instant.

They buried Joseph Senior in some country cemetery in the village of Kozino, out by Solntsevo. It was done simply and very cheaply. No priest, no mourners, only her little son was with her as she stood over the fresh grave and struck a toy drum like a shaman playing a tambourine.

Dasha had no way of knowing that, on that very same day, on the other side of Moscow, a young woman had died of an undiagnosed illness. She was exactly the same age as Joseph Senior and she had left a daughter behind . . . It must also be noted that the dead woman was the daughter of a certain Maria, better known as Masha. The same Masha from the foreign currency store, with whom the young Iratov had spent a most enjoyable night, back when life seemed eternal . . .

An orphaned life awaited Dasha and the young Joseph. The milky river in her breasts dried up, and her suffering made her thin and bony; only her face stayed round. She dreamed of her dead Joseph every night. She tormented herself with guilt over not saving her son and husband, realizing that it was her ignorance that had caused this tragedy. She would howl quietly into her pillow so she wouldn't scare the boy, but, to her increasing surprise, he never mentioned his father.

"Don't hold it in!" Dasha said, embracing Joseph. "Let the bird of death fly free, you'll feel better."

"There's no bird inside me."

"You just don't want to remember your father, but you have to—he was your father, after all. I think about mine all the time—your grandfather, Joseph Brodsky, the Nobel laureate. He was Jewish."

"I don't think about mine, though."

"Why? Why don't we go to his grave on Sunday?"

"It's cold out there, and there's nothing in the ground."

"Your father is buried there."

"My father's body may be buried there, but he is somewhere else."

"With God?" Dasha asked.

"Who's God?"

"The one who created us."

"Then he's with God. So why would we go to some grave where my father left his broken space suit when he went . . . to

God? We just buried the suit . . . If it was valuable, my father wouldn't have left it here, in some hole . . ."

Dasha had never heard such mysterious talk from her son, and she looked at him as if he had been reborn. She had probably missed the development of Joseph's mind, absorbed as she was with her sick adopted son, her physical relations with him, and his future.

"Listen, son," she imparted. "I wasn't born smart, so when knowledge came to me, I did not let it in, didn't know what it was for. So what you're saying isn't something I can understand."

"You're my mother!" Joseph said, his tone strangely adult. "There is nothing more important in this life than one's mother and father. My father has left us, and now I only have you. How much intelligence you were endowed with is of no consequence to me . . ." The boy drew closer to his mother, put his arms around her waist, and nuzzled against her breasts, the safest place there was. She cradled his head, kissed it long and passionately, as if she were kissing two Josephs at once, or even three, including her father the poet.

"I've got no brains," Dasha said, beginning to cry. "Neither did your father. It was all mixed together and set aside for you. It's all in your head . . ."

Life went on, and they hardly noticed the passage of time. Dasha stopped mourning quite so deeply, released the bird of death beyond the bounds of the universe, and delighted in the fact that her biological son was doing tremendously well in school, winning all the academic contests he entered and medaling at several adult chess tournaments. Former world champion Valery Estin once came to their school and held a simultaneous exhibition. He had been doing that less and less often lately— he wasn't as energetic as he once was, and his interest in the game had been long since satisfied . . . Both the students and the teachers took part. They all lost, including Joseph Brodsky. But the youth made such an unconventional move in the middle-game that Estin had to spend three nights sitting at the board to realize that it was a revolutionary innovation that would change how people thought about the Sicilian Defense. Later on, this fantastic opening strategy was sold to the current world champion, who used the novelty move to retain his crown in a match against a challenger. Estin sent his friend Mitya Schwartz, who had a doctorate in theoretical mathematics as well, to the boy's school in Belyaevo. The forty-year-old academic's task was simple: determine the youth's IQ.

The assistant principal, of course, could not turn away people who had so much influence—not just in their country, but around the world. A whole classroom was set aside for Joseph to meet the mathematician, and the first-graders were sent home early to accommodate the testing. A quiet day was declared throughout the school.

Joseph went into the classroom, where Schwartz, the mathematician, had already made himself quite at home, eating the last of an éclair, the crumbs of which had already settled all over the room. The scholar had a mop of red hair, a freckly face, and eyes hidden behind thick glasses.

"Mitya," said the scholar, extending his hand to the youth.

"Joseph."

Now acquainted, they got settled in at a long double desk in the back row. There was some odd resemblance between the two of them, though Mitya Schwartz could hardly be called handsome.

"It's all quite simple," the mathematician explained. "I will give you the Eysenck Test, which you must complete within thirty minutes. True, the questions are in English, but I'll translate for you."

"No, that's fine."

"How do you know English?"

"From our school curriculum . . . Well, and I've read a few things in English. Books." That was enough for Mitya to give his blessing.

"Then go for it! Remember, exactly half an hour. In the meantime, I'll step out for a smoke. The clock starts now."

When the mathematician returned twelve minutes later, Joseph gave him the stack of papers.

"Too tricky?" Mitya, still smelling of tobacco, wasn't surprised. "Don't be upset. Most people can't make heads or tails of it."

"No, these are my answers." Then Mitya was surprised, but not terribly so. He took Joseph's work, sat down at the desk, and looked through his answers. Schwartz looked at the boy for a few minutes, then held out his hand.

"I have to go!" Joseph nodded, not venturing to accompany the scholar to the door; he just turned to the window to watch him walk away. Mitya Schwartz wasn't walking away, though; he was running. The mathematician dashed across the school grounds like a top-notch sprinter and disappeared through the gate.

Just an hour later, he met Estin at their training camp. Chewing on a high-calorie bun, he gave the world champion his answer.

"180!"

"Very high. He's a genius."

"But at what?" Schwartz wondered, picking a raisin off the bun. "You don't need me to tell you how many people with that IQ have vanished into oblivion."

"He's certainly not a genius at chess," Estin noted. "He could have drawn, at least . . . Yeah, he has the kind of mind that can memorize three thousand pages of text, but what for? If they don't have a vocation, these kids become the unhappiest of people. If he worked at some design bureau, they wouldn't know what to do with him. He thinks so quickly that a computer can't keep up. He'll think he's speaking accessibly, but a PhD will lose the thread two words in. It's like an adult trying to explain the theory of relativity to a one-year-old."

"Agreed. If he were a precocious mathematician, we would have seen some evidence by now, but he got a B at school. What should we do?"

"Nothing," the former champion replied. "We'll watch, we'll monitor him . . . Maybe he'll become an actor, like James Woods."

Well, there you have it.

Joseph graduated with high honors but didn't go to drama school. Actually, he didn't even apply anywhere. He mostly sat at home and read some thick book in a language Dasha couldn't understand.

"They'll draft you if you aren't in school!" she warned him. "And you won't be able to hack it!"

"People get by wherever they are . . ."

His mother was worried about him. Sometimes, when she looked into her son's eyes, she saw his father, Joseph Senior.

Six months after he completed his high school finals, the young man started going to the town of Istra, where he visited the yeshiva and begged for permission to audit some classes on the book he'd been reading at home. Joseph demonstrated deep knowledge of the text and real maturity in his thinking. He spent his evenings with the rather elderly teacher, Rabbi Yitskhok, stunning him with his unexpected interpretations of a few passages in the book that the Almighty presented to Moses on Mount Sinai.

"Where did you find that midrash?" the teacher would ask. "A most curious interpretation!"

"I have practically no literature, just a couple of booklets . . . I think . . ."

"How do you know the Torah?"

"Believe it or not, it was in our school library, somewhere between Chukovsky and Ilf."

"What's not to believe? The Torah is to be found wherever it is needed! So you *borrowed* the book, right?" the teacher asked, winking.

"That would be wrong!"

"It was no sin—the Torah was there for you to find."

"I thought it would be better to memorize it."

"You can memorize anything!" the old teacher said with a smile. "But that isn't necessary. This book isn't read, it's studied, every day, and the Lord—may he make his face shine upon you—will honor your efforts! I will give you the book."

"Thank you."

"We have quite a few copies here . . . Are you Jewish?"

"My birth certificate says so. That was why I took an interest."

"What is your mother's ethnicity?"

"She's either a Buryat or . . . I don't remember for sure. She was definitely from somewhere up north."

"Not Jewish, then," said the teacher, displeased for some reason.

"You know better than me."

"Do you want to become a Jew?"

"I thought that I already was, but now I don't know . . ."

"Yes," the teacher said, his beard shaking. "We know who is Jewish by their mothers."

"But I read that it's only been that way since the Babylonian captivity, when they were trying to decide whether or not to take gentile wives and children from mixed marriages with them to the Holy Land. They decided to leave them in Babylon, so they wouldn't dilute their Jewish blood. That was the only reason they adopted the law that one can only claim Jewish ethnicity via the maternal line. Before that, it was on the father's side, of course. After all, it is said that the man is the progenitor of both son and daughter."

"You've dug deep!" said the teacher, almost angry now. "Was your father Jewish at least?"

"As far as I know."

"Do you still have your birth certificate?"

"My grandfather was Joseph Brodsky."

"The poet?"

"He received the Nobel Prize."

"That was a personal tragedy."

His backpack stuffed with books of every kind, Joseph decided to stop visiting the Istra yeshiva; studying independently would be much more effective. At the end of the fall, Joseph Josephovich Brodsky was drafted.

Dasha seemed inconsolable as she said goodbye to her son, as if she were seeing him for the last time. She hung on him for a long while, enormous tears falling from her narrow eyes.

"You don't even know how to shoot!"

"Mom, there's no war right now . . . And they'll teach me to shoot!"

Dasha watched the buses full of new recruits receding into the distance. Like all Russian women, she waved her kerchief and shouted after him.

"Be safe, son!"

Joseph was sent to boot camp for six months so the army could acquire one more sergeant. When he arrived at his assigned service location, he instantly found himself being interviewed by one Major Belic, who took an interest in the intellectual development of this shaved-bald recruit with the face of a model.

"How'd you do in school?"

"Fine, all A's and B's."

"How come you didn't go to college? Or did you flunk out?"

"No, I didn't apply anywhere. I wanted to join the army."

Belic looked at the soldier suspiciously. The old officer didn't trust patriots, especially in those unpatriotic days.

"Athlete?"

"No."

"Know how to draw? We need a guy to do the wall newspaper."

"No."

"Well, what *can* you do?" the major asked, already sounding indifferent.

"Play chess . . ."

"Earned a category?"

"Yes, sir."

"God, this is like pulling teeth!" said the now irritated Belic. "*Which* category? Come on."

"First category."

The major sank so deeply into his old faux-leather armchair that it almost flipped over. His years of training had not gone to waste, though, and he kept his balance without even noticing, rubbing his hands together in satisfaction.

"I've got one colonel here who's a real chess nut. I always have to play with him, even though he's head and shoulders above me. Then he gives me grief about it afterwards, like,

'Come on Belic, were you born with no brains?' If you beat him, you can eat in the officers' mess for six months!"

"I'd rather have my books back. I don't need to eat in the officers'—"

"Those books are in a foreign language!"

"Two foreign languages, actually."

"Well, there you have it," said the major, throwing up his hands. He reached into a desk drawer, pulled out a piece of candy, neatly unwrapped it, stuck it on his protruding lower lip, adroitly flipped it into his mouth, and asked the recruit if he liked his trick.

"Why does it matter that they're in foreign languages?"

"It could be enemy propaganda for all I know!"

"But who are our enemies now?" Joseph asked. "We're friends with everybody these days. They announced that whole conversion program. They say the army doesn't even have bullets anymore."

"Yeah, because they kept them in leaky warehouses! You wouldn't believe the money the government's sinking into defense now!"

"Well, if I can't have them, I can't have them. I quit chess a long time ago anyway."

"Hang on, I haven't decided yet. What are those books?"

"The Old and New Testaments, plus secondary sources."

"Are you religious?'

"No, but I know there is a God."

Belic rummaged in his drawer, fished out a handful of mint hard candies, and offered Joseph one. The soldier accepted it, and they were both soon crunching away.

"Everybody's gotten really into religion lately. It's all Gorbachev's fault! The country started falling apart on his watch! And there is no God!"

"Yeltsin's the one who really made it fall apart."

"And the new guy is religious, too!" The major pulled a wry face, making his wrinkles stand out and revealing two tufts of hair in his nostrils. When his features resumed their former shape, the flora disappeared entirely. Joseph smiled.

"So, will you play?" Belic asked.

"The books."

"Alright. You are permitted to read in the Lenin room! You are dismissed!"

"Yes, sir!" Joseph turned neatly on his artificial leather bootheels and strode to the exit.

Army life rolled on for the young man. Classes on military hardware, physical training, then the mess hall where they would be fed meagerly, almost always pearl barley with fatty herring. Belic seemed to have forgotten about Joseph, and the latter was quite content with that situation. He spent his free time with his books, searching, underlining, and mumbling to himself in some language nobody could understand. That was very nearly hazardous to his health when the other guys thought it was Chechen. The two wars were fresh in everyone's memory, so Joseph took a few punches to the face from the soon-to-be sergeants.

"What was that for?" he asked, spitting out blood. The soldier remained imperturbable, and the tone of his voice was almost indifferent.

"For being a dirty Chechen!" his comrades answered. Then Slipperov, the smallest trainee, gave his enemy a juicy slap.

"Just a second," Joseph said calmly. "First of all, I'm not a Chechen, and even if I were, there's nothing wrong with that now, being a Chechen is perfectly honorable."

"I'll show you 'honorable'!" the little guy wailed, suddenly emboldened, like he had just become Goliath. He wound up for another blow, but Joseph rose to his tiptoes, so he caught the jab in the shoulder instead of the face. It was funny, and the future noncoms burst into laughter.

"If you hit me again, you'll die." Joseph warned him.

The soldiers fell silent in anticipation.

"What did you say?" Little Slipperov was jumping up and down like a monkey.

"By the way, our president loves the Chechen people you call dirty." He had some fearful words in store for the runt. "And you have a growth hormone deficiency!" The runt was about to pounce. His cheek was twitching, but Joseph's voice stopped him. "Hang on! Cool it! Let me tell you something. The lack of growth hormone has launched a slow-burning chain of changes in your body, specifically protein regression, which has led to a chemical imbalance in your immune system, so now you have an aneurysm building up in your brain!"

"What!?"

"You got a bomb in your noggin, and it could go off any second. You have this messed-up blood vessel in your brain, with a little lump on it. If that lump bursts, your whole brain will drown in blood. If I were you, I wouldn't jump around like that. I'd lie down on the asphalt so our buddies can call a medic."

Joseph described little Slipperov's condition so dispassionately and matter of factly that the company believed every word he said. The little guy went pale and slowly lay down on the asphalt. Someone bolted off to find a doctor.

Medic Juliet Adamian strode across the parade ground in ratty slippers unhurriedly, waddling like a foie gras duck.

"Please, Ms. Adamian!" went the soldiers, trying to hurry her along. "He's dying!"

She was a fully-loaded tanker, not some swift rescue cutter.

A tanker doesn't speed up; it reaches cruising speed and gets there when it gets there. The medic swept through the waves, and it seemed an eternity would pass before her hips stopped their entrancing swaying and she dropped anchor by the poor fellow's little body. The soldiers could feel the blazing midday sun on the backs of their necks, birds hollered in the nearby woods, drunk from the heat, and there wasn't the slightest breeze.

"Well?" She held up her great arms. The soldiers carefully lowered her boundless body to the asphalt, alongside the little guy.

"So who said this was an aneurysm?" she asked, drawing back his eyelids and feeling his pulse.

"Me, Comrade Captain of the Medical Corps!" Joseph confessed.

"'Ms. Adamian' will do. Are you a doctor or something, sonny? You look a little young . . ."

"No, ma'am!"

"Why do you have to be such a nuisance? Little Mr. Yerevan University X-Ray thinks he can see into the guy's skull . . ."

"I am not from Yerevan, ma'am."

"What'd you bring me out here for, sonny?" The medic continued, still half sitting, half lying on the ground. "There's always the disciplinary barracks . . ."

"I assure you, it's an aneurysm! And if he dies here . . . well, you know. Plus, you have problems to think about in Karabakh!"

Captain Adamian was an intelligent, levelheaded woman. She did indeed have grandnephews in Karabakh; she had to help them out, send them money . . . Sitting there on the hot asphalt, she thought that if this pretty-boy type really was just messing with her aging head, she'd find a way to get even. But if this guy lying on the asphalt really did have an aneurysm and die, she'd be the one with problems . . . They could force her into early retirement, and she didn't have her own place in Russia. She'd be awfully sorry for the soldier's mother, too; she sent her son off to serve the Motherland and got back a zinc coffin . . . She arrived at a rapid and correct decision.

"Stretcher!" the medic commanded. "Quick-quick-quick!" Her voice sounded forth across the base like the trumpets at Jericho, and orderlies appeared almost instantly with the stretcher. "Vehicle!" she commanded, then spoke more quietly to the soldiers standing around her. "Pick me up nice, boys, nice and easy—we don't drop old Armenian ladies in this woman's army!" They took the little guy to a military hospital, while Joseph sat across from the tired medic in the base infirmary and answered her questions.

"Where are you from? What's your name?"

"Moscow. Joseph."

"That's a nice name. How'd you get the notion it was an aneurysm, Joseph-jan?"

"I could feel it."

"I wish I could 'feel' things!" She followed that with a few curses in Armenian. "I'm always wrong! The wrong men, and gal pals that weren't any kind of pal. Are you hungry?"

"Yes."

"Second shelf on the top," she said, gesturing toward a cabinet. "Wrapped in gauze. Can you see it?" Joseph groped blindly.

"I can feel it."

"Take it out." The soldier grabbed something hard that smelled intoxicating.

"Basturma. Hamlet from Kotayk sent it to me." She produced a knife and instructed him to start slicing. "Nice and thin, though!" They chewed the miraculous meat and made small talk.

"This is delicious . . ."

"Hamlet makes it himself! He makes the wine he soaks the meat in, too! He's really something!"

"I'm Jewish, but they took me for a Muslim," Joseph told her, without even knowing why.

"And I'm Armenian, but I only spent the first two years of my life there. My daddy was in the service, so I became a medic. I know the *Daredevils of Sassoun*, though!"

"Who?"

"It's an Armenian epic poem, sonny. I know it by heart."

"I know a lot by heart, too," Joseph confided, finishing a piece of basturma. Captain Adamian didn't hear that last phrase, though. Her head drooped, and she slept the sleep of the elderly, snoring and wheezing. Joseph put his hand behind his head, leaned back, and looked out the window at the sun-drenched parade ground, watching a wagtail with its beak slightly open. It was wagging its tail, two feathers fluttering, obviously thirsty. The soldier felt sleep creeping up, blinked, and, unable to resist, dozed off. He dreamed of Dasha . . .

They were both jerked awake by a deafening ring.

"What's that?" went the medic, still half asleep. "Alarm?"

"It's the phone," Joseph reassured her.

"The phone!" Captain Adamian shook her finger at him. "It's your time to shine, recruit! Gimme that phone! Captain Adamian here . . . Confirmed? They did an X-ray, right? That bad? Oh God! What now? They're already operating? Well, thank you. Thank you!" She put the phone down and wiped the sweat from her forehead. "Good going, you! C'mere." She hugged Joseph like the universal mother, big and smelling of sweet sweat, filling him up inside with kindly Soviet nostalgia. "My boy, my dear, you saved your comrade! Your buddy! No need to look his poor mother in the eyes now! May you live three hundred years, Joseph!" Tears of joy ran from her eyes, falling like living water on the soldier's shaved head.

He didn't tell Ms. Adamian that death would come for her in just three springs, at roughly this time of year. She would get hot again, then doze off, just like today, and go to God quietly. He didn't tell her anything, just stroked her fleshy arms.

"Am I dismissed?"

"Run along, sonny!"

After that day, the other boots constantly nagged Joseph with questions about their health. The soldier refused to answer, assuring them that his diagnosis had been a lucky guess, and he wasn't psychic or anything. They offered him money and cigarettes. One guy even promised a liter of Georgian chacha if Joseph could heal his father's hernia remotely . . .

Major Belic rescued Joseph by sending a special courier.

"The colonel's coming! Time to make good. You get as much chow as you want all day. They're making you fish, for the phosphorous! Just don't eat too much and don't shit the bed! The match is tomorrow at eleven."

Colonel Jamin turned out to be a military intelligence officer of the old school. In those days, people didn't hold them in high regard, or even fear them. They were just mildly wary of them. No need to slip up; you could land yourself in a little pile of shit that way. He was a colorful character. A big man with large features and a voice like Chaliapin. As a cadet in Leningrad, the colonel had once auditioned at the Mariinsky Theatre. They received him cordially, but didn't cast him, suggesting that he study at the conservatory instead. His father, a KGB general, delivered a stern message, as one would expect of a fearless knight with unblemished honor.

"What, do we not have enough fags in our family?"

It was that utterance that sealed his son's fate.

Colonel Jamin arrived with the grandeur of a tsar inspecting his army. He pulled up in a twenty-three-foot-long Chrysler, blue as the sky above the Motherland, the bestial roar of its twelve-liter engine commanding respect. The soldiers were in awe of this miracle of engineering. Then the rear door was flung open and the rider of the mighty steed appeared, first his chrome leather boots, then the entire personage, clad in full dress uniform with an imposing medal bar holder on his chest.

"We wish you good health, Comrade Colonel!" the boots chorused in perfect unison, marking his arrival.

"'Mr. Colonel,' please! Times have changed!" Jamin corrected them. "Have you heard how they address the president these days? They call him 'Mr. President!' The time of comrades has passed." He looked around, his tenacious eyes searching for Major Belic, but he was already approaching from the colonel's right side in a freshly ironed uniform.

"I-wish-you-gd-heth-Comra-Conel!"

"Enough with all these formalities!" Jamin held out his hand, but he was eyeing the young women who worked in the kitchen and had come out to gape at his classic American car.

"Is there any chow?"

"Boy is there!"

The two of them had lunch in the officers' mess, their table talk echoing hollowly all through the giant room. They had a few shots, paired with herring in milk, plus some cucumbers that grew right behind the mess hall—compliments of the major. Then the cooks brought in trays of fried fish straight from the River Loogie, which ran through the base, and finally some nice cold kompot to finish it off.

"I will be very cross if I have come out here for nothing, Belic."

"I wouldn't do that to you, Comrade Colonel!"

"Enough with the 'comrade!'"

"I like to do things properly. And yeah, this kid's a chess whiz."

"Want to make this a little more interesting?"

"If he loses, I'll give you 70 pounds of sun-dried bream, Com . . . Mr. Colonel."

"And I'll put up a case of vodka. Russian Standard! They only just started delivering it to our neck of the woods."

"Best of three," the major announced.

"Five," Jamin countered, pouring another shot into himself. Then he began singing an old folk song, "The Floating Ax Head," in his luxurious bass voice.

"Seems like a respectable guy," the major thought to himself. "But get a few shots in him and he's as drunk as a schoolgirl."

"How about a moment to relax?" Belic asked, his tone servile.

"Ah, I love napping in the hay up above your sauna! The smell of fresh, crinkly sheets . . . And send me that . . . what's her name? The cook with the pink hair."

"Goodness, Comrade Colonel!"

"That's Mr. Colonel! I'll give her a hundred—in dollars!"

"The match is tomorrow . . ."

"A big, warm ass never hurt anybody!"

"I'll ask her," the major promised, then turned around and shouted for his subordinates. "Manuilov! Steklov!" Two yefreytors appeared instantly. "Escort Mr. Colonel to the bedroom above the sauna at once!"

They fed Joseph—good food and lots of it. The pretty young cooks huddled around the handsome man with the deep black eyes and looked at him reverently. They liked the way he ate. The soldier boy paid no attention to the chicks; he was lost in his own thoughts. After he drank the kompot, Joseph shivered, covered his eyes, and whispered something in a language the cooks didn't understand. They listened, though, like teeny-boppers to a hit song.

"What was that? Were you singin' somethin'?" one of the civilian employees inquired when he had stopped whispering.

"It was a prayer."

"What kind of prayer?"

"For the dead . . . Slipperov just died."

The next morning, at eleven o'clock sharp, in the Lenin room, Colonel Jamin moved his king's pawn and pressed the clock. The intelligence officer didn't have any prepared opening lines for the match (or any at all, for that matter), so he was looking at Joseph with a certain degree of pity. This piece-of-trash recruit would have to drink enough bromine to wash away the Ostankino Television Tower, while he'd had that big-assed, pink-haired cook breathing in his ear all night. Jamin disappeared into his erotic reminiscences, making his moves mechanically, like he was playing through some memorized book variation, while time ticked away, and he imagined his nighttime hetaera à la doggy. Then suddenly, a short, cold word crashed into his brain—"mate!" The colonel came to his senses and stared at the board, not understanding how his opponent had managed to capture his king so quickly . . . It was a sight how happy Belic was! The major was practically jumping for joy, making faces, on the verge of giving Joseph a French kiss. The victor retained his usual demeanor as he set up the pieces for the next game and turned the board around so he could play white. When Colonel Jamin finally realized that he had been defeated by a private, his face turned crimson and he broke into furious sweat.

"Are you Jewish?" he asked, unable to contain himself, pointing at Joseph, who was already prepared to play white.

"Yes," the soldier answered. "What does it matter?"

"I'll tell you later," the intelligence officer promised. "Make your move, Jew. Where's your yarmulke?"

The next game lasted thirty-two moves. Eventually, white had three major pieces versus black's vulnerable king shielded by a couple of pawns. Joseph could have put an end to his opponent's torments at any moment, but he tried to make him resign himself and avoid the utter shame denoted by that word— "mate." The intelligence officer fought on doggedly. Sweat dropped on to the board as he moved his king back and forth, but Joseph kept checking him over and over again, until Belic finally nodded. Wipe me out!

"Mate," Joseph declared, sliding his rook along the file. The major looked like he was about to crouch down and burst into a dance. His face was as red as Jamin's, but from joy—the colonel looked like he was about to have a stroke.

"Yid!" the intelligence officer raged. "Kike!"

"Anal sex maniac!" Joseph snapped back unexpectedly.

"How dare you, you little bitch!" The officer sprang to his feet, medals jangling, sweaty hand moving to his holster. "I'll whack you in the toilet, you fucking bastard! I'll shoot you right in front of Lenin! And, by the way, why the hell haven't they taken Lenin down?!" At that point, the major had to step in.

"Later, Mr. Colonel! The next item on the agenda is the third game! A deal's a deal! Then you can shoot Lenin himself, if you want!"

"I'll whack you, too, bitch!" Jamin growled. "Damn you, Belic! You're a yid too! You're all yids here!"

"Sure, sure," the major agreed. "Everybody's a yid, just move your pawn or whatever . . ."

The colonel took a few deep breaths, trying to calm down. He strained his brain, like he was putting the pedal to the metal in his mighty Chrysler and moved so fast sparks flew: E2—E4.

An elegant, absolutely crushing combination ended the third game on move 15.

The instant Joseph uttered the word "mate," Major Belic shouted.

"Get outta here, kid! Run!"

In white-hot fury, with blood rushing to his brain, the colonel sprang up, clawing at Joseph's chest, but the quick, nimble youth slipped away and was already running across the parade ground toward the gate leading to the woods, Jamin's voice booming after him.

"Halt! I'll kill you, kike!" Gunshots and four-letter words rang out. Hell, five-letter words, six!

Joseph was unharmed for the time being. Jamin and Belic got into a rather primitive fight and busted up each other's noses . . . When they broke apart, breathing hard, blood gushing, there was a sudden summer thunderclap. Buckets of rain came down; plump white mushrooms would sprout tomorrow.

"I'm from Machulishchy," Belic explained, the wind accompanying his voice. "That's in Belarus!"

"I know this trick by heart," said the colonel, adjusting his uniform. "You're a secret yid!"

"Would you be so kind as to pay up . . . mister?" The irony was deliberate. "By the way, our president is inviting yids to return to our country. He promised to welcome them with honors!"

"What are you showing off for, Belic?" Jamin's heart had slowed, and his once hot skin had cooled; there was just a little blood left around his nose. "You can't win yourself, so you brought in a Jew! That's why the boys upstairs are inviting them back, to edge everyone else out once and for all! Those bastards did all their science abroad and left us fuckin' high and dry!"

"You're the one who challenged him!"

"But you're the one who told me about him!"

"Did anybody put a gun to your head?"

"You know I have a temper!"

Those who had lived on that base for a long time and seen Colonel Jamin invited for chess matches knew it always ended the same way: the most primitive of fights, then reconciliation. These officers weren't enemies, just the opposite—they were comrades whose lives were missing something. One didn't have enough opportunities to torture people, the other didn't have enough stars on his shoulder boards—so they sublimated their real desires into games, the fair sex, and busting each other's noses. Jamin lugged the case of fashionable new vodka out of his Chrysler and shook Belic's hand.

"Until next time, Comrade Colonel!"

"Sure . . . Comrade it is. We're as far from misters as a Jew is from a general." Jamin got into his car, where the air conditioner was already running, and bade the driver get moving.

The following day, Slipperov's coffin was brought out to the parade ground for the service. The departed seemed to have gotten even smaller; his face had dried up and the sight of the little cloth covering his head was heart wrenching. His skull had been opened neatly but then closed carelessly. A dead man doesn't give a damn!

Belic received a call from the command center—he was not being held responsible; they were surprised that they had even managed to diagnose an aneurysm on a military base. The major explained that he was trying to keep morale high in these difficult, anarchic days, to maintain Soviet standards, especially in medicine. An ounce of prevention is worth a ton of cure!

The soldiers crawled up to the coffin like drowsy flies but then sped up to get away from the strange smell.

"Formaldehyde," Mrs. Adamian explained. She seemed to have aged another ten years. She wouldn't leave the coffin, just stood there on legs riddled with varicose veins, stroking the cloth on Slipperov's head . . . That evening, they escorted the old Armenian lady to her room, poured her some valerian, and let her be. Under cover of darkness, the kitchen girls hauled bucket after bucket of rapidly melting ice to keep Slipperov's body cool. His parents would be arriving the next day, and everything had to look presentable.

Belic drank the Russian Standard all night, getting pretty raucous, constantly inviting Joseph to knock one back to Slipperov's memory and his victory over Jamin. Joseph abstained from drinking, but he sure did eat. The kitchen girls had fried up a whole heap of fish . . .

"Well, yid, ol' buddy . . ." the major said to Private Brodsky in parting. "There ya have it!" Then he retired for the night.

The next morning, a black Volga arrived for Joseph. It was the general in command of their military district and Mitya Schwartz. Belic was instructed to provide Recruit Brodsky's file without delay, as well as Brodsky himself.

"He didn't do anything wrong!" The agonizingly hungover major did his best to defend the kid, thinking Jamin was up to his old tricks, but the general harshly ordered him not to interfere.

"Don't worry, they're going to give him a medical discharge," Schwartz reassured him.

They took Joseph to Moscow and improved his mother's living conditions. They had found a vocation for this young man with the 180 IQ after all and, with it, the meaning of his life. As if he didn't know it himself.

12

Every year, at the end of winter, I run a marathon in honor of a
Roman named Pheidippides who never existed. Those Romans
made up a lot of things in their long history—gods and idols to
teach their wives and children, to sleep with them and cheat
on them. Boy, those guys were a creative bunch. They changed
the world. They stunned the Creator himself. Basically, I like it
when it's really coming down, and all the puddles . . . I put on
my track bottoms with the stretched-out knees, some sneakers
preserved since the fifties, a T-shirt with a Moscow Dinamo
stencil on it, and . . .

Well, long story short, I start running. I'm slopping through
the melting snow, and all the people are gawking, like there's
something wrong with me. Maybe I'm not dressed right, who
knows? I really like the way I look, though. It just so happens that
contemporary activewear fashions tend toward the retro. Adidas
and Fila both have retro lines. The people of Moscow are a peculiar lot. The best way to get a smile out of them is to slip on the ice
and smack your head. Just slip and go face first right into the dirty
snow. I brought so much joy into the world! The college girls
started laughing, then the guys copied them out of habit, using
my misfortune as an opportunity to flirt, even though they'd
already suffered their own misfortune in their pants! Yesterday
morning, they had all discovered that they were eunuchs. Even
an old lady who had just a day and a half to live showed her gums
in a toothless smile when she saw how elegantly I run.

"You will be forgiven!" I promised her, then looked at
the world around me and added, "but not the rest of you," in a
whisper.

I trotted to the Boulevard Ring and started running where they'd plowed. I unexpectedly encountered an elderly man I recognized; it was Medvedev, the bachelor from that long-ago communal apartment, the one who'd once tried to evict me and enlisted the support of those other scumbag neighbors. I came up beside him and started running a little slower.

"Do you remember me, Medvedev?" I asked calmly. He was carrying a bunch of bags, probably from the local Pyaterochka—must have been coming home with groceries.

"Sure, you're EE." He looked at me like he'd seen me yesterday.

"Precisely."

"You really don't change. It's like aging just isn't for you."

"Try running, Comrade Medvedev. Especially now that there's nothing between your legs to get in the way." My neighbor clearly didn't want to listen to what I was saying, so he stopped, pretending he needed to rest. I could not stop, of course; I was running a marathon and could not disrupt my graceful progress, so I had to leave Medvedev behind, but a chain of associations led me back to that disgusting apartment where they would never let me live in peace . . .

Just as I had promised, I set up a table in the common area, one of the little mommies covered it with a white cloth, and then I loaded it with such fanciful delicacies in such quantity that even Old Lady Morozova started drooling.

"I bet you stole it all, Mr. Eskimo!"

"Why 'Eskimo'?" I wanted to ask. Suckling pig, pressed black caviar, three grilled chickens, Olivier salad, Moskovsky salad, a bunch of cans of all kinds of fish, Stolichnaya vodka, enough to drink until you burst, plus Alazani wine for the ladies—a rare commodity back then.

They sat, they ate, they drank. Old Lady Morozova

single-handedly put away a whole grilled chicken but still managed to look displeased. Those representatives of the Russian people grew more kindhearted and raised a glass to me as the son of Comandante Che. They sang all the old songs: the "Seven Magpies," the one about the horse, and the one about the partisans . . . Then the apartment burned down. It was Old Lady Morozova's fault. She mixed vodka with red wine, got in bed with a lit cigarette, and dozed off. Her cotton blanket caught fire, and a lick of flame jumped to the synthetic curtains. After that, it was just a matter of follow-through . . .

The mommies, along with their children and partners, burned like witches and warlocks in the fire that spread from that wayward flame. Only Medvedev the Bachelor managed to miraculously escape, and he stood outside and watched it amble up and down the whole height of the building, holding Old Lady Morozova in his arms, who was cursing for the whole neighborhood to hear, proclaiming that the bankbook for an account worth a million rubles was still inside.

"I wanted to make a donation for repairs to the mausoleum of the great leader of the proletariat!" she yelled. "I saved up for so long!"

She lived out the rest of her days in a quiet unit at Kashchenko Psychiatric Hospital—not half bad—since she had contrived to become the secretary of the Building 2 Party chapter . . . Well, to hell with that apartment! There were so many of them, some better, some worse. At least now I was sitting pretty at Senescentova's place. Nobody bothered me. I kept running, trying to not think about anything, just meditate. The sky was swollen, gray-black, like a boil that was about to burst and send a black hole sluicing out.

I run out on to Petrovsky Boulevard, startling the pigeons— and bam, I see this old man, one leg up on a bench, tying his shoelaces. The old man's wearing the same sneakers as me, except red, plus track bottoms and a shirt with CSKA stenciled on it. Dinamo's rival team. I recognize this flabby athlete, but who is he? Why, it's my barber, my favored provider of tonsorial services, the silent Greek with the scissors! Antipatros! Then he starts running in the same direction as me. He's as swift as a donkey on steroids!

"Hey!" I shouted. "Wearing a CSKA shirt is beating a dead horse!" Their first stadium was built where Moscow's old horse track once stood, so that was an easy dig. Antipatros turned around and, for the first time in my memory, answered aloud, his voice coming through his fluttering beard.

"Dinamo is a sty! A *pig* sty!" He was answering my jab in kind: Dinamo has a reputation for recruiting from the police force. "Dina-noooo!" he booed, as if he were in the stands.

I was astonished. He was speaking! This man who had been silent for decades, and perhaps longer!

"My dear Antipatros, your years of silence are over!" I exclaimed joyfully.

"What's it to you?"

"Blood brothers, hey, hey! Oh, smell the hay! Oh, hear them neigh! CSKA is here to play!" I belted out his team's official song.

"Blood brothers? People have blood," the Greek squeaked, his sneakers sloshing along the boggy ground. "You aren't a person."

"You never ran before!" I said.

"You're the one who never ran!"

"I always run in honor of Pheidippides! What's your assistant's name?"

"Zoika—but what's it to you? Butt out! Anyway, I am Pheidippides."

"He's a fictional character! I'm just asking because she's a pretty girl—"

"You're a fictional character!" The old Greek wasn't lying, I could see that in his eyes. I felt sorry for Antipatros. My heart contracted into a nut and beat fast like a hammer.

"How long have you been here?"

"You do the math!"

"A long time. What're you in for?"

"Don't butt in! I'm not asking you, so don't you butt in, piggy!"

"My apologies . . . But Pheidippides died at the end of his run to Marathon! Stone-dead, ready for the glue factory! Get it? Like a horse?"

"Then he was resurrected! For real, not like what certain fantasists have concocted."

"Do you have a telephone too?" This was a most surprising conversation with my kinsman.

"Gee, I don't know. Did the Romans have phones?"

"But how will you know when it's time for you to go back?"

"They have their own methods there," the Greek chuckled. "So you're always waiting for a call?"

"Yes, I will admit it. Sometimes I call, too, when I'm feeling despondent . . ."

"And you're just waiting and waiting, like you called tech support!" Antipatros laughed, and his laughter was like a cough from ages past. "Which way are you going?"

"Following the Boulevard Ring."

"Garden Ring for me." The old Greek laughed again, or coughed, and ran to the right, away from me.

I'm no fool either. I've known for a long time that something grand is in the works, and the fact that the old Greek has parted his lips at last only serves to confirm my conclusions.

I ran, dreaming that something revolutionary, along with that something grand, would happen to me . . .

The sky ruptured at last, and a wall of rain assembled from all over the world fell on Moscow. I looked for an awning to stand under so I could wait out the storm and found one in front of a restaurant. I stood under its protection, or, more accurately, continued my run there, but just did it in place.

Then I saw her. Perfection. The tender oval of her face appeared through the wet plate glass of the eatery, and not even the rain could wash that miraculous image away. She had a coffee cup in her hand, white against her white sweater with a neckline somewhere between nakedness and attire . . . Verushka! I couldn't see who she was sitting with, conversing breezily and flirting lightly. Her Iratov, I dare say—but how could that be? What good was he to her now?

I took a step under the ocean falling from above and saw a young man—indeed, a *young* man—a little over twenty, strikingly similar in appearance to the old Iratov. It wasn't him, though! It wasn't him, even though they were like two peas in a pod! His son? Impossible! I know all of Iratov's children: Alevtina's son, Joseph, God rest his soul, his scion born of Svetlana, and the girl Masha from the foreign currency store had . . . No, it was an outsider! I looked at the stranger and felt enmity toward him. Even through the glass, my nose picked up the scent of their recent illicit copulation. Forgetting about the marathon, I grabbed the massive door handle and entered the restaurant with a warlike cast to my face. I even felt sorry for the older Iratov, who had suffered such misfortune. I would have approached the young man, but then my chest collided with the huge hand of the manager.

"Where you goin'?" the shift boss asked with a scornful squint, studying my admittedly drenched raiment. He kept poking my chest, trying to push me back into the mighty downpour.

"Well, to the restaurant, of course."

"Whaddaya want?"

"Just some tea—it's cold out there on the broad boulevards of Moscow. I must say, this isn't what I'd call service."

"Make tea at home."

"Why?" I was getting annoyed.

"Because I say so! We have a dress code! Beat it!"

"How about some hot water?"

"Out!" The manager shoved me in the chest with both hands, but I was not disposed to give in, so I stood there like a stone statue, not even flinching. The eatery employee, a man with the physique of a bodybuilder, was surprised at this. He looked at his ham-bone arms, then at me. "Resisting, huh?!" He hit me again, this time in the solar plexus. His knuckles struck the steel of my stomach; he groaned and stepped away from me, looking down at his mangled fist. I can take a few hits when necessary, and even defend myself if the situation calls for it.

"Don't lose your cool," I warned him.

"I'll call the police!" the manager warned me right back, still cringing in pain.

"Go right ahead! They'll find out about your illegal second credit card terminal that sends money to your own bank instead of the one that's supposed to service this business. Tax evasion! The owners will be over the moon! But you, young man, how will you make a brilliant career after running someone else's business into the ground over a cup of hot water?"

"We have a dress code . . ."

"You're just a broken record! Well, simply seat me behind that curtain then!"

The bodybuilder led me to where the staff ate and personally brought me a cup of tea. A waitress hurried after him, carrying a staff lunch on a tray: pale hot dogs with buckwheat and a bowl of borscht with a chicken leg in it.

"Not quite Michelin-star fare," I commented. "Now, if you would be so kind as to leave me to my solitude!"

"I'll be right here, watching," the manager warned me, but glanced at his fist again. It had ballooned to twice its normal size.

After my hurried run, I was hungry to the point of spiritual desolation, so I swallowed the borscht in three spoonfuls and sucked on the chicken leg until the bone shone. The hot dogs turned out to be made of soy, and the buckwheat had been crushed, not peeled! Still, my belly was full at least, and the first sip of hot tea flowed through my insides and warmed my body.

Of course, even when I was eating, I had been observing my dearie and the impudent young man with Iratov's face. It was stunning how much the young woman's body language had changed. She was pulling faces like a teenager. Vera, whose beauty I have worshipped for many years, was fluttering her eyelashes and sticking out her breasts, which had nearly escaped from the neckline of her white sweater. The young man would occasionally reach out to her face, stroking her cheeks. His eyes, black and bottomless, were home to utter indifference. The cold of space, if you will, radiated from within him. His fingers were indifferent, too, waxy. He stuck one of them in Vera's mouth; she bit his phalange and all of her, from head to toe, exuded pheromones. If I were interested in erotic matters, it is unlikely I could have withstood that onslaught of love molecules. I would have had to retreat immediately. Since all of those physiological delights had no bearing on me, I strained my ears to hear the substance of their conversation.

"You know, Eugene," she said, her intonation so saucy it made me shudder. "I'm not afraid of these changes I'm experiencing anymore."

"Great," said the young man, who I now knew was named Eugene. What a fucking nasty name. "I told you that all your needless anguish and torment would pass. Iratov isn't your whole life!"

"Yes," she agreed submissively. "You're my life now!"

Oh, great Padishah! I can't sit here and listen to this stunning woman making these sappy proclamations to a man who is just using her! Now she was whispering something so vile it cut me to the quick.

"Take me."

"We're in a restaurant," replied the young man with a name fit only for a stripper, rather gruffly.

"So what? There's nobody here, and the stalls in the ladies' room are as well-appointed as any boudoir."

"Let's go," he agreed with a shrug.

I was squashed like a mouse by an elephant. Coupling in a public place! Pah! That's too much, even for the snot-nosed, sophomoric, snorting set! How bottomless the fall she had opened up before him! "Well, she certainly doesn't understand what's going on," I thought. "She's doubtless under the influence of some malevolent charm and is thus not responsible for her actions . . . Some trick of yours perhaps, kinsman?"

The couple got up from their table, then Vera took Eugene's hand and drew him toward the ladies' room. I could not permit this to occur, so I foolishly appealed to the bodybuilder manager, informing him that a man and woman were about to bang in the restroom.

"What's it to you?" asked the uncomprehending waiter.

"You'll have problems!" I was losing my mind. "The health inspector will impose fines! A threat to respectable businesses everywhere!"

"You gonna call him or something?"

"If you fail to put a stop to this intolerable behavior, I will nip it in the bud myself without hesitation!"

"Oh yeah?" The Slav-shithouse waiter blocked my way. I had to get up and meet him with a foot between the legs. No reaction was forthcoming. Realizing that things weren't what they once were downstairs, I seized his bull-like neck and squeezed his carotid artery. I had about twenty minutes. I ran out from behind the curtain and giant kangaroo leaps carried me to the facilities.

Charging into the bathroom, I detected the repugnant sounds of hasty coupling, then saw the personages themselves by the mosaic window. She was seated on the sill, her legs boundlessly open, and he was digging into her like the very scarabs of Egypt! Scarabs! And she was moaning shamelessly, oblivious to the world around her, and he was glancing at the cover of a yachting magazine that lay nearby. My conviction that this matter could not be explained without recourse to sorcerous influence grew yet firmer, that there are no mere falls, just shoves into fiery Gehenna! This Eugene was the manifestation of a passionless weapon, destroying a woman in the highest sense of that word. This beetle with the long mouthparts was part of my enemy's dark design.

She suddenly saw a stranger observing their amorous convulsions from the sidelines and wanted to stop their runaway train, but the brakes had long since burned out, so all she could do was cry out ferociously—lewdly, to my ear—giving me a beckoning stare. Before it was destroyed, reduced to mangled metal mixed with flesh, the train sounded a frantic blast on its horn, as if in farewell. She sang out the final note . . .

The moment had come for the vile youth to cease the movements of his loins; he turned around, scrutinized me, then smirked and winked.

"What, old-timer? Found something fun to watch?" Vera kept looking at me, but her eyes were full of madness, her body absorbing the enemy's seed, her numb mouth still open, her cheeks blushing a hellish red. "Well?"

"My darling Vera . . ." I pronounced her name with calm pity. "Leave this place at once!"

"Do you know him?" Eugene asked in surprise.

"No," she answered hoarsely, finally lifting her hand to cover her breasts, which had worked their way out of the neckline of her sweater, and closing her legs tight, as if I meant to lay claim to the shredded prize between them.

"Who are you, old-timer?" he asked again.

"Vera, leave this place forthwith! How will you ever be able to face your husband?! On a windowsill in the shitter, letting an impostor know you!?"

"You know Mr. Iratov?" she asked in drunken surprise.

"I have for many years!"

She was about to get scared, but then she remembered the events of the past few days, her husband's disability, how he had then fallen so low, observing her and Eugene with sickly passion rather than killing the thief on the spot, the fact that she could never have children with him—all of that erased her fear, making room for the strongest feeling to take shape . . . love. I realized that she truly did love this monster, that she had been remade, whether by sorcery, charms, or curses.

"Oh Vera . . ." I began to weep.

Eugene continued looking at me as he zipped up his jeans. Something alarmed him about this peculiar person with the spiky white buzz cut and no eyelashes or brows crying there in front of him; Eugene could sense some threat to his existence, but he attributed it to a chemical imbalance or a failure to interpret his own distemper.

"Get out of here," he commanded.

"Oh Vera . . ." I said, wiping the tears away with my sleeve. "You could have been . . ." I threw my hands high, toward the bathroom ceiling. "You could have been . . . You were my Verushka . . . my dearie . . . now you're just some Vera, one of thousands!"

"Listen, old-timer," Eugene said threateningly, lightly hugging his consort around the shoulders. "If you want to stay in the ladies' room, nobody's stopping you. Just let us by, please! Or else I'm going to have to . . ."

Yes, I did let them by, then stood there for a moment before I returned to the main room. They were back at their table, where she was daintily holding a tea fork, eating a fruit tart.

I wanted to brand her as a harlot in front of the whole restaurant, but then I heard police sirens. The bodybuilder had apparently called for backup. I had to leave via the staff entrance, and I did it like a true professional . . .

I had to clear my head, so I ran for the next three days, racking up nearly 400 miles.

Then I went back to Senescentova's apartment, took a shower, wanted to make a call on the landline telephone, but remembered Antipatros; I exercised some self-control and went to bed for a week, with an alarm set to awaken me in due course. Even as I was falling asleep, I found myself thinking that the planet would soon face events of historic import.

Instead of withdrawing from this world so I could experience my former nature, or memories of it, at least in the illusory world of dreams, I saw pictures from the lives of ordinary Muscovites.

I dreamed of Masha, the one from the foreign currency store, whom the young Iratov had once used in passing.

I saw her with a little girl in her arms, fair-haired and

blue-eyed. Masha gave birth to her in utter solitude, deprived of any opportunity to find decent employment, cut off from her friends and even her father, who turned his back on her because of the efforts of Photios Prytki, that spook and denouncer of innocents. He adroitly manipulated everyone close to Masha, claiming that she had prostituted herself for foreign currency. The striking word "hooker" had only just come into popular usage. It resulted in banishment from the Communist Youth League, blacklisting, and all the associated delights. Masha never had a mother; she had run away from the maternity ward, leaving behind everything superfluous, everything she didn't need in her life . . .

She named her daughter Iseult. What disposed her to choose such an obscure name remains unknown. On the other hand, Masha herself was a spiteful personage, spiteful in the extreme; her only dream was to marry a foreign citizen. She hated this country with all her heart, hated the pressed cotton she had to use instead of real tampons, the meager diet available, the unkempt, depressed men; she couldn't stand this land's emblematic white birches and watching *Seventeen Moments of Spring* infuriated her. If she were Stierlitz, the superspy in the movie, she would have stayed in Germany and surrendered to the Americans. But in the movie, all that prick got for all his heroic efforts was a tiny little dacha made of about three planks, and it seemed like he was happy with his wife, just like Tikhonov, the actor who played him. She'd seen him in his Moscow-made suit at a screening of a French movie about the trials and tribulations of the self-indulgent bourgeoisie at Dom Kino. He smiled at everyone who recognized him; everyone else found him touchingly gentle, but to her, he was another worthless Russian sissy. To hell with all those local Delons, Belmondos, and Richards!

She learned perfect English; by eighth grade, she already

knew that there was no way she was going to stay in the USSR. She educated herself independently by visiting museums and theaters so she wouldn't look uncouth in front of whomever from wherever. She would show just how well-rounded she was. She learned to prepare European dishes from a cookbook by Vasilisa Zudova, the chef at a restaurant called "Prague"—who, it must be noted in passing, had never been to a single European country.

For as long as she could remember, she had devoted her life to backbreaking self-improvement, all so one day some rotten malefactor, some worthless playboy, could negate her work and her future, rob her of all her hopes! Worse still, she was left utterly alone, with a pretty-boy swindler's child in her arms. How could she not be spiteful?

First it fell to her to sell everything in the house she had accumulated during her time at the foreign currency store to feed and clothe her daughter, Iseult. The child turned out to have a good appetite, and she grew at a remarkable rate. By the age of three, tormented by her mother's hatred for everyone and everything, she had already lost all her loveliness and was an overfed, blue-eyed mediocrity. The illegitimate child grew up surprisingly lazy and indifferent to everything. Whether it was her strange name weighing her down or sloth passed down from her ancestors remains unknown and, in truth, unimportant.

Never once in her whole adolescent period did she bemoan the fact that her mother brought men home—men who, by the time she was sexually mature, were shaking the hardwood floors down to the foundation as they trod the path to her mother's bedroom. Iseult understood that it was Masha's men—she called her mother "Masha"—on whom her prosperity and ability to live as she saw fit depended. At school, she was considered a disadvantaged child, and there was nothing to be found on

her report cards but Cs, with only a single A in physical education shining among them. Realizing that her excess weight made
her unattractive, and given her lack of any prospects whatsoever,
she cajoled the teacher to work with her after class, and after
a few years of tenacious exercise, she was pretty again. A new
haircut, a manicure, and her mother's push-up bra improved her
appearance, making her a lure for the opposite sex. Her sloth
evaporated in her early youth, but her indifference remained
with her forever. She soon learned the ways of intimacy, losing her virginity to the gym teacher, obviously, thereby repaying
him for all his extracurricular work. Her mother had taught her
well: she always had safe sex, so as not to wind up with her own
unplanned Iseult or Brunhilda, forcing the boys to wear product no. 2, with no concessions, not even for her regular clients.
If the local youth lacked the experience to put on a rubber, the
girl was always ready to offer commensurate assistance—just so
she wouldn't get knocked up. Iseult didn't experience any disgust from intimacy with men but took no pleasure in it either,
which made her doubly surprised that her mother saw her work
as a way to recharge her emotional energy, as well as make
good money. Iseult never had to charge herself; her battery was
always empty, but she collected material compensation from
boys and teenagers for the use of her insensate body, which she
spent exclusively on herself, never giving her mother a penny.
Her clients did not pay with money alone, of course; the young
prostitute also used the barter system: panties, T-shirts, foreign
cigarettes, alcohol—even if it was Bulgarian—all kinds of stuff.
One time she even got paid with a one-hundred-piece package
of cherry-flavored gum . . . Iseult sold what she didn't need at
the flea market near Leningradsky Station, and, by the age of fifteen, she already had a tidy sum in her savings account. Iratov's
flesh and blood tirelessly forged her happy little future. An initial

analysis would suggest that Iseult, indifferent to the world as she was, was toiling away like a draft horse in the domain of illicit intimate services. She was, in a manner of speaking, the second in a dynasty. Her mother, Masha, and her. The only person the girl wasn't indifferent to was herself, though.

With her wretched transcript, she didn't even apply to college; she could have bribed her way in, but she preferred to spend that money paying off the cops at the big hotels where she paraded her firm ass around the bars and restaurants to pick up men on business trips. Iseult acquired foreign currency, said a brief goodbye to her mother, and rented an apartment right by Patriarch Ponds, where she was visited by a pair of cultural attachés, one consul, and the ambassador of one of the smallest African countries, who wore a big gold buckle on a sash across his chest. Iseult wasn't like her mother at all. She didn't hate her country, and thus had inherited very little of Masha's spite. She was perfectly happy with her life in Moscow. All the brand-name foreign products that speculators once traded could now be sold openly, and there was plenty of food in the stores; Iseult even tried crocodile at a reception with her African ambassador. It tasted like chicken. You could even fly to America . . . if you had the money. But what would she do over there with no English or other skills? Turn tricks? She was already offering paid admission to her loveless temple in Moscow and receiving an embarrassment of riches from her clients. Iseult grew more beautiful with time; she got thinner without any fancy diets and her cheeks burned with a natural pomegranate glow. She had a steady customer base, her own foreign car parked out in front of her building, and a fully stocked refrigerator—she couldn't complain. It was just that she was feeling tired more and more often, and not just on the job; it was happening at home, too. Iseult didn't pay any attention to those trifles, though. She was planning to go to

Italy in the summer and spend two whole weeks not working, just soaking up the Neapolitan sun.

During one of their rare phone calls, Iseult's mother advised her to go in for a checkup.

"Regular physical examinations are key for girls in our profession!"

"Are you still in the business?"

"Yeah, but now I have some girls working for me. I only see clients when I feel like it."

"Maybe I should come on board?"

"What kind of mother would sell her daughter?! Keep working on your own."

"How come you're still in Russia?"

"I'm saving up to buy a house in Spain, then . . ."

Iseult went to the gynecologist and was surprised to learn that she was pregnant.

"But how? I always use—"

"You're nearing four months." The specialist clearly was not interested in a lengthy conversation. "You will have to register, undergo a series of tests, and take vitamins."

Iseult was such a mess on the drive home that she almost crashed into a fire truck. She kept wondering who could have caused this misfortune, where she had slipped up, whose flesh was swelling in her leavening dough. All the evidence pointed to one of her clients, the ambassador from the small African country . . . Iseult had no intention to profit by this conclusion, however; she didn't plan to blackmail the ambassador or anything. She kept receiving visitors, just significantly less often.

Then men came to her apartment. A full squad of cops, the district officer, and a man in a wrinkled white coat. The district officer pressed himself against the wall as if she were a leper, while the man in the white coat identified himself as a doctor from the public health department and asked her to come with them to the hospital at Sokolina Gora.

"Why?" Iseult asked, startled.

"You'll find out at the hospital," the policeman replied.

It turned out that the hospital specialized in infectious diseases. Iseult was no fool; she realized that meant she had picked up syphilis or something. If it was just gonorrhea, they wouldn't have dragged her all the way out there. Now she was in for a heap of trouble. She'd really put her foot in it . . . but when, with who?! They'd try to preach to her at the hospital, but who cares? And the pregnancy on top of everything else . . . She was taken from office to office. They probed every orifice, shined a light in her eyes, and did ultrasounds. They wouldn't even give her a towel to wipe off the gel. They did tell her it was a girl inside her, though. She figured it had to be syphilis; that was why they kept giving her those scornful looks. They stuck her in an MRI machine bearing a label with the peculiar name "Image 1." The doctors chatted among themselves, mentioning that this imported machine had been sitting in the basement for a year. Nobody even knew how to set it up, much less use it. They had planned to bring in some Americans to teach them, but the money had apparently gone toward the foundation for a little country home. A mere ten thousand square feet.

A woman general practitioner listened to her heart and asked her questions.

"How's your weight?"

"I've lost a little recently."

"How much?"

"I don't really weigh myself, but I can tell by my clothes."

"Weakness? Sweating?"

"Well, I am pregnant. The sweating is mostly at night."

After all the examinations, she had to sit in a chair out in the hallway for four hours, driving herself to the brink of madness. How had she gotten pregnant? How had she gotten the syph? She'd get through it, one way or another.

What Iseult heard in the chief physician's office first drove her into perplexity, then plunged her into a primal whirlpool of indescribable fear.

"You have contracted the human immunodeficiency virus!" the department head said, pointing to her MRI scans for some reason.

"What's that?"

"AIDS."

Iseult lost consciousness and slid down the wall on to the chlorine-smelling floor. Nobody picked her up or tried to wake her.

"Dirty tramp," the department head stated simply.

"Yeah," said the resident.

"You have a daughter, right?"

"I'd kill her!"

"But she isn't even in school yet."

"Yeah, but just thinking about it . . . I'd kill her!"

"How'd the tramp let it happen? She's a professional . . ." the department head said, thinking out loud "Anal sex," he answered himself. "Those airheads think only one hole needs protection! He went in a little low and spurted too fast. That's how she got HIV, and it probably explains the pregnancy, too."

"Serves her right for doing anal!" the resident declared.

Iseult regained consciousness and instantly remembered the sentence the doctor had passed on her. She was about to slip into unreason again, eyes rolling back in her head, when the resident gruffly interrupted the process.

"Hello! This isn't a brothel. Quit lying around!" She managed to get up, breaking the false nails on her right hand, then breathed deeply, moved to an armchair like a somnambulist, and sat down without asking permission.

"What is your name?" the department head asked. "Never mind, I have it here." He flipped through his papers and informed her that the first order of business would be getting rid of the child.

"But it's already been four months!" Iseult forced out, her voice hoarse.

"Induced labor then. We'll shove him out!" the resident announced. "You'll pop out yet another AIDS gremlin!"

"Doctor, please!"

"Why . . . why 'AIDS gremlin?'" She was moving her tongue with difficulty, as if her mouth were full of modeling clay. "And it's a girl. They told me—"

"Because the chances that he will be born healthy are almost nonexistent," the department head said, agreeing with his colleague. "And even if he's lucky enough to be HIV-negative, who would take care of him? And what if he isn't lucky?"

Running on autopilot, Iseult repeated that it was a "she" not a "he," a girl, and she had a mother. Then she snapped out a question.

"How long do I ha—" The department head rose from his desk, picked up a pointer, and began to poke at the MRI images.

"Do you see this? And this?"

"What?" She was barely holding herself together, mechanically licking up the tears rolling down her face.

"This! Your lungs! No, those are hardly lungs anymore! Your liver? Nope, not what I'd call a liver. Same goes for your kidneys, and you have the heart of a dwarf!"

"Yes, yes, I understand . . ."

"Oh, you understand, do you?" Then the department head suddenly seemed to see this sick, pregnant, utterly lost woman for the first time, and he felt pity for her. "We all die sooner or later . . ."

"Sooner, in your case," the resident noted.

"Leave the room immediately, Doctor!"

"Huh?"

"Get out of here, close the door behind you, and go see your patients!"

The resident's face turned as purple as potassium permanganate mouthwash. He got up and left, deliberately jostling Iseult's shoulder along the way, firmly convinced that forced euthanasia was the way to handle people like her . . .

"What's your name, honey?" the doctor asked again when the door had closed behind his colleague.

"Iseult . . .

"My name is Vasily, Vasily Stepanov . . . Listen, you waited an awfully long time to seek medical help . . ."

"How much longer, Doctor Stepanov?"

"You're a professional, I'll give it to you straight. Up to a year, but that's if you are under strict medical supervision and you take all of the necessary foreign medications. Without the medications, you may not last that long. They cost thousands, though."

"I have a little saved up," she said, wondering why he had called her a professional. Was it her professional attitude toward death?

"It will cost tens of thousands of American dollars!"

"I have the money . . ."

"Thank God! Really, that does my heart good." He went back to his desk and sat down. "I will oversee your case."

"Okay."

"Let's get ready for induced labor. The proper authorities will deal with your . . . let's just say 'sexual partners.' We have to track all of them down . . . I just can't believe you managed to get infected from heterosexual contact."

"No induced labor. I'm keeping the baby," Iseult fired off, and she instantly felt better, as if someone had freed her from an immeasurable load. She breathed in deeply and wiped away her tears. "I will not give my partners up. They are all foreign citizens and are protected by diplomatic immunity."

"But who will you leave him wi—"

"It's a girl. Try to do everything the way I want it done and I will be very grateful, Doctor Stepanov."

The department head looked at her, internally dismissing her as an idiot, but simultaneously feeling sorry for this woman struggling under the weight of the name Iseult. He also understood perfectly well that she had just offered him money.

"The decision is yours, naturally! Ten thousand dollars for me to set everything up for you."

"Agreed."

"Terrific. You won't be staying at our hospital, of course. Anonymity cannot be guaranteed here. I'm afraid our specialists are rather untutored when it comes to such matters . . . I will give you the address of a gynecologist. He's also a urologist, in case that proves necessary. He will prolong your life as much as possible. He has a private department affiliated with the hospital for employees of the Ministry of Transportation. He has grand plans, too—building his own clinic! I'll write it all down for you . . . the doctor's name is Eldar Edgarovich Sytin . . . He's actually a descendent of the famous Sytin, the publisher!"

"Okay."

Stepanov could see that she had never heard of Sytin, and she didn't give a damn about anything at that moment.

"They will take you home in an ambulance. Give my guy the money. He'll drive back with the siren on. I'll whisper your instructions right in the doctor's ear. You can have the baby at his department, by the way. He has private suites that are up to Western standards."

Then Iseult lay in bed for two days, her face burrowed into the wall. She wasn't depressed, but what fear there was seemed to be splashing around at the bottom of her stomach, letting her breathe free. She disappeared into herself, trying to feel her tiny little girl down below her heart. The girl didn't make her mother wait and responded to her summons with faint, nearly imperceptible movement. That ethereal movement awakened the whole of her soul into a smile, as if she expected tremendous happiness in the time left to her.

She even managed to eat a little something, and by evening, she felt able to call her mother. Masha was as strong as marble when she instructed Iseult to keep it together. A whole year to live! She would help with the money.

"It'll be a lot!"

"We have enough."

"What about your house in Spain?"

"We have enough for that, too! Don't you worry. Ask your foreigners for help. They knocked you up and infected you. They owe you!"

"Masha, you know our profession. Nobody owes anybody anything. They all paid me . . ."

"You're right . . ."

Iseult visited Doctor Sytin, and they drew up a plan, one centered around giving birth soon and getting the right HIV treatment. Sytin showed her his private suites and invited her to die there if it struck her fancy.

"That's not for a while, of course," Sytin said with a wave of his hand.

Iseult bought all sorts of prenatal vitamins, spent everything she had on medicine, and shed her indifference for the first time in her life. She loved her little girl madly and had long conversations with her, apologizing for her recklessness. In return, her daughter projected astounding dreams for her: there was always an endless table covered in a white cloth, beginning on earth and ending in the heavens. Righteous people sat at the table, clearly celebrating. Iseult struggled to understand the reason for this perpetual feast, but she couldn't figure it out. She had a place at that table, and there was an old man with a patchy beard who looked Greek sitting to her right. He never said anything but always looked up there, into the endlessness of the celebration, paying no attention to Iseult. Then one Friday night, he suddenly turned toward her.

"I will take care of everything!"

She often got calls from her former clients, but she would tell them that she had retired because of an injury. Iseult's sympathetic foreigners stopped disturbing her. The ambassador from the small African country was nowhere to be found, though. Only after a full month had elapsed did she receive a precious parcel containing his golden buckle and a little note, in which the envoy imparted to her that he had been compelled to return to his homeland because of his faltering health.

"I hope you'll forgive your father, too," she uttered aloud for her daughter to hear.

In her next dream, the silent old man addressed himself to her again, nearly ordering her to devote more attention to her mother the following week.

"Be gentler with her!"

Iseult went to visit her mother at work, and the sight of her brought home the fact that they had not been together for many years. Iseult embraced her mother, pregnancy belt pressing against the latter's withering body.

"I love you, Masha!"

Masha found this display of daughterly affection off-putting, but she attributed it to Iseult's illness and perhaps a hormone imbalance. Untangling herself from the embrace, she showed her daughter a private enterprise consisting of eight rooms and four large halls, where hetaerae of every trade and every tribe of the collapsed Soviet Union toiled away indefatigably.

"It's all legal. This is a strip club, it's called the 'Gabon.'"

"Why 'Gabon'?"

"I don't know. It's a cool word."

"It isn't a word, it's the name of a country."

"Yeah, I know . . ."

Of course she knew. The ambassador from that small African nation with the golden buckle on his chest had frequented her enterprise when it was still illegal. He invested some serious money into the place to turn it into a strip club—obviously, it was all in her name, though. In addition to honoring him by calling the place the "Gabon," the grateful hostess had passed on her daughter's contact information. That's where the ambassador with the golden buckle came from, the man who would become the father of Iseult's daughter.

"What was his name again?"

"Who?"

"The black guy."

"Adiu. Why?"

"It's nothing, never mind."

"By the way, I gave him your phone number, but he got attached to this place . . . sorry . . ."

"So does that mean everything's okay, Masha?"

"Yeah, you can see that . . ."

Iseult was happy that the baby would have a grandmother to take care of her after her mother passed on. She made Masha give her word that she would never encourage her granddaughter to follow in their footsteps and extend their dynasty of currency whores. Masha promised that she would raise her with the mores of Chekhov's time and send her away to an international school in Switzerland when she was fourteen. At home later that evening, Iseult, contented and draped in a comforter, was half collapsed in an armchair, devouring sour-cream-and-mushroom chips, when she suddenly heard the voice of a television anchor through the wall, from the next apartment over. A Chechen man whose identity had not yet been established, apparently unsatisfied with the service at the Gabon strip club, had produced an automatic weapon of foreign manufacture from his bag and shot the owner of the establishment dead, along with seven other people: four strippers and three clients. A manhunt was underway in Moscow and an investigation had been launched.

The pregnant and increasingly weak Iseult had to identify her mother's body, take care of all the paperwork, and have her buried. She did it all with resurgent indifference as her body used the last of its strength to hold the line for the life growing inside. Iseult didn't even arrange for nine days of mourning, to say nothing of the traditional forty; she was already in Sytin's private suite by then. The doctor was afraid that his patient would not make it to her due date, since the disease was eating away at her at record speed. Sytin visited her and, trying not to meet her eyes, recommended that they perform a C-section as soon as possible.

"I won't live long enough?"

"No," the doctor answered honestly.

"When do you have to do it?"

"Your pneumonia is progressing and your heart's giving out."

"When?"

"Tomorrow."

Iseult had the dream that night, and the old man with the patchy beard promised her that, in the fullness of time, her daughter would be higher than all the kings and queens of the earth put together, that she would be exalted above all humanity, he would see to that . . . This time, it seemed to her that guests were sitting at the table in perpetual quantities, and that Jesus must be somewhere among them. She cast her eyes about for the Savior, but the old man had seemingly guessed at her hopes, and promptly demolished them.

"Just not at this table. He is not here."

She woke up when they were taking her into the operating room. Doctor Sytin was walking beside her, his hand resting on her frail shoulder. She was having trouble breathing, and her heart was sputtering impotently, dying.

They started to give her an anesthetic, but there was no need. The vitals monitor was emitting an uninterrupted squeak, announcing that Iseult was no longer in this world.

"Faster!" Sytin commanded. "We only have a few minutes before oxygen deprivation sets in!"

For some reason, they started putting iodine on the dead woman's belly. Sytin cursed at the nurse, repeating that she was dead.

"Fucking idiot!" He made a confident incision with his scalpel while another pair of hands inserted the forceps, and a few moments later, Doctor Sytin carefully extracted a tiny girl from the lifeless body. "Cut the cord, stat!"

Then Sytin placed the infant on a table for newborns, branded with the insipid name "Stork," while the midwife cleaned her mouth and nose with a tiny squeeze bulb, lifted her by the legs and slapped her tushy. The long-awaited cry was heard in the operating room, and everyone burst into joyous applause. Someone noticed that the girl had dark skin and black hair.

"It's a baby African!" Sytin announced, then left the operating room, carrying the daughter of Iseult and Adio the Gabonese ambassador out into the land of the living. Everyone else followed him.

The mutilated Iseult lay on the table, eyes open and belly dissected. Trained staff would soon enter the operating room to clean and disinfect everything . . .

The newborn ate well and didn't require any further medical assistance. Many of the hospital employees came to see the little miracle, the mixed-race baby with blue eyes as piercing as laser beams.

A week later, Sytin decided to bring social services in, but that proved unnecessary; a strange, elderly man with a patchy beard and harsh eyes came to see him before he could make the call. The old fellow, dressed in a tuxedo and sneakers, presented all the documents necessary to adopt the little girl. All the obstetrician/gynecologist/andrologist could do was put the newborn in the elderly man's arms.

"How old are you?" Sytin inquired.

"Ten thousand . . ."

"What?!"

"Kidding. Fifty-two."

"He's lying," Sytin thought. "He's gotta be over seventy. What does he have to do with all of this? Well, I did my job honestly. Why not let the girl have a grandpa? Even if it'll just be for a little while . . ."

"Well . . . good luck!" said the doctor. "Boy, you have a funny name . . . Antipatros . . ."

"Your good deed will be rewarded," the old man promised and coughed into his beard. Or maybe he was laughing.

•

I woke up, and, when my head cleared, I realized in horror that I'd slept for a month instead of a week. As I was brushing my teeth, I thought in panic that I'd missed some key events and incidents! How could this be?! Then I remembered my dream in the minutest detail and a tiny crack revealed a complex, multifaceted image. I realized that was where Zoika, the mixed-race girl with the blue eyes, had come from, sensing that an understanding of the whole grand design would soon take shape in my head. His adopted daughter or granddaughter . . .

I turned on the television and spent two hours straight absorbing the news. What I saw astounded me!

13

Mr. Arseny Iratov had abandoned his architecture firm and was spending more and more time at home. Sytin visited him frequently, and they discussed how to get out of their situation, whether they should resort to surgical intervention or try something else. They played cards, and Iratov often used the skills he remembered from his former life to cheat, without the doctor ever noticing his nimble fingers . . .

As the days went by, Iratov became more and more convinced that they should leave everything as it was. They were no spring chickens; they had more pressing interests than sex.

"What about that young wife of yours?"

"She's all set. Found herself a young stallion named Eugene. He's probably my illegitimate son, but he says he's my member. Haven't I already told you this?"

"What a bunch of bull . . ." Sytin replied rather limply . . . and was surprised by his own flaccidity. "And hormone replacement therapy doesn't work. Very strange!"

"Your therapy sucks dick!"

Two days later, the World Andrology Organization, headquartered in New York, made a sensational announcement. According to their data, 80 percent of adult men, teenagers, and boys, as well as male infants, had lost their sexual organs within a single month. A representative of the State Department confirmed their findings, and every stock exchange in the world plunged by the same percentage. Only one-fifth of the male population, consisting of old men with untreatable erectile dysfunction, still had their primary sex characteristics.

Hundreds of talk shows all over the world switched their

focus to this incredible, seemingly fantastical, unimaginably sensational topic. They discussed the possibility of some sudden genetic glitch caused by a black hole swallowing the gas cloud at the center of the Milky Way, concluding that some situation on the quantum level was being reflected in the male half of humanity. Males of other species were examined, beginning with apes; the organs in question were found right where they belonged, working and producing.

The world was surprised by this new state of affairs, but not frightened. Men, no longer burdened by testosterone, discoursed on the matter rather limply, while feminists instantly saw it as a reversal of the poles of human civilization. The female sex developed a new conception of itself as dominant. Numerous ethical and political questions emerged. For example, how could heads of state—the presidents of Russia and the USA, let's say—be expected to control their potent nuclear arsenals when they had no potency of their own? One wag quipped that a man with nothing to scratch when he's lying on the couch isn't a man at all. Men had less testosterone in them than a tea rose or the passionate sculptures of Rodin.

Obviously, a demographic question also arose, giving the world a nasty scare, but then it was announced that sperm banks could provide enough material for several more generations. The stock markets rebounded considerably at this news, but then crashed to historic lows in response to the tragic information that all of it was unviable, nothing but dead spermatozoa . . . Fortunately, this grim announcement led to a good idea. Man is so full of optimism, so convinced that he is the king of the earth! Kerry Smith, one of the world's leading family-planning specialists, the director of the Breim Institute (an organization originally sponsored by the Rockefellers), announced that semen was not at all necessary for human reproduction. They had already practically completed a research project that demonstrated, without the slightest doubt, that the material necessary to reproduce an individual could be acquired from nearly any cell in the body. The markets started climbing again. Kerry Smith left out one detail: those pregnancies would only produce girls. One thing leads to another . . . this information promptly led to the creation of a secret world government headed by Angela Merkel, since the planet would be populated exclusively by women within a century, and they would have to run it . . .

I couldn't help but be astounded by news like that, and I didn't know what direction this world was rushing in, this world where I no longer knew what to do, what my function was. I rushed to the barbershop to see Antipatros, who was still carrying out his tonsorial duties as usual.

I was so impatient that I nearly jumped into the antediluvian chair. Antipatros used the pedal to lift me up slightly, then began trimming my barely noticeable hair.

"What does all this mean?" I asked, unable to contain myself.

"You will find out when the time comes," the barber stated gratingly. He was Pheidippides and God knows who else . . . Zoika emerged from the back room, smiling at the world, then set about sweeping up the hair, sparks flying from her big blue eyes.

"I know who she is to you!"

"Well, at least they put *something* in your head! They gave the wretch prophetic dreams!" He didn't say anything else until the end of the haircut. "You will be faced with the necessity of acting soon. Be ready!"

Back at Senescentova's apartment, I made myself calm down and tried to formulate a picture of the world at large as it then stood, but despite my best efforts, however I strained my brain, no answer was forthcoming, just disparate pieces from the mosaic of human affairs that teased my imagination . . . I picked up the phone and made a call . . . All I heard was the endless, monotone ringing . . . Strangely enough, it actually comforted me, and I stretched out on the sofa, hands behind my head. Determined not to fall asleep and miss something essential, I thought back to how I had interrupted my retelling of the story of Joseph Josephovich Brodsky, the grandson of Alevtina Vorontsova and Arseny Iratov, whose fate happened to have been coupled to my own, but I also found myself thinking that his story no longer held any significance. It was a secondary plot, of little use to anyone, but the recollections were already appearing, igniting my brain, gradually becoming my waking reality, and I no longer held sway over them.

Valery Estin didn't meet with Joseph again, even though the young man was brought to his personal estate outside of Tver and put up in the guest house. Estin, like any great chess player, took an interest in everything that went beyond the boundaries of ordinary human understanding. Psychics, telepaths, people who could levitate or see the future. They helped him win—at least that's what he thought—so he created an institute for paranormal studies. Absurd as it sounds, it made over a million a year . . . Mitya Schwartz was exclusively responsible for handling the discharged soldier.

"Do you know why you were removed from your noncommissioned officer training program?"

"No," Joseph replied.

"You'll find out in a few days. In the meantime, let's get some food in you. You can watch some movies and catch up on sleep. There's a phone right there. You can call your mother as much as you want."

"But she can't come here?"

"No, especially now that she's busy decorating the new apartment . . ."

"Fine."

They didn't bother the young man for three days. He slept splendidly and watched endless Hollywood movies—fortunately, the house was equipped with an amazing sound system. He ate well, watched more movies, and slept without nocturnal visions. There was only one night when he saw a picture of the dead Slipperov lying in his coffin. He awakened instantly and saw Mitya Schwartz's face above him.

"Did you see Slipperov?" he asked, already knowing the answer.

"Yes," Joseph answered.

"How did you know that he had an aneurysm?"

"I didn't know." Joseph sat up in bed, stretched, and yawned.

"But you—"

"I predicted it."

"Predicting something is almost exactly the same as knowing it!" Mitya said, keeping up the pressure.

"Almost," Joseph agreed. "Did you put that picture in my head?"

"What gave you that idea?"

"It's the first dream I've ever had."

"What, you mean you've never even dreamed about naked girls?"

"No."

"You don't happen to be gay, do you?"

"No."

"Strange. All people dream . . . you apparently just can't remember."

"I remembered Slipperov . . . By the way, could you bring me my books?" Joseph asked.

"No problem . . . So you're interested in Judaism?"

"It's hard to say . . ."

"There's a synagogue not too far from here. Would you like to go?"

"Sure . . . So you put Slipperov in my head?"

"Let's just say it was me . . . Listen, go take a shower, and . . . you know, freshen up, if you need to. I'll meet you downstairs in the dining room."

While Joseph stood under the hot water, washing the image of his dead comrade from his consciousness, Mitya Schwartz was peeking into his bag for some reason, rummaging around. Then he went over to the bed and looked under the pillow. He even sniffed the pillowcase, just like a working dog . . .

They sat at a round dinner table, where Joseph breakfasted on fresh farmer's cheese with berries, drenching the dish with condensed milk and thoroughly enjoying himself . . . Mitya had eaten a while ago, so he was mixing five spoonfuls of white sugar into the impenetrable gloom of his coffee, giving his young charge a sideways glance.

"There's some excellent sausage. We make it ourselves! Want to try it?"

"No, thank you. I don't mix meat and dairy."

"You keep kosher?" Mitya asked, surprised.

"No . . ."

"Then how come you don't mix them?"

"It gives me an upset stomach . . . Maybe I'll have some curd fritters, though, if you don't mind."

Mitya Schwartz was finding him more and more irritating, this handsome, well-built youth with the eyes of a wise old man and the hair he'd grown out since his discharge shining like blue steel. The mathematician's own IQ was off the charts, too; he had made a name for himself by applying mathematical analytics to new developments in quantum theory, but he knew very well that he was no Einstein. He wasn't a genius, and his looks were nothing to write home about either. This new charge of his wasn't exceptional, but Estin had sensed something in the kid, like he had with Mitya himself in his day, so he had bade him work with him. He was to do it gently, though, without all the psychological bells and whistles he was so adept at using.

A song by the Nikitins about a town in Uzbekistan resounded into the summer, variations on its name forming the cheerful refrain "Brichmulla, Brichmelja, Brichmalla, Brichmiga," but the mathematician heard it as "Brit Milah, brit major, brit mama, brit bigger!"

"Gah . . ."

"Is everything alright?" Joseph asked with a smile.

"I don't like this song. Well, you probably realize you weren't just brought here to get you out of doing your duty to the Fatherland?"

"I do," Joseph said with a nod, wiping his mouth with his napkin. "I take it I'm not here to play chess?"

"Only in your free time."

"So what can I do for you?"

In addition to the enmity he was experiencing toward his guest, the mathematician could not shake the feeling that it was the new guy who was in control, not him. That made Mitya suddenly feel hot.

"Well, what do you need me for?

"What's the hurry? You'll know when you need to!"

"I'm not in the army anymore, right?"

"Right."

"Why exactly are you speaking to me as if I'm your property?"

"You can go back to the army today if you want!" Schwartz was barely containing his emotions.

"I was discharged."

"They'll call you up again."

"That won't go anywhere."

"Why not?"

"They'll find my arrhythmia . . . And I've been accepted to the Moscow Institute of Physics and Technology, so I have a five-year deferment."

Mitya did not have that information—a serious oversight for which he could face a serious punishment. He also thought of Olga, a girl he'd been in love with for seven years now. It was mutual, but she was born the daughter of an FSB general, and her father, Photios Prytki, wasn't especially enamored of people with curly hair and big noses. The lovers were limited to extremely rare trysts. They would possess each other with Shakespearean fury, but Prytki's people almost always found them, and it would end with Mitya getting his face busted up and Olga throwing a fit . . . Schwartz thought about trying to use the new apartment Joseph's mother was living in as leverage, but he refrained from doing so for the time being.

All the while, the radio relayed retro joy for people born in the USSR, the refrain ringing out: "Brichmulla, Brichmelja, Brichmalla, Brichmiga . . ."

"When did you manage that?"

"Well, I was with my mom for two days. I went over to the institute and submitted an application. I graduated from high school with a gold medal, so I got an automatic acceptance."

"What department?" The mathematician was sweating, thinking about what he'd tell Estin. Brit bigger, bitch!

"Quantum mechanics . . ." Joseph rose from the table and did some calisthenics to limber up. "You are a nervous, servile type, Mitya. I'll tell Estin that I applied while I was still in the army. So you calm yourself down somehow, please. You will not be punished."

"Are you a telepath or something?" The mathematician twitched, threw his head back, and started sniffing the air for some reason.

"Are those the people that can read minds?"

"Why can't I smell it on you?"

"You have abnormally sensitive olfactory perception. You're like a dog. That's very rare! I'm not a telepath, though."

"What, then?" The mathematician was on the verge of barking.

"I'm just a person who knows how to read books. I read about you a long time ago, back in the army . . . Estin didn't find a use for you. He probably just didn't think of it. But you could find truffles with that miraculous nose of yours. The black ones are worth their weight in gold, you know."

"Are you comparing me to a pig?"

"Better yet, why not just go out in the taiga and dig up ginseng? What do you need Estin for?"

"Now listen here—"

"Why are we arguing anyway, Mitya?" Joseph said with a smile. "Nothing good will come of it. I'm not your captive and you're not my jailer. Shall we reach an amicable agreement? Ask me whatever you want, and I will give you answers, but not to every question. Estin will be happy, and you will get paid. By the way, you won't get to marry Olga Photiosevna Prytki, no matter how badly you want it."

"So you *are* a telepath!"

"No, I told you! I repeat—all of my knowledge comes from the book."

"You're lying! Why can't I marry her?"

"You know why—she's a general's daughter and you're a Jew."

"That bastard has to retire eventually!"

"There's no such thing as an ex-FSB general. You know that, too." Mitya fell silent, looking inward, trying to squeeze out his negativity, hoping that there was some other variation, some parallel universe where everything would be different for him . . .

"When will Estin die?" he asked.

"I have no idea," Joseph replied with a shrug.

"It isn't written in the book?"

"Everyone is in the book."

"And?"

"I don't read about everyone. Why would I? I know every thing about myself and my mom. That's enough for me. Well, and I know about the events going on around me . . ."

"Well, that's where the money is," the mathematician stated, rather sadly. "But you aren't interested in money, right?"

"Only as a means to exchange essential goods."

"So all I can do is work as a truffle pig?!"

"Don't get bent out of shape! Let's just reach an agreement. People who are prepared to reach honest agreements can live side by side and help rather than hinder one another."

"What are you offering?"

"Well, what does Estin need?"

"Information on any subject, provided he can use it to gain a competitive, material, or political advantage."

"You can tell him that I have telepathic abilities . . . in a loose sense. Let's say I sometimes have epiphanies. They don't happen often, though, and I have no control over them. You can also tell him that you'll have to work with me intensively, and it will not always produce real results. But I will have answers to some of his questions."

"So you *are* a telepath!"

"No! Come on . . . I tell the truth and nobody believes me. If I just lied, everyone would be fooled! I spend all my free time studying and I find answers to my questions."

"In the book?"

"Precisely."

"Maybe I can find the answers myself? I have books, too."

"If you are capable of that . . . of being consumed with a book, if it is fated to open up to you, then . . . But you're meant to do something else."

"Well, what is it?" In that moment, Mitya Schwartz was weighing the idea of sticking a fork in the eye of this haughty, handsome youth in the role of cut-rate prophet.

"Digging up ginseng!"

Mitya lost control then, obviously. He leapt on Joseph, swinging his fists. The mathematician had a funny way of fighting, leaning backward, head bent away so he could hardly see his opponent, but he kept repeating, "Take that! Take that, you frickin' prophet!" He was throwing punches with gusto, but Joseph dodged the blows, saying that Schwartz could make up to ten thousand dollars a day hunting for ginseng with a nose like that!

"Take that, bastard!"

"What are you doing?" Joseph was indignant, avoiding yet another jab at his nose. "Since when do Jews start brawls? Come on, Schwartz, you're a scientist! Stop it! You should be ashamed of yourself!"

Tired of throwing punches at nothing, Estin's assistant collapsed on to the leather sofa, where he couldn't catch his breath for some time. He had never been in a fight before, so he had no idea it was so strenuous. His blood pressure was running high, his face red. The mathematician rummaged around in his pockets, took out some medication, and swallowed it dry.

"I agree," he said suddenly.

"To what?"

"Your offer."

"Well, that's great! Why get all bent out of shape, why throw down like that? Two smart people can always reach an agreement, and between the two of us, we have an IQ of 360!"

"Yes, yes," said the flushed Mitya. "We'll reach an agreement."

That was when Joseph began working with Estin, the former world chess champion. The day after the altercation, he appeared in person, flying in on a light helicopter accompanied by an enormous mastiff named Fischer. It was a little hot for the dog; his enormous, blood-colored tongue nearly dragged along the ground, and drool flowed abundantly from his chops . . . First they all had lunch together. Estin inquired as to how Joseph's compulsory military service had gone, and whether he liked the new apartment, then asked if he had any physics-and-mathematics-related news, and what major he had chosen. Joseph gave him exhaustive answers, but in response to the last one, he evinced a desire to specialize in . . . Well, Estin and Schwartz listened to Joseph Brodsky's ten-minute monologue without managing to understand a single sentence. Oh, they'd heard those words before, but they had no idea how he was using them!

Then Estin talked to Mitya, rubbing Fischer the mastiff's enormous ear and griping to the mathematician that those 180 IQ points Schwartz had been so enamored of made him feel like an idiot. Had he gotten anything out of what the young man was saying?

"Yes, I could follow it," Mitya lied. "It was terminology from quantum mechanics. I think he was speaking Hebrew some of the time, though, so I couldn't follow then . . . Perhaps he's another Einstein?"

"We don't need an Einstein! It's all very simple. I'm a curious man, but I keep my feet on the ground. I have a ton of questions and very few answers!"

"He agreed to give us answers. But not very often . . ."

"So when will I die?" the chess master asked his assistant.

"He doesn't know."

"Or he won't say . . ."

"Perhaps you should speak to him yourself? You may fare better."

"I'll try. I have to do everything. What are you good for anyway?" Estin wiped the dog drool from his hands with a monogrammed handkerchief, then gave it to Schwartz.

They spoke that same evening in the chess master's study, its large windows offering a view of an artificial pond where two black swans lived. Someone—apparently the designated fisherman—was pulling nice fat carp out of the water. Scales shone, sunrays ricocheting as the latest one flopped on the hook. Joseph figured it was for dinner. They talked about various things, while Estin played on a miniature mother-of-pearl chessboard until he moved the white queen four squares and toppled the black king with a flick of his finger.

"So, how long do I have to live?"

"I honestly don't know," the young man answered.

"Can you find out?"

"The answer will be imprecise."

"How imprecise?"

"Do you remember how the Lord promised Abraham that he would die at a venerable age, in perfect peace and satisfaction?"

"Vaguely . . ."

"Abraham had a grandson named Esau who grew up to be an excellent boy, but he was fated to change and become a criminal by the age of sixteen. Then the Lord shortened the life of his righteous grandpa by five years."

"I don't follow . . ."

"Well, He promised Abraham that he would die in peace and satisfaction. But can it truly be called peace if your grandson is a robber? By the way, that is the only instance of a man's life being shortened for the future sins of his descendants."

"I don't have any grandchildren," the former champion declared.

"All I can do is tell you if you will suffer a sudden death soon, if that interests you."

Estin tensed up. The mastiff smelled his master's fear and began to growl.

"Knock it off, Fischer!" He leaned his whole body forward.

"Don't worry. You will not die suddenly, and your life will not be short." Estin relaxed, thinking for a moment that this kid was just a swindler, so he asked how much he would like to be paid, expecting him to name a tidy sum. "I don't need money. I'd just like to repay you for that apartment somehow . . ."

"You want to work for free?"

"I'd just like to go back to my mother. You can send me your questions in an envelope through Mitya, and I'll write my answers. Okay?" Estin thought for a moment, looking Joseph right in the eye, as if he were trying to find evidence of a common or garden variety scam there, but all he saw was the silent black ocean of eternity.

"I don't know . . ."

"The organizers in Japan will give in. Don't take the million, hold out for a million and a half."

"How do you even know about that?" Estin lunged forward. "It's confidential!"

"Isn't that precisely what you wanted from me? It's the perfect way to make sure I am not a swindler."

"When will they sign the contract?"

"Your match with Deep Fritz will take place in November. Three weeks from the present day, you will agree on a million and a half dollars."

The information Joseph was somehow privy to was remarkably specific, and so confidential that even Estin's assistant Schwartz had been kept in the dark. The chess master clenched his jaw in anticipation of some strange euphoria. He did not intend to smile at his informer, though—that would make him look too gullible.

"Why don't you want to live here? We have all the amenities and it's all free . . . There's a training camp for rhythmic gymnasts on the other side of the woods . . . Some of them are pretty adventurous . . ."

"I'd like to go back to my mother, if you don't mind."

"Are you gay?"

"It's funny, Mitya asked me the same thing. No, I'm not gay. I just want to live with my mom. She needs my help."

"Deal." Estin got out of his chair, forcing Fischer to rise from the floor, and extended his hand to Joseph. The titanic dog let out a loud bark, putting the seal on their handshake.

The young man went to Moscow by helicopter, delighting from the height of the faint clouds in the great living picture of the world the Creator had made. He flew over Istra and spotted the yeshiva where he had studied. Joseph's soul fluttered, thirsty for this proximity to the Lord's creation that grew with every second. They landed near the Moscow Ring Road, then a Mercedes took him to his new apartment downtown, right by Pushkin Square.

Dasha just couldn't get enough of staring at her now grown son, hugging and kissing him all the while. Even when he was sleeping soundly, she looked at him, thinking how funny life was—it can go from the awful, insane racket of a shaman's tambourine to an all-encompassing flute of happiness. Anyone can be happy, even a Jew and a Buryat. The sun is for everyone, after all; it warms even the worst of scumbags . . .

The following day, they went to the cemetery and paid tribute to his father, Joseph. Dasha cried in memory of her adopted son and husband, lamenting that life had been so merciless to him. It never gave him anything nice, not even a measly scrap of brain. Life hadn't been like that to her, though . . .

"Dad's okay now," Joseph informed his mother, smiling tenderly. "You have nothing to worry about. Believe me, he's much better off there than he was here."

Once they were back in the city, they went to the Rossiya Cinema and saw a foreign film packed with sex and violence. After that, Joseph would never visit another movie theater, museum, or stage production, realizing that such entertainment was unworthy when he had big books and big thoughts in his head. He did not even try to persuade his mother that such cultural institutions were unacceptable. Dasha liked movies; they were a kind of outlandish depiction of a life that didn't really exist. Everything that was good for his mother was good for him. When she asked her son to get his hair cut, calling him a "hippie," he did not defy her. He just found a barbershop on Petrovsky Boulevard, a three-minute walk from their building, where his long, peculiarly beautiful hair was trimmed by an old man with Greek features and a patchy beard who kept smiling and trying to look into Joseph's eyes.

Then Joseph saw a girl of about ten, with dark skin and bright blue eyes, standing by the door to the back room, smiling slyly, one dainty leg bent at the knee, and his soul filled with certain knowledge . . .

"Come again!" the barber said invitingly, nearly giving the manicurist a heart attack; for the last fifteen years, she had been convinced that Antipatros was mute.

"I most certainly will."

Three days later, Joseph went out to the yeshiva in Istra, where he begged for permission to audit classes until they relented. The teacher remembered him, but warned him that it was just a primary school.

"I doubt you will find the classes with the children interesting. If I'm not mistaken, you have memorized the book?"

"I can actually claim to know it a little now," Joseph replied, with appropriate modesty.

"Very well," said the rabbi. "Come three times a week at five o'clock. I will try to talk with you . . ."

On Mondays, Mitya Schwartz delivered the envelopes containing Estin's questions. Joseph would meet the messenger in a public cafeteria. In the first letter, he inquired if it might be a good idea to ask the match organizers for a little more. The young man replied that it would not, since they were holding negotiations with Kasparov and Kramnik, and they were both asking for more.

No more letters from Estin were delivered for a whole month after that. Joseph went to the yeshiva in Istra to see the teacher. Anything might serve as a topic for their conversations. Time, for instance.

"Yes," Joseph replied when Rabbi Yitskhok asked if he remembered the first lines of the Torah, then recited them: " 'In the beginning of God's creation of the heavens and the earth. Now the earth was astonishingly empty, and darkness was on the face of the deep, and the spirit of God was hovering over the face of the water.' "

"So what did the Almighty—may His name shine—create first?"

"The heavens and the earth," the student replied.

"What does the word 'beginning' itself tell us?"

"First of all?"

"You know, of course, that there is nothing accidental in the book, nothing that could have been phrased better than it is in the text?"

"I do."

"So what does this phrase 'in the beginning' tell us? What did the Lord create before the heavens and the earth? Time!" he answered himself. "That is the meaning of the word 'beginning.' That is why, my dear Mr.—pardon me, I've forgotten your surname."

"Brodsky."

"Yes, that's right. Well, my dear Mr. Brodsky, a parrot can memorize. Admittedly, it's good to have the book memorized so when you're old, you can find new meanings, if you're capable of doing so. The text itself is not as important as the key to it, the key to understanding. There was one Jew who was only repatriated to the Holy Land when he was as old as Methuselah. He decided to learn Hebrew so he could read the Torah in the original. He studied and studied, but he only managed to read one page before he died . . . but that was enough for him to become a righteous man. It all comes down to how you make yourself better. The book is about uninterrupted study—every second of every day—discovering more and more new things about your soul in lines already pored over for decades . . . The old man who read a single page at the cost of titanic effort changed himself, made himself better. We come into this world to make ourselves better . . ."

Estin sent a second letter, which Joseph read in front of Schwartz over a cup of hot chocolate.

"What medicines should I take to make sure I feel good?" went the chess master's first question. Joseph promptly replied

that the sensible thing to do would be to take medicines pre-
scribed by a doctor, ideally a good doctor.

"So what was his little question?" Mitya pried, through a
protracted yawn.

"That's confidential!" Joseph replied.

"Oh yeah . . ."

"When will the world end?" went the second—rather
strange—question.

"In two hundred and thirty-eight years," Joseph replied,
promptly, again.

The young student loved to goof around with the children
at the yeshiva; he would often bring them sweets or little toys,
and he especially enjoyed celebrations, like the upsherin, when
a three-year-old boy's hair was cut for the first time. Everyone
who was invited received a lock, and a wish was made on every
curl. A thirteen-year-old's bar mitzvah was the happiest celebration at that age, when a child becomes a man and takes on an
adult's responsibility before the laws.

Rabbi Yitskhok once came upon Joseph with a book in
ancient Aramaic. He was rather at a loss himself when it came to
reading older texts, so he was quite surprised.

"You read Aramaic?"

"Yes."

"Remarkable!" the teacher exclaimed.

"I know other languages, too . . ."

"How many?"

"Seventy or so . . ."

"The Lord is infinitely generous! But you must know, my
dear Joseph, that what the Lord has given you is a gift, but that
realizing this gift will do nothing for your soul. For your soul,
you must seek a different nourishment entirely . . . You know,
of course, about the schools of Hillel and Shammai, which have

debated for centuries on end and arrived at different answers to the same questions?"

"Even your primary school students know about that, don't they?"

"But do they know about the debate on whether or not man should have come into this world?"

"Probably not."

"Well there you have it. The debate—or discussion, in this case—continued for a long while, but for the first time, both schools arrived at the same opinion. Man should not have come into this world! But since he has, he must put himself right!"

Estin's next letter arrived in November. It was delivered by a woman who looked to be a secretary and declined to have a hot chocolate. She was somewhat haughty and apparently upset that she was being used as a messenger. That wasn't quite so, however: the chess master used Bella for a variety of purposes. Sometimes she would agree to some quick sex, but she mostly answered his calls, harshly repelling the superfluous ones.

"What's wrong with Schwartz?" Joseph asked.

"Pneumonia," Bella replied.

"Tell him I say hello! He got sick in Germany . . ."

"He'll get better in Germany, too."

"What will the price of gold be in the medium term?" came the first question. "What geopolitical conflicts or changes in government will the world face? Devaluation of the dollar? Gold?" On and on it went. Joseph answered with a laconic "I don't know." The second batch of questions pertained to the chess master's personal life. He requested that Joseph look into his prospects with the messenger, Bella Pushkina, and provide an answer to the question of whether or not they would make a good match. Joseph looked up at the woman with a gaze worthy of Lenin. The young man replied that she was indeed suitable for him . . . There followed a postscript, in which Estin wrote that he had tried to track Joseph down at the Moscow Institute of Physics and Technology but had been told that the student in question was not attending classes, even though he had received an automatic acceptance due to his stellar high school transcript. He hadn't even filed the paperwork to drop out . . . What happened to studying quantum mechanics? Joseph replied that he was studying somewhere else and that Estin shouldn't worry; he was doing fine and he would continue to answer the questions to the best of his ability.

Once the messenger had received the envelope, she took it to her car and broke the seal, since she had already familiarized herself with the questions beforehand. The fact that her fate might soon be decided in the best possible way briefly turned the professional-minded individual into a regular, happy woman, humming the "Hymn of the Democratic Youth" all the way home.

. . . A few years went by, but nothing about Joseph's life changed. He visited the yeshiva, began to grasp the meanings of the book, and answered Estin's meaningless questions.

He attended the bat mitzvah of Antipatros the barber's daughter, Zoika, who was no longer a funny little girl but a young woman, accepting all the responsibilities of adulthood. She had hair like Angela Davis, a great big ball that looked to him like a black dandelion. Her father had shaved the letter "V" into it. The girl looked fixedly at Joseph, and the light from the magical turquoise of her eyes filled up his heart like a warm and tender current.

"A sun with blue rays," he thought. "Truly, I behold an unearthly miracle!"

. . . I would sometimes meet Joseph in person. I would just sit next to him on a bench on Tverskoy Boulevard and sit in silence as he devoured his latest book. I couldn't understand why the young man spent his time on that chess master, Estin, trading the significant for the valueless, but I just couldn't work up the nerve to ask him.

One cold winter, I encountered Joseph sitting on a ledge near the entrance to Moscow's underground transportation system. He was engaged in his typical activity, turning the pages of an ancient tome, immersed in the text like the moon in the ocean. I heaved myself up on to the cold granite beside him, holding an ice cream I'd bought from the frost-covered kiosk. It used to cost forty-eight kopeks . . . not anymore! I ate noisily—one of my shortcomings, I shall not deny it!—and Joseph favored me with a brief glance.

"Bonjour!" I said and smiled in greeting at the spitting image of Iratov.

"Good afternoon," the reading youth said, smiling briefly in reply.

"Do you find my noisy eating funny? I have an overbite. It used to be lot worse, though!"

"Certainly not! I'm smiling because I'm reading about you."

"How?" I asked, so startled I dribbled ice cream on my lap. "Do you have the book of fates?"

"I was speaking metaphorically, of course . . . It's just that the entity described here bears a striking resemblance to you."

"What do you mean? You don't know me at all!"

"You are quite right, we have not met, but you do often sit next to me on the bench on Tverskoy Boulevard."

"So this resemblance is purely external," I reasoned.

"I think so." Joseph tore himself away from the book and looked at me attentively as I finished my ice cream, thoroughly slopping my pants with it. I have never known the sensation of embarrassment, so I met my interlocutor's gaze calmly. "You are the one who gave my mother money for my father."

"Is that written in the book?"

"No, it came to me just now . . ."

"Your mother told you?"

"No . . ." He seemed lost in thought for a moment. "The event came to me, but not in a dream . . . in waking."

"My appearance is rather unusual. Many people take me for some old acquaintance of theirs. By the way, have you ever been to Prague?"

"No . . . what's in Prague?"

"Nothing, really, I'm just asking. I've never been there before, but I will certainly go."

"Well, I'll look in my reference books!" Joseph promised.

"Until next time!"

"Until next time . . ."

Then Joseph's mother died. She was sick for just three days, and, in the waning hours of that Friday, she passed away, even though Joseph did everything he could to save her. If he could save anyone, let it be his mother; he thought he had the inner strength to make her life long and tranquil.

On the first day of her illness, she told her son that she would be dead by Saturday. He stroked her round face and said that nobody could be granted such knowledge, that she had a perfectly ordinary cold . . . She was as bright as the moon, but she was extinguished quickly, and she asked her son not to grieve for her, since she would go to deer heaven, and all her relatives would be there. Joseph's grandfather, the Nobel laureate Joseph Brodsky, would be there, and she was eager to see him . . .

"Bury me beside your father," she requested.

Standing over the grave of Yevdokia Brodsky, his mother,

Joseph felt for the first time in his waking life that someone else wielded some unlimited power over the world, which he could not break or understand. He was not afraid of death, but Dasha passing away so soon made him a vulnerable child once again, left alone in the great big world, and the one who ruled over it had still not extended his hand to him . . .

A year later, I met Joseph in the Eliseevsky Store. He didn't buy anything, just sat on the radiator and read, as was his custom.

"I haven't seen you for some time!" I said, approaching him. "Have you moved?"

"No," the young man answered. "My mother died."

"Oh yes, I heard . . . Mourning . . ."

Joseph's eyes were like oceans full of sorrow; I tried to buck him up by saying that the one who ran everything, the big building superintendent upstairs, had already extended his hand, but Joseph just hadn't noticed.

"Why haven't I noticed? Do you know the answer?"

"You lack focus. You are an information desk for that idiot Estin. Your gi-i-i-f-t! You're scattering your gift to the wind."

"Who are you?"

"I am the one who has scattered himself worst of all. And I am an acquaintance of yours . . ."

In his next letter, Estin asked if Joseph was willing to continue answering his questions. The young man replied that he had fulfilled all of his obligations to Estin, that his answers had tripled the chess master's fortune, and that there was no further need for him.

"I now consider myself at liberty," he wrote, "inasmuch as I no longer require the apartment in which my mother and I lived. I spend most of my time outside of Moscow. Reclaim the apartment if you wish. You may act however you deem just . . ."

Estin must be given his due. He may have been desperately

angry, but it was his spouse, Bella, who did not wish to let this suddenly cocky "prophet" go.

"What made him so cocky?!" she shouted . . . In the name of fairness, it must be noted that Estin, despite himself, released Joseph to the four corners of the earth and let him keep the apartment . . . It was due to that action that the chess master would live a rather long life in material comfort, without any great personal tragedy.

Joseph almost completely moved into the yeshiva, signing the apartment over to the Jewish community. On the day he'd set aside for the paperwork, he hung around Bannyy Lane all morning, signed the deed of gift, then went to the barbershop. After a routine haircut, Antipatros permitted the young man to enter his private room above the shop, where he seemed perfectly comfortable leaving him alone with his adopted daughter, Zoika. Without saying a single word, they conversed with smiles alone. Her thin fingers lay in his strong palm, and the two young people felt that they had become a single whole. Their emotions, their shared origins, melded them into a single sunray. Their breathing nearly froze, and, for a few brief moments, they were suddenly outside their bodies, as if they had stepped out the door of a house and now they stood there, stunned, watching themselves from the sidelines. They liked this picture . . . This uncommon state the two young people found themselves in, and their divine ichor, were detected by the aquiline nose of the old Greek Antipatros, startling him so much that he sliced off my neighbor Ivanov's earlobe—the one who had once burned down Tamarka's corner store and thereby become a wealthy merchant. Ivanov shrieked, but Antipatros spat on the rejected flesh and stuck it back on. The earlobe instantly reattached itself, as tight as death, but the customer continued to whimper and demand compensation.

"Have you completely forgotten who you are, you bastard?!" Antipatros hissed into the newly restored ear with the rage of a primitive pangolin. "You've only been here for a hundred years longer than me, but you've already assimilated, you scumbag."

Ivanov the merchant did not understand why Antipatros was treating him like that. He asked if he could get out of the chair, and the Greek lashed him across the cheeks with a hand turned wooden by age, like he did after he gave him a shave and a hot towel treatment.

"Remember, you son of a bitch! You ruined the purest day of my life!"

Finally, he awarded Ivanov a thump on the back of his flat head and sent him into the street with a kick. The door slammed, and Antipatros sat in the chair designated for his customers to enjoy the sensations coming from the merging of kindred souls. The manicurist, who was coming back from her lunch break, would've been frightened that the old man's heart had given out, but the Greek gave her a thumbs-up.

"Can we decide who is a sinner and who is not?" Joseph once asked his teacher.

"Of course."

"Who endowed us with that right?"

"No one. The answer to that question is very simple. Everyone is a sinner! We must start from that assumption."

"But there are also great sinners, those who commit crimes or bloody deeds."

"There are indeed," the rabbi agreed.

"But even those monstrous creations have all done something good at some point in their lives: loved their children, fed the birds, supported someone financially . . . Shall their good deeds not be weighed in the balance when they are judged? And what is to be done with righteous people, pure and enlightened people, who have also made some poor decisions in their lives, perhaps even accidentally?" Rabbi Yitskhok let Joseph finish before replying.

"The good deeds of great sinners will also be weighed in the balance, as will the mistakes of righteous men. It is simply that those who have sinned gravely are rewarded for their kindness here, on earth, in this virtual world defined by time. They are rewarded with money, long lives, and other earthly pleasures, while righteous men are punished for their mistakes, here, on earth, punished with poverty, illness, and so on. In his eternal existence, the sinner goes to hell, while the righteous man, who has paid for his mistakes in our world, sits at the table with the Almighty and has everything he might wish at his disposal for eternity—in a spiritual sense, of course."

"I have read that hell is shame, that when a human soul goes to hell, it experiences monstrous shame. It is visited by the souls to whom that person did ill. That must be why people say someone is 'burning with shame.' What do you think, Rabbi?"

"Everyone, even the most sinful, goes to heaven eventually. Twelve months in hell, then on to heaven. Every day in hell, however, will be equal to all the suffering Job endured in his entire life. Those who realize this, who understand that time does not exist there, or hardly exists, that a year in that place is equal to a thousand years on Earth, those are the truly God-fearing men . . . Yes, it may indeed be said that hell is shame and heaven is enjoyment. There is so much mixed up in people that oftentimes there is no knowing if one is a good person or scum, or what comes from where, or how to judge, how to create the scales for it . . ."

A rabbi from the USA once came to the yeshiva, talked to Joseph briefly, and then withdrew into a conversation with Rabbi Yitskhok, which occupied the wise and knowing men for half an hour. Next came lunch; the American rabbi ate well, drank wine, and laughed a great deal. When he'd had his fill, he grabbed Joseph's hand and pulled him into a dance, singing the tune himself, and so intoxicatingly that the kids in the kippahs began dancing along with them, but Rabbi Yitskhok kept sitting, stupefied, just mimicking the dance with his hands. When he'd had his fill of dancing, the American whispered in his partner's ear that the latter would soon marry and snow would fall on his kippah, then unexpectedly said his goodbyes to everyone and set off for Moscow.

"Do you know who that was?" Rabbi Yitskhok asked Joseph when the kids had been sent to bed and they were alone.

"Rabbi Cohen."

"And do you know who Rabbi Cohen is?"

"Do I need to know any more than that?"

"Not necessarily. You in particular don't need to know. But he came to Russia for one day, just to see you!"

"Me?"

"Precisely. He said that you have a vocation."

"What is it?"

"He did not share that information . . . One does not talk about that."

"Everyone has a vocation!"

"But in your case, he knows what it is! But you have still not been circumcised!"

"Well . . . I honestly don't know how to tell you . . ."

"Are you having doubts?"

"No . . . Of course not . . . I was just born . . . born circumcised. Without a foreskin, I mean. My mom said that doctors have found cases like that, and, well, my father was one. He died when I was very young, but I apparently inherited it. I'm Jewish on my birth certificate . . ."

Rabbi Yitskhok was awake all night, thinking that the one everyone was waiting for might be right here. For minutes at a time, he even wept with joy, but by morning a critical thought overcame his euphoria, a harsh reminder that there was no need to put the cart before the horse, and that looking at the face of the one holding the reins was extremely dangerous . . .

I accompanied Rabbi Cohen to the airport, following his car in a taxi, to make sure nothing happened. I waved to him when he met his coreligionists getting off a bus, a group of people with payots and fur hats. Somewhere in that interval, I encountered my neighbor Ivanov, well-dressed and sitting sadly on a bench near the entrance to the apartment building.

"Did Tamarka die in the fire?" I asked.

"Boy, the way it went up . . ."

"What about Zinka?"

"Zinka inherited a warehouse full of goods and a location for a new store."

"Looks like you're moving up in the world!" I said, looking my neighbor Ivanov up and down. "Brand-new jeans, a pullover, and a haircut!"

"This prick almost chopped my ear off while he was cutting my hair. Some fucking barber he is! I'll burn his shack to the ground!"

"You're a regular Nero!"

"Who?"

"He was this emperor who liked starting fires . . . Are you drinking?"

"Yeah," my neighbor admitted, but he suddenly snapped to seeing himself not as the lowlife alcoholic he had once been but as a person of means, someone with power in the world, but with the weakness of a Russian man. "Hey, have you been tailing me or what?" this inebriated Rothschild asked with the crudity of Ham.

"Me? No . . ."

"My brother?" Ivanov asked. "My parole officer?"

"Did you buy new briefs?"

"Huh?"

"Briefs. Undergarments."

"No . . . Why waste money on something nobody's gonna see? You're weird, neighbor, and you ask weird questions!"

"Sometime you're gonna have to bang some fancy broad, but you haven't washed your undies in seven years! How 'bout that?"

Ivanov thought for a moment, then admitted that there was some truth to my words. Broads were going to be putting out now that he had money. Well, we live and we learn!

Then I called and called . . .

Earth called the international space station. The stream was transmitted all over the world. The NASA administrator, a close-cropped career man who had earned his high rank, asked the astronaut if the crew was following what was happening on Earth.

"Yes, sir," replied the flight engineer. "There is a small time-lag, but we've been watching the news."

"So you are aware of what has happened to the men in every country on every continent?"

"We are . . . Have you checked the Pygmies in Africa?"

"Every variety of man on the planet has been checked!" the NASA administrator stated. "Including the Pygmies."

"And none of them have . . . Everyone's . . . ?"

"Absolutely."

"What about animals?"

"Fruitful and multiplying! Now please show me your genitalia."

The whole shocked world held its breath in preparation for watching a critical outer-space striptease. The astronaut, however, refused to remove his suit, since his instruments supposedly showed that his sexual organ was intact.

"What instruments, Mr. Culkin?" the administrator asked indignantly. "What are you up to?"

"Um . . ." Culkin replied. "An instrument . . ." And he swam into another room like Ichtyandr—a room with no video cameras. It was time for the commander of the Russian space agency's mission control center, Butcherov, to try.

"Bovinov, show me your prick!" he commanded crudely.

They managed to bleep out the last word in Russia, where it could have brought astronomical fines on the networks. Bovinov, without a second's hesitation, pulled down his track bottoms, and the world gasped. Bovinov had his tool.

"Boom!" the Russian cosmonaut exclaimed. "How do you like that?" The connection was unexpectedly terminated when he asked that question, but the world lit up with hope.

NASA and the leadership of Russia's space industry both analyzed the footage independently and came to the conclusion that Bovinov had mocked up his genitalia with Mold-It-Yourself-brand modeling clay, which was always kept on the station to make sure the astronauts' fine motor skills didn't deteriorate. Upon magnification, the specialists spotted the tub in the corner of the frame. Analysts in both countries noted the quality of the clay forgery attached to Bovinov's body by a thread tied in clever little knots. He had nailed both the color and the texture, but had significantly increased its size. On the other hand, who was to say what he was packing before this global drama? His fine motor skills hadn't deteriorated, no doubt about that . . . The entire global community soon found out about his lowly deception, while hundreds of millions of women who had been yearning to meet Bovinov simultaneously sank into despair, realizing that they would have to content themselves with marital aids. The lesbian community was the least disappointed, however; they had begun to lay claim to the right to govern all of humanity. There was a certain logic to it, since they were the only group whose sexual orientation had the potential to be fulfilled. Nearly all of the women on the planet soon joined that sexual minority, turning it into a majority of almost 100 percent. Their sex lives were still a source of delight, that hadn't changed . . . The president of the United States, a woman elected as a Democrat, proclaimed the hegemony of feminism, dug Monica

Lewinsky out of obscurity, and made the dumb, fat broad the secretary of state. The American leader also called for global elections, in which only women would participate. She also sorrowfully stated that humanity had no more than one hundred and twenty years left, if one counted the infants born that day. FYI, all of the newborn boys lacked sexual organs and already looked a lot like girls . . . The good news was that the planet had abundant resources, and, given these circumstances—just a measly hundred years to account for!—every inhabitant would be set for life. The markets nearly doubled in response to this announcement, while retail prices plummeted . . .

The only opponents to this female hegemony were the leaders of the world religions, most of whom hadn't been using their male assets because of monastic vows or celibacy requirements. These hierarchs insisted that power be transferred to the Church, and specifically to untainted men.

The women guffawed in response and used the newspapers to lampoon the religious leaders who were knee-deep in the sins of homosexuality and pedophilia. One especially zealous lesbian argued that religious institutions were unnecessary, since the Lord had clearly indicated that it was His will to nullify the human race. Her position was challenged by a woman researcher who held that a hundred years was enough for women to learn to have children without male spermatozoa playing any role in the process.

The situation was calmer in the Third World, and in Russia. Aside from the lesbian groups, women here did not raise a storm. Despite what Lenin said, they had historically chosen the role of kitchen maid over president. They were already satisfied with their husbands coming home on time now that they had lost their desire to play dominos and watch limp, homosexual soccer. They used to say there was no sex in the Soviet Union, but now there really was no sex, not that it had been that great to begin with. The ballet was theirs, too!

The world's men had lost their testosterone. Their blood was water, their brains were fatty nodules. The entire male population of Europe spent most of their time in movie theaters, where they ate popcorn by the ton and marveled at how passionate the men on the screen were. Why kiss someone's breast or grab someone by the ass? That was as uninteresting as it was unhygienic. The porn industry collapsed within months, despite the lesbian market.

Radical Muslims blamed the way the world had changed on Jews, Christians, Taoists, and Hindus. Basically, everyone except themselves. This declaration was nothing more than that, however, because of the loss of martial spirit and desire for self-sacrifice. The last shahid snuck into Paris, planning to blow himself up on the Champs-Élysées, but when he heard a speech at a rally there about the superiority of women, he decided not just to embrace their ideas, but also to remake his body into a female one. He still did wind up exploding that evening, in the garage where he lived, when he started trying on women's underwear.

Gender reassignment surgery became widespread, especially in the developed countries. Men everywhere voluntarily subjected themselves to vaginoplasties, while *The Vagina Monologues*, once a hit, was no longer viewed as relevant and soon disappeared from the stages of the world. Alcohol sales remained at their previous level, however; people of all genders still needed endorphins, so they continued to drink prodigiously. Plus, spending on food products tripled. After just a few months, men were up to 30 percent heavier, and some ballooned to twice their original size. Uncounted talents were discovered among the plump male herd. Two out of ten developed magical singing voices and lined up for auditions at all the world's opera houses, but opera was soon abolished entirely. What the hell good was it, when there were dozens of countertenors on every street, driving their neighbors into blinkered hatred? Baritones vanished into oblivion, to say nothing of basses . . . Ballet didn't last long either, obviously. The newly flabby male dancers could no longer jump around and do grand battements. Art degenerated. Museums were deserted. Nobody wanted to look at meaty, varicose-vein-riddled women like the ones Rubens painted. The world was unisex, and medieval-style street theater was revived—fat women and former men enacting scenes of bygone days so the audience could get some yuks at the expense of the characters' attempts to couple. Men's sports disappeared. The fate of soccer has already been described, but one could also recount the disappearance of hockey, all combat sports, etc. The new vacancies were filled by women, who were now rooting and playing for Real Madrid and Barcelona, lifting weights, and doing mixed martial arts. Many other human achievements vanished into oblivion, but the greatest loss was scientific thought, which had always been steered by sheer genius, multiplied by testosterone. The world community just didn't give a damn about that, to put it mildly. What on earth did they need science for, if there were only three generations left? Everyone was perfectly satisfied with the gadgets they had; they didn't need the newest iPhone! And studying the universe was just a waste of time . . .

On the other hand, war practically came to an end. A couple of lesbian gangs started duking it out among themselves, but the police soon lowered the temperature by imposing long prison sentences on the offenders so they would not prevent humanity from living out its last century in peace and friendship. Surprisingly enough, there was not even a hint of anarchy. Nearly the entire population of the earth became law-abiding citizens and supported the planet's peaceful order. The hospitals and banks were still operating, the trains ran on time, the planes were flying, and the restaurants and saunas were open . . . True, there was a revolution in the world of religion. Priests, rabbis, church fathers, muftis, and Brahmans of every stripe were dramatically drummed out, but it was done with the clear and recognized goal of building a new, ecumenical religion in their place. But without all those churches! It was clear to the entire population that there was one Lord for all of them, since He had not spared a single denomination.

So things settled down and life went back to normal. People worked and earned money. Petya Savushkin, the newly obese trauma specialist, had kept his old job, while Lilia Zolotova had become an activist, elected herself to the sexual majority, and begun riding around on a Harley with other bellicose lady motorcyclists. The club elected her as their leader, while the Therapist, former president of the Daylight Dragons, was removed from office. He went to work at the botanical garden, where he'd gotten a job as a nightingale—he'd really gotten lucky in the voice department!

Mr. Arseny Iratov stopped taking his pills, despite the fact that withdrawal had almost killed him so recently. His soul was at peace, even without his medicine, and he slept as sweetly as he had in childhood. Iratov limply attempted to continue designing his peculiar buildings, but his heart wasn't in it anymore; it was just a habit. Nothing really came of that, and he abandoned his office and his assistant, Vitya, without regret, retiring to live on his investments and spend most of his time playing cards with Sytin. He cheated from force of habit, and the fattened-up andrologist didn't notice. His clinic went under, since it specialized in a branch of medicine that was no longer necessary, and he had neither the energy nor the desire to go into a different one. His savings were intact, plus his friend Arseny was not tightfisted and gave him large sums of money on various occasions. Mr. Iratov would sometimes go to the floor above and visit Vera, though he acted like a relative toward her now. He provided her with funds as well, and she would serve him tea, though Eugene did not like their little get-togethers. The young man ruled the young woman as he saw fit, harshly and tyrannically, only tolerating Iratov for his money. During their sexual play, he sometimes simply flogged her tender kidskin tushy with a whip, but he was also wont to bite her breasts like a dog, and when she said he was hurting her and asked him to be gentle, Eugene would haughtily warn her that one percentage point of unexhausted patience stood between her and losing him.

"Do you know how many women in the world are yearning for me without even knowing that I exist?"

"Yes . . ." Vera answered submissively, but tears of misery were flowing from her eyes.

She resolved to leave Eugene several times, but only in her imagination; she was not strong enough to do it in reality. Her will was as soft as paraffin wax. The lower parts of her body always defeated her brains, and she indulged her lover's every whim, giving him all the money from Iratov, desperately hoping she would get pregnant, even going out on to the terrace naked in the dead of winter to amuse her lover. In those moments when he was drunk with power, Eugene would smile and feel that he was growing fangs. It only felt that way, though. As the last young man who still had real, natural primary sex characteristics, he was waiting for the moment to announce himself to the world—"Behold, I am the savior of the human race, and only my seed can combat God's decision . . ." He was not hungry to become a deity, though he thought he could if he wanted. What he wanted, and ferociously, was to defeat the Almighty, break His will and live according to his own!

I met him one more time. In the hope of saving my fallen

Verushka, I waited for the young man outside of Iratov's apartment building. He recognized me, even stopped and looked me up and down attentively. Then he moved with a sudden jerk and tried to grab my crotch but encountered emptiness.

"What do you want?" he inquired condescendingly.

"Let her go."

"Go to you, you mean?" Eugene guffawed. "Your pants are empty! What would you do with her?"

"My pants have always been empty. I was born that way, and I don't want her the way you do."

"Oh, so you're an angel? A sexless angel?!" He released his grip on my pants. "So what do you need her for?"

"She's my Verushka-a-a-a . . ." I said, softly exaggerating the 'a.' "She is the fruit enjoyed illicitly, the reason the world is the way it is! Let her go!"

"I could kick your ass right here, angel, but I won't. I'm an angel, too, I just have balls. I'll give it to you straight— you'll soon be able to collect your . . . what do you call her? 'Verushka-a-a-a'?"

"Precisely." I looked at him for a moment, then punched him in the face. He had no idea how powerful the blow would be, so he didn't really try to dodge. That misjudgment left his nose jammed between the fractured bones of his face. Eugene grabbed at his ruined features, looked at me—with horror, now—and ran back inside, abundantly dripping blood on the green summer grass.

He'd let me come a little closer to her . . . I sighed heavily, mourning my lost illusion, and thought that the fruit could be driven by its own will to seduce a man into tasting it, illicit as it was. That was what had happened in this case . . .

Back at Senescentova's apartment, I collapsed into bed without even setting an alarm. When I closed my eyes, I thought about Major Belic and Colonel Jamin. Once the army was abolished, they collected their nice officers' pensions and settled in a little dacha community called "the Orioles," building their houses next to each other. They played chess and drank vodka every day. Juliet Adamian lived nearby and would pay the retired officers rare visits; she would always bring them dolmas . . . The ex-chess champion Estin finally realized that he had sufficient funds to be at ease for the rest of his days. He was still married to Bella Pushkina, who found that the lack of shortages more than made up for his plentiful shortcomings. She attended the small local parish of the new ecumenical church. The son Iratov had with his first love, Svetlana, was part of the same majority as all the other men on the planet. The elderly and peeling Gryazev tried to talk Svetlana into letting him live with her, saying that he still had everything. Well, not everything, but he joked lewdly that the façade was still intact, and who needs to pitch a tent when you have a façade? The pathetic old man was mercilessly exiled and instructed to fuck the hell off for the rest of his days.

Almost every day, Alice, young resident of the village of Kostino in the Vladimir Region, would go outside wearing a white dress, bearing a small bouquet of cornflowers, and stand on the dusty country road, her eyes following it through the flowering fields and the neighboring villages, waiting for her unforgettable prince with maidenly trepidation. Only the hot wind came to meet her, wrapping Alice's unneeded wedding dress tightly around her knees . . .

Then they called me.

I lunged for the phone. If I'd had a human heart, it might not have been able to withstand so much tension and emotion. Hundreds of years of expectation and hopeless suffering.

Crushed under the fear of complete annihilation, it might have stopped like the mechanism of a clock or exploded like a nuclear bomb.

Obviously, nobody said anything on the other end of the phone pressed to my ear, but the necessary information, a deposit of silence into my expanded consciousness, proved all-encompassing and opened all of its meanings to me.

"Thank you . . . thank you . . ." I whispered as I raced off to Belorussky Station. "Thank you . . ." I got in line at Window 4 to buy a ticket to Prague.

"Adimus!" I felt a heavy hand on my shoulder and turned around to see the aged Antipatros with his eternally patchy beard. "So they finally called you!"

"Yes," I managed, full of love for my kinsman who had lived in exile for so long, even longer than I had. "Yes, they did . . . and, unless I'm mistaken, they called you, too!"

"And do you know what to do now?"

"I have the plan in my head."

"Excellent! We'll get round-trip tickets with flexible return dates."

"Oh yes," I agreed. We had already nearly made it to the front of the line when, of all people, my former neighbor Ivanov crashed into us from behind. Can you imagine?

"Why are you here?" I asked in surprise.

"Me?" My nervous neighbor exhaled the stale scent of alcohol. "I'm, you know . . . going to Prague . . ."

"Going for the beer, Mr. Homegrown Merchant?"

"They called . . ." my neighbor disclosed. "They called me."

"Welcome, Angel Ivanov!" Antipatros greeted him. "Is your brain back in working order?"

"Yeah . . ."

"So you really are my brother?" I spoke with difficulty, absolutely astonished.

"Kinda . . ." Ivanov answered shyly.

"Yeah, yeah, he's your brother," Antipatros explained as he approached the window and put his money down. "Three economy-class tickets to Prague! He isn't your parole officer, though!"

"Reserve a whole luxury sleeper car," Ivanov demanded with the grandeur of a hussar. "What good will money do me now?" he elaborated, skewing his mouth into a smile. Then we spent half the day sitting in a nearly empty café, talking and drinking vodka like regular people.

"So what are you in for?" I asked Antipatros.

"Why'd they exile me, you mean?"

"Precisely."

"I got in a fight with Jacob, Abraham's grandson. How about you?"

"I poked fun at the boss . . . tried to get a rise out of Him about Job. I said he could only be so faithful and observant because he was rich and happy."

"Gotcha . . ." Antipatros parted his beard so he could pour vodka into his mouth. "And now you've suffered enough?"

"Sure have . . . I served out my sentence, from beginning to end . . ."

As we followed the vodka with crepes, we both turned to my former neighbor Ivanov with an unspoken question. He took another shot—his penalty for being late—oinked, as was his custom, and admitted that he had been the seventh cloud of glory but had shirked his obligation to wash the clothes of the numerous people wandering the desert.

"And sometimes I'd go AWOL to enjoy some earthly maidens."

"So you have a prick?" we both asked, almost in unison.

"Yes," the Angel Ivanov said, his eyes downcast. "I am not of your . . . brotherly . . . Christian . . . breed." We all drank to that.

"What are we going to do about Iratov?" I inquired.

"Nothing . . . He has nothing to do with this. Selected at random. But do not forget, however random he may be, he is Joseph's grandfather! Remember the city of Zoar, which was not destroyed along with Sodom and Gomorrah because Lot, the nephew of the Prophet Abraham, was hiding there!"

We all agreed on that, yet, in the depths of my soul, I would still always hold my Verushka against Iratov. At that moment, it all seemed like a meaningless detail, though.

For half the evening, we sat there in silence, feeling an immense, universal celebration in our souls. We didn't want to go our separate ways, but the café had supplied us with more than a thousand crepes, overfulfilling their plan by 300 percent, so they had to close.

"Does everyone know what to do?"

"Yes," I replied.

"I don't!" the Angel Ivanov admitted.

"You take care of what grew between Iratov's legs and exercised the right of self-determination, like Crimea!" Antipatros chastised him.

"His name is Eugene," I elaborated. "A vile genital!"

"I'll take care of him," Ivanov promised. "What's the method?"

"You're the pyromaniac around here! If you can't handle the laundry, handle the fire!"

"That store burned to the ground!" the inebriated angel agreed. "With Zinka's sister Tamarka inside!"

"Right, you figure out how . . ."

"Why are we going to Prague, guys?"

"What, you don't know?" We were surprised.

"No," he replied, puzzled.

"Prague is the brother city of the Eternal City itself!" Antipatros informed the uninitiated Ivanov. "When we are called up to sit at the table, we go!"

"Ah . . ."

I went to the yeshiva in Istra, where I found Joseph teaching a class for the youngest kids. He was telling the children about the meaning of some part of the book so beautifully, so elegantly that they were listening with bated breath, and Rabbi Yitskhok, seated by the wall, was almost weeping.

Joseph did not seem at all surprised to see me. When the lesson was finished, he came over and said hello like we were old acquaintances.

"Have you come to see the rabbi?" he asked.

"I've come to see you."

"Has something happened?"

"We're off to buy you a tuxedo!"

"A tuxedo?" The young man was clearly surprised.

"I'll give you the details in the taxi."

Joseph looked at Rabbi Yitskhok, who nodded in encouragement, thereby giving his blessing for him to leave the yeshiva. When the car was rolling into the tunnel under the Moscow Ring Road, the driver, a man as old as Methuselah, suddenly spoke to me.

"I remember you . . ."

"Me?" I was surprised, catching his eyes in the rearview mirror. "Or the young man?"

"You . . . Around thirty years ago, you saved my Svetlana

from inevitable death," the driver explained, but he saw my bewilderment and tried to jog my memory. "You were all beaten up, and you tried to pay me with a three-ruble bill from before the reform . . . My little daughter, Svetlana, with periostitis. Do you remember now?"

"Oh yeah!" I slapped myself on the forehead. "Now it's coming back to me! How is Svetlana?"

"She's given me three grandsons! Thank you! My wife Elena, God rest her soul, sends her thanks, too!"

Joseph looked at me in surprise, so I explained things.

"The tuxedo is for the wedding!"

"What wedding?" Now the young man looked even more surprised.

"What do you mean, 'what wedding'? Your wedding!"

"But . . . I . . ." Joseph stumbled.

"Hush now, your wedding will be on Thursday." He apparently did not like my little scheme, and he asked the driver to stop.

"Pardon me, but I would like to get out! Your sense of humor is too weird."

"The plane's already in the air, you can't get out! A man without a wife is like half of a coin—he has no value."

"I categorically insist!"

"Alright, alright, keep calm . . . If you don't want to marry Zoika, that's your prerogative."

Joseph's expression instantly transformed. An apple-red glow appeared in his cheeks as blood ran back into his pale skin.

"Zoika who?"

"That's doesn't matter anymore!" I turned aside but kept my attention focused on the bobber that was slowly but surely sinking into the water, indicating that the fish would soon be caught. "You might be a little young to get married . . ."

"Z-z-oika w-who?" Joseph stammered.

"The one from Petrovsky Boulevard . . . She tidies up the barbershop. Perhaps you're right . . . Perhaps she isn't a good match for you . . ."

"I'll do it!" the young man shouted, so thunderously and unexpectedly that the driver was startled, and the taxi almost crashed into a truck. I myself nearly soiled my pants.

"Alright, I got it, I got it . . . What are you scaring people for? How are you, sir? God, you gave him such a fright!"

"I'd like to give him a smack!" the elderly driver replied, then continued unexpectedly. "It's just a shame there won't be any great-grandchildren!" Joseph grinned from ear to ear, like a complete idiot, sadly resembling his deceased daddy.

"But w-who are y-you?" he asked, still stammering.

"Me? Well . . . in traditional Russian weddings, if the groom's father was not able to participate in the ceremony, another man would be brought in to play his role. I'm someone like that . . ."

"Did her father give his b-blessing?"

"Why on earth would we be buying a tuxedo without his blessing? That would be utter foolishness! Antipatros gave us the money out of his own pocket."

"How do you know him? Does he c-cut your h-hair, too?"

"Oh, my dear boy, who don't I know? But yes, that's it precisely. I am an old customer of his. And that's enough stuttering!"

The owner of the Central Universal Department Store unexpectedly appeared in the fitting room and commanded that Joseph be furnished with a tuxedo completely free of charge. He also received the accompanying white dress shirt, black tie, and polished shoes.

"Why?" Joseph asked, still surprised. "What for?"

"He is a God-fearing man!"

"He just gives everything away to everyone?"

"He's no fool. What kind of business would that be, if he just gave everything away?" The Lyonchik brothers, the owners of numerous jewelry brands, gifted us with the wedding bands and escorted us all the way to the exit, shedding tender tears . . . Then we set off for Joseph's apartment, where we spent two days preparing for the most important day of his life.

The Angel Ivanov stood on the Old Arbat in a Grim Reaper costume, complete with a real scythe. God only knows where he procured it. Perhaps he pilfered it from the Vakhtangov Theatre?

From time to time, Ivanov would light a stream of alcohol and send a tongue of flame into space from his mouth. The passersby just went about their business, paying no attention to this homegrown fire-eater/flamethrower.

As he walked out of his building after a night with Vera—he was sick to death of her by then—Eugene suddenly realized that he would never return. He was transfixed by the thought that this was the day to make himself known, to elevate himself above the masses like a fireworks display, an explosion of hope, to soar above the world. Held captive by his thoughts about how to rise to the peak of triumph, he stepped on to the Old Arbat from the Smolensk Market side and headed down toward the metro. His thoughts bounced from one method of elevating himself to another, but then it became clear to him that it would all happen here, on this street, that this was the place where unnumbered gawkers would see his might and carry the glad tidings of humanity's salvation to the whole world. Pale from the grandeur of the moment, he stopped in front of a jewelry store.

"I am with me!" he declared, seizing his belt. Yanking on the leather tongue, he was about to release his pants into free fall, but then someone started whispering some incomprehensible words in his ear, pouring in some fluid that felt warm and brisk at the same time. He turned around and saw Death. Death was short, just like in the fairy tales, the polished metal of the scythe shining in the sun. Eugene was about to shove the mummer aside, but the latter suddenly showed him two pieces of silicon in his hands.

"Take that, pussy!" uttered costumed Death, striking the pieces of silicon together to produce an overpowering spark.

Eugene didn't go up like a torch, as one might have imagined; instead, his whole body trembled faintly, feeling heat advancing on all his innards. The heat turned into an inferno, an internal fire as ferocious as in the pit of perdition, and the figure of the young man began to smoke, a trick unusual enough to attract the tourists' attention, then his clothes sloughed away, baring a body overcome by flame from within. Eugene's last thought was a simple statement—"It didn't work out!" His ignited flesh expanded, as if someone had filled a rubber product with air, and, in a moment, the blazing object came to resemble a sizzling sausage, sending the juice intended for billions of human souls squirting in every direction. To the accompaniment of the crowd's hooting, the phallic sausage burned and spat for some time but eventually collapsed into a heap of ashes on the pavement.

The Angel Ivanov heard the applause, but he muttered that it was no trick, that a magician really had worked an illusion, then quickly retreated to Starokonyushennyy Lane, where he disappeared in an unknown direction, leaving his scythe in the gutter . . .

The wedding was held at the Crocus City Mall, where

thousands of guests had come to celebrate. Neither Joseph nor Zoika knew where they had all come from or who had paid for the ceremony. The young couple were led out on to the street, where the children of the yeshiva held a chuppah above them.

"You are hereby betrothed unto me with this ring in accordance with the laws of Moses and Israel," Joseph intoned, then gave his bride the ring. At the very instant he put it on her finger, snow began to fall from the sky. Those in attendance applauded in delight, marveling at the miracle of this August snowfall. Rabbi Cohen read the marriage contract, then the groom was lifted toward the heavens in a chair, and thousands of men danced with such fury that the floorboards would have to be replaced the following day. Only after all of that did Joseph make love to Zoika in his mother, Dasha's, apartment, which was proper and in accordance with the law. Black was tinged with white, and the expression of her blue eyes was coy and submissive . . . She conceived that very night and felt the joyful presence in her belly ere break of day.

That same morning, Vera stood facing the rising sun, its myriads of warm rays penetrating her thin nightgown. She knew, she felt, that Eugene would never return, but, for some reason, she did not lament that fact, just smiled guiltily at the sky.

"Ah!" she exclaimed, feeling some kind of movement below her stomach, and grabbed the softest spot, what makes a woman a woman. "Ah!" Vera cried out, flabbergasted, thinking for a moment that she, like Mr. Iratov, had become sexless. From under the hem of her nightgown there flew a butterfly of hitherto unseen beauty. It described a circle around the young woman, grazed her hair, as if in farewell, then lightly flapped its turquoise wings, flew through the open window, and soared into the sky. Vera! Verushka!

At the same instant, as Alice stood on the white country

road awaiting her sweet Eugene, a cabbage butterfly suddenly emerged from under her dress, flapping its little wings so quickly, rising toward the peculiar, shaggy clouds.

"Hey!" Alice shouted, grabbing her stomach. "Where are you going, butterfly?!"

Lilia Zolotova was riding her Harley that morning, enjoying the speed. She didn't even notice the large swallowtail butterfly crawling out from under the men's belt holding up her tight jeans, trying not to break its wings, but she suddenly felt that the spot touching the leather motorcycle seat had become insensate, as if an anesthetic had been administered. The butterfly was swiftly carried away by the headwind, and it suddenly soared aloft like a kite breaking loose from its reel . . .

In that instant, billions of butterflies soared above the world. They spun and bored into the air, rising on their wings toward the sun. Tiger moths and swallowtails, cabbage and sulfur butterflies, oeneis tarpeja—the tender and fragile creatures blotted out the whole sky. The world went dark, black, like it only does in the hour before dawn.

Moscow, 2016

Dmitry Lipskerov is a playwright and author whose novels have been met with international success due to their vivid, intense portrayal of Russia through both fabulism and realism. He has been awarded the Moscow Komsomol Prize and the French Imaginales prize in 2019, and was shortlisted for the Russian Booker Award. He cofounded two Russian literary prizes: the Debut prize for works of fiction by young Russian writers and the Neformat prize. *The Tool and the Butterflies* is the first novel of his to be translated into English.

Reilly Costigan-Humes and **Isaac Stackhouse Wheeler** are a team of literary translators who work with Russian and Ukrainian. Among their published translations are two books by contemporary Ukrainian author Serhiy Zhadan: *Voroshilovgrad* (Deep Vellum, 2016) and *Mesopotamia* (Yale University Press, 2018).

PARTNERS

pixel ||| texel

ADDITIONAL DONORS, CONT'D

Mark Haber
Mary Cline
Maynard Thomson
Michael Reklis
Mike Soto
Mokhtar Ramadan
Nikki & Dennis Gibson
Patrick Kukucka
Patrick Kutcher
Rev. Elizabeth & Neil Moseley
Richard Meyer

Scott & Katy Nimmons
Sherry Perry
Sydneyann Binion
Stephen Harding
Stephen Williamson
Susan Carp
Susan Ernst
Theater Jones
Tim Perttula
Tony Thomson

SUBSCRIBERS

Audrey Golosky
Ben Nichols
Brittany Johnson
Carol Trimmer
Caroline West
Chana Porter
Charles Dee Mitchell
Charlie Wilcox
Chris Mullikin
Chris Sweet
Courtney Sheedy
Damon Copeland
Derek Maine
Devin McComas
Francisco Fiallo
Fred Griffin
Hillary Richards

Jody Sims
Joe Milazzo
John Winkelman
Lance Stack
Lesley Conzelman
Margaret Terwey
Martha Gifford
Michael Binkley
Michael Elliott
Michael Lighty
Neal Chuang
Radhika
Ryan Todd
Shelby Vincent
Stephanie Barr
William Pate

FORTHCOMING FROM DEEP VELLUM

MARIO BELLATIN · *Mrs. Murakami's Garden*
translated by Heather Cleary · MEXICO

MAGDA CARNECI · *FEM*
translated by Sean Cotter · ROMANIA

MIRCEA CĂRTĂRESCU · *Solenoid*
translated by Sean Cotter · ROMANIA

MATHILDE CLARK · *Lone Star*
translated by Martin Aitken · DENMARK

LOGEN CURE · *Welcome to Midland: Poems* · USA

PETER DIMOCK · *Daybook from Sheep Meadow* · USA

CLAUDIA ULLOA DONOSO · *Little Bird*, translated by Lily Meyer · PERU/NORWAY

LEYLÂ ERBIL · *A Strange Woman*
translated by Nermin Menemencioğlu · TURKEY

ROSS FARRAR · *Ross Sings Cheree & the Animated Dark: Poems* · USA

FERNANDA GARCIA LAU · *Out of the Cage*
translated by Will Vanderhyden · ARGENTINA

ANNE GARRÉTA · *In/concrete*
translated by Emma Ramadan · FRANCE

GOETHE · *Faust, Part One*
translated by Zsuzsanna Ozsváth and Frederick Turner · GERMANY

JUNG YOUNG MOON · *Arriving in a Thick Fog*
translated by Mah Eunji and Jeffrey Karvonen · SOUTH KOREA

FISTON MWANZA MUJILA · *The Villain's Dance*, translated by Roland Glasser · *The River in the Belly: Selected Poems*, translated by Bret Maney · DEMOCRATIC REPUBLIC OF CONGO

LUDMILLA PETRUSHEVSKAYA · *Kidnapped: A Crime Story*, translated by Marian Schwartz · *The New Adventures of Helen: Magical Tales*, translated by Jane Bugaeva · RUSSIA

JULIE POOLE · *Bright Specimen: Poems from the Texas Herbarium* · USA

MANON STEFAN ROS · *The Blue Book of Nebo* · WALES

ETHAN RUTHERFORD · *Farthest South & Other Stories* · USA

BOB TRAMMELL · *The Origins of the Avant-Garde in Dallas & Other Stories* · USA